THE TROUBLE WITH CHARLIE

THE TROUBLE WITH CHARLIE

A Novel

Merry Jones

Oceanview Publishing
Longboat Key, Florida

ISBN: 978-1-60809-074-7

Published in the United States of America by Oceanview Publishing, Longboat Key, Florida

www.oceanviewpub.com

10 9 8 7 6 5 4 3 2 1

PRINTED IN THE UNITED STATES OF AMERICA

To Robin, Baille, and Neely

Acknowledgments

Heartfelt thanks to Rebecca Strauss at McIntosh and Otis; Robert and Patricia Gussin, Frank Troncale, David Ivester, George Foster, and Susan Hayes at Oceanview Publishing;

Fellow Philadephia Liars Club members Jonathan Maberry, Gregory Frost, Kelly Simmons, Marie Lamba, Solomon Jones, Don Lafferty, Dennis Tafoya, Jon McGoran, Keith Strunk, Keith DeCandido, Ed Pettit, and Stephen Susco;

Friends and family, especially my husband and first reader, Robin.

THE TROUBLE WITH CHARLIE

PROLOGUE

Sometime before Charlie moved out, I began reading the obituaries. It became a daily routine, like morning coffee. I didn't just scan the listings; I read them closely, noting dates of death, ages of the deceased, names of survivors. If there were photos, I studied faces for clues about mortality even though they were often grinning and much younger than at death. Sometimes there were flags at the top of notices, signifying military service. Salvadore Petrini had a flag. Aged sixty-four. Owner of Petrini's Market. Beloved husband and father and stepfather and brother and uncle. Viewing and Life Celebration at St. Patrick's Church, Malvern.

Some notices were skeletal, giving no details of the lost life. Sonia Woods went to be with the Lord on August 17. Viewing Friday, from nine to eleven, First Baptist Church. Service to follow. These left me disturbed, sad for the deceased. Was there, in the end, really nothing to be said about them? Were their lives just a finite number of breaths, now stopped?

For weeks, I followed the flow of local deaths and funerals. I tried to surmise causes of death from requests for memorial contributions in lieu of flowers. The American Cancer Society. The Vascular Disease Foundation. The American Heart or Alzheimer's Association. When there were details, I read about careers accomplished, volunteer work conducted, music played, tournaments won. Lives condensed to an eighth of a page. Less, usually.

Though the notices were brief, the words and patterns of language had a gentle, rolling rhythm, comforting, like prayers, like nursery rhymes. And between listings, stark and straight lines divided one death from another, putting lives neatly into boxes, separating body from body. Soul from soul. Making death quantifiable and normal, a daily occurrence neatly announced on paper in black and white, on pages dense with ink, speckled with gray smiling photos. Smiles announcing that death wasn't really so bad.

I don't know why I was compelled to read those listings every day. At the time, I'd have said it had to be about the death of my marriage. After all, my own life, in a way, was ending. My life as Charlie's wife was dying, but there would be no public acknowledgment of that demise. No memorial service. No community gathering to mourn. Maybe I read the listings to remember that I wasn't the only one grieving, that others had lost even more. Still, I would have felt better if the obituary page included dead marriages and lost identities: Mrs. Charles Henry Harrison (nee Elle Brooks) ceased to exist on (date pending), when the couple's divorce became final. Maybe it would help to have some formal recognition of the demise of my former self. Maybe not.

It's possible that my own losses brought me to the daily obits. But I doubt it. Looking back, I believe what drew me was far more ominous. A premonition. An instinct. For whatever reason, though, every morning as I chewed my English muffin, I buried myself in the death notices, studying what I could about people who were no more, trying to learn from them or their photos or their neatly structured notices anything I could about death.

Of course, as it turned out, the notices were useless. None of them, not one, prepared me for what was to happen. According to the obituary columns, the circumstances of one's life made no difference in the end. Dead was simply dead. Final. Permanent. Without room for doubt. The pages I studied gave no indication of a gray area. And the boxes around the obituaries contained no dotted lines.

OCTOBER

Bottles glowed amber and jade along the mirrored wall. Toned bartenders did their signature dance: reaching, pouring, swirling. Gliding along the narrow, dimly lit alley of spigots and glassware, serving up alcohol-laden concoctions to a thirsty crowd clustered along the bar. Music amplified to too many decibels pounded percussion without melody. Happy Hour at a mostly singles bar. What diabolical cynic had come up with that name? Dubbing as "happy" the dire, loneliest moments before dark, the time when people cling to each other in primal desperation.

I was no exception that night; I was among them.

"You have to start sometime," Becky had nagged me. "You can't just sit home forever."

It had only been a few weeks, I'd argued.

"It's been almost three months."

But I wouldn't know how to act, what to talk about. Hadn't been out on my own in a decade. I was rusty. Didn't know how to flirt.

"Just be yourself. You don't have to flirt. Just let go. Dance. Have fun."

Great. I hated dancing, wasn't good at it. I reminded her.

"Don't be so defeatist. What else will you do—stay home and watch *NCIS* reruns?"

Why not? Mark Harmon was kind of hot, for an old guy.

"Fine. Don't complain when you're eighty and dying alone. Remember what you told me after I broke my engagement?"

"Which one?"

"Very funny, Elle. But any of them—all of them. You said, 'The best revenge against a man who breaks your heart is to celebrate your life without him.'"

She was right. I had said that. Good advice, too.

"So now it's your turn. Come out with me. Celebrate." She'd kept it up, having an answer for each of my excuses until I'd caved, and there I was, standing in a bar, staring at glowing bottles, feeling clumsy and conspicuous and not very successful at celebrating my life. The Miller Lite in my bare wedding-ringless hand was empty again. I waved for another over the pounding music, its thumping bass relentless, reminding me with every slamming beat, of sex. Which, with Charlie out of my life, I might never have again. But that was absurd. Of course I would. Someday. Right?

The bartender put another bottle in front of me and I put a few bills in front of him, still thinking about sex with Charlie, his bare chest and shoulders poised above me in bed. Trying to stifle the images. Lord, I could kill him. Sometimes fantasized about it. Had even discussed it with various sympathetic girl-friends, most recently at lunch just the day before.

"You'd have to make it look like an accident," Susan had admonished. She was a criminal defense attorney, always practical. "Overdose him on his blood pressure meds. It'll look like a heart attack. And an autopsy would be inconclusive. They couldn't prove he didn't accidentally OD." She'd forked grilled tuna to her mouth, brows knit, thinking.

"No. Make it look random. Like a mugging or a carjacking." That had come from Jenny. Blonde, a body that poured into her clothes, eyelashes so long you could trip over them, a voice like silk. "Shit, if I was going to kill Norm, that's what I'd do." Jen's husband Norm owned things, including most of some NBA team. Or was it NHL? Her fingers glittered with diamonds. "I'd definitely shoot him and make it look like an RGB.

RGB. I'd had no idea.

"RGB?" Susan had apparently no idea either.

Jen had rolled her eyes. "Robbery Gone Bad." As if the meaning were obvious.

"Shooting's too violent." Becky had lowered her voice, looking around cautiously. "But remember, women usually use poison." I'd wondered how Becky knew that. She was a kindergarten teacher. How did she know this about poisons? Was it common knowledge that had somehow passed me by? I'd watched my share of cop shows, had learned my share of forensic science. "So don't poison him."

"And if you stab him, remember to restrain yourself." Jen spoke with authority. "Be efficient. Too many wounds looks like a crime of passion, not just random."

"And have a good alibi. Cops always assume the spouse did it."

They all nodded and agreed. My best girlfriends: a lawyer, a teacher, a rich housewife. Experts on murder.

"But even if she gets arrested, no jury will convict her once she tells them about Charlie—"

Somehow they'd begun talking about me as if I weren't there. The conversation had stopped involving me, had become about me. "Right. They'd let her off with time served. How many years were they married? Ten? That's a long enough sentence."

They'd laughed. They'd gone on, concocting detailed scenarios. I was to lure Charlie over in the dead of night, shoot him, and claim that I'd mistaken him for a prowler. Or hide in his condo's parking garage until he came home, shoot him, and take his wallet and his watch. Or hire someone to do it for me. All the ideas seemed familiar, like *Law and Order* reruns, but I'd drifted in and out of the conversation, watching from various distances as my friends had brainstormed from salads through coffee, offering and amending ideas with enthusiasm and delight. Not one had expressed disapproval at the thought of my killing Charlie. Not one had seemed the slightest bit appalled or surprised. They'd seemed comfortable with the idea, regarding Charlie's murder as a reasonable, even a positive alternative to divorce.

But, of course, the conversation hadn't been serious. It had merely been lunchtime amusement. Entertainment, like the bar's pounding music. Except the music was more painful than entertaining. It shook the floor, hurt my head. Made me remember what I didn't want to remember: the rhythmic whamming and thrusting of Charlie's pelvis. Damn.

Above me now was no pelvis, just a big screen playing football highlights.

Happy Hour. Did other people feel as self-conscious as I did? Or did they think this was fun? I looked around. Saw toothy smiles and drinks. Body heat. Commotion. Mostly I saw need. Maybe I was projecting. Lord, I felt uncomfortable.

The place was called Jeremy's. On Main Street in Manayunk, pronounced "Mannyoonk," a Native American word meaning, "the place to go to drink." And, for many professional single Philadelphians, it was. People were. I stood at the bar like a grinning stunned doe, watching people wander and cluster. I gulped Miller and nibbled carrot sticks from the array of free munchies, trying to pretend that I was in fact having an excellent time and that anyone who talked to me would also have one. With a cheerful semismile pasted onto my face, I determined not to look like a wallflower as I watched Becky wag her hips to the music and shimmy and shake with a skinny guy who had fashionable facial hair. She smiled at me, gesturing that I should join in. "Come on, Elle. Dance with us."

Becky was in her comfort zone. Happily single, twice divorced, she was cute, breezy. Short. With a pert little nose, wide grin, breasts like big feather pillows. Men flocked to Becky, and she took care of them as she did her kindergarteners, a mother duck with swarms of hungry ducklings.

Not me. I stood untalked to. Undanced with. At five foot nine, I was too tall to be "cute." In fairness, though, a few guys did approach me. One was stocky, wobbly on his feet, as tall as my chin, wearing a thick-lipped grin. His gaze fixed on my chest. "I'm Pete. Wuzs yrr name?"

He watched my bust as if he thought it would answer.

"Wann' dance?" He shouted over the music, his voice gruff.

My breasts didn't reply, but Pete didn't notice. Already distracted, he craned his neck to ogle some other woman, rotating so that his back turned to me. I stepped away, looked for Becky. Again, she waved me onto the dance floor. I shook my head. The music pounded on, jangling my bones. I stepped out of myself mentally, viewing the bar from above. Saw myself, a woman out of sync with her surroundings. Gawky and out of place.

"Nothing can be that serious. Come on. Give me a smile."

The guy had a strong jaw, broad smile. I felt a jolt, something like fear?

"Oops, look at this—" He reached out, lightly tapped my earlobe, and produced a quarter. He feigned surprise. "Here. This was in your ear!"

The stranger had shiny, playful eyes. Too shiny, too playful. Maybe dangerous. I felt the urge to run. But he held the quarter out, watching me until I took it. Then, eyes still on mine, he cupped his hand and—poof—produced a red chiffon scarf, looped it around my neck.

Wait. He was a magician? The place had a floor show? Oh Lord. I thanked him, stuffed a couple of dollars into his pocket, lifted my beer in a silent toast.

He frowned, retrieving the cash. "Hey, I don't want money. All I want is your smile."

My what? My face got red-hot. I steadied myself. Why was

my adrenalin pumping? He stared at my mouth, waiting. I smiled. Actually, I laughed. Nervously.

"Success!" He grinned, put the money back on the bar. "I'm Joel." He yelled above the din.

"Elle."

His eyebrows rose. "Elf?"

I blinked, shook my head. Charlie called me Elf. No one else ever had. "Elle. Like the letter."

"Your face lights up when you smile, Elle."

More blushing. More inexplicable panic. In the dim light, maybe he couldn't see. "So you're not the house magician?"

"No, no." A broad grin. "I create illusions for fun. To cheer people up."

"And help you meet women?"

He laughed. Nice lips. Strong jaw. Good teeth. Carnivorous. "Sometimes."

I smiled. "So. Does it work?"

"You tell me." His eyes twinkled. Playing.

I looked into my beer, drank. Tried to think of a clever response. Couldn't.

"You seem tense." He studied me, as if reading my body language. "Recent breakup?" his voice roared above the music.

He could tell just by looking at me? Oh Lord. I hesitated, not wanting to admit it. I rubbed my temple. "Just a headache."

His eyes softened, sympathetic. For a heartbeat, they reminded me of Charlie's. Odd, since Joel's were grayish and danced, and Charlie's were dark brown and dared. Their eyes looked nothing alike. Maybe it was that he'd called me Elf.

"Press here." He took my hand to show me. His touch was warm, firm. Unfamiliar. "What happened to your hand?"

I looked at the bandage. I'd cut myself earlier, had forgotten about it. A kitchen knife had slipped while I was cutting fruit, slicing my palm. And it must have been deeper than I'd thought because blood had seeped through the gauze. "No big deal. I got attacked by an orange."

As if from the ceiling, I watched myself talking, smiling. Letting a man touch her bandaged hand. Seeming to enjoy herself. Flirting.

Joel smiled and, avoiding the gauze, squeezed a precise spot, just between my forefinger and thumb. And poof—magically, the pulsing in my head eased. "If you press this spot, you relieve pressure. You slow the blood flow to the brain. Something like that."

"You're a doctor?" We were shouting in order to be heard.

His smile was sly. "No. Not a doctor. Just intrigued by anatomy."

He let go of my hand. The headache started up again. Immediately. I set my beer on the bar, began squeezing the spot. Relief. Amazing.

"I'm pretty good at reading people, Elle. Know what I see when I look at you?"

I didn't answer.

"I see a beautiful woman who's very sad."

He did? I looked at his eyes, didn't know what to say.

"Remember, life's full of surprises. Everything can change suddenly—presto. Like magic." From thin air, he produced a single red rose. He held it out, his eyes still on mine. "It's for you. Take it."

I did. Impressed. And unsettled.

Somebody jostled me on his way to the bar, and I glanced away, regaining my balance.

"See you around, Elf. I mean, Elle." Joel squeezed my shoulder, then moved on, disappearing into the crowd, leaving me shaken. A rose? A single, long-stemmed rose? It was another coincidence, nothing more.

Alone again, I stood sandwiched between warm bodies at the bar. Holding a beer and a rose.

Okay, I decided, I'd done enough for one night. Had taken the first step, proved I could go out, even talked with a hot guy. So I could go home. With luck, I'd get there in time to catch the end of *NCIS*. I located Becky on the dance floor and waved to her, mouthed the words, "I'm going."

"Behind the bar." She pointed to the ladies' room.

"No," I moved my lips. "Home."

"What?" She cupped her ear, gyrating. The guy she was dancing with now was swarthy and buff, mesmerized by her backside.

I made my hand into a telephone, held it to my face. "Later."

She looked disappointed. "You're leaving?"

I nodded and, before she could protest or pout or even miss a grind, I'd pushed my way through the crowd, dashed out the door, and escaped into the chilled evening air. At the corner, I hopped into a taxi, thinking of Charlie who, until that night, had been the only man ever to give me a rose.

~

The night was warm and the cab stale, so I cracked the window, watching couples walking hand in hand or arms circling each other. We inched slowly through traffic on Main Street, passing crowded upscale clubs, boutiques, and restaurants. Manayunk had grown in the hills above the Schuylkill River, had housed mill workers, but now it was gentrified. Populated by young professional types. I lived only a few miles away, near the Philadelphia Art Museum, in the townhouse that had been Charlie's and mine. Now it was just mine, or would be when our divorce was final. I played with my empty ring finger. There was nothing to regret. Nothing left to save.

Nor was there a reason to feel so raw about attending a Happy Hour. There was no shame in being single again. In looking for companionship. Divorce didn't make me a loser or a failure. Or unattractive. It didn't mean I sucked at life. All that it meant was that Charlie and I hadn't worked out. Millions of women were separated or divorced. Millions of men, too. I didn't like bars, that was all. There had to be other, quieter, more comfortable venues to meet men. Like health clubs. Supermarkets.

By the time the cab pulled up to my house, I'd almost convinced myself that I had hope. It wasn't definite that I would grow old lonely, sad, and celibate. I was an educated, professional woman, a second grade teacher. When I stood up straight and held my stomach in, I was kind of stately. I had big hazel eyes and full lips. Charlie used to say I was striking; other men must think so, too. But, then again, finding a new man wasn't the answer. What I needed was a new passion, something fulfilling that I could do alone. Maybe I'd take classes in Italian. Or Portuguese. Or Tae Kwon Do. Or opera or skeet shooting.

I exited the cab with more dignity than I'd entered and stood tall as I unlocked my front door, only to slump again when I stepped inside, confronting what was left of my home. The blank spaces on the walls where Charlie's art had hung, the empty corner where he'd kept his aquarium, the half-vacant shelves that had held his books, the bare corners where his philodendra had clustered. Everything was a reminder that Charlie was gone.

Never mind. Spaces could be filled. I'd redecorate. Get new stuff. I set my bag on the hallway table and took a deep, cleansing breath. Maybe my head was aching because I was hungry, had eaten only carrot sticks for dinner. On the way to the kitchen, I stopped, sniffing. I wasn't imagining it. The scent. I knew it, had lived with it for ten years. The air smelled of Charlie. Old Spice. Had he been in the house? Was he still here?

"Charlie?" I stood still, listening. He still had keys. Our divorce wasn't final; I hadn't changed the locks. Even though he shouldn't and, as far as I knew, hadn't come in, he still could.

"Charlie?" Louder this time.

Silence. He wasn't there. Of course, he wasn't.

Even so, I stepped into the living room again, checking, seeing no one. Nothing out of place. Obviously, I was imagining the scent. Or maybe the house had just held onto it, absorbed it in walls, in floors. I went back to the kitchen, suddenly drained. My arms felt leaden, making it difficult to open a bag of Spring Mix. My hands were stiff, fingers sluggish, struggling to add chunks of bleu cheese. Slicing an onion, forgetting about the cut on my hand, I pushed the knife as if slicing through bone. Felt the wound reopen, a warm gush. What was wrong with me? I stopped cutting, pushed on the bandage to stop the bleeding, leaned on the counter to rest. Sensed movement behind me, a tickle on the nape of my neck. A light kiss—

"Charlie, dammit—" I spun around, knocking the knife to the floor.

No Charlie.

Again, I called his name. Heard no reply.

Finally, I decided there hadn't been anyone moving behind me. And the tickle hadn't been a kiss, had been just a tickle. I gave up on slicing the onion, added a few cherry tomatoes, a sprinkle of walnuts. Poppy seed dressing. Dinner for one.

Head aching, hand stinging, arms inexplicably wooden, I lifted my plate to go to the study, thinking about which rerun would be my dinner companion. *NCIS* or *Criminal Minds*.

"Elf."

The voice was definite. Clear. And Charlie's. He was there, after all. What the hell was he doing in the house, sneaking up on me? I turned around, annoyed.

But no one was there.

"Charlie." Not a question this time. I'd heard him say my name, knew he was in the house. Saw movement in my peripheral vision. I set the plate on the counter, looked down the hall. "What are you doing? Cut it out."

Silence.

I glanced into the study, went back to the living room.

"What the hell, Charlie? Do you think you can just come in any time you want, like you still live here?"

I checked the front closet. The powder room. Yelled up the stairs. "Charlie, dammit. Answer me."

But he didn't.

My headache raged. Arms hung heavy, weighed tons. As if their muscles had turned to concrete. Moving, walking took unusual effort. What was wrong with me? Was I having a stroke? I tried to remember the symptoms. What were they? Headache? Yes, I had that. Fast pulse? Had it. Stiffness, or was it limpness on one side? Either way, I had both on both sides. Oh dear. Was I having a double stroke? Could that even happen?

I told myself to calm down, stop being dramatic. Nothing was wrong with me except that I'd listened to music that was hundreds of decibels too loud and imbibed too many beers on an empty stomach. Clearly, I'd imagined Charlie's voice and the flicker of movement behind me. I wasn't having a stroke, and he wasn't in the house. My nerves were simply jangled. Calming myself, taking deep, even breaths, I wandered back to the kitchen, picked up my plate, opened the fridge for a Diet Coke, and got an overwhelming whiff of Old Spice.

"Elf."

My dish clattered to the floor. I pivoted, shrieked a curse.

Where was he? This time, there was no doubt. I was certain I'd heard him. Scanning the room, I stomped across the salad-strewn floor. "Dammit, Charlie. Is this a game? Hide-and-seek? Because, trust me, I'm not in the mood."

My words sliced empty air. Charlie wasn't there. But improbably—impossibly, something else was. On the floor, in the middle of the kitchen doorway.

A single long-stemmed red rose.

~

I stared at the thing. It couldn't be there. And yet, there it was. A cold tremor began at the base of my spine and slithered upward. I grabbed my shoulders, holding onto myself for reassurance. Closing my eyes to make it go away. Opening them again to see it still there.

Okay, I told myself. You're okay. It's only a rose.

Yes, but there was a problem with that rose. And the problem was that I'd left it with my bag on the table near the front door. And I hadn't seen it on the floor moments earlier when I'd gone to check the living room for Charlie. And roses didn't move by themselves. So, obviously, someone had moved it. But why? To let me know that I wasn't alone? To scare me? Why would Charlie want to scare me?

"Charlie?" It was an angry bellow. "Where are you?"

I shivered, chilled. Unnerved. I told myself that Charlie wouldn't hurt me, not physically. He'd wronged me a thousand times, but he'd never been violent. Then again, he'd never played hide-and-seek with me, either. Had never refused to answer me, never snuck up from behind to tickle me, never moved objects around the house just to alarm me. Charlie simply wasn't acting like Charlie.

Then again, how did I know what Charlie acted like? With all the tales he'd told me, what did I really know about him? Not much. Almost nothing. But I did know that he was angry about the divorce, unhappy about losing half his assets to me. But how unhappy? Enough to hurt me? Or to hire someone else to do it?

Lord. Had Charlie hired a hit man? Was someone in the house to kill me?

Every instinct in my being told me I shouldn't stick around to find out. That I should just get my handbag and go. Fast.

As in a nightmare, though, my legs were stone. Even though I told them to move, they wouldn't. My heart sped, my pulse soared, but my legs were stiff and stubbornly still. Rooted, like tree trunks.

I remained there, frozen in place, gaping at a rose. Completely exposed and vulnerable. Unable to move. Slowly, cautiously, I twisted my head, checking the room. The shadows. The corners. The empty spaces under the kitchen table and behind the trash can. My eyes did a careful 360, but saw not a trace of Charlie or a hit man. Not a footprint. Not a hair. Just my salad splattered across the kitchen tiles. And the rose.

"Okay," I repeated the word aloud, assuring myself that I was panicking over nothing. There was no hit man. I'd recognized Charlie's breath, his scent, his voice saying my name. Obviously, Charlie himself was in the house. Lurking. Toying with me. Not intending to kill me. Even so, just in case, I bent over and reached for the knife drawer. Rattled around for something long and sleek, something that would give even a hit man pause. Ended up with something short and serrated that I used for chopping celery. Still, I was armed.

"Okay." I needed to stop saying that. To find out what he wanted. "What do you want, Charlie?" I kept my voice deep so it wouldn't tremble. "Talk to me. Stop acting like a child."

No one answered. The house stood perfectly still. The silence was thick, tangible. Smothering. I was trembling, kept staring at the rose. I told myself that a thorn in the stem must have caught onto my clothing, that I'd inadvertently carried it to the kitchen myself. That it had simply fallen off.

Knowing that it hadn't.

Charlie was there, in the house. I could feel him.

"Charlie, where are you? If you don't tell me, I'm calling the police."

Silence.

"I swear. I'll do it."

Nothing.

"Charlie? Last chance!"

No answer.

Of course, I didn't call the police. What would I have told them? That I'd found a rose in the kitchen? That I'd felt a tickle on my neck? Heard a disembodied voice? The cops would have smelled the beer on my breath and laughed about me all the way to the donut shop.

No, calling the police would have been useless. I was better off simply ignoring Charlie. Whatever he was up to, I wasn't going to reinforce it by letting it get to me. Still, my hands shook as they picked up shards of a broken plate and globs of salad. And I was cold, shivering as, with the knife wedged under my arm, I mopped salad dressing off the tiles and rebandaged the cut on my hand. Finally, no longer hungry, chopping knife in hand, I started upstairs to go to bed.

I was halfway up the steps, unbuttoning my shirt, when I stopped, remembering. When I'd cleaned the kitchen floor, I'd scooped up walnuts, tomatoes, blue cheese, greens. I'd mopped up dressing and soda. But there was one item I hadn't picked up, one I hadn't even seen: the rose.

～

Even with limbs of cement, I ran back down the stairs, down the hall, straight to the kitchen. I turned on the lights, surveyed the room, saw no rose. I opened the broom closet, examined the mop and the bucket. I opened cabinets and drawers, looked inside the microwave and the oven. No rose.

My hands were ice cold, holding the knife. My spine was jangling. Where the hell was the thing? And how had Charlie managed to move it without my seeing him?

"This isn't funny." I spoke to the air. "If you're trying to scare me, Charlie, you're not succeeding." My voice was thin and shrill, scared. "All you're doing is pissing me off."

Silence.

"Okay." I turned off the light. "Fine. Sit in the dark alone and hide. Knock yourself out."

Do not tremble so much, I told myself. Do not let him get to you. Keep walking to the steps, do not stop.

I kept walking, shaking only slightly, still clutching my

kitchen utensil/weapon, and I made it to the steps. In fact, I made it all the way up to the top. Then into my bedroom.

Where I stopped, staring. Not breathing.

Impossibly, there it was. Delicate, yet dangerously armed with thorns. Red as blood. Perfectly displayed on the pale-cream pillowcase, where Charlie used to leave them.

∿

A low growl gurgled in my throat as I turned and stumbled backward out of the bedroom and turned to run down the steps. The stairway seemed endless, treacherous in the dim light, but I made it to the bottom, where I raced to the front door, still clutching my stubby little knife, grabbing my handbag, heading out onto the front stoop.

Standing outside, panting, I wondered how he'd done it? How had he picked up the rose and moved it all the way upstairs without me seeing or hearing him? I had no idea. Couldn't figure it out. But clearly, he'd managed it. And had succeeded in scaring me right out of the house.

I grasped the railing, collected my breath, and considered what I was going to do. Was I really going to run to a neighbor's house, frazzled and jittery, in the middle of the night? What would I say? And what good would it do? If I let Charlie run me out of my home once, he'd do it again and again. I'd never be done with him. No, I couldn't allow it. Wouldn't run away.

Still, I didn't go back inside. I stood on the porch, holding my knife. Wondering why I was so scared. It wasn't Charlie. I wasn't afraid of him. Of being married to him, definitely. But of the man, definitely not. Disappointed, furious, hurt, frustrated, yes. But afraid? No, never. Not once until that moment. I'd come to know Charlie as a liar, manipulator, charmer, sleazeball, and cheat. But, in his defense, he wasn't mean. Wasn't impulsive. Didn't have a temper. His intent wasn't to hurt others; it was merely to help himself. I had no idea why he was pulling this bizarre prank, but I was convinced he wasn't planning anything violent or cruel. Why should he? Just by moving a flower and saying my name, he had me dropping my plate, stuttering and cursing, running up and down the steps clutching a kitchen knife—all of which was probably cracking him up. Making him reel with laughter. No, I was done. The only way to get Charlie to stop was to calm down and ignore him. And change the locks.

For a while longer, I stood outside in chill October air, watching the starless night sky, the streetlights, the line of parked cars in front of the row houses across the street. Quieting my breath. Then, deliberately calm, I opened the front door and went back inside. The house was dark. Had I turned out the lights? I didn't think so, but never mind. Turning them off was just more of Charlie's mischief. I simply turned them back on and, instead of going up to bed, headed for the bar in the study. I deserved a drink.

Snapping on the light, I set my knife down on the counter, grabbed a tumbler off the shelf, and pulled out the Johnny Walker Black. Poured a generous few fingers. Drank. Closed my eyes, taking it in. Feeling its heat work its way through my body to my nerves. Relaxing me.

When I opened my eyes and turned around, I saw him right away. Charlie wasn't hiding any more. He was reclining on the gray velvet couch, big as life, watching me.

～

I didn't flinch. Didn't blink. I simply turned away again, opening the minifridge, getting some ice. Charlie liked rocks. "Drink?"

Charlie didn't answer.

I poured him one anyhow, swirled the Scotch to cool it. I made myself a refill, too. Took another long swallow, let it slide down my throat. Savored its burn. Or maybe the burn was my temper.

"So." I held his drink out. "I didn't get the memo—why have you called this meeting?"

He sat still, staring at me. Not reaching for his drink. Not answering.

"Okay, Charlie. Enough." I set both drinks down on the liquor cabinet and walked over to him. "Tell me what you're—"

I'm not sure when I finally realized something was wrong. Maybe it was when I saw the slackness of his jaw. Or when I noticed that his brown eyes didn't move, didn't follow me as I approached, just stared fixedly at the wall.

For sure, though, I knew when I touched him, when I took his hand, intending to lead him to the door. When I felt it, cool and gripless, offering neither resistance nor acceptance, just hanging there on the end of his arm, a couple pounds of meat.

These events—seeing his jaw and eyes, touching his hand—happened in a flash. Too quickly for my mind to register or interpret their significance. So I persisted in challenging him, tugging at Charlie's hand, harping at him to explain himself, unwilling or unable to grasp the truth that he was never going to do so. In fact, I continued scolding, didn't stop even as he slowly tilted and slumped onto his side. Even when I saw the blood soaking his Polo windbreaker. God help me, I was still yapping when I saw the handle of a carving knife, one I recognized from my own kitchen, protruding from his back.

～

Seconds? An hour? A century? I have no idea how long we remained there, Charlie dead and me yelling at him, pulling and tugging, slapping and shoving at him. For a while, my mind floated away, and I watched myself, my frantic futile struggle to deny the truth. But at some point, I remember the doorbell ringing. At first, I had no idea what the sound was. An irritating repetitive clanging chime. Distant. Irrelevant, because it was unrelated to the sole focus of my being: the act of rousing Charlie. But it persisted. And eventually, it penetrated the thick walls of hysterical confusion and denial engulfing me.

It made me stop yammering, come back to reality, and let go of him. It made me listen and pay attention. Identify the sound. Alarm clock? Smoke alarm? Cell phone? Microwave? Doorbell? Oh yes, doorbell. And, during that process, my mind had time to reach the semicoherent, if unacceptable conclusion: Charlie was dead.

Dead? My mind wasn't working. Couldn't process. The thought ricocheted, bouncing and rebounding, reverberating against my skull. Charlie was dead? Dead? Charlie was dead.

The bell kept ringing. And my cell phone began singing. A symphony of signals. I squatted beside Charlie, watching him. Hearing Elvis belt out my ringtone. "We're caught in a trap—" And the door chime. Dinnnng Dong. Charlie had chosen the bell; it was nothing elaborate. Just basic and classic: two simple and distinct bells, the first one longer than the second. Dinnnng and dong. Elvis sang. "Because I love you too much, Baby—"

But Charlie's mouth wouldn't close. Nor would his eyes. He stared at air. And I at him.

Another dinnnng. Another dong. Elvis stopped singing, started again. Why? How long had the doorbell been ringing? Nothing made sense, not Charlie's body, not the reason for phones or doorbells. My mind was at a full stop. Entirely useless. Finally, I got up and went to the door, but not to answer it. I just wanted to locate the noise, the terrible dinnnnging and donging, and make it stop.

~

"Damn, Elle. I was about to call the cops."

Becky. It was Becky at the door. Pounding and ringing until I opened it, when she charged in, raving.

"What's wrong with you, Elle? Why didn't you answer? I've been standing there ringing your bell for ten minutes."

Ten minutes?

"You've got to be more responsible. You can't just pull Elles like that."

"Pulling Elles" meant spacing out, drifting, getting lost in time. Apparently, I did it so often that my friends had given it a name.

"You didn't call when you got home, so I got worried. You didn't answer my texts, either. What's wrong with you? You know our deal."

She went on, scolding. Our deal, she said, was nothing to take lightly. We were women living alone in a city with a high crime rate and, when we went out at night, we needed to check in with each other. It was irresponsible of me not to. When she hadn't heard from me, she'd called. When I hadn't answered, she'd come all the way over to my house, seen my bedroom light on, and rung the bell. When I hadn't answered, she'd called my phone again. She'd been about to call the police.

As she ranted, Becky stomped in circles around my entry-way. Finally, she threw her phone into her bag and dropped the bag emphatically on the table by the door. When she finally looked at me, she froze, silent. Her mouth opened. Her right hand rose to cover it. "Oh my God. What happened? Is all that from your hand?"

I didn't know what to say. Didn't have an answer.

"Oh God, Elle. You're bleeding."

I looked down. Saw dark stains on my hands, my shirt.

Becky gave orders, rotating me, looking at my belly, my arms and back. Finding only the old, no-longer-bleeding bandaged wound on my hand.

"Elle? Say something. Are you hurt? Talk to me. What's all this blood?" She held her phone, dialed a number, gripping my arm while talking into it. She was panting, and her eyes darted, looking down the hall, into the living room, up the stairs. She told someone to come to my house, to hurry. When she ended the call, her voice got quiet. "Elle. Tell me what happened."

Becky was short but sturdy. I thought about how strong she was as I leaned on her, as she put an arm around me, supporting my weight.

"Okay. You're in some kind of shock. Come sit down." She led me to the living room. Sat with me on the red leather sofa. Good, I thought, that it was red. Blood wouldn't stain it like the one in the study. That one, the fabric was ruined.

Becky held onto my hand. "Whose blood is this, Elle? Is somebody hurt?" She watched me.

I nodded. Felt proud of myself that I'd managed a response.

"Oh God, who?" Her grip tightened. "Are they still here? Now?"

Another nod.

"Are we safe? Are you okay?"

More nods. I was on a roll.

"Where are they? Who is it? Were they shot? Do we need an ambulance? God—" She held up her phone. "I'm calling 911."

Becky was taking too much time. I had to get back to Charlie, couldn't leave him alone with my carving knife in his back, so I tugged my arm out of her grasp and headed back to the study, Becky trailing behind me.

～

Somehow, time continued to pass. I had moments of clarity when vivid details carved their way into my mind. Cops in my house. Susan appearing. Television trucks out in the street. Neighbors clustering. Lights flashing, red, blue, white. Then, the sick green hue of fluorescent lights. The jutting steel edges of swinging doors. The coarse black eyebrow hairs and stubble popping from a sergeant's pores. Details assaulted me in hordes, overwhelmed me. So I drifted willfully. Letting events carry on around me. Letting myself think about Charlie, that he was dead. Murdered. In my house. And that, despite that, I'd heard him call my name, felt him kiss my neck.

I was not superstitious. Did not believe in ghosts. Knew that dead men could neither talk nor kiss.

But clearly, from the coolness of his body, Charlie had been dead for a while. Longer than the few minutes I'd been in the house before finding him. So how had he called my name? Or played his irritating game of hide-and-seek when he was in the study, dead with a knife in his back?

It made no sense. Dead men didn't play hide and seek. Didn't move roses up and down stairs. Clearly, the whole experience was impossible.

And yet, I hadn't imagined it. It had happened. I was sure. After all, I'd been startled enough to drop my salad, hadn't I? And disturbed enough to grab a knife?

The police took me to the Roundhouse to talk; Susan came along as my attorney. I answered their questions, but didn't mention the rose or the kiss or the voice. Didn't mention the whiffs of Old Spice. I told them only what I thought they'd believe while my head battled to make sense out of impossible events, including the fact that Charlie was dead.

Even as I talked to the police, my memories surged. Charlie's orgasmic foot rubs. His pecan chocolate chip pancakes and fondness for Shiraz. His bare chest against mine in bed. His terrible, uninhibited shower arias. His credit card charges for travel to Russia, the first of the lies I discovered. The tidal wave of discovered lies that followed, washing away our marriage. I felt once more the disbelief, the loss. But I kept on answering questions. Not letting on what I was thinking. And somehow, after a fog of time, it became morning. And Susan and I were no longer with the police. We were at her house, in her kitchen, bathed in the aromas of cinnamon and fresh-baked banana bread. Rays of sun flitted through her lace curtains, and Becky was swirling honey into her tea when Jen charged in, pouting and, as usual, cursing. Prada bag slung from her shoulder.

"You BFBs!" Jen's term for Big Fat Bitches. "I can't believe you didn't call me."

"Jen, it was the middle of the night." Susan didn't even look up. She sprinkled flour on the piecrust she was rolling out. "We didn't want to wake Norm."

"Bullshit. Norm wouldn't wake up if they turned fire hoses on him."

"Well, there was no point bothering you. There was nothing you could do." Susan motioned for her to sit. "Tea?"

"There was nothing I could do, but you and Becky were essential?"

Rivalry was an inherent part of our foursome. Like siblings, each wanted to be the best most important prima favorite donna in every situation. Susan scowled. "I'm a criminal defense lawyer, Jen. There was a reason for me to be there. And Becky was there because Elle didn't call when she got in. Believe it or not, this situation isn't about you."

"FU, Susan." Jen rushed to me, kneeling in her skinny jeans. I wondered how the fabric could stretch enough to allow her legs to bend. "Elle, sweetheart, are you all right?" She put her arms around my neck, her eyes in my face. Her monster lashes blinked, tickled my cheeks.

"Don't even bother," Susan snapped. "She's not all there."

"Doing her Elle thing?"

Was I? Pulling an Elle? I wasn't sure. I was drifting, but not far away. Hovering close by.

"No. The doctor gave her pills." Becky came over, tried to edge Jen away. "She's just groggy."

I was. Very groggy. I liked the word, too. Groggy. But it confused me. If foggy meant full of fog, did groggy mean full of grog? What was grog? I inhaled Jen's exhaled air. It was warm, secondhand. But, being full of grog, I didn't care.

"And she's exhausted. The cops kept her all night."

"Those dickheads were questioning her? You poor thing." Jen stroked my head. Wouldn't let go of my neck, felt like a ninety-pound boa. "So, from the top. What happened?"

"It's mostly in the newspaper." Susan tossed it onto the table where it landed in a puff of flour.

"I knew something was wrong because she didn't text me when she got home." Becky started talking, but I couldn't listen. Not because of the pills, though. I just couldn't bear to hear any more. I'd been up all night going over and over what had happened. I felt sore, bruised all over, and preferred to sit still, letting my mind float, hearing the comforting buzz of conversation but not the actual words. It was as if I was both in the room and watching from the ceiling, simultaneously in my skin and out.

Susan poured Jen a cup of green tea. Well, it wasn't actually green, more of a yellow. Maybe chartreuse? I'd never understood what color chartreuse was. But Susan had read somewhere that green tea was good for us and she'd been urging us to drink four cups a day. She'd even made her husband, Tim, down a cup before taking their daughters to school. He'd been obedient, knowing better than to resist Susan when she had a cause.

Jen hung onto me as Becky talked. Susan fluttered around the kitchen, unable to stay still. When she was upset, Susan whirled into motion, cleaned, gardened, shopped, cooked, exercised, sued somebody, or did whatever lawyers did. The minute we'd gotten back from the police station, she'd pulled out bananas, nuts, butter, and flour to bake bread. Now, in addition to serving tea and running the dishwasher, she was making a pie. I didn't know what kind. Maybe apple. Maybe peach.

I watched Jen and Becky sit with me at the kitchen table beside a platter of sliced banana bread. Lord knew I couldn't swallow any food. But I sipped tea, mostly because lifting my cup to my face made Jen take her arms off my neck. The tea was mild, mostly tasteless. Like chartreuse-tinted water. So I took another sip, swished it around my mouth, and set down my cup.

And realized everyone was looking at me.

Staring. Why? I focused, paid attention to what they were saying.

"She's out of it, poor thing." Becky's voice was almost a whisper.

"Elle? You in there?" Jen's face was too close to mine, searching.

Of course I was. Somewhere. Maybe.

"Let her be, Jen. She's had a shock. And pills."

"And she's Elle."

Whatever that meant.

"But they can't actually believe she's involved." Jen backed away, blinking rapidly, eyelashes flapping like blackbird wings. "Morons. Are they crazy?"

"They're cops." Susan brushed flour off her hands. "They know that Elle was alone in the house with him. And that there was no sign of forced entry. And, look, the two of them were involved in a nasty divorce. If anyone had a motive to kill Charlie, she did. Plus, the knife came from her kitchen. And, statistically, it's often the spouse—"

"But we're not talking about statistics." Becky sat straight, sounded indignant. "We're talking about Elle. She's a second grade teacher, for God's sakes, not some Jack— Jill the Ripper."

"And, face it, Charlie was a bastard. Elle couldn't have been the only one with a motive to kill him." Jen jammed banana bread into her mouth. She weighed nothing, but ate incessantly, even more when she was emotional. Never gained a pound.

"Guys, the cops are just doing their job." Susan's voice was flat. Authoritative. "They have to look at Elle, if only to rule her out."

Good, I thought. They were just ruling me out.

Becky sighed. "But Jen's right. Tons of people must have had issues with Charlie. Not just Elle."

"Yeah." Jen chewed. "Like what's his name? That douche bag he worked with?"

"Derek Morris." Becky offered.

"I bet he had issues with Charlie, right? Partners probably off each other as much as spouses, right?"

Did they? I pictured Derek Morris. Charlie's business partner was smooth shaven, looked great in suits. His eyes were a tad too close together, his bottom teeth crooked. But his fingers were long and elegant. Could fingers like that shove a knife into someone's flesh?

"Or maybe it was an unhappy client." Becky was saying it might not have been Derek. "Some investor who was angry about his money—money's the motive in lots of crimes."

"Or it could have been a woman." Jen rubbed her forehead with diamond-laden French manicured nails. "Someone he dumped."

Susan raised an eyebrow. "Doubt it. True, stabbings can indicate passion, but they also imitate the male sexual act—"

"Oh, come on—"

"Stabbing is penetration, Jen. Often it's an impotent man—"

"Cut the crap, Susan. Women don't have dicks, but we can get pissed off enough to screw someone, too. Look. The guy was out there, single again. Who knows who he was messing around with?"

I winced, wondering.

"So say the babe stalks him, sees him visiting his ex-wife, and gets jealous, so bam, she sticks him."

"Jen, you realize you're basing this on nothing."

"It's not nothing. It's based on knowing Charlie. He had SA." Sex Appeal. "He liked the babes. Don't tell me he never flirted with you? Squeezed you a little too long and tight when saying good night?"

Really? Charlie squeezed Jen? I wanted to kill him.

"No, I'm betting it was an obsessed woman."

"Or maybe it wasn't a woman but about a woman," Becky pitched in. "Maybe a jealous husband."

"Right. Chances are he was cheating on Elle even before they separated."

Really? I'd never said a word about him cheating.

"And that Elle isn't the only POS."

"Jen, good God!" Susan erupted.

"Pissed Off Spouse." Jen translated.

But Susan was fuming. The oldest of us by three years, a senior in high school when we were freshmen, Susan was as usual the big sister, the mother hen. "Elle is sitting right there. She's not deaf. Don't you think she can hear you? It's one thing to make things up, but you don't have to say stuff that will make her feel even worse."

"Shit, Susan. I'm just saying—"

"Well, stop saying. We can theorize all we want. But we can also give the cops a chance to do their jobs, can't we? It's possible that they might actually know what they're doing."

"The hell they do, Susan. Get real."

"If they knew what they were doing," Becky agreed, "they wouldn't have kept Elle at the station all night."

"I've already explained. They had to talk to her. The body was in her house. She was the one who found him. It was her knife. And coincidentally, she had a knife wound on her hand."

I sipped tea. Thought about the police, their questions. Detective Swenson, broad shouldered, ample bellied, maybe forty. And Detective Stiles, a little older, disarmingly handsome, even with a scarred face. The walls had been pickle green, without windows. The furniture, a dirty bolted-down table and some straight-backed chairs. A camera on the ceiling. "How'd you hurt your hand, Mrs. Harrison?" Swenson asked the questions. Stiles just watched.

"What was your husband doing in your home? Did you invite him over? You know, you two going through a divorce and all, maybe you wanted to settle things privately, without the lawyers. So you talked, and things started out fine, but before you knew it, there was an argument. Things got out of hand. Maybe he got rough with you and you had to defend yourself. That's understandable. Was that how it went?"

I'd paid close attention to the questions and answered them, determined to sound rational, composed, and straightforward, not mentioning the tickle of a kiss on my neck or the voice calling my name. Not referring to the traveling rose. Not revealing my inability to accept the idea that Charlie, my Charlie, was, in fact, dead. Instead, I'd concentrated on acting normal, even though I had lost all sense of what that word meant.

But they'd kept at it for hours. Began changing subjects quickly, asking random questions. Did I work out? Was my health good? Had I been drinking? How often, how much did I drink? Was I seeing anyone romantically? What bar had I been to earlier? Did my husband drive a car? Did I? How long had we been married? Why were we getting divorced? What business was he in? Who were his clients? When had I last seen him? How much money did he make?

The questions had begun politely, but Swenson's tone had suddenly changed. "Your husband was a good-looking guy, Mrs. Harrison. Just because you were separated didn't mean you two weren't still, you know, attracted to each other." I'd felt my face get hot. Pictured Charlie naked; could almost feel his kiss. "It's understandable. Were you still getting it on? Is that why he was there?" My neck had gotten hot, too. Blotchy. I saw them notice.

"But your husband still had keys, you said. Odd, because we found no keys on his body. Neither to your place nor to his. Do you know where his keys are? Did he come over for sex? How often did he stop by? Was he involved with anyone else? Another woman? A man, maybe? You said your husband was a venture capitalist, right? What exactly is that? How were you involved in his business? Tell me again how you found him? What time was it? And how much had you been drinking,

again? How much life insurance did he have? Are you the beneficiary? How did his blood get all over your clothes?"

"And tell me again, how did you cut your hand?"

Hours had piled onto hours. At some point, I'd stopped caring about being present and composed or rational or straightforward or mentioning the disembodied kiss and voice. I'd
struggled simply not to poke my eyes out or smash my skull
against the green, windowless walls. Finally, Susan had been
able to get me out of there and, since my house was still a crime
scene, to take me to her house near Rittenhouse Square where
she turned both our phones off to avoid calls from the press,
and I sat drinking tea with my best friends.

Susan told the others not to worry about the police. One of
the detectives—the good-looking one, Stiles, was married to her
friend, Zoe. I'd met Zoe a few times, found her intense and demanding. But still, if Detective Stiles was married to Susan's
friend, it might help somehow.

"Look at the paper." Susan pointed to the article. "He's quoted
as saying the investigation is open and Elle is not a suspect."

"At this time," Becky corrected. "It says they've talked to
Elle but are making no arrests 'at this time.'"

I looked at the newspaper.

A picture of my Fairmount row house graced a double column on the lower right of the front page. With an inset of Charlie. A headline announced his murder: Prominent Investor
Fatally Stabbed. I stared at the page. Read that the weather was
warm, high seventy-five. That gas prices were up again. And
that it was Thursday, October fifth.

Wait—Thursday? A school day?

"Oh God—" I was on my feet, looking for my bag. "Where's
my phone?"

Six eyes blinked at me.

"I—I have to call. School." Why didn't they see the problem? "To get a substitute."

Still, they gawked. Dumbstruck.

Slowly, Susan grinned. "Welcome back, Elle." She put down her rolling pin, came around the table, and hugged me. Her eyes were sad.

"Elle! You're talking?" Jen actually clapped her hands.

"Don't worry," Becky embraced me as soon as Susan let me go. "I called and got subs for us both. I said we had the flu. But it's in the news. By now, everyone knows the truth."

The truth. I sat again, released a breath, wondered what the truth actually was.

The three of them still watched me. Warily.

"I'm okay. Really." As if to prove it, I took another sip of tea. "You can stop worrying. I swear. I'm fine."

They looked away, but nobody said anything. No point. Everyone knew it was a lie.

~

We sipped tea. Jen devoured more banana bread.

We sat in silence. We had been friends forever, didn't need to talk. Susan kept moving, opening cabinet doors, putting away shortening and flour.

Becky stared out the window. I followed her gaze, saw a blue sky dotted with clouds. A single oak in the tiny backyard. A sparrow or two flitting around. A brick patio with two Adirondack chairs, potted plants. A small patch of grass. Hedges lining the wooden fence. Peace.

Finally, Becky broke the silence. "No matter how he died or who did it, the hardest part is that he was one of us. Charlie's, like, the first to go."

"No, he's not." Susan dismissed the comment, checking the oven temperature. "We've all lost people—Jen's dad died, and my mom. And we've all lost our grandparents. That guy from our class—George Evans—he OD'd, remember? Christy Morrison—in Honor Society? She died of breast cancer. And I've dealt with tons of—"

"But no one so close," Becky argued. "Not from our own private circle. Charlie was Elle's husband—and poof. He's dead. Gone. Just like that."

"Unless you believe in hell." Jen chewed. "He's probably doing push-ups down there—"

"Jen, stop—" I began, God knows why, to defend him, but Susan cut me off.

"Look. Dead is dead." Susan lifted the crust and plopped it into a tin. "Hell or no hell, Charlie's gone. It's just that simple."

"Actually, I'm not so sure it is." I swallowed tea, stopping myself. Not certain I wanted to tell them. They wouldn't believe me. Hell, I almost didn't believe me.

"What do you mean?"

"Huh?"

They watched me warily, triplets with identical expressions of pity and concern.

"You'll think I'm crazy—"

"We already think you're crazy." Susan opened the refrigerator, took out Tupperware filled with blueberries. Another food that she said would make us healthy.

I looked out the window, then into my teacup, and decided, what the hell. There was no risk in telling them. I might feel better if they knew. These were my closest friends. We knew each other's worst flaws and most embarrassing secrets. I could trust them. Still, I hesitated. Took a deep breath. Another. Saw Susan put down the container of berries, fold her arms. Saw Jen's lashes flap, Becky lean so far forward that her breasts rested on the tabletop. They were all waiting, watching me.

"Let me be clear." I paused. "I don't believe in ghosts or paranormal stuff. And I'm not delirious, even though I might be a little in shock. What I'm about to tell you is the God's honest absolute truth, and I want you to promise to believe me."

Three sincere nods. Three voices promising.

I took one more deep breath. Closed my eyes, opened them

again. Okay. "Charlie isn't gone. He's still there. He's still in the house."

~

"Elle? What kind of pills did that doctor give you?" Susan picked up her Tupperware, shaking her head.

Becky and Jen said nothing. Becky looked away.

"No. Susan. I swear." I went on, hearing how loopy I sounded. "I smelled his Old Spice. He kissed me on the neck. Talked to me. He said my name."

An audible sigh from Becky. Susan dumped the berries into a pot. Jen stuffed her mouth with a huge wad of banana bread.

"You don't believe me."

A pause.

"I do." Becky reached out, touched my arm. "I believe you, Elle. Things like that—I believe they happen. But you have to be careful—"

"Christ. You're both delusional." Susan pushed a floury hand through her hair, left a streak.

"No, Susan. Don't dismiss us. After my grandpa died, my grandmother continued to see him all over their house for years. She talked to him, held conversations, even argued with him."

"But, Becky," I insisted, "this wasn't just wishful thinking. It was real."

"So was that."

"Becky's right," Jen's mouth was full of bread. "Stuff like that happens."

"Oh, please." Susan shook her head.

"It's funny that we've never talked about this stuff before," Jen went on, ignoring Susan. "But when my dad died—I mean the moment he died," her eyes got big, "I was seven hundred miles away at college, but I suddenly got the worst headache of my life. And my arms got heavy and stiff, almost paralyzed."

Like mine had when Charlie died?

"So I went to lie down, dozed off, and dreamed that my dad

flew away. Just jumped off the sidewalk into the sky, like a bird without wings. What was that? Why did my body get weak just when he died? Why did I dream of him leaving the earth? I'll tell you why: life energy. A loss of life energy."

Susan snorted. "Hocus pocus, Dominocus."

"Shut the F up, Susan." Jen's eyes glowed.

"But it's hooey—"

"Hell if it is. Life energy connects us with the people we love. When a loved one dies, we lose energy. That's what gave me a headache and made my arms weak. And that's what happened to Elle last night. She lost Charlie's life energy. And some of it must have lingered around her even after he died."

Susan laughed out loud. "Jen, that's pure crap."

"But it wasn't just energy, Jen." I needed to explain. "Charlie called my name. He said, 'Elle,' just as loud and clear as my voice now." The kiss on the back of my neck had been physical, and his voice real enough to make me drop my plate. "It was not just a loss of energy. There was more."

"So, if he could say your name," Susan dumped sugar over the berries, set the pot on the stove, "why didn't he mention who killed him?"

Susan relied on visible, tangible evidence. Her career was about concrete facts. If you couldn't prove it, it didn't exist for her. But at that moment, I needed her to believe me. "Susan, I'm serious. There was a rose in the house. Charlie moved it. He took it from the front door to the kitchen, then up to my bed-room."

"God, Elle." Susan closed her eyes. "All of you. Get a grip." She turned down the burner and sat beside me. "Elle, someone you loved has suddenly died." She spoke with authority, as if she were some kind of sudden-death expert. "It's understand-able. There's nothing supernatural going on here. You don't want to accept the death. So part of your mind refuses the facts. It fights them by keeping Charlie alive and—"

"Susan. I did not imagine this—"

"No. No, you didn't imagine it. You hallucinated it. There's a difference. Hallucinations seem real."

I opened my mouth to argue. Closed it. Realized there was no point.

"So, Susan, what about this?" Jen wasn't giving up. She crossed her elbows on the table. "I swear, this is the truth. My mother's uncle always kept his shoes beside his closet door. After his stroke, he was bedridden, so his wife put the shoes inside the closet. When he was dying, my great aunt and their kids were standing around his bed, saying goodbye when, suddenly, there was a thump. They turned and, guess what? His shoes were right back where he kept them. Beside the closet door. That was no hallucination. It was him, his energy saying he'd crossed over."

Susan groaned. Wiped her hands on a dishtowel. "Jen, I had no idea you were so—"

"So what?"

Susan scowled. "I don't know. La-la? Delusional?"

"Fine. You don't believe it? I've got another one." Jen's voice lowered as she told us how her mother's friend's niece had died a few years earlier in a car accident just before her sixteenth birthday. Every year since, on the birthday, the woman makes a cake, lights the candles, and the girl's spirit comes by and blows them out. "I'm dead serious. It's the girl's energy," Jen said. "It remains with the mother."

"Bull," Susan disagreed. "If it's anything other than a tacky ghost story, it's the mother's own energy. She wants her daughter to be there so badly that she creates the situation. Not consciously, maybe. But she does it herself."

"Either way." Jen sat up, arms crossed like a petite blonde guru. "It's still energy. Linking us. You don't have to be dead, either. Like my friends Luke and Riley—you met them, Becky—at the shore."

Becky had been oddly quiet, but she nodded. "The twins?"

"Right. Twins. One was in a ski accident in Jackson Hole one winter. At the very moment he broke his femur, his twin had terrible leg pains and couldn't walk. It's the same thing. Life energy. It links us."

For a few beats, nobody said anything. Becky shifted in her chair, looked from Susan to Jen. "Does anybody but me think Elle should talk to a priest?"

I wasn't Catholic; Becky knew that.

"A priest?" I was baffled.

"Just because this thing smells and sounds like Charlie, doesn't mean it actually is—"

"Becky, stop." Susan rolled her eyes, half laughing. Not joking. "I mean it. Stop."

Becky sat up, petulant. "Why should I—"

"I see where you're going, and it's absurd. What are you saying, that Elle's got a loose demon in her house and needs a priest to do an exorcism?"

"I didn't say that."

"Even Jen didn't get that wacko."

Now Jen was in it. She and Becky both went after Susan. "Excuse me? Just because you don't agree with me doesn't mean—"

"I was just making a suggestion."

"That I'm wacko. And who said you're the one to judge."

"Neither one of you is helping Elle."

"I just thought she should talk to someone with more experience."

"Or to decide what is or isn't true?"

"EVERYBODY STOP." It was my voice, bellowing.

They did. The bickering stopped, and they sat suddenly quiet, although disgruntled.

"I know you want to help. Just, please don't fight."

Nods. Shrugs. Agreements. And then Jen went back to presenting more stories. People reacting to a shift in energy when loved ones were endangered, injured, or killed. People sensing the energy of those they'd lost. And Susan continued to debunk the stories as wishful thinking or perceptual phenomena involving the subconscious mind. Reminding everyone that, no offense, but I was distracted and forgetful even under normal circumstances, that the shock might have made me even more so. No matter their reasons, they both made it sound completely normal that I'd sensed Charlie around me. And completely impossible that he actually had been.

There was no point trying to convince them. They hadn't been there, couldn't grasp it any better than I could.

Finally, Jen and Becky left around one thirty. Susan's blueberry pie was out of the oven, cooling, and she was folding her third or fourth load of laundry, talking to some opposing counsel on the phone. I went to the spare bedroom and lay down on the floral comforter.

I wasn't sure I could fall asleep, but behind closed doors, away from cops and friends, at least I was alone and finally would have a chance to cry.

∾

The next days passed in a haze dotted with more press coverage, police and legal interviews, muddled memories, and fleeting moments of clarity when I grasped unacceptable facts. Charlie was dead. He had been murdered. The murder had been committed in my house. And, at least partly because of the cut on my hand, the police suspected me.

At some point, it occurred to me that the killer might still have been in the house when I'd come home. That the killer, not Charlie, might have kissed my neck, called my name, moved the rose. Played with my mind. I began to doubt my own perceptions of that night. Questioned my memories. Slipped back into my protective haze, watching life from a safe distance. As time passed, I wasn't sure anymore what I'd seen or heard. Probably

Susan was right; my mind had been playing tricks. Probably I was jumbling events and distorting impressions because I wasn't able to absorb or bear the truth.

By Saturday, the police had finished examining the crime scene. I could go home. But I was in no hurry. In fact, I dreaded going home. Charlie's blood would be on the sofa. It would have dried, darkened. Might look black. And the drinks I'd poured would still be there, the ice melted. Water marks on the cabinet.

But it wasn't just the study. I dreaded the kitchen, too. The lingering odor of spilled dressing. The pieces of lettuce or cheese drying out, rotting in the sink.

And the whole house might smell of death. Or of Old Spice. Either way.

So, I remained in exile from my home. Exile seemed better than confronting the mess of Charlie's murder. For two days after the crime scene was cleared, I stayed at Susan's. I would have stayed longer, but the fact was that by Monday, I couldn't take another day in her house.

It wasn't that I didn't like kids—I taught seven-year-olds, for God's sakes. And Charlie and I had been trying to get pregnant when we'd fallen apart. In theory, I still hoped to be a mom someday. But, honestly, I didn't know how Susan could stand it. Her husband, Tim, was almost never around, traveled for business. And her home was in constant uproar. Noise. Clutter. Thundering, bellowing commotion. Three girls bickering, shouting and whining, their music and the television blaring nonstop.

After three days, I needed to escape. So, despite Susan's generosity and hospitality, and regardless of her concerns about me going back to the place where Charlie had been murdered, I insisted on going home. I craved stillness and quiet. Needed privacy and space.

Even so, I felt uneasy. The police and crime-scene crew would have gone through everything. The place would be a disaster.

Charlie's blood would still be on the sofa.

And who knew where the rose would be.

In the end, I had to go. I had no choice. Monday morning, I told Susan I'd be leaving. She didn't argue. Merely commented that she thought I should wait a little while so she could go with me. "You shouldn't go back there alone."

In truth, having company made it easier. Susan took the top down on her BMW. The sky was clear, the weather warm. Optimistic. When we pulled up, I understood why Susan had asked me to wait. She'd needed time to rally Jen and Becky, who were on the porch, waving. Welcoming me home.

Bolstered by friends, I unlocked the door and stepped inside, tentatively sniffing, anticipating the smell of rotting flesh or Old Spice. Sensing neither, just the fresh scent of pine. Pine? As in cleaner? I was puzzled, but said nothing. Becky watched me, smiling slyly. Jen led the way.

"Come on, Elle." Jen hurried to the back of the house. Straight to the study. Why? Did she want me to face the blood right away? Why was she grinning?

I followed slowly. Passed the living room. Wait. Something was different in there. And the kitchen. When had I done the dishes? Picked up the salad? Cleared the countertops? I had no memory of cleaning, must really have been in a daze.

Jen and Becky rushed into the study. Susan stayed behind me, her hand on my back. Pressing me on.

At the study door, I stopped, remembering Charlie, the slackness of his jaw. The knife in his back. I wasn't ready, didn't want to go in.

"Dammit, Elle." Susan shoved me forward. "Move."

So I did, slowly. Cautiously. And became confused. The room smelled fresh, faintly of leather and chemicals. In a moment, I realized why: There was a new carpet. Cream-colored. And a new chocolate-brown upholstered sofa where the bloodied old gray one had been.

Three faces grinned at me, expectant and proud.

"Susan's housekeeper came and worked all day yesterday—"

"And Jen got the couch. And there were stains on the carpet, so we pitched in—"

"You did this? So fast?"

They had.

I didn't know what to say. How to thank them.

"She's FBA." I knew that one: Fucking Blown Away. And Jen was right, I was. I remember hugs and tears. I remember flopping onto the sofa, taking my shoes off to feel the thick soft rug. I remember going to the bar, pouring drinks, ordering pizza, and laughing too much and too loud. And sometime in the middle of the raucous sisterly bonding, I remember Elvis singing, "We're caught in a trap—" and picking up my phone.

Charlie's body was ready for release. I was listed as next of kin, and the coroner's office wanted to know when I would have a funeral parlor pick it up.

~

Becky offered to stay the night, but I couldn't let her. She'd done enough, needed her own time. And, sooner or later, I had to face being in my house by myself again. And, truly, by the time everyone left, I was grateful for the quiet. I hadn't been alone for days. Needed stillness and solitude. Time to settle.

And I had phone calls to return. My voice mail was overloaded. I'd put off answering for four days, but now there was no excuse. Charlie's partner, Derek Morris, had called repeatedly. As had many of Charlie's colleagues, clients, and acquaintances. I had to respond. And Lord. I had to get in touch with his mother, Florence, his brother, Ted, and sister, Emma. They'd have seen the news, read the papers. But I had to tell them personally what had happened.

I made a list and, Johnny Black in hand, I made the calls, one by one, repeating the same words. Yes, it was horrible and shocking. No, the police had no idea who did it or why. No, I hadn't seen anything. Yes, I'd be fine. Yes, I would let them know if there was anything they could do, and when the funeral would be.

Derek, as usual, was frantic, aggressive. Intense. He barraged me with questions. "What time did you find him? Did he say anything before he died? Did he have anything on him that would explain what happened? Were things messed up? Was anything missing from your house? How did the killer get in? Who knew Charlie would be in your house?" He was worse than the police. No, not worse. But as bad. And he wanted to come over right away, help me go over details. I said I was exhausted. He kept pushing. Obnoxiously. Until I told him that he needed to back off and that I'd talk to him later. Intending not to.

After Derek, the only people I had to call were Charlie's family. As his undivorced wife, I was still next of kin. It fell upon me to contact them. These calls would be the most difficult, so I'd saved them for last. I called his mother first, but spoke to Tina, her caretaker. Charlie's mother, Florence, lived nearby, in Center City. She was eighty-one years old, a widow who suffered from severe dementia, had no short-term memory whatsoever. There was no point in telling her that her son was dead, she wouldn't remember it. But Tina needed to hear what the other callers had. There were no suspects yet. I hadn't seen anyone. I'd let her know about the funeral.

Next call was to Ted, Charlie's brother. Ted was fifteen years younger than Charlie, lived in Virginia Beach, hadn't seen Charlie in years, but contacted him often to borrow money. I thought he gave water-skiing lessons and did body piercing, suspected he sold drugs and used more than he sold, needed the money to pay for them.

Ted answered on the first ring. His voice was a croak. "Ch-Charlie?"

Charlie? Why would he think it was—oh, of course—caller ID. He'd recognized the number on his cell phone screen.

"Is it you?" He sounded incredulous.

"No, Ted. It's Elle."

"Elle?" I could hear his burned-out brain whirring, probably trying to figure out who 'Elle' was. He sounded stoned. Shaky.

"Charlie's wife." Ten years earlier, at our wedding, Ted had been the best man.

"Okay. Right. But technically—no offense—you're not his wife any more. I mean you guys split up."

"That's right." I bristled, decided not to react. There was no point. "We split up, but we weren't divorced yet—"

"What are you talking about? Of course you were—he called you his 'ex.'"

He did? "Well, I am his 'ex.' But legally, I'm still his wife. Divorce takes time." Why were we talking about the status of my marriage?

"Oh, man." Ted sounded wasted. And disappointed. But not even a little curious about why I was calling. "Damn it—Charlie said he was single."

"Ted." I interrupted, not sure why he cared about Charlie's marital status. "I have some bad news."

"What. Somebody die?"

Good guess. But then, why else would I call? "Yes." I swallowed Scotch, took a deep breath. "Charlie."

"Charlie? For real?"

I thought he'd already have heard. But the murder might not have been on the news in Virginia Beach.

"Yes, for real."

"Well, son of a gun." He didn't say anything else. Didn't ask what happened.

"Ted—" I took a breath. The words didn't have meaning any more. I'd repeated them so many times that I felt like a recording. A computerized voice. "Charlie was murdered."

Ted made a sound, kind of a cluck. "Murdered? Huh." He stopped talking. "So did anyone—do they know who did it?"

"No."

"No suspects? Really?" He didn't ask any more questions. Not how Charlie was murdered. Not when. Not if he suffered. Nothing.

"He was stabbed. Thursday night." For some reason, I felt compelled to tell him. "I thought you'd want to know."

"Yeah. Sure. Thanks, Ellen."

"Not Ellen. Just Elle."

"I thought it was Charlie calling when I saw the number on my phone." Ted coughed, deep and hoarse. "I couldn't believe it. That it was him. But I really thought it was."

Charlie never called Ted. It was the reverse. Ted called Charlie. Regularly. Whenever he needed money. Whenever he was desperate.

I pictured Ted, rubbing his tangled hair, his eyes. Hanging his head. Brain fried from whatever he'd smoked. Or swallowed or injected. Probably more upset about losing his cash cow than about losing his brother. "So. Will you come to the funeral?"

"In Philadelphia? You mean go up there?" The thought seemed to baffle him. As if he'd forgotten there were roads.

"Well, Charlie was your brother."

"Yeah. I don't know, Elle." He remembered my name. "It's a long way and gas costs a lot of dough."

Silence. I had nothing to say. Did he expect me to pay for his trip? Should I?

"So. Do you think—are they going to have like a reading of, you know, his will?"

What?

"Because there's a chance he might have left me something. Do you know? Would I have to be there for that?"

I said I didn't know. I didn't pressure him to come up. Hadn't expected him to. Didn't know what I'd do with him if he showed. I said something about keeping in touch and refreshed my drink before placing the final call.

～

Charlie's sister, Emma, and I had never been close. She lived in Connecticut with her insurance company CEO husband, Herb, had a busy social life, sat on the boards of philanthropic organizations, belonged to a variety of book, garden, and country clubs, sent her kids to prestigious private schools. She and Charlie had been tight, but she and I hadn't spoken at all since the separation. In fact, I wasn't sure when we'd last talked—at least a year ago. Probably two. Even so, she wasn't surprised to hear from me, answered the phone, saying, "Derek already called."

"Derek? Really?" Well, okay. At least I didn't have to break the news to a second sibling. "I'm sorry I didn't get to you sooner, Emma. It's been crazy. You must be pretty shaken up."

Emma didn't confirm or deny her condition, didn't ask if I were shaken up, too. She didn't ask for details about the murder either. What she asked was, "So, do they have any suspects, Elle?" Her voice had an edge. And when she said my name, the edge sliced, razor-sharp.

"None that I know of." I didn't like her tone. And I was tired. Had repeated the story of Charlie's death eight or ten times in an hour. I swallowed Scotch.

"So, Elle," again the cutting tone, "don't you think it's odd that they found him in your house?"

"What? Of course I do—"

"And that the murder weapon belonged to you? Derek said Charlie was killed with your knife? Have they read his will? Who was Charlie's main beneficiary? You, right?"

Her implications were as subtle as a hatchet blow. Obviously, she thought I'd killed him. I sat up straight, indignant. "Emma. Is there something you want to say to me?"

She paused. "Yes. Actually, there is." She drew an audible breath. "Honestly. I've never especially disliked you, Elle. But I never especially liked you, either."

Okay. I didn't like her either, but that wasn't news.

"If Charlie wanted to be married to you, that was his business, not mine. But what was my business was that after he married you, my brother changed. Especially these last few years, Charlie became someone I didn't know. Morose. Troubled. Something happened to him, Elle, and it happened on your watch. First, his joie de vivre got taken. And now, his life."

"Wait just a goddamned second, Emma—" I was seething. "Who the hell do you—"

"So, bottom line, here's what I want to say to you." She continued evenly, calmly, as if I hadn't interrupted. As if immune to my anger. "If you played any—and, Elle, by 'any,' I mean even the remotest, minutest most indirect part in my brother's death—forget inheriting his estate. Forget his life insurance. Forget getting one cent of his money. I swear I'll see to it that you rue the day your sorry eyes first fell on him. I'll make your life so unbearable, so full of misery that a mere knife in your back will seem like tender mercy."

When she finished, I was sputtering. Stuttering. Unable to come up with a coherent syllable, much less a fitting response. Emma, with her porcelain skin and delicate tea sets, had just bitch slapped me, and, frankly, I was stunned. Maybe I said goodbye. Maybe I simply hung up. But afterward, I stayed in my kitchen, holding my drink, seething, staring at the phone.

Clearly, Emma was convinced I had something to do with Charlie's murder. But why? We'd separated, true, but that didn't mean I wanted to kill him. I mean I'd talked about it, but jokingly. Privately, with my friends. No one would take those conversations seriously.

"Women usually use poison," I remembered. Who'd said that? Becky? Susan? Jen had suggested staging a robbery gone bad. And someone had warned against making repeated stab wounds, I forgot why. But Emma didn't know about the conversations I'd had with friends. Couldn't know. Maybe her suspicions arose from her dislike of me. Or wait—she'd talked to

Derek, Charlie's partner. Had Derek told her I might be involved? Did Derek suspect me, too?

And if they suspected me, other people must as well. Including everyone whose phone calls I'd just answered. And the police.

Oh God. Obviously, people would assume I'd killed Charlie. I was the spouse. Worse. The estranged spouse. And statistically, spouses were guilty. And, as Emma had so graciously reminded me, Charlie had been killed right here—with my knife. I pictured the detectives, how their eyes had narrowed, studying me. Oh God. I wasn't just a suspect. I was Suspect Number One.

But how could people honestly think I'd kill Charlie with my own knife in my own house? Did they think I was that stupid? Of course not. At least the police didn't. Did they?

I stood, needing to move, woozy from the Scotch. I put my glass in the sink. Opened the fridge, took out bread and Swiss cheese. Made a sandwich. Added a pickle and mustard. Picked it up. Put it down. Wondered why Charlie had been in the house. And who had been with him. Who'd killed him. But I had no idea. Charlie had known a lot of people.

I carried my sandwich back to the table, set it down. Realized I wasn't finished yet, had one more call to make. Picked up the phone again, hoping the place was still open.

For all of her fierce familial loyalty and sisterly venom, Emma hadn't offered to help with Charlie's funeral. Nor had any of his shocked and caring friends. Nor had his concerned partner. No, that part was left to me, Suspect Number One.

~

And so, I called W. J. Sloane, the parlor that had handled Susan's mother's funeral and made an appointment for the next day. Turned my phone off. Swallowed my sandwich, still bristling about Emma. How had she dared to speak to me like that? Why had I simply sat there taking it? And how could I prove I hadn't murdered Charlie?

I thought about my alibi—Jeremy's bar. That guy Joel, the magician, if I could find him, he'd confirm that I was there. And Becky, of course. And the cab company could confirm my ride home. I could prove I'd been out, no problem. Even so, Emma's assumptions and implications riled me, and I headed upstairs reciting things I should have said to her. Like, "Emma. Your head's up your ass." Or, "Charlie didn't change, Emma. He just stopped pretending to tolerate you." Or, "Emma, you ever talk to me like that again, I'll do to you exactly what I did to Charlie."

Even as I muttered those feeble comebacks, though, I realized Emma had been right about one thing: Charlie had changed. Especially over the past few years. Sorrow washed through me as I remembered the old Charlie, my Charlie. But I couldn't dwell on that, and hurried upstairs to quiet my mind.

I ran the bath, added jasmine-scented bubbles. Finally sank into warm water, relaxing, soaking in silence. Lying back, closing my eyes. Again, I thought of Charlie, how he'd sometimes kept me company when I'd bathed. Brought bubbly wine or bonbons. Sometimes, he'd lit candles and turned out the lights. Sometimes, he'd put on music. Sinatra. Beethoven. The Stones. Whatever suited his mood.

Oh God, why was I remembering those times? They were finished. Even if Charlie weren't dead, those times would be. It was the bath, probably. The tiny popping of bubbles, the embrace of hot water. The jasmine scent. Memories were linked to those sensations. Or maybe it was even deeper—maybe the house itself held memories. Maybe the walls, floor, stairway, bathtub—maybe they all held images of what had happened inside them. Meals, music, laughter, lovemaking. Maybe not just bubbles, but also memories floated in the tub.

I closed my eyes, engulfed in quiet and warmth, and let the memories surface, almost feeling Charlie beside the tub, leaning against the wall, holding his drink. Almost hearing his voice.

"Derek brought in big bucks today. I mean big. Somerset Bradley."

I'd never heard of him.

"Guy owns half of New England. Hotels, commercial real estate. He's giving us the whole enchilada. He says he's done working, just wants to travel. So Derek—got to give him credit—he lured him in by putting a whole trip together for him. Russia. The Far East. It cost a wad, but it was worth it."

Lord, why was I remembering that conversation? It was boring, had no significance. Why, when I let my mind drift, wasn't I remembering steamy sex? Or spooning cozily in our sleep? After all, these were my memories, too. Why was I resurrecting Charlie talking about business? And out of all his clients, why a twit like Somerset Bradley?

The water cooled; the bath ended. I wrapped myself in a terry robe that had been Charlie's and went to bed. It was barely nine o'clock. But I lay down, clean, on fresh sheets, turned out the light, and lay quietly listening, watching. Maybe he'd say my name again. Or put the rose somewhere. Or kiss me. Or brush by, leaving his scent.

For a long time, I didn't let myself sleep. I lay still and alert. Waiting for Charlie.

∻

No kisses. No scents. No rose. No voice. No Charlie. At least, not while I was awake, which was, I think, until after one.

But then, I remember walking into the study, stepping on something sharp—a tack? Wincing. Looking down at the floor, seeing not a tack. A rose. Thorns. A speck of blood on my foot. And, in the shadows, a man.

"Charlie?" I was surprised. Delighted. He was back. Home. Everything was okay.

"You're smiling." He didn't move, just turned his head my way. "Don't smile, Elle. Don't pretend."

But I was glad to see him and felt my smile widen. "See, I

thought you were—" Wait. What had I thought again? It flittered away, but I knew it had been something bad. Something awful.

"Oh, please, Elf. There's no need to say it." He looked pale, and I wondered if he'd been drinking again. He'd been drinking so much lately.

I went to him, sat beside him. Leaned over for a kiss.

But Charlie didn't kiss me. He sighed, but didn't move. Didn't even put an arm around me. Dread washed through me. Why was he being so cold? What was it I had forgotten?

His expression was blank. "Please. Don't make it difficult. Don't pretend." A slow, twisted smile.

I was cold. Shivering.

"You were the love of my life. But I could never make you happy." Charlie stood, towered over me. "Goodbye, Elf." He leaned down, his lips brushing mine, tickling like butterfly wings. And then he turned away. Leaving me.

I opened my mouth to call him, but could make no sound. Charlie was going. Almost gone. No—no way. He couldn't leave me.

A knife was in my hand. I raised it. Drew a breath. Closed my eyes. Felt a rush, a thrust. And distinctly, independently: The taut resistance of fabric, the smooth separation of flesh. The scrape of steel against bone. The handle slipped. The blade cut my hand as I adjusted my grip and tugged at it until with a sucking sound it came suddenly free. Then another plunge. And another.

～

I tried to open my eyes, to shake my head, to say "no," but couldn't. I tried to sit up or move my legs. But couldn't. In fact, I could move nothing, not my toes, not my eyelids. I was paralyzed. You're asleep, I told myself. Not awake. Stuck in a dream. But blood was warm and sticky on my hands. And I still heard gurgling, the rasps of Charlie's dying lungs.

Don't fight it, I told myself. Go back. Change it. Make it so you didn't kill him. Because you didn't. You know you didn't. Charlie, my mind called to him, and I saw him, stumbling onto the sofa in the study, staring at me. It wasn't me, I told him. I didn't kill you. You must know that. Didn't you see who did? Tell me, who was it?

But Charlie blinked at me, stunned, as if surprised to be dying.

And he mouthed a word. Only one syllable: Why.

Why? Why what? Why, as in, why am I dying? Or as in, why did you kill me? Didn't he believe me? Did Charlie think I killed him? He stared at me from the couch with accusing eyes as I blithered my innocence. So far, going back into the dream wasn't going well. But it was my dream. Shouldn't I be able to steer it the way I wanted? It wasn't me, I repeated. I didn't kill you, but Charlie was gone, and I was lying immobile in my bed, struggling to open my eyes. This time, I insisted, pulling myself out of a well of deep sleep, making my eyes open, my limbs come back to life. Even when I could move, I didn't get up right away. I lay there, actually checking my hands. My cut was healing, and they were both free of blood. Finally, my mind still immersed in the dream, I looked at the clock, remembered my appointment. Made myself get up to make coffee. My left foot was tender. When I looked, I saw a tiny red sore there, as if I'd stepped on the thorn of a rose.

∼

Nonsense. The mark on my foot was probably just a scratch. Not a prick from the stem of a rose. But some dreams are so vivid, so intense that coming out of them is like pulling out of quicksand. As I brushed my teeth, I could still feel the knife in my hand, still smell Charlie's blood. And, as I made coffee, I was still shaking off the accusations in his eyes. I knew the dream was merely that, and that I had to get on with the day. Meet with the funeral director. Make plans for Charlie's body to be picked up and buried. I was thinking about epitaphs when the doorbell rang.

It couldn't be Becky. She was teaching. Maybe Jen? I opened the door still wearing Charlie's robe, my hair disheveled, face unwashed. And faced Detective Stiles, the handsome one with the scar. Married to Susan's friend.

No Swenson this time; a uniformed officer was with him. A woman. They had yet more questions to ask. Could they come in?

"Coffee?" I offered. "I'm just having some."

They followed me into the kitchen. On the way, I realized that the kitchen might not be a good idea. Charlie had crammed it with expensive appliances—a fridge bigger than my closet, stainless steel top-of-the-line everything, but the room was tiny. Before we'd added the study and powder room, it had been the back end of a row house in Fairmount. Sitting down together would mean crowding chairs around a protrusion of granite just big enough for Charlie and me. Not built for three. Three would mean that at least two have their knees or even thighs bumping each other, depending how the bodies were arranged.

When they saw the room, the officer—her name was Moran—hung back, standing at the door, declining coffee. Detective Stiles and I sat.

I refreshed my mug, poured his. Offered milk and sugar. Stiles drank it black. He sipped it. Complimented it, said it was nice and strong.

Good. So he liked my coffee. I sat, trying to seem relaxed. As if I hadn't just committed murder in my sleep.

"Just a few more questions, Mrs. Harrison."

"Elle—please call me Elle. We were getting divorced. I don't think of myself as Mrs. Harrison."

"Okay, Elle. I know it's a difficult time for you. But chances are we're going to be showing up here repeatedly during this investigation."

"No problem. I understand." I sipped coffee. He had clear, blue eyes. Penetrating.

"Good. So. Let's begin by going back to last Thursday. The day of the murder. You said you went to Jeremy's bar that evening. What did you do before that?"

Before going to the bar? "Nothing. I took a shower."

"I mean, all that day."

All that day? Why? I heard Emma's accusing voice, saw Charlie's eyes. Stiles probably believed I'd killed Charlie, too. I held onto my mug, eyeing the handcuffs on Moran's belt. Suspect Number One.

"Should I call my lawyer, Detective?"

The side of his face without a scar smiled. "You can, of course. But that will slow things down. All we need for now is a timeline."

Just a timeline. Well, there was no harm telling them what I'd done on Thursday. Besides, calling my lawyer would antagonize them; that's how it was on every cop show that ever aired. "I worked. Left the house about seven thirty a.m. Came home from school about four." I paused, trying to remember. What had I done next? Probably reviewed the next day's lesson plan—that's what I normally do. "Oh—I remember. I was upset. It was Benjy's birthday, and his mother sent chocolate cupcakes. Well, Aiden and Lily, two of the kids in the class, are allergic to chocolate." Why was I telling him about the cupcakes? "Anyway, I remember writing a memo to all the parents about being careful with birthday snacks."

"And then?"

And then? Why couldn't I remember? "I think I graded some arithmetic papers."

"You think?"

I stiffened, not accustomed to having my language examined. "No. I know." I did, didn't I? "I graded some arithmetic papers."

"Where were you while you did all this? In what room?"
His eyes drilled into mine. Almost punctured my corneas.

"Probably the bedroom." Damn. I sounded unsure again.

"You're not sure?"

"I was in the bedroom."

"You're sure."

"Yes." Kind of.

"Okay." Stiles glanced at Officer Moran. Just the tiniest, quickest glance. "So. You graded arithmetic in the bedroom. Then what?" He set his mug down, empty. Crossed his legs with some difficulty; they were long, didn't fit easily under the extension of granite.

"I was tired. I took a nap."

He nodded. "And what time would that have been?"

What time? I didn't know. If I'd come home at four, written a memo, graded papers, it must have been—what? Almost six? "I'm not sure. Six?"

"When did you cut your hand?"

I had no idea what time it had been. "Right before I left for Jeremy's, I was slicing fruit—"

"And the knife slipped?"

"Yes. I've already told you what—"

"And what time was it when you left the house?"

He'd asked all these questions before. Several times. Why did we have to go over all of it again? What difference did it make? "Detective, really—I don't see—"

"We're trying to establish a timeline, Elle. That's all."

A timeline. Okay, of course. That made sense. "I met Becky about a quarter to nine. Left here about fifteen minutes before."

Stiles didn't say anything. He sat still, legs crossed. Watching me. Officer Moran also watched me. Armed, guarding the door. I cleared my throat, drained my second cup. Needed to go to the bathroom. Shifted my weight, deciding whether to excuse myself. "So, is there anything else, Detective?"

He uncrossed his legs, slowly leaned forward, arms crossed on the table. His face was too close. I wanted to move back. "Well, Elle. There's likely to be more. Because it turns out that the time of your husband's death was between six and ten p.m. Which means, he might have been killed after you left for Jeremy's." Stiles paused, making me anticipate the finish. "But also, he could have been killed while you were still home."

∾

While I was home? Asleep upstairs?

"No way. I couldn't have been here. I'd have heard him come in—" Wait. Stiles was implying that I must be the murderer. Oh God. Was he going to arrest me? The handcuffs on Moran's belt—were they for me?

"Did you go into the study at all, Elle?"

I tried to remember. But now, everything that happened on Thursday seemed dim. My only vivid memory was of finding Charlie's body. Everything else—even being at Jeremy's appeared in momentary flashes, like snapshots. "No. I didn't. I had no reason to go in there."

"You'd need a reason?"

"I didn't go into the study." Had I?

Of course not. But if I had, would I have seen Charlie in there? Was he already there when I came home? Why didn't he say anything? Unless—was the killer in there, too, keeping him quiet? Killing him?

"Again, Mrs. Harrison—sorry. Elle. Do you have any idea why your husband was here?"

No idea. I'd already told them that.

"Is anything missing?"

Nothing I'd noticed.

Stiles went on, eyes piercing, his voice hammering. He had questions about Charlie, his business acquaintances, his will, his insurance policies, his women and friends. I floated away inside, overcome with the sense that my life had stopped being real.

That it was a bizarre play being enacted on stage. I watched myself talking with police. The scar on the detective's face darkened, looked dangerous, sinister. I remembered my dream. The stiffness of the knife, the penetration of clothes and skin. The streaming of blood, the slicing of my hand. Don't let on, I told myself. Act like nothing's wrong. It was just a dream. Remain in character. Smile, be normal. Wait, no. Smiling wouldn't be normal, not in this situation. Not when the detective's thinking I killed Charlie. Not when he's zeroing his attention on me, studying my reactions.

Instead of smiling, I offered Detective Stiles more coffee. He declined. If he was going to arrest me, he ought to get it over with. But he didn't. He just kept questioning me until, finally, I made myself tell him I had to get to the funeral parlor, that I had an appointment there. Instead of arresting me, he apologized for taking so much time. Stood up to go as if it had just been a friendly visit. He thanked me for the coffee, said he'd see me soon. His smile was crooked, eyes sober.

I watched them go as if they were exiting the stage, as if I were sitting far up in the second balcony.

After they left, I told myself that Stiles didn't really think I'd killed Charlie. He couldn't. The police were just being thorough. I rinsed out the cups, went upstairs, showered. Stood under the stream of hot water, replaying the visit, over and over again. No matter how I tried to deny it, though, it was clear. The police suspected me. Otherwise, why the multiple questionings? Why the intense stares? Why all the questions about my hand, my activities on Thursday?

Oh God. I closed my eyes. Why had answering those questions been so hard? I'd given my best guesses, made assumptions about what I must have done. Didn't have complete concrete certainty. My memory was misty. And it had gaps; the chain of events lacked links.

Obviously, that was to be expected. I'd been in shock on

Thursday. Suffered a trauma. Memories of minor tasks I'd performed earlier had been blown away by the murder. It was understandable that I couldn't recall details. Wasn't it?

Hot water pounded my face, my hair. And thoughts pounded my head. Someone had killed Charlie. In my house. The police had narrowed the window of time of the murder. I'd been home at least for part of it. Even had that damned knife wound on my hand. Obviously, they thought I was guilty, were gathering evidence against me. Probably weren't even looking at anyone else. I was the spouse, and it was almost always the spouse. Especially the estranged spouse. As soon as they could build even a circumstantial case, they would arrest me.

Oh God. Really? They'd arrest me?

I saw Officer Moran's handcuffs closing around my wrists. Felt the cold metal, heard the locks clink. Would they come for me here at home? Before work? Surely, they wouldn't take me out of school, not in front of twenty-four second graders. But maybe in the parking lot—

Stop it, I said out loud. Startling myself. Realizing that I was no longer standing, but curled under the streaming water against the shower wall, on the floor. Hiding.

No. Shaken, I climbed back to my feet, turned off the water. Smoothed my hair. No one was going to arrest me. They didn't have evidence, not a scintilla. They couldn't, since I didn't do it. It was that simple.

Good. So why didn't knowing that make me feel safe?

Maybe because innocent people had gone to jail before. For years. For decades. For life. Lord. Innocent people had even been executed.

No way was I going to sit passively and watch the cops weave a web around me, trapping me in a net of suspicion. Stepping out of the shower, I wrapped myself in a towel, faced myself in the mirror, met my own wary eyes. And understood. There was only one sure way to get the police to back off and accept the fact that I hadn't killed Charlie. And that was to find the guy who had.

But first, I had to plan a funeral.

～

"Shit, Elle. I cannot believe you didn't call me. You just let them in?" Susan was exasperated. She'd called as I was about to leave for the funeral parlor, and I'd told her about the visit by Detective Stiles. She scolded me, furious. "And you served them coffee and chatted like you were best friends. And told them everything they wanted to know. Please, Elle. Do not tell me that."

Why? Had talking to them been so wrong? "But I thought Detective Stiles was your friend."

An audible sigh. "Yes, Elle. Nick Stiles is my friend. Mine. Not yours. To you, the man is a homicide detective." She spoke slowly, as if to a moron. "Elle, listen to me. Detective Stiles did not come to your house to socialize. He came to interrogate you. Swear to me you will not let the police in again without a warrant."

She stopped, waited for a reply.

"Okay."

Not good enough. "No. Not just 'okay.' Swear."

"Okay. I swear."

"And do not answer any more of their questions, not a single one. If they have questions, tell them to contact me. Get it?"

I got it. "So I guess you think I'm a suspect?"

A pause. A tsk. I pictured an eye roll. "Elle. You're kidding, right? Yes. Definitely. You. Are. A. Suspect."

"That's insane—" Something hot flew up my rib cage. "Susan, I didn't—"

"I know that. Anyone who knows you knows that. But the cops don't know you and don't care. Unless they have compelling evidence leading them elsewhere, they'll go after the easiest, most likely person."

"Which would be me?"

"Sad to say. The estranged spouse."

I shivered. Sat on a step in the hallway. The police seriously suspected me. The facts pointed my way. I looked down the hall, saw the door blur. Felt tears pool around my lashes. What the hell was happening? Nothing seemed real. Not the murder. Not the suspicion. Not my life. I grabbed the banister to make sure it was solid.

Susan was still talking. Asking questions.

"Sorry."

"What exactly did they ask?"

My nose was running now, and tears were sliding down my cheeks, dripping off my jaw. I needed a tissue. Didn't want to get up and look for one. "They were making a timeline, they said. Checking what I did all day, what time I left, what time I came home."

"Okay."

"Turns out I might have been home during the murder." My voice sounded unfamiliar. Like a cough or a choke.

"What? Time of death was while you were—"

"That's what they said. I was here only for part of the window, but still—"

"Shit. If you knew the time of death, why did you tell them you were home? Why didn't you call me?" She was yelling.

"I didn't know the time of death, Susan. How was I supposed to know why they were asking me what time I got home? Besides, that wasn't the only thing they asked. They wanted to know what I'd done when I got home. What rooms I'd been in." And why couldn't I actually remember all of it? I stood, desperate for a tissue, headed into the kitchen.

"Okay. Whatever. The damage is done. Damn, you're crying, aren't you?"

"No."

"Yes, you are. Stop crying, Elle." Her voice softened, became maternal. "I'll do damage control. We'll get through this."

I took a deep breath. Swallowed. Nodded. Yes, we would get through this.

"So what did you tell them you did after school?"

I grabbed a tissue from the box on the windowsill. Paused to blow my nose. Told her what I'd told the police. And then, I told her the truth.

"Wait, you don't remember anything? But you said you wrote that memo—"

"I know I wrote it because I have it. So I must have written it that afternoon. But I don't remember writing it. Same with the arithmetic papers. They got graded. But I don't remember doing it."

"It's shock, that's all. It's normal."

I let out a breath, slowly. Letting Susan reassure me.

"People don't process memories in traumatic situations. That's why eyewitnesses are so unreliable. The brain shuts down in crises. Memories get distorted or don't get recorded at all."

I nodded, dried my face. She was right. Just as I'd suspected, the gaps in my memory were normal. The result of a traumatic situation. My mind had been scrambled.

"Besides, you probably weren't paying attention to what you were doing. Lots of times, we do stuff on automatic, without thinking. If you ask me whether I did laundry yesterday, I'll have trouble remembering. I don't pay attention to laundry. I just do it. Sometimes, I'm amazed that I have clean underwear in my drawer because I have no recollection of putting it there. So, you came back from school and did what you normally do. You didn't know you'd have to remember it, so you didn't pay particular attention. You were tired and your mind wasn't recording. That's why your memories are so vague. No big deal."

No big deal. Good.

But Susan wasn't finished. I pictured her pushing her hair behind an ear, straightening her posture as her tone became formal, businesslike. "We have to meet, Elle. Attorney and client. We need to get to work and to get you off the suspect list."

I wrote the appointment on my calendar: Susan. Wednesday. ten a.m. My handwriting looked strange. Unfamiliar, as if it belonged to someone else. But then, so did the rest of my life. And I couldn't stop to think about strangeness. I was late for my appointment at the mortuary.

～

Edward, the director of W. J. Sloane, was an expensively dressed fortyish guy with freckles and ginger hair on his hands and a practiced soft-spoken voice. He was skilled with euphemisms, never once said the word "death," let alone murder. He was sorry for my "loss," especially for the "circumstances." And he hoped he could make the "process" go as smoothly as possible. He wanted me to know that my husband was in good hands, that the "home" would treat him with care and respect.

Edward ushered me into the office, a cheerful, brightly lit modern place with cushioned furniture and a conference table. He offered coffee or tea. I declined, and sat, hands folded on the table, not knowing what to expect. Never having planned a funeral before. Glad to be with Edward, who dealt with funerals and dead people on a daily basis. Oddly, he didn't seem grotesque or the slightest bit Igorlike. He might have been a banker, or an insurance executive. A pharmaceutical rep. His suit was a subtle pinstripe. His haircut expensive. Nails manicured. A successful businessman. Whose business just happened to be death.

Edward guided me, much as a car salesman would, to a showroom where I could see the latest "models." Which meant coffins. Coffins were everywhere. A dozen or more of them. Open and closed. Wooden or metallic. Shiny or matte. Dark or light. With bars or grips for pallbearers. Some understated, sleek as a boat's hull, others ornate, intricately carved. I'd never shopped for a coffin before. Never even thought about them. Didn't know the desirable—or undesirable—traits. Price would probably be a good indication. Expense would reflect quality. I touched rich, glowing wood. Was it mahogany? Edward whispered that the cost of that model was ten thousand dollars. I withdrew my hand. Why would someone spend that much on a thing that would be stuck in the ground and never seen again? I had no intentions of spending that kind of money on Charlie. Still, I couldn't very well bury him in a plain pine box. People already suspected me of killing him. Putting him in a pauper's coffin would only reinforce that idea.

I looked around, from coffin to coffin, couldn't tell which one suited Charlie. And I doubted Charlie would give a damn what I did with his body now that he was done with it. Edward stood patiently, hands clasped in front of him, butlerlike. Not intruding. I had to make a decision. I looked from price tag to price tag. Coffin to coffin. Couldn't help but imagine lying in one. Being closed in. Wasn't there a short story—by Poe—about being buried alive? The air thickened, made it difficult to breathe. Death, being buried—it was all too intimate, too close. I didn't want to think about in which box Charlie would be closed up, or on which cushion he would rest his decaying skull. But, surrounded by coffins, I could hear his voice, as if he were there beside me.

"I never skimped on anything for you, Elle."

It was true. Charlie had indulged me. Had always provided us both with generous material comforts. Like my refrigerator—a small, if chilly, family could set up house in that thing. But I wasn't as materialistic as Charlie. Or as rich. And, besides we hadn't been together when he died. There was no reason to splurge.

"Whatever happened between us, Elle," Charlie whispered, "for the moment can't we get past who did what to whom?" I could all but feel his breath on my neck. "You hold the cards. I know you won't deprive me of a first-rate send-off. One last luxury ride. I'm in that box forever, Elle. All I'm asking is for a cushy place to rest."

I drew a breath, pressed my hands against my eyes. Was Charlie's voice just my imagination, like Becky's grandmother seeing her dead grandfather? Or was I actually losing my mind? Edward glanced at his watch. I needed to get out of the funeral parlor, to see the sky. So, with Edward's excellent advice, I selected an elegant smooth walnut coffin with a plush satin cushioned lining, priced at a cool $5,000. Then, back in the office, urged by Charlie, I bought Edward's ultradeluxe product line. The highest-priced, tightest, most moisture-proof encasement for the coffin, to prevent leakage. Or was it seepage? Whichever, I didn't want to think about it. I just proceeded, following Edward's recommendations as if he were selling not death compartments, but vacation time-shares or luxury condos. I signed forms approving postautopsy embalming procedures, but balked at the escalating costs. The funeral—without the burial plot—was already into the five figures. I hesitated at the optional cosmetician and a hair stylist.

"Elle. Come on. This is my last public appearance. Give me a break." His voice was so loud, so clear, that I thought Edward had heard it. But he gave no indication as I caved, approving every optional service the funeral parlor provided, hoping Charlie would leave me alone if I let him go out clean shaven and well trimmed.

Edward compiled the names of guys who might serve as pallbearers: Charlie's partner, Derek; his brother-in-law, Frank; brother Ted if he came in; some tennis buddies, Mort and Andy. A couple of clients, Jonas Walters and Philip Wendell, who'd belonged to the Union League with Charlie.

Edward recommended and arranged for a pastor. He helped me pick out an organist, music, and poetry readings Charlie would have liked. He brought in a florist to create opulent arrangements for the viewing and service. He sold me the premier high-gloss program and guest book. Charlie was in my head, insisting. And finally, with almost twenty thousand dollars spent and with neither Edward nor me having uttered "death" once, all that was left was to write the obituary.

That part should have been easy; I was an obituary expert, after all. I knew the standard structure and vocabulary. But after filling in Charlie's name, I stared at the form, unable to go on.

"Beloved husband?" Edward suggested.

Charlie's voice was silent. Probably waiting to see what I'd come up with. Probably smirking.

I shook my head, no, and searched for appropriate words. How could I encapsulate our relationship, let alone Charlie's life in a simple paragraph? Charles Harrison, 43, heartbreaker, manipulator, wheeler-dealer, and expert backstabber, finally stabbed in his own back on October 5 by person or persons unknown.

No. Too wordy.

How about: Charles Harrison, aged 43, went to final judgment by his Maker, poor bastard.

I kept at it. In the end, I chose: Charles Harrison, venture capitalist, aged 43. Suddenly on October 5. I listed information for the viewing, funeral, and interment, and thought about a charity to receive donations in lieu of flowers. Obviously, there was no American Knifed in the Back Association, so I chose the SPCA and World Wildlife Fund.

After that, all that was left was the "survived by" part. It was supposed to list the bereaved, the people devastated by his loss. Charlie's mother couldn't remember that he was dead long enough to be devastated. His brother wasn't even curious about what had happened. His sister was annoyed with him, and his murder had only annoyed her more.

For all his contacts, Charlie didn't have many who would mourn him. Most of his relationships had been functional, formed around particular activities: making money, having sex, playing tennis, betting on football. They weren't about kinship or love. Well, I'd once believed we'd been about love. But never mind. Charlie's relationships or lack thereof weren't my problem. I listed the names of his family and left it at that.

Or I almost did. One name wasn't on the list.

Should it be? If so, what should I call myself? His wife? Former wife? Estranged wife? Almost ex-wife? Lord, what difference did it make? The man was dead.

And his voice—even if I'd been imagining it—was mute, offering nothing.

Edward was patient, but the obituary was taking a long time, and the newspaper had a deadline. And he had another appointment. The dead kept coming. He advised me to keep it simple. So I called myself Charlie's wife, which didn't feel right, but was technically and legally accurate.

The obituary, finally, was one of the simplest, lacking details. No "beloved" or "dear." No American flag, no career summary. No cause of death. But it was done. And I thought I was, too.

But Edward reminded me that I had one more task. Before the funeral, I had to select the clothes Charlie would wear for the viewing and the funeral. And for eternity.

∼

Soft breezes rustled through green, red and golden leaves above Rittenhouse Square. Speckled by tree-filtered sunlight, people sat on benches lining the paths, reading, talking on phones. Enjoying the scene. I didn't stop to admire foliage or fountains, though. I was on a mission and wanted to get it over with. Go in, grab the suit, and leave.

I'd never been in Charlie's apartment. Hadn't been invited. Wouldn't have gone if I had been. Didn't want even to glimpse his life after me, let alone to find out if the bathroom held extra toothbrushes. Or tampons. No, I didn't want to know. But the police had already been there, searching. Would have found whatever there was to find and removed it. Hopefully, they'd found stuff to take suspicion away from me. I made a silent prayer, asked God to help them find the real killer and leave me alone. Made my mind up to sprint in, grab a suit—any suit—it didn't have to be the perfect suit, and leave.

Charlie's was one of those high-rises right off the square. Ritzy and glitzy. The doorman knew I didn't live there, asked if he could help. Eyed me when I said no, that I was Charlie Harrison's wife. I held Charlie's key up, told him the apartment number: 21C. And he backed down, told me how upset everyone was about the murder, offered his sympathies. Stifled his questions. Probably suspected me.

The elevator lights glowed softly. My feet sank deep into plush hallway carpets. And then, there I was, putting Charlie's key into the door of 21C.

∿

I recognized the art. He'd stripped it off the walls of our house. But I was surprised to see my art deco stainless floor lamp. It had been my grandmother's, had stood in the corner of the living room. Odd, I hadn't missed it. What else had Charlie pilfered? I glanced around, saw the aquarium, the philodendra. The sparse furnishings, all new. A modular leather sofa. An enormous flat-screen TV.

Keep moving, I told myself. Do not get sidetracked. But, passing the kitchen, I couldn't help looking in. Noticing the wine rack. Charlie had stocked up on Williamson's, his favorite Australian Shiraz.

"Go ahead. Help yourself."

The voice was so clear that I actually looked around. Saw no one, of course.

"Go ahead. I bought it with you in mind."

Even dead, Charlie was lying to me. And no way was I going to have a glass of Shiraz or anything else in his apartment.

"Remember the first time you tried it?"

Of course, I did. Two feet of snow had fallen, a record in Philadelphia. Everything had shut down. We'd done what newly married couples do: made love, ate, drank wine, repeated the process. I remembered it vividly. But I also remembered the last time I'd had that wine. About eight months ago. The onset of our implosion, before I'd found out about the missing money. The night I'd found a piece of paper in the bag with the bottle.

A receipt for that day, from The Four Seasons Hotel, Philadelphia. "What's this?" I'd held it up, frowning.

"Huh?"

I'd brought it to him. Shoved it at him.

"Oh. Nothing. It's Derek's."

"Derek's? Derek can't charge his own hotel rooms?"

"It was for a client. It's complicated."

My jaw had tightened. I'd said nothing.

"What? You think I'm cheating on you?" A puppy-dog face. Big innocent eyes.

"How can you think that?"

I'd held the wine bottle in one hand, the receipt in the other. Charlie had reached out, tried for a hug. I'd resisted, pulled away.

"Elf. Seriously. It was just business."

Just business? As in a professional? "A hooker?"

He'd chuckled. Shook his head, crossed his arms, sighed. "I swear. The room wasn't for me."

My hand had tightened around the neck of the bottle. "It's your credit card."

"I paid for the room. But it's complicated." Charlie had leaned against the kitchen counter, watching me. Breathing heavily. "I can't talk about this, Elf. It involves important clients. Just trust me."

Trust him? Seriously? He'd been acting oddly. Brooding. Secretive. Distracted.

"Look at me, Elle." I'd looked, glaring. He'd looked back, directly into my eyes. "I didn't take a woman there."

Not a woman? Something had hopped against my rib cage. "You took a guy?"

Charlie's mouth had opened, then closed. And exploded as he'd laughed out loud. Not a happy laugh. A sad, heartbroken laugh. But he didn't answer.

"I don't see what's funny, Charlie."

His demeanor had changed. He'd gone on the offense. "You really want to pick a fight with me? You're jealous, aren't you?"

I hadn't answered.

His eyes had laughed. He'd darted away, dodged my questions, avoided the issue, made my suspicions seem like a personal flaw. Was I really that insecure? Didn't I know that he loved me? Why was I checking his receipts, anyhow? What was next? Would I stalk him? Read his e-mail? Examine his phone records? His eyes had danced, enjoying himself as he'd turned things around, making it my fault that I'd found the receipt, that there even was a receipt, that I'd wondered why.

He'd escalated, mocking me until suddenly the wine bottle wasn't in my hand anymore. It was flying. Aimed right at Charlie's smug and smirking head. Which at the last moment, ducked deftly, so that the bottle missed him and smacked the cabinet behind him.

Amazingly, the bottle hadn't broken. Charlie'd caught it before it rebounded off the cabinet and fell onto the counter. Without comment, he'd opened it, poured two glasses, handed me one. Toasted us, our commitment to each other. Our love. We'd eyed each other warily, silently declaring a truce. Then, tentatively, maybe reluctantly, we'd kissed. Neither of us apologizing.

And the night had moved on.

❧

I wasn't going to drink Charlie's Shiraz. And I didn't want to hear his voice in my head or see what else was in his apartment. I hurried down the hall, ignoring the art that had hung in our home, the bubbling aquarium, the new upscale furniture, the lingering smell of Charlie's Old Spice. I left the kitchen, passed a spare bedroom that was his home office. Found his bedroom at the end of the hall on the left. My breathing was shallow, heart rate too fast. Kept going, passing a new king-size bed. Why had Charlie needed such a big mattress? Never mind. Not my business who slept there. Or who'd inspired the new Ralph Lauren comforter and sheets. I avoided the bathroom, not wanting to see feminine toiletries. Or Charlie's, either—didn't want to remember him coming out of the shower, or standing in a towel by the mirror coating his face with shaving cream, or talking to me with a toothbrush in his mouth. So I crossed the room without turning my head, went straight past the dresser to the closet, had my hand on the doorknob before I stopped and looked back. At something on the bureau.

Our wedding picture? Charlie had it on his dresser? Good Lord, what for?

No. I wasn't going to wonder about that. There was no point. I wasn't there to ask unanswerable questions or drag myself yet again through the reasons we'd split. I was there for one reason: to find a suit. Determined, I made myself stop staring at the photo, turned back to the closet, and opened the door into a space larger than my kitchen. The midnight-blue silk robe I'd bought him last Christmas greeted me from a hook. I turned on the light and stepped in, faced a wall of shirts, shelves of shoes and sweaters, a rack of slacks, another of jackets and ties. Enough for a dozen men. But, strangely, there were only six suits.

Charlie had liked clothes, looked good in them: tennis whites, khakis, and polo shirts. But especially suits. Nobody wore a suit like Charlie. He'd had them in every shade: gray, black, charcoal, navy. Solids. Pinstripes. Jackets that were vented and not. Slacks that had cuffs and didn't. Different shapes of lapels and numbers of buttons. Vests. Tuxedoes. Blazers in navy, forest-green, burgundy, tan, chocolate. And he'd had them in every texture and fabric: tweeds, cashmeres, gabardines, wool, linen, flannel, corduroy, camel hair, even leather and suede.

But now, all that hung in his closet were half a dozen suits, and they looked new.

He still had his hundreds of shirts, shoes, sweaters, and jeans. I stood in his closet, surrounded by his clothes. Dizzied. Where were his other suits? They couldn't all be out for cleaning at once. Had he given them away? Moved them into a girlfriend's house? No. He'd have taken everything, not just suits. Never mind. It didn't matter where they were. I needed to select one suit, only one. I closed my eyes, spun around, reached out. Found my hand on a black pinstripe.

"Seriously?" I heard Charlie complain. "That's so somber. I'll look like I'm going to a funeral."

Funny. Very funny. "Okay, Charlie." I may have spoken aloud. "Then tell me what you want to wear."

No answer. Charlie would offer only vetoes.

I looked at a charcoal suit. Pictured him going to work in it, smelling fresh and spicy. The tailored jacket fitting his shoulders, cut just for him. The fabric reshaping itself with his movements, hinting at the muscles underneath. Stop it, I scolded myself. Just pick a suit and go. Damn. I shouldn't have come alone. Should have brought Jen. She was good with clothes. Never mind. I could do this. I'd simply take the light gray.

"Not that one. Fabric's too soft." Charlie nixed it as I put my hand on the hanger.

Too bad. I wasn't going to argue with the voice in my head. I simply replaced the light gray and grabbed a different suit, a darker pinstripe.

"Elle, that's so boring—it's the ultimate gray flannel suit."

I ignored him. If he wasn't going to tell me what he wanted, he'd have to deal with what I chose. I took a white shirt, red tie. Charlie whined. I changed the tie to a blue one. Pulled a pair of Jockey shorts—did they bury people in underwear? And some black knee-high socks from the bureau under our wedding picture, which I refused to look at. I threw everything into a hanging bag, headed into the hallway without even glancing at the wedding picture. And stopped.

A key was rattling in the front lock, and the knob began to turn.

For a few rapid heartbeats, I considered greeting the person openly. I had every right to be there and to question theirs. Besides, it might not be his killer. It might be the police. Or Derek. Or his cleaning service. Or a girlfriend. But before I finished the list of possibilities, I was back in Charlie's closet, the door shut behind me, huddling among his few remaining hand-tailored suits.

~

I don't know how long I crouched there, not moving, barely breathing, listening. But it was long enough that my muscles began to burn and cramp. Charlie's thick carpets muffled footsteps. And with the closet door closed, I'd have no way of knowing where the visitor was. Or who. Or what he wanted. Unless he was a she. It might, of course, be a she. I remembered the king-size bed. Did Charlie have a girlfriend? How long had he been seeing her? I tried to picture what she'd look like. Tall, like me? How old?

"You're still jealous, Elf?"

No. Of course not. Wait—was Charlie reading my thoughts?

"Well, you don't need to be. You never needed to be. You were the only one who mattered. The love of my life."

Shh. I put my pointer over my lips, the symbol for quiet.

"Why? No one can hear me—"

"Somebody's here," I whispered. "It could be your killer—"

"My killer *is* here, Elle." I could smell him, felt his breath on my neck like a shiver.

What? Where?

"We both know who killed me."

"Wait—you think it was me?" My whisper was too loud. "How can you think that?"

He didn't answer.

"It wasn't. Charlie, I didn't kill you." Still too loud.

Still no answer. But, since we were talking, maybe I could learn something.

"Charlie, who has keys to your apartment?"

Charlie remained silent. He offered nothing. Not a peep. Great. I was crouched in a closet behind hanging fabric, talking to air. My legs were numb. My lower back burned. I had to move. And it occurred to me that, if I couldn't hear the visitor, the visitor probably couldn't hear me. So, slowly, I set down the hanging bag and emerged from the blockade of suits. Straightening my back, I stood, limped on feet I couldn't feel to the door, and put my ear against it. Listening.

Hearing nothing.

More minutes passed. At some point, I realized that, if the intruder left, I wouldn't know. In fact, he or she might already be gone. Sooner or later, I'd have to check. Which would mean opening the closet door.

I didn't right away. As blood flowed back into my legs, I prepared, rehearsing various encounters. If the intruder were a policeman, I'd explain why I was there. No need to say more. If Derek, I'd find out what he wanted. I didn't trust him, didn't like him, didn't want him sneaking around Charlie's apartment. I'd tell him to leave. But what if it were the killer? Oh God. I looked back to the suits. Maybe I shouldn't risk it. No. I had to, couldn't stay in Charlie's closet forever. But, just in case, I'd need a weapon. Maybe there was a shoebox? A small case that held a gun? Nothing. But wait—I was in a closet. Could make my own weapon. I grabbed an empty wire hanger and, despite the raw wound on my hand, untwisted it.

I bent the wire, winding it, doubling it, reshaping it, forming a dangerous tip. Imagined myself bursting out of the closet, charging. And finding neither a killer nor a cop, but a woman. Crying, sobbing about her dead lover. She'd found out from the news, from TV. I tried, but couldn't see her clearly. I pictured red hair—or, no. Brown. Olive skin? A tan? I kept shifting features, but none of the faces or bodies seemed right. Of course they didn't; none of them were my own. Damn. Would I ever let go of him? Of being his wife?

The hanger had become a shiv. Maybe not sharp enough for a surgical incision, but good enough to do damage. One more time, I put my ear against the door. Heard nothing. Reached for the knob and, carefully, soundlessly, turned it. Cracked the door just an inch. Peeked out. Saw no sobbing woman. No masked murderer. No one at all.

Good. Another inch. And another.

Soon, the door was open wide enough for me to leave. I poked a tentative foot out the door. Another. Tiptoed into the bedroom, looking left and right, in front and behind. Listening, clutching my hanger weapon, ready to strike. Looking around, seeing nothing amiss. No rifled drawers. No tossed mattress or upturned furniture.

I moved into the hall, more confident. Almost convinced that the intruder was gone. That maybe there had been no intruder, that I'd imagined it, just as I'd been imagining Charlie's voice. That the sound of a key, the sight of a turning knob had been nothing, just emotions, nerves. The effects of trauma and loss.

At the front door, I exhaled, realized I'd been holding my breath. I relaxed my shoulders and opened the door. Feeling foolish but relieved, I stepped into the hall. Where I stopped. Pivoted, catching the door just before it closed. Cursing.

The funeral clothes. I'd left them in the closet. I'd almost left without the stuff I'd come for.

This time, I didn't stop to look around, just hurried back to the bedroom. Which is probably why I didn't see the figure lurking in the office doorway.

I hit the floor hard. Felt the jolt of impact. Heard a scream.
Mine? Pain bolted through me as someone grabbed me from behind, tugging, and I rolled, resisting, seeing, in my bandaged
hand, a wire shiv.

~

I blinked, squinted, tilted my head. But still, I didn't recognize
the man. Well, even his mother wouldn't, not with a mangled
wire hanger buried in his eye. Not with thick blood clotting all
over his face. But, lying on the floor, half under, half beside him,
I kept staring, wondering who he was. Whether I'd seen him before.

I wasn't sure what time it was. How long we'd been lying
there. What exactly had happened. I knew he'd attacked me,
knocked me on the floor. But then? Obviously, we'd struggled.
The cut on my hand had reopened, seeping and stinging. And
when I touched my head, I felt a sticky bump. So, we'd fought.
I'd hit my head. And I'd stabbed him.

Oh God. I'd killed a man. Self-defense or not, I'd killed him.

Okay. I had to get up. Had to call 911. The police. Oh—and
Susan. Susan would know what to do. She lived just a block
away. Could be at Charlie's apartment in a minute. The guy's
one good eye was open, staring. Watching me. Who the hell was
he? It hurt to sit up, to move. But I did, slowly, grunting. Pulling
my legs out from under his. Aching, I edged over to my purse,
to get my cell phone. Didn't take my eyes off the guy, just in
case he wasn't really dead. Just in case he'd spring up and come
after me again.

But he didn't. He lay there, one eye wide, the other a mess
of jellied gore. Exploded under a clump of twisted wire.

My hand hurt as I reached into my bag, feeling for my
phone. But I found it, grabbed it, made the calls. Susan then
911. Or the other way. Don't know. Don't remember. Either
way, I didn't get up. My head hurt. And the walls swayed when
I moved. So I just sat, waiting for help to arrive. Seeing myself

from far away, watching the dead guy as his one good eye was watching me.

~

Susan got there first, spouting Oh my Gods. She helped me to my feet, sat down beside me on the new living room sofa. Handed me a water bottle. A water bottle?

"Quick," she touched my arm. Comforting. "Before the cops get here. Tell me how you know this guy. What happened. And what the hell you're doing here."

I listened for sirens. Watched for police to storm in. This time, for sure, they'd arrest me. Oh God. I'd killed a man. I could see him in the hall. Lying on the floor. Arms splayed. But Susan was scowling, demanding answers. I needed to focus, to tell her the basics. About getting Charlie's funeral clothes. About hiding in the closet because someone had come in. About shaping a weapon out of a hanger.

"So the guy jumped you?"

"He tackled me. Pounced on top. Slammed my head against the floor." He must have. I had a lemon-size lump on my temple as evidence.

"And you don't know who he is? Really?" She frowned, doubting me.

"No. Why? Do you?"

"Well, yes. He's pretty well known around here. And throughout the entire Northeast U.S." She looked at him. "That's Somerset Bradley."

Somerset Bradley? I remembered, knew the name. Had pictured him older, bulkier. Not nearly as limber.

"He was a client. Charlie mentioned him, said Derek brought him in." I saw Charlie sitting beside the bathtub, keeping me company. The lights low. The water warm, bubbly and scented. My head woozy from drink. And Charlie's eyes glowing. About Somerset Bradley.

"The guy was a big developer," Susan spoke quickly, glanced at the front door. "He owned everything. Malls. Hotels. Sky-rises. Commercial real estate everywhere."

"So what was he doing here?"

Susan shrugged. Got up. Looked at the body. "Somebody gave him a key. Did Charlie often give his clients keys to his apartment?"

Why would he? "I don't have a clue."

She eyed the body. "He looks like a cat burglar, those black running clothes. But why is he dressed like that? Somerset Bradley sure didn't need to rob anyone. So what was he up to?" She twisted her neck to look at his face. Grimaced. "Man. You sure did a number on him."

I didn't know what to say. Made kind of a moan.

"Okay." She stood straight, all business. "Here's the deal, Elle. The press is going to be all over this, especially after Char-lie. Ignore them. Do not speak to them under any circumstances. More importantly, when the police ask questions, I'll advise you about whether or not to answer. We want to cooperate, but not self-incriminate, understand?"

I did. Sort of.

"We'll explain that you were attacked in your husband's apartment. No matter who this guy is, you were the victim here. You acted in self-defense. Although—"

Although?

Susan pushed a lock of hair out of her eyes. Folded her arms. Stood up straight. "They may argue that you had time to think. You know, to plan to stab him. I mean, you had the time to make this hanger thingie—"

"Susan. I wasn't planning to kill him. I was hiding. I thought Charlie's killer was here. I made that to protect myself. I was scared."

"I know, Elle." Susan sat again. Touched my arm again.

Tilted her head. "Of course that's what happened. And that's exactly what we'll tell the police."

For the briefest moment, I wondered if she believed me. And I probably would have asked her, but just then Charlie's front door swung open, and police swarmed in.

～

An EMT looked me over. Checked the swelling on my head. Recommended a trip to the hospital. Susan agreed. In fact, even though I didn't see the need, she insisted.

Detectives Stiles and Swenson had arrived. Looked at the body. Looked at me. My insides flipped and blood drained from my head, but met their eyes. Susan stood with them, spoke in a low voice, her head bent toward Stiles. His eyes warmed, listening to her. Friends.

I waited on the sofa. Watching the commotion. Wondering if they would take me in. If I'd sleep that night in jail. If I'd be able to shower, wash off all the blood. An officer stood beside me, watching the EMT take my blood pressure.

Swenson, not Stiles, finally came to talk to me, Susan at his side like an extra sleeve.

"You want to tell me what happened, Ms. Harrison?"

I looked at Susan. Did I?

She nodded. "Just briefly, Elle. I've already explained the basics to the detectives, and they can see you're in no condition for a lengthy conversation."

Detective Stiles stood within hearing range. Listening. Swenson took notes. I was shivering, teeth chattering. The EMT wrapped me in a blanket, mentioned the word, "shock." Susan scolded Stiles, said I needed immediate medical attention. Swenson argued that if I would just answer his questions, we could all move on. Susan looked at me, her face a question. I nodded, yes; I could do it. Told them what happened. How I'd gone there to get funeral clothes, and seen the doorknob turn, heard a key in the lock. How I'd run back, hid in the closet. And made myself a weapon, just in case it was the killer. And finally had left, but forgotten Charlie's clothes. Gone back for them. And boom. I'd hit the ground.

I stopped, not sure what else to say.

Swenson leaned close, breathing on my eyes. Frowning. "You didn't mention stabbing Mr. Bradley in the eye."

"Hold on, Detective. Why should she? Clearly, it was self-defense." Susan stepped in, stood in his face.

"We'd like to hear her account, nonetheless. That is, if you don't mind." Swenson stood nose to nose with Susan, sarcastic, facing her off.

Stiles watched, silent.

"Elle?" Susan didn't take her gaze off Swenson's eyes. "Are you up to this?"

My thoughts were jumbled. Even so, I knew I shouldn't say I didn't remember what else happened. That would sound like I was lying. Maybe about everything. No. I had to tell them something that would satisfy them. Had to improvise.

"He knocked me down. We fought," I touched the lump on my head. Winced. Looked at my hands. The EMT had rewrapped the cut on my palm, but there were still stains of dried blood. "He bashed my head against the floor. I don't remember how many times. But somehow, I rolled over and pushed to get him off me. I couldn't. And he put his hands on my neck, like he was going to strangle me, so as hard as I could, I jabbed him in the face with the hanger." Six eyes focused on me. Waiting. Not blinking. Ten eyes, if you counted the EMT and the uniformed officer standing beside the sofa. "I honestly wasn't aiming for his eye. But there was kind of a slip and a pop. A spurt. And he let go of my throat and slumped down."

There. Finished. Was that good enough? I looked from face to face, measuring the reactions. Did they believe me? Was it too much detail? Not enough? Would they check my neck for strangle marks?

Swenson moved closer. Too close. So close I could see into his pores. "Ms. Harrison," he growled softly into my ear, "Detective Stiles here says I should take it easy on you. So I am. For now. But just so you know? Something about you isn't right. I know it—"

"Detective," Susan actually shoved him, "if you want to speak to my client, do it within my hearing."

Swenson backed away but kept his eyes on me. I sat straight, didn't look away. I knew about eye contact, that if you looked away first, you were admitting weakness. So I didn't. I stared back until, finally, he turned away. And then, I let myself drift.

Susan was talking again, her voice still stern. Stiles had an arm across her shoulders as if to calm her. The three of them— Stiles, Susan, and Swenson stood in a huddle, buzzing. And then, I saw myself flat on a stretcher, being rolled down the hall to the elevator. I watched the fancy light fixtures of Charlie's building until they became the lights of the elevator, or the sun in the open sky, or the sterile white roof inside the ambulance, and I could see the ambulance racing through the city, passing cars, going through red lights, siren blaring. Then strong arms helped me onto a bed, from which I watched the drop ceiling in the emergency room. And dozed. Until a voice—Susan's?— asked what my room number would be. Repeated it, telling someone on her phone that I had a mild concussion, would be fine, had to stay overnight for observation.

A while later, I sat up in bed. Saw the room spin. Had a headache. In front of me was a tray of roast chicken, peas, and mashed potatoes, a slice of apple pie, a pot of brewing tea. *Jeopardy!*— *Jeopardy!* Teen Tournament played on a television near the ceiling. And, seated in a row, facing me, looking somber, frightened, and frantic, were the three most beautiful women on earth. Susan, Becky, and Jen.

︙

They watched me eat. They brushed my hair. Becky rubbed skin cream onto my feet. I thanked them over and over. Told them they were the best friends ever. That I didn't deserve them.

"You're right," Becky agreed. "You don't."

"We're just here so when we want something you'll owe us." Jen grinned. I could see her aura: golden pink.

Alex Trebek read categories for Double Jeopardy!

I tried to get up to go to the bathroom.

"Don't move." Becky put a hand on my shoulder. "You have a concussion."

"Just a mild one."

"Nevertheless."

"But I have to pee."

"Let me call the nurse."

"No, let me get up."

Jen reached for the call button, Becky pressed on my shoulders, to push me back onto the bed. Susan grabbed the tray so the food wouldn't spill.

"I'm fine. I don't need a nurse." I lifted my head off the pillows. The walls shimmied.

"You're not supposed to jostle yourself."

"NFW, Elle." No Frickin' Way. "You're not getting up. Pee in a pan."

I was surrounded. And they weren't giving in.

"Guys. I'm not going to do cartwheels. I'm just going three steps to the john."

They considered it. Silent groupthink.

"Fine. If you're careful. But you have to lean on me." Becky offered her arms to pull me up.

"And go slowly," Susan added. "Very slowly."

"Glide smoothly, Elle. So you don't rattle your brain." Jen stepped along with us for the distance, maybe two yards from the bed to the bathroom door.

The walk, though short, was unsteady. Wobbly. Nauseating.

My body ached all over, probably from fighting. But Becky was solid, and we made it. The walk back was less urgent, still a little dizzying.

"Does your head ache?"

"Jen, don't make her talk," Susan scolded. "We agreed not to ask her questions."

"Back off, Susan. I just asked if her head hurt."

They squabbled, like normal. Made comforting background noise. Alex Trebek's answer was the university whose students were called, "Elis."

Becky mumbled, "What is Yale?" as she helped me back into bed, replaced the food in front of me.

I gazed at the clotting gravy on the cooled mashed potatoes. Felt woozy.

"You going to eat that?" Jen pointed at the pie.

Ever so gently, I shook my head, "No." Watched her grab the plate, inhale the pie. Lay back.

Drifted. Closed my eyes.

And remembered. Oh, damn—

"Charlie's clothes!" I sat up. "The funeral parlor—"

"Don't worry. It's all done." Susan nodded toward Jen.

"Everything was in that bag, right?" Jen's mouth was full. "I took it over before, while you were being admitted."

Really? "Thank you."

"No problem."

Alex's answer was, "The university whose team is The Big Red."

"Oh, I forgot—the funeral director gave me this."

"What is Cornell?" Becky asked.

"It was in Charlie's jacket pocket."

"Don't bother her with that now," Susan frowned.

"I'm not bothering her," she snapped. "I'm just giving her an envelope."

"She needs to rest."

"It's okay," I said, but neither listened, in bickering mode again.

I reached for the envelope that Jen had pulled from her enormous Louis Vuitton handbag. Held it as I lay my head back down. Thought about the man I'd killed. And Charlie. The gaps in my memory. And the police.

Final Jeopardy was over. The teen on the right, Tyler, had won, had nailed the Shakespeare category with "What is King Lear?" Alex was shaking hands. Becky kissed my cheek, "You'll be okay, Elle. See you in the morning."

Jen squeezed my shoulder, gave me a peck, whispered. "They say you'll probably get out tomorrow. If not, the funeral director said he can run another obit and postpone the—"

"Jen." Susan actually pulled her by the arm. "Not now."

Jen stiffened, whirled around. "You are a real PIA, Susan." Pain in the Ass. "Elle needs to know what he said."

"Fine. She can know it tomorrow." Susan, the oldest, bossing us around. Just like when we were kids. "Elle's in no condition to deal right now. Let her be."

Jen backed down, looked at me. Back at Susan. "Fine. You decide what she should know. You tell her." And she stormed out.

Leaving Susan and me by ourselves.

~

Susan sat on the reclining chair beside the bed. Sighed. Rubbed her eyes.

"It's going to be okay." She wasn't convincing.

"Are they going to arrest me?"

"No—for Somerset Bradley? No. He might be a big shot, but he was trespassing. And you were defending yourself—"

"But what about for Charlie? Detective Swenson just about threatened—"

"I know. It's just bullying tactics. Ignore him." She crossed her legs, leaned an elbow on her knee. Pursed her lips.

"What?"

"Nothing. We should let this go until you're—"

"Susan. I need to know what's going on."

"It's better to wait—"

"Bullshit. Talk."

She bit her lip. Brushed hair out of her eyes. Nodded. "Okay. But just briefly. I talked to Stiles. The police do consider you a person of interest in Charlie's murder, but for now, they aren't arresting anyone."

"For now?" My mouth went dry. "What the hell is a 'person of interest'?"

Susan sat up straight, looked away. "It means they want to look at you more closely, but they don't have enough evidence—"

"Susan. They think I killed Charlie. And now I've killed another person. To them, I'm, like, a serial killer."

"That's ridiculous."

"No, it's not. I took a man's life today." Saying it out loud seemed to make it more real. More definitely true. Oh God. What was happening to me? Who was I really? Until this week, I'd been a second grade teacher. Now, I was a killer?

I looked at Susan, deciding how much to tell her. She'd always been like a big sister. A few years older, she'd always been the one I'd gone to for advice. And now, she was also my lawyer. If I was going to confide in anyone, it would be her. Still, I hesitated. She wouldn't believe me. She'd say I was imagining things, just as she had when I'd told her about hearing Charlie's voice.

"What?" She had such soft brown eyes. "What's on your mind, Elle?"

"Susan. Can I trust you?"

"What?" Her voice rose, insulted. "After all these years, you're asking if you can trust me? Elle. This is me. Susan."

I guessed she meant yes.

I considered how to continue. Studied her face. A vein stuck out in her forehead, a sign of stress. And her eyes strained with concern. Bloodshot. Reminded me of another eye, red with an embedded hanger.

The fact was I had no choice. I had to trust somebody. And Susan wasn't just my friend; she was my attorney, so, legally, she couldn't breach a confidence. But she looked exhausted. Needed to go home to her family. I'd taken up too much time already. Should let it go.

"Hello?" Her voice was loud. "Where are you? Are you doing an Elle?" She thought I was drifting.

But I wasn't. "I'm thinking how to put this."

"Don't think. Just tell."

Okay. "I know the cops think I killed Charlie—"

"Not necessarily—They just have to—"

"Don't deny it. We both know I'm the obvious suspect. So, before this thing today happened, I was thinking that the best way to get them off of me was to figure out who really killed him. And I was going to make a list. But I didn't. Because I had to wonder: What if it really was me? What if I killed Charlie?"

Susan's jaw actually dropped. She pushed her hair back. Licked her lips. Uncrossed her legs. Leaned forward. Scowled. "Elle. I'm only going to ask this one time. What the fuck are you talking about?"

"What am I talking about? I'm talking about maybe I did it and just don't remember—"

"That's absurd. It's—"

"No. Listen. Maybe it was such a trauma that my brain blocked it out and didn't record it."

"Beyond absurd. It's ridiculous. You would never kill anyone, Elle. Let alone Charlie."

"I'm serious, Susan. My entire memory is full of holes. Big gaps. Blank spots like a piece of Swiss cheese. You guys tease me and call me spacey. But this isn't just daydreaming. It's like

I've skipped chunks of time. Maybe I have early onset Alzheimer's. Or a brain tumor. Or some mental disorder that takes me away. Protects me from recalling things I don't want—"

"That's crap."

"No. Listen. The detectives asked me what I did after school on the day of Charlie's murder, and guess what? I couldn't remember."

"What do you mean, you couldn't remember? That makes no sense."

"That's what I'm trying to tell you. I remembered only snapshots. The rest was blank. I filled in the rest by deduction. By best guesses."

"Sorry." She shook her head. "No way you killed him."

"Fine. But Susan. What if I did?"

I looked at her. She looked at me. Blinked. Sputtered. Shook her head. "That's simply not a possibility."

"Look at the cut on my hand—"

"But you said you did that cutting fruit—" She stopped midsentence. Realizing that maybe I didn't remember the cut any more than anything else.

"There's more. Susan. I dreamed it. I dreamed I was killing him. I felt the knife in my hand. Cutting through his jacket. His skin—"

"So you had a nightmare. It's understandable—Even with your separation, Charlie was your husband. His murder horrified you."

"But the details? How would I dream such vivid details if I hadn't done it?"

She shook her head. "Sorry. I'm not listening to—"

"No. You have to. I meant it about a mental disorder, Susan. You all tease me about 'pulling an Elle.' Drifting off, not paying attention. But maybe pulling an Elle isn't just a quirk. Maybe it's serious. And the gaps in my memory—maybe they're part of it, and I do things and then don't remember them. Like that rose—remember how it moved around my house? And how I thought Charlie was moving it because it kept showing up some-place else?"

She nodded, yes, she remembered. "But that wasn't Charlie—"

"No. I know that, Susan. Because maybe it was *me*. Maybe I moved the rose myself and just don't remember. Just like I don't remember killing him."

Susan let out a breath. She sat perfectly still, watching me, with only her eyelids moving, blinking rapidly. "Listen to me, Elle. I don't know about the stupid rose. Maybe you moved it, maybe not. But of one thing, I'm very sure: you did not kill Charlie."

I wanted to believe her. "How do you know that?"

She smiled. Tentatively. "Because I know you. You're an air-head, yes. You float in and out of conversations like dandelion fluff. But you are not violent or dangerous. You're simply not a killer."

"Tell that to Somerset Bradley."

A tsk. "That was different."

"Maybe. Maybe not. Truth is, I don't remember."

Her head tilted. "You don't remember that either?"

Slowly, without disturbing my mildly bruised brain, I shook my head, No. "Not a second of it."

A sigh. A silent moment or two. "Well, the evidence leaves no doubt. You acted in self-defense. But I get what you're say-ing. If you really don't remember, maybe it's about trauma. When you're under extreme stress, Elle, maybe you just check out. Some kind of defense mechanism. Part of your brain shuts off, maybe, and your memory stops recording. Actually, to some degree, that happens to everyone. Eyewitnesses to traumatic or violent events can't remember anything accurately. People watching the same event will swear that the getaway car is green and that it's also silver. And the perp is both fat and skinny, black and white, old and young, even male and female."

I knew about eyewitnesses. But they didn't forget what they did after work. Didn't find roses moving around their homes. Didn't forget killing a man.

"Do you want to see a shrink?"

I blinked. A shrink? Lord. Tears gushed, rolled over my eyelashes. I smeared them across my face.

Another tsk. "Elle. Don't cry—" Susan put a hand on my arm. Tenderly.

"But Susan—" My chin wobbled. "What if—" I swallowed, finding my voice. "What if I'm not who we think I am?"

"Who are you, then?" She sounded maternal, soothing.

"I don't know. Some multiple personality? Somebody with a killer living in my body?"

"A serial killer living in your body? Really?" She chuckled. It did sound pretty wild. "Poor Elle. You've been all alone with this, giving this some serious thought, haven't you?"

I sniffed. She handed me a tissue.

"Well, you're not alone with it anymore. You told me. And I'm glad you did. Feel better?"

Not much. Maybe a little. But I said, yes, I did.

"Good. Now, here's the deal. If you want, we can get you evaluated by a psychiatrist. I'll even arrange it for you. But at least for now—and I mean this seriously, Elle, don't talk about this to anyone—I mean anyone but me. Not Jen. Not Becky. Not a soul. Get it?"

I did. Susan didn't want the police to find out about my memory gaps. Because the gaps invalidated my statements about what had happened. Made it look like I'd lied about the events surrounding Charlie's murder and Somerset Bradley's death. Which, actually, I had.

⁘

A woman in green came in for my dinner tray. "You not like?" She eyed the untouched chicken.

"I wasn't hungry."

"Maybe tomorrow. You feel better, missus. God bless." She smiled, took the tray, waltzed out of the room.

I looked up. Pat Sajak was saying goodnight. Wheel of Fortune was over. We'd been talking for a whole half hour.

Susan stood. "Look, I've got to go—Emily's bedtime. But I don't want you lying here thinking you're Jekyll and Hyde. You're not a serial killer and you don't have a multiple personality. What happened today was that your survival instincts kicked in. If Bradley hadn't attacked you, he'd be alive. You are a beautiful, kind woman and good-hearted, generous friend who has always been there for me."

"Susan, please—"

"No. Who took me to the hospital when Tim was away and Emily came early? You. Who helped me breathe through labor? You. Who drove me to my father's when my mom had her stroke? Who stayed with Julie when Lisa's camp bus—"

"Okay, Susan. Enough."

"Point is you've always been there for me, Elle. You're not some murderer—you have gerbils in your classroom, for God's sakes."

Hamsters, actually. Romeo and Juliet. But Susan's voice was husky, impassioned. Reassuring. I smiled. I thanked her. We hugged.

"They're going to keep waking you up all night, so don't expect to get much sleep." Like a mom, she tucked me in and kissed my forehead, near my lump.

I lay there after she left, in and out of sleep. The nurse came in sometime later, checking my vitals. And asked me about the envelope I was clutching in my hand.

‿

Becky showed up, carrying a dry cleaning bag, just as breakfast arrived. I'd already been up, and I'd managed to get around all by myself. Feeling much less wobbly, I'd stepped into the shower. Washed my hair. Scrubbed my body. Wondered how I would make it through the day. And the next.

She examined my so-called food. "Yum."

I was actually hungry. Held a forkful of scrambled eggs in my hand.

"I guess you're better."

I chewed, nodded. Regretted the nod when the walls kept bobbing after I'd stopped.

"Good." Becky sat on the foot of the bed, watching me eat.

"Want some?" I offered her a pancake.

She shook her head. "Already ate." But she kept watching me.

Never mind. I shoveled eggs into my mouth, chugged the juice. Wanted comfort, settled for eggs.

"So I have your clothes. The black suit, like you said."

I didn't remember telling her what I wanted to wear, or asking her to bring it. But the suit is what I would have chosen, perfect for a viewing. Why didn't I remember? Another memory lapse? No. It was normal. I had a head injury, after all. Had been groggy.

I swallowed fruit cocktail. "Thanks, Becky."

"So," she pointed at the table, "was that anything interesting?"

I followed her gaze.

"Love letters? Or a wad of hundred dollar bills?" She was looking at the envelope.

Oh, the envelope. I tried to sound indifferent. "Just some travel documents."

"Charlie was going somewhere?"

I chewed, swallowed. Told myself the itineraries were nothing. "No. They're actually not his. They're for Derek and some other people." Other people like Somerset Bradley. Whom, in fact, I'd just killed. But I didn't want to talk about that.

"Must be business."

"I guess." Except Charlie and Derek had never done business anywhere near where the flights had been going. As far as I knew, Somerset Bradley hadn't built any malls in Moscow. Or condos in Kiev. I remembered Charlie telling me that Derek had wooed his new client with a fancy travel package. But the travel plans didn't matter. Not any more.

"Wow, Becky—" Jen whooshed in, decked out in black Gucci. Dismayed. "Elle's still eating? She's got to get ready. We need to get her to the—"

"Relax. She'll be fine."

"Are you kidding? Look at her. Her forehead is purple. And her hair—"

"Jen, please." Why did my friends so often talk about me as if I were inanimate? "Let me eat. Then I'll do some makeup and fix my hair. We have time."

Jen huffed, pouted, crossed her arms, tapped her foot. Looked at Becky, eyed her deep-purple floral dress. "Ann Taylor?"

Becky reddened. "On sale. Forty off."

"Nice." Jen's fingernails tapped the wall. She watched me and the clock, waiting. Impatient.

I hurried. Wolfed down a wad of pancakes, gulped some tea. And sat passively while Jen and Becky swirled around me, styling my hair, understating my makeup, covering my bruises. They doted on me, pampering, fussing as if they were preparing a bride for her wedding.

But, that day, there would be no wedding. That day, I'd dress in black.

～

Edward greeted us at the family entrance, guided us into the comfortable waiting room for the bereaved. Several plump leather sofas and easy chairs. Lots of tissue boxes. Hard candies.

Coffee, tea. A private bath, stocked with soft towels, mouth-wash, amenities. Soft-green walls, a few innocuous paintings. A plush carpet. No windows. It was a room where people whis-pered, if they spoke at all.

Edward asked how I was doing, took my hands in both of his. I introduced Becky and Jen, told him to let Susan in when she arrived. Hesitated when he asked if I wanted to see Charlie alone before doors opened for the viewing, which would go on from noon until four.

"You don't have to, of course—"

"No. I appreciate it. Thank you."

And then, he led me through the double doors into the view-ing room. To the walnut box I'd selected. And the floral arrange-ments I'd picked out. And Charlie. Wearing his pinstriped suit.

Edward left us. He closed the door to the family room, blocking Jen's and Becky's views. Leaving Charlie and me alone.

He didn't look dead.

Then again, he didn't look alive. Cheeks were noticeably, ar-tificially rouged. Lips shut too tight. Had they sewn them closed? It looked like maybe they had. Or glued them? Charlie smelled of heavy makeup, sweet and unnatural. And the skin on his forehead was too pale, too still. No blood running through it, massaging it from within.

"Charlie?" I whispered, lest someone hear me talking to a dead man. "Charlie." His name was all I could think of to say. I put my fingertips on his cheek, tried to rub away some of the makeup. Gave up. Let my palm rest on his face. Felt the absolute quiet of his skin. His coolness. Empty as a rock.

Well, obviously, he felt empty. Charlie was gone. Not in his body. I remembered his body, its weight on me, its heat. Oh God, Charlie. I could almost feel his breath on my face, half ex-pected him to open his eyes and profess his love again. Or ac-cuse me of killing him. But Charlie just lay there, looking almost, but not quite, like Charlie. Doing nothing.

"I don't understand," I told him. "What happened? Why are you dead? Who killed you?" I stroked his stony forehead, as if it might soothe him. I asked questions he couldn't answer. I apologized for my part of our problems, promised that I'd loved him and probably always would. I was leaning over the casket, kissing him goodbye, when the double doors swung open, and children barreled over, surrounding me.

Emma and her family had arrived.

~

"I've brought Mother," Emma announced, brushing past me, dabbing a tissue at her eyes, peering with what looked like disappointment at her dead brother. Two of her children wriggled in front of her, pressing against the coffin, gaping at Charlie's body. "She thinks she's at church. Has no idea what's going on. She thinks I'm her sister. It's just as well. This would kill her. Is Ted here?"

I said, no, I hadn't seen him. Didn't think he was coming.

"Because it's time for us to line up for the viewing. People are in the lobby waiting to come in. There's quite a crowd. We ought to get started—I'll tell the director to open the doors. Kids, say goodbye to your Uncle Charlie."

The kids looked at each other, wide-eyed. "Goodbye, Uncle Charlie."

Emma gazed at him for a moment. Dried a tear. Sniffed. "We're closing this, aren't we?" She meant the casket.

Were we? I hadn't thought about it.

"We don't want people gawking, considering how he died." Emma met my eyes, squinting slightly, as if to intimidate. "I'll go get Mother." And, taking her children by the hands, wordlessly stomped away.

Edward joined me shortly after Emma left, asked me if I was ready. My head throbbed as I nodded that, yes, I was, and I watched Charlie's profile until the lid went down, forever sealing him in.

~

Susan stood close by, near the reception line. With Becky and Jen. My shoes pinched, and I wondered how I'd bear standing in them for the next two or three hours. I greeted Florence, who called me by her dead sister's name and asked where I'd been for so long. I took a spot in line as far from Emma as possible, putting Florence and her wheelchair, Herb and the children Gavin, Ashley, and Liam between us. Emma, however, moved at the last minute, stepping right beside me with an air of entitlement. As if she thought proximity to the coffin was an indication of rank.

Edward opened the doors, unleashing a throng. Like a mall opening the day after Christmas. The parlor filled with Charlie's people, all greeting each other, mixing, talking. Like a party. Florence apparently assumed it was a wedding, asking repeatedly, "What's taking the bride so long?" and, "Maybe she's not coming. Maybe she's had second thoughts."

I glanced around, still a bit unsteady, recognizing only a few people. Derek, of course, was at the head of the line, red-eyed and gaunt. And Mort and Andy, from tennis, looked bereft. Andy quipped that Charlie had only died so he wouldn't have to lose to them in the upcoming tournament. Mort leaned close, whispered, "No matter what they say, I know you didn't do it, sweetie," and then he moved on.

The principal of my school was there, and a bunch of my fellow teachers. Even a big cluster of my students' mothers—including Benjy's. Oh, dear. I hoped she wasn't mad about the cupcake memo.

The line kept moving, a convention of everyone Charlie had ever known. And some he hadn't, like Detectives Stiles and Swenson, who stood near the entrance, observing, all but snapping photos. People stopped at the casket, some talking or praying, some silently touching it. Tons of strangers, leaning over to hug me, leaving traces of their scents. Chanel N°5. Burberry.

Opium. Some of the faces belonged to old friends—like Charlie's college roommate, Jake. He'd gotten fat. And our neighbors from our first apartment, Mr. and Mrs. Shannon. They'd aged well. Mike, the guy who worked on Charlie's car, was there. And Sophie and Lauren and a woman whose name I didn't know from my spinning class at the Y.

Lots of people. They knew Charlie from his investment firm or from charities, professional organizations, health clubs, favorite restaurants, civic groups, childhood, school. Everyone was upset, offering sympathy and support. Despite the warm wishes, I was aware that many, if not most of them, suspected I'd killed Charlie. And more than once, I wondered if the murderer was there, in line, offering heartfelt condolences like a friend. Which one was it? Would I know by his eyes? His scent? For a while, I watched, but people kept flowing by, a river of whispers and touches, and I got lulled into a rhythm of nodding and thanking, of drifting along semiaware, returning hugs. Not focusing on details, not differentiating faces.

So when Joel came by, offering a sympathetic squeeze, and a warm whisper not to lose hope, to remember that life could suddenly change for the better, I didn't react in any particular way. But my face tingled where his cheek had brushed it, and I found a silk handkerchief in my hand. By the time my mind registered who he was, he'd already moved on, past Emma, Herb, and Florence. Out of reach.

Flustered, I twisted, searching, trying to find him in the crowd. Messed up the timing of my responses to well-wishers. Had that really been Joel? The magician from Jeremy's Bar? What was he doing here? How had Joel found out that Charlie had been my husband? Or heard about his death?

What was I thinking? The story of the murder, as well as my name and picture, had been all over the news. Joel must have heard about it the same way half the other people at the viewing had. But still, why had he come? I mean, we weren't friends.

We'd met only once. That didn't give him cause to come to my husband's viewing. Gooseflesh rose on my arms. Traveled up my back. I recalled the rose he'd given me. His cryptic words—he'd said them twice now. About how life could suddenly change. Was Joel—with his teasing eyes and strong jaw—was he interested in me?

I greeted one of Charlie's clients—Jonas Walters, returned his hug. And felt my face heat up. I was at Charlie's viewing, thinking about Joel. About flirting with another man. What was wrong with me? I focused, got back into the flow.

At least until a few minutes later, when the woman came up to me. She was dressed wrong, in black leggings, a tight, belted red sweater, too-high heels. Dark-blue eye shadow. Long, dyed platinum hair. She didn't take my hand or express any sorrow. Still, I thanked her for coming, expecting her to move on. But she didn't. She remained there, staring at me, silently halting progress, blocking the line. Did I know her? I wasn't sure. Couldn't place her. She was tanned, with good cheekbones, strong jaw. Maybe thirty. And determined to remain where she was indefinitely.

Finally, Emma reached an arm out to guide her along.

Fast, like a springing cobra, the woman slapped Emma's hand. Emma yelped.

"Ma'am—" I stepped forward, protecting Emma.

The woman met my eyes. "You didn't really know him. Not like I did."

What?

Emma walked in circles, indignant, looking for help. "Herb—do something. Where is Edward? He should be here."

"Still, I had to see you, face to face."

Emma's kids wanted to know what was wrong, why she was whirling. "Mom?" They followed her like baby ducks. Or a dog's tail. Around and around. Herb saw his kids and wife fluttering, began fluttering, too. Wringing his hands.

I faced the woman. "What for? Who are you?"

"Just tell me. Why couldn't you let go and let him move on? Why couldn't you let him be happy?"

"Excuse me?" Who was this woman? Why was I being so polite?

People in line stirred, confused by the commotion and the bottleneck. Detectives Stiles and Swenson stepped over from across the parlor as Susan intervened, Becky at her side. "What's going on?"

"This—that person assaulted me, that's what's going on!" Emma sputtered. "Where is the help? Why is nobody here to supervise—"

"I'll find Edward." Susan seemed to think Emma was exaggerating, but she went off, Becky trailing, while Jen reassured the people still in line, and Herb calmed Emma. Stiles and Swenson moved to escort the woman away, but she resisted.

"You're not like I expected." The woman was oblivious to the detectives standing at her side. Wouldn't budge. "In the picture you were much younger."

The picture? "What picture?" Who the hell was she? What was she talking about?

"From the wedding."

I blinked. My wedding picture? This woman had seen my wedding picture? When? Where? And then, I knew: the picture at Charlie's. I'd see it there, too. On the bureau in his bedroom.

So, this woman had been in Charlie's bedroom? Who was she?

She had huge hazel eyes. Fiery. Fixed on me. "You stand here like a grieving widow, but I know better. I know the truth—"

Detective Stiles took her arm. "Let's move on, ma'am."

"Get that person out of here—" Emma was squawking. "Who is she? She's disrupted the entire viewing!"

Edward appeared from nowhere as Detective Stiles took her by the arm and led the woman away.

"Look!" Florence pointed as she cried out, delighted. "There she is! The bride! With the groom! Finally." She clapped her hands, singing the wedding song. "You want to know the truth? I thought she'd flown the coop."

Gradually, the line dwindled. By four o'clock when I left, my feet were burning and swollen, head aching, and hand sore. I was still bothered by, and Emma was still ranting about, the woman. But out of all of us, only one had any idea who she was: Florence, who was disappointed that she hadn't caught the bouquet.

∿

Thank God for Becky. I was too exhausted to move, and the doorbell kept ringing. Neighbors, stopping by with casseroles and lasagnas. Or fruit bowls. Delivery men bringing flowers. Derek hand delivered a gigantic sweet tray from Tartes, laden with delicacies of crusty tortes and nutty brownies and buttery pastries that put pounds on if you even glanced at them. He wanted to talk to me. Becky took his tray, told him I was resting, that he could talk another time. He persisted, said he just wanted a minute.

"It's okay," I called from the living room sofa. My feet were up. I was sprawling on red leather.

I heard Becky warn him not to tire me as he strode in on spindly long legs which, as always, reminded me of a spider. I didn't move to make room for him, so he sat on the chair beside me.

"Something to drink?" I had no idea why I offered. I wasn't going to get up if he wanted anything. But my mama, rest her soul, had raised me properly. When someone came to your house, you offered something to drink.

Derek didn't want anything to drink, though. He wanted to ask questions.

"I know this is an awful time for you, Elle."

I waited for the "but."

"But I'm probably just as upset as you are, in my own way."

And?

"And I'm going over it and over it. What was Charlie doing that night? You said last time we talked that you hadn't expected him. So why did he come over?"

Really? The day of Charlie's viewing, the evening before his funeral, Derek wanted to discuss the circumstances of the murder. Typical Derek. Whatever was on his narrow self-absorbed mind was all that mattered.

"I have no idea, Derek." I bent my knee, rubbed the ball of my foot, let out a small moan. Those shoes needed to go.

"You said he still had keys."

"Yes."

"So he let himself in. Why?"

I kept massaging.

"Was he meeting someone here? Doubtful. Why would he arrange a meeting here of all places? He wouldn't. And you said—and, by the way, I believe you—that he wasn't here to see you. So, scratch both those possibilities, and what do we have?"

We? I didn't know what Derek had, but I had a headache, sore feet, and a dead not yet ex-husband to bury. I let go of my foot. "You tell me."

The doorbell rang again. I saw Becky hurry to answer.

"I think he was here for one of two reasons, Elle. To get something he'd left here. Or to leave something hidden here."

Really? "Like what?"

"I'm not sure. Have you seen anything missing? Or found anything new?"

"The police went through everything. They'd have seen anything unusual—"

"But this might be something they wouldn't notice—something small, maybe. A detail, like a computer flash drive. It might be tucked away. Have you noticed any—"

"Look at this!" Becky poked her head in. "What an incredible cheese platter. From the school—everybody signed the card. Oh my God—even Lois." Lois was in charge of the cafeteria, never contributed to birthday cakes or shower gifts. Her participation was a big deal.

"Wow." My voice was flat. "How nice."

"I'll try to make room for it—the fridge is full." She hurried off.

Derek cracked his knuckles, impatient.

I sat up. "Derek, what are you saying? Why would Charlie have to hide something here? Or anywhere, for that matter? There are safety deposit boxes for valuables—"

"Maybe he didn't have time to get to the bank. Most banks close at three—"

"You're not making sense—"

"Okay. I'll be frank. There's no polite way to say this, Elle. Charlie took something. From the business."

Something hot hit my rib cage. Seared it. "That's absurd." Why was I defending him? "Charlie would never cheat you." Well, I wasn't absolutely sure of that. But Derek was probably among the last people Charlie would cheat.

"I don't mean it that way. He didn't take money." Derek leaned forward, clasped his hands. Lowered his voice. "Okay. He took client information, Elle. Highly confidential information. Potentially, very damaging information."

I took a breath. My chest felt raw. Why would Charlie take client information? Unless—wait. Was Derek accusing Charlie of blackmail?

The doorbell rang again. I didn't want to know who was there. I was thinking about blackmail. And about Charlie. Not for even one second did I jump to his defense. Not a single breath protested that he'd never stoop that low. I simply accepted the word of Derek, a man I'd always found too slick and more than a little slimy, and his implication that Charlie was a blackmailer. Maybe because I was tired. Maybe because Charlie had disappointed me too many times. At any rate, I didn't defend him. Didn't throw Derek out of the house for maligning my newly dead, not yet buried never-to-be-ex-husband, who couldn't dispute the accusations.

Instead, I thought about what he'd said. "How did Charlie get the information?"

"By accident. A client trusted me. Charlie found the records. It was quite a while before I realized what had happened."

"So. Why are you telling me this?" I knew very well why. He wanted me to find the stuff.

"Because you might be able to find what Charlie left here. And return it. Elle, if this stuff gets out, not just investments and careers, but actual lives would be destroyed. The results would be—irreparable."

Irreparable?

Bad enough to kill over? Was that what had happened? Had someone killed Charlie because he'd been threatening to expose their secrets?

"Which client was it, Derek?"

"What?" His smile was twisted. "You know I can't tell you that, Elle."

"But you have to. Think about it. If Charlie was blackmailing someone—someone powerful and important—they might actually have—"

"Have killed him?" He was laughing. "Seriously? Elle, if people like our clients wanted to kill Charlie, believe me, it wouldn't have been so clumsy or so messy. He wouldn't have turned up bleeding all over your house with a carving knife in his back. No. It would have been delicate. An undetectable event. In fact, I doubt his body would ever have been found."

His voice had a thin, vibrating timbre, sounded like a threat. Was Derek implying that, if I didn't come up with the information he wanted, I could encounter some delicate, undetectable event? Smug, slick bastard. I'd never liked Derek.

"You know what, Derek—" I was about to say that I didn't appreciate his implications about Charlie or care about his precious client's information, and that I would appreciate it if he'd remove his slimy butt from my house, but I didn't have to. At that very moment Becky came in, handing me a small envelope and a mug of steaming tea. Scolding him.

"You have to see the flowers that this card came from. Who sent them? They're amazing—"

"Open it." I had no interest in flowers.

She opened it while scolding Derek. "Elle needs to rest, Derek. Can't you see that? Leave her alone. Visit another time."

"You're right." Derek looked my way, raised an eyebrow. "As I said, this is a difficult time for all of us. Thanks for the talk. And let's keep in touch on this matter, Elle. Keep an eye out, will you?"

On his way out, he pecked my forehead. I tasted bile.

Becky held the card up, reading. "If some roses on a cloudy day can make your troubles lift away, then let them come from whom they will, and go outside, and see the sun—" She stopped and looked at me, brows knit. "Elle? Who's Joel?"

∾

"Her name is Sherry McBride." Susan talked with her mouth full of a corned beef on rye from a deli tray someone had sent over. She'd just rushed in from an informal off-the-record talk with her pal Detective Stiles, who'd done some research about the woman who'd been removed from the viewing. I wanted to take her aside. To tell her in private about Derek and what he'd said about Charlie, but she was bursting with news. "She's single, thirty-three years old. And a receptionist at Multicor."

Derek's and Charlie's investment firm.

"So that woman—Sherry McBride. She and Charlie were—they were dating?" Why did I have trouble even saying that? Charlie and I weren't together anymore. Were almost divorced. Had been free to do whatever we wanted. Even so, I felt a pang.

"MFB," Jen swirled the ice from her diet soda. "I mean, so she was screwing him. So what? That entitles her to absolutely nothing. What kind of person would make a scene like that? Confront a widow? At the viewing?"

"Actually, that's pretty standard behavior for her." Susan licked coleslaw off her lips. "Sherry McBride has a history of stalking. Making threats. Ambushing people. Just last November, an old boyfriend took out a restraining order against her."

"Really?"

"Wow."

Silence. Probably, we were all sharing the same thought. That this woman was unstable. Might have been obsessed with Charlie. Might even have killed him?

It was just the four of us. Well, five. Susan's husband, Tim, was there, too, but he was snoring softly in the easy chair. We were spread out in the living room. I hadn't left, except to visit the bathroom or grab food off a tray. I hadn't gone near the study, though. Didn't dare. Despite the new sofa and fresh carpeting, I knew I'd see Charlie's body there. Wondered if that image would ever fade.

"So why did she come to the viewing?" Becky sounded angry. "What did she want? Some kind of recognition for sleeping with him? Like to stand in line next to his mother?"

"She said she wanted to face me." And she'd asked why couldn't I let go and let Charlie move on. As if she'd thought I was still in love with him. Or, worse, that he was still in love with me. "I think she's jealous of me."

"Of course, she's jealous of you. Look at her—she could never compete with you. Charlie blew it and messed up the marriage, but no way was he over you." Jen sounded convinced. "If you'd have let him, he'd have come home in an eye blink."

I doubted that. "But why would she be jealous now? There's no point. The man is dead—"

"Yeah. And, given her obsessive jealousy, maybe she's the

one who made him that way." There. The possibility was in the open. Jen had said it out loud.

And Becky agreed. "I bet she was stalking him. Like her last boyfriend. She probably followed Charlie to Elle's house—"

"But why did he go to Elle's?"

"Who knows? It doesn't matter." Becky dismissed Jen's question with a wave of her hand. "Maybe he left a book here—"

Or maybe, like Derek said, he was hiding evidence so he could blackmail a client.

"But here's what I think happened. What's her name again? Sherry?"

"Yes. Sherry."

"So Sherry follows Charlie, because she's an insecure psycho stalker by nature." Becky leaned forward, animated. "And when she sees Charlie going into Elle's house, she goes bananas. She assumes he's there to cheat on her, that he's been seeing Elle all along behind her back. So she rings the bell. Charlie looks out to see who's there. When he sees it's her, he lets her in. They argue. She accuses him of cheating. He accuses her of being a lunatic. 'What are you doing? Following me?'" Becky imitated Charlie's baritone. Did a good job. "You know Charlie. He's not going to take any shit. He gets pissed. He dumps her, right there, and walks away. She's not going to be treated like that. She goes after him, asking, 'What's so special about her? What's she got that I don't?' Charlie ignores her, goes about his business. Maybe he tells her to get out, but she won't leave. She tails him, yapping, until maybe he shoves her. Or maybe not. Either way, she grabs a knife in the kitchen and stabs him in a final fit of mad envious rage."

Becky's eyes glowed. She was breathless, panting. Pleased with herself.

For a moment, nobody said anything.

Then Susan nodded, "It's certainly possible." She took another bite of corned beef.

"Is that what your detective friend thinks?" Jen asked. "Because if Becky can figure that out, the cops certainly should."

Becky bristled. "What's that supposed to mean? 'If Becky can figure it out.' As if I'm the least likely to—"

"No. Becky, QD." Quiet Down. "I just meant that they're professionals—"

I stopped listening to the words, let myself float upon the back-and-forth of voices. I couldn't help it. I felt relieved. Hugely relieved. Because, clearly, Sherry provided the police with another suspect. In fact, between her and the client Derek had been talking about, the number of possible killers had tripled in a matter of hours. And I was no longer the only person on their radar.

≀

I was in bed, unable to sleep, events whirling in my mind out of sequence. And, like a rotten aftertaste, Derek's assertion kept coming back. Was he right that Charlie had come to the house to hide stolen files? I hadn't found anything. Didn't believe Derek anyway.

But then I sat up. If Charlie had hidden something in the house, I thought I knew where he'd have put it.

No one knows a house like the people who live in it. Within walls, above rafters, beneath staircases are secret spaces, cloistered corners, nooks known only to inhabitants.

And so it was with our house. Charlie and I knew her skeleton, her flaws and facades, the bare beams under her painted and papered walls. We'd seen her guts when we'd redecorated, redoing the old kitchen and bathrooms, adding the powder room, replacing crumbling old walls and woodwork, enlarging closets.

When we'd rebuilt the front closet, we expanded it into the foyer, leaving the old, smaller one behind it as storage space for luggage and miscellany. Snow shoes. Old golf clubs. Charlie's bowling ball. Picnic baskets. Beach umbrellas. The storage cubby extended from the rear of the new closet to the underside of the stairway to the second floor. It was a place no one else knew about. A place Charlie might put something he didn't want found.

I stepped into the front closet, shoved through coats and cleaning bags into the storage space. Turned on the inner light. Smelled mothballs and stale air. Peered into the dimness. Saw nothing remotely resembling a flash drive. Or an envelope. Or a printout. Or anything not covered with dust.

I picked up snow boots, turned them over. Nothing fell out.

I opened a shoebox, found old photos. Charlie as a baby in a pram. His parents at Niagra Falls. His grandma holding him on her lap. Little Charlie on a tricycle.

I sneezed. Closed the box. Knelt and felt under the steps where the light didn't shine. Found only cobwebs.

Stood. Gave the storage space one more look. Saw nothing but clutter. Boxes and suitcases, a cubby crammed with discarded memories. Wiping off my hands, I turned out the light, pushed through the coats, closed the closet door, and went upstairs to bed. Derek's words still lingered like the taste of spoiled milk.

～

The first row was reserved for family. I sat apart from Charlie's blood relatives, to the left of the aisle. Across from me was Florence in her wheelchair, her hair done perfectly and nails newly manicured. Beside her were Emma, Herb, and their children, and beyond them were a few of Charlie's cousins, people I'd met a decade ago at our wedding and hadn't seen since. Ted never showed up.

I was alone on my side of the aisle, preferring not to sit with Emma's brood. Without children, siblings, or parents to buffer me, I felt exposed. Felt the lasers of staring eyes, and the weight of the unspoken allegations that, if I'd killed Somerset Bradley,

I must have killed Charlie. "That's her over there—she looks guilty, doesn't she?" Or, "That's his ex, the one I told you about." But Susan and Tim sat right behind me. Jen and her husband and Becky sat close by in the same row. Surrounding me like family, even without blood ties. I felt a pang, missing my parents, gone now for fourteen years. Aching, I wondered again if they'd seen the drunk careening toward them, if they'd realized they were going to crash. Had they screamed? Prayed? Cursed? Thought of their daughter? But no, I wasn't going start that spiral. Today was about Charlie. Only Charlie.

The coffin looked polished and tasteful. The flowers were graceful. The room filled to capacity. When I glanced around, I saw people standing along the walls. Charlie would have been pleased, I thought, that so many had turned out to send him off.

The pastor adjusted his spectacles and began the service that Edward and I had planned. Nondenominational. Mostly poems.

"We begin with Three Ecclesiastes." His voice rang out, nasal and affected, reminding people to follow the programs on their seats. "To every thing there is a season, and a time for every purpose under Heaven—"

I lifted my program on which Edward had printed our selected readings. Tried to follow along. Mumbled, "A time to be born and a time to die—"

Someone took a seat right beside me. Well, who cared? Why should people stand when there were open seats in the family row?

"A time to plant, and a time to reap what has been planted. A time to tear down and a time to build up—"

"You're not crying."

Without moving my head, slowly, I shifted my eyes to the left.

"Why not, Elle? Can't you shed one goddam tear?"

Charlie was indignant.

"Look around you. Everybody—even my ice bitch sister is

crying her brains out. Even my buddies, tough guys like Mort. The only dry eyes in this whole place are yours."

He was sitting right beside me on the pew. Openly, not even trying to conceal himself. And he was talking out loud, right over the preacher. I glanced around, making sure no one else was seeing him. Susan noticed me squirming, mouthed a question, "What's wrong?"

I whispered, "Nothing."

Nothing except that the deceased whose life we were there to celebrate had decided to attend his own funeral. Of course, no one else knew that. Charlie was, after all, my own personal hallucination. Or my imagination. Either way, it didn't matter. He wasn't really there, and I knew it, even though I could see and hear him perfectly, could probably touch him if I'd tried.

The pastor finished his readings, and Derek went to the podium to make a personal statement.

"Those of you who know me know that Charlie and I were more than partners. Charlie was—" Derek's voice broke, and he drew a breath, looked at the ceiling, bit his lip, collected himself. "Charlie was the closest thing I've ever had to a brother. I trusted him completely—"

"Elle, I gotta tell you." Charlie leaned close, spoke into my ear. "Dry eyes don't look good. At least fake it. Think about it. Not crying only makes you look more guilty than you already—"

"Stop it. I'm not guilty." I whispered. "I just don't cry in public. You know that—"

"Did you say something?" Susan sat forward on her seat, touched my shoulder. Whispered, "I didn't hear you—"

"It's nothing." I told her. I glared at Charlie, annoyed. He wasn't, couldn't be there. I was seeing what I wanted or needed to. Hearing him because some sick part of my mind couldn't let him go. I needed to ignore him, make him go away.

People were chuckling. I looked around—saw that, thank God, the laughter wasn't about me. Derek must have told an amusing anecdote, something about Charlie's unbreakable competitive spirit. Or his uncanny ability to sniff out profitable ventures. Or his unwavering determination to excel—

"And there was Charlie, just like the guy said. Flat on his face, passed out cold under the sprinklers, wearing the Easter Bunny suit." More laughter.

"Do you believe that?" I asked Charlie. "He's making fun of—"

"It's okay," Susan whispered. "He's just reminding people of the good times."

Charlie sat impassive, saying nothing. But then, Charlie wasn't really there.

Across the aisle, Florence asked, "What's that man talking about? Talk, talk, talk, talk. Enough talk." Her voice was shrill and loud, and it interrupted Derek's poignant closing comment. Emma and Frank hushed her, but Florence kept on, demanding to know how long she had to sit there. "When the hell's lunch?"

Snickers rippled softly across the chapel. Emma scolded Florence, "Mother, keep your voice down," and stood to eulogize her brother.

As Emma began talking about her childhood and brother, Charlie got up and went across the aisle to his mother. I saw him kiss her cheek. Then he stood behind her and rubbed her shoulders until Florence relaxed and, smiling, nodded off.

～

I didn't see Charlie again during the service. He wasn't with his mother after Emma spoke. Wasn't around when the pastor led the final prayers, when pallbearers carried his coffin to the hearse, or when Edward escorted the bereaved family to a limousine. Charlie wasn't there, but others were.

Like the ever-present Detectives Stiles and Swenson. Standing in the corner, as they had been at the viewing. Watching. Conferring. Even as the limousine drove off.

We followed the hearse, led the parade of cars going to the

cemetery. I watched Emma's children, felt regret that I hadn't seen them in recent years. Doubted they remembered me. I wondered if this was their first encounter with death, if they remembered the living Uncle Charlie. They seemed subdued, stared in moody silence out the window. The youngest wriggled a bit, annoying his sister, but they didn't squabble. Just grunted.

Frank and Emma sat stonily, Emma no longer weepy. Stoic, now. Long-suffering. I considered telling her that she'd given a touching eulogy, but couldn't, and not just because I hadn't listened to it. After her rampage to me on the phone, blaming me for her estrangement from Charlie, all but accusing me of killing him, I wasn't going to say anything to Emma. Not about her speech or anything else. Ever, if I had my way.

Florence was the only relative of Charlie's for whom I had true affection, and she was snoring, sound asleep. So I kept to myself as the limo moved out of Center City onto the Schuylkill Expressway, heading toward Bala Cynwyd and West Laurel Hill Cemetery. And then, through the gates, into the burial grounds.

A perfect funeral day. Crisp, cool air. Cumulus clouds dotting the sky. The leaves turning orange. An ominous hint of a chill, a reminder of coming winter. Of inevitable death.

The parade of cars snaked along to the gravesite. And from there, my memories are snapshots. A tent beside the open grave. A large machine, some kind of device to lower Charlie into the hole. People gathering around the hole in the ground, making statements, reading poems.

I clearly remember Susan reciting one. "I Did Not Die," by Mary E Faye. She cleared her throat. "Do not stand at my grave and forever weep. I am not there; I do not sleep."

What an appropriate poem, I'd thought. Given that Charlie had not slept much since his death, popping up even at his funeral service.

"I am a thousand winds that blow. I am the diamond glints on snow. I am the sunlight on ripened grain."

Suddenly, Emma wailed as if in pain. Herb comforted her. Florence didn't stir.

I remember Becky and Jen, side by side, reading the Twenty-third Psalm. Herb reciting the Lord's Prayer. And later, the coffin being cranked lower and lower into the ground.

I stood graveside, noticed muddy water puddling at the bottom of the hole. Was glad I'd bought the most expensive vault, so Charlie would stay dry.

And then, people were leaving, returning to their cars. Cemetery workers began dumping earth into the hole. Covering Charlie.

I remember Emma hurrying her children. They had a plane to catch, after all. And Florence waking up, confused about the commotion, thinking once again that Emma was her dead sister, Dorothy. Still hungry for lunch.

As I climbed back into the limousine, I remember stopping to look back one more time, half expecting to see Charlie climbing out of the ground.

Instead, I saw someone else. Sherry McBride. Her dyed hair blowing in the breeze, she was standing beside the grave. And she was watching me.

~

Finally, everyone was gone. I had the house to myself. People had come back after the burial, drinking, eating, talking, congregating to erase the proximity, the awareness of death. I'd been amazed at how many people cared about Charlie. And, despite the suspicions and rumors, how many people had come out to support me. From school. From the gym. From the neighborhood. From the past.

For two solid days, I'd been surrounded by good intentions. People had hovered around me, touching and consoling. Blanketing me with good wishes. The truth was I felt smothered. Needed air. And solitude.

The last to leave, of course, were Becky, Jen, and Susan.

They'd wrapped leftover cold cuts in plastic. They'd run the dishwasher. They'd sprawled out on my red leather sofa and matching easy chair, helping me put away the better part of a bottle of Scotch.

Becky, once again, had offered to stay the night.

"You shouldn't be alone," she'd insisted.

"It's okay. I need to be."

"Not yet. You'll have plenty of time to be alone."

I hugged her. "You've done enough for me, Becky. You've been here for me nonstop. Go home. Pamper yourself a little. All of this has been hard on you, too."

She stood her ground, all five-feet-maybe-two-inches of her. Head high. Feet apart. Hands on hips. "What about that woman, the stalker? You said she was there, graveside. What if she comes after you?"

"She won't. Not tonight."

"You don't know that."

True. I didn't. "If she comes, I'll call the police."

Becky stood up straight, trying to get in my face. Coming up to my chin. "This is serious, Elle. For all you know, she's who killed Charlie. Which means she might have Charlie's keys. The police still haven't found them, have they?"

No, I didn't think they had.

"And you still haven't changed the locks?"

No, I hadn't.

"So she can come in while you're sleeping—"

"And, if you're here? What'll you do to stop her?" Becky wasn't terribly imposing.

"At least we'd outnumber her."

We'd argued. But I had to stop depending on my friends. Becky looked exhausted, pale. She needed to stop worrying about me and rest in her own bed. Finally, I'd promised to double bolt the doors. And keep a hammer under my pillow. And have my phone ready on the nightstand. Even then, Becky had been reluctant to go home.

But she did. I closed the door after almost forcing her down the front steps, and leaned back, embracing the stillness of my empty house.

For a while, I stood in the entranceway, listening to the quiet. Letting go. And then, slightly tipsy from the Scotch, I wandered from room to room, reclaiming my house, my privacy. Feeling the air settling, the scents fading. Turning the light out in the kitchen, letting it sleep. Making my way down the hall, passing the powder room, stopping at the door to the study. Drawing a breath.

Maybe I wouldn't go in. Maybe I'd wait until the next day. But why was I so hesitant? Charlie was not, would not, be in there. He'd been buried. He was gone.

I probably shouldn't have been drinking with so recent a head wound. But a drink was exactly what I wanted. Not Scotch. Wine, this time. Just one glass to help me sleep. Shiraz, finally, was what convinced me to go into the study. The bottles were in there, on the rack above the bar. So, I ignored the fine hairs on my arms and the nape of my neck, the ones that stood up and danced out warnings. I paid no mind to the shiver of air that chilled me as I stepped into the room. I was determined. Despite what had happened there, I marched in, straight to the bar, where visitors had left an open but not empty bottle. And poured.

Something moved in the periphery of my vision. But I didn't react, knew that whatever I'd seen wasn't really there. Couldn't be.

The wine splashed around in the glass as my hand trembled. But slowly, I turned around, lifted the glass, silently toasted Charlie, and drank.

Okay. I'd done it. Gone into the study again. Not seen a ghost or had any hallucinations. Reclaimed it. Now I could leave.

I drained the wine. Rinsed out my empty glass. Recorked the bottle, tossed an old cork into the jar where we—where I collected them.

And noticed that one of the corks looked odd.

∿

Because it wasn't a cork.

It was a flash drive.

And it had no business being in my cork jar. Actually, it was Charlie's cork jar. After he'd left, I'd just kept filling it.

"Why do you save corks?" I'd asked him way back in the beginning.

"Well, you can't just throw them out."

I couldn't?

"Wine isn't like soda pop." Charlie had been impassioned about wine. "It's alive—it's living and breathing right up until we consume it. Wine dies for our pleasure, and the cork? Well, the cork is a reminder. A marker of the life sacrificed to our enjoyment."

I'd found his concept macabre. But we'd been drinking and he'd probably been half in the bag when he'd said that. Not entirely serious. Even so, we'd kept the corks. A row of full jars lined a shelf beneath the bar. And a not quite full one sat on the bar's end. Holding not just corks, but a flash drive.

I heard Derek, pressing me. "Have you seen anything out of the ordinary? Maybe a flash drive?" And after the funeral, he'd come back to the house, wandering around, looking into vases and behind books. He'd gone into the kitchen, ostensibly for ice cubes, but ice had just been an excuse. He'd been snooping. Probably opening drawers and cabinets, checking canisters. Looking for the client information he claimed Charlie had taken.

And now, there it was, in the best hiding place of all: right out in the open. I had no doubt I'd found what Derek had been searching for, what Charlie had been hiding when he'd died.

I looked at the jar, but didn't reach inside. Something held me back, though I didn't know what. After all, the flash drive was nothing to me. Whatever was on it concerned some rich client of Derek's whom I didn't even know.

So why was I wary? The flash drive was small. Innocuous. The size of a car key or a lipstick.

Maybe I'd just leave it there. Pretend I hadn't seen it.

In fact, that was probably the best idea. I had enough problems without Derek's flash drive. The thing didn't affect me, wasn't my business. Whatever was on it was between him and Charlie and some client. I wanted no part of it.

I was still telling myself that as, up in my bedroom, I opened my laptop and plugged the thing in.

∾

A password? It wanted a password.

Again, I told myself to leave the flash drive alone. My instincts agreed, warning my body to stop. My mouth went dry. My stomach churned out warnings: Stop. Leave it alone. Don't mess with this. My fingers trembled as they typed out guesses. Missed keys as they tried to produce the magic minimum six digits that would unlock the drive and reveal its contents.

What was wrong with me? Why was I so afraid to find out what Charlie had hidden?

Well, that was a stupid question. I'd lived with Charlie for over a decade. Knew that, while he dressed like a gentleman, he loved playing dirty. Taking risks. Pushing limits. And, according to Derek, the information Charlie had put on the drive was seriously limit-pushing. Bad enough to merit blackmail.

Maybe bad enough to merit murder?

And, if I opened the drive and saw the information, would my murder be merited, too?

Ridiculous. No one would know that I'd seen it. No one even knew I had the flash drive. Besides, I had no proof that the flash drive was connected to the murder. I thought again of Sherry McBride. She might have stalked Charlie, tailed him to the house, gone inside, and fought with him. Killed him.

I tried another password: Jehosaphat, the name of Charlie's favorite tropical fish. It didn't work. Nor did his birthday. Nor our anniversary, no surprise. The password wasn't Cornell, his university. Or Ithaca, its location. It wasn't Cape Cod, where he'd once had a beach house. Not Florence, his mom's name. Or Nathaniel, his father's. It wasn't Multicor, the name of his investment business. Or its address. Or Beemer, like his car. Or "money" or "profits" or "finances" or "funds." I tried all kinds of wines, at least the ones I could think of, like Zinfandel. His favorite: Shiraz. Pinot Noir. Cabernet. Nothing. I tried team names. Charlie always bet on sports. But it wasn't Eagles or Broncos or Saints. Also not Flyers, Phillies, or Sixers.

I knew I should quit. No question. It would be better not to know what was on the drive. And even if I saw it, the information might be highly technical, or financial. Or encoded. After all this effort, I might not even comprehend what I saw.

I gave myself just three more tries. Three only, and then I'd stop.

Okay. The password had to have at least six digits. And something that would have been second nature to Charlie, something that he wouldn't have trouble remembering. His first car? Mustang. No. It didn't work.

Two tries left. I closed my eyes. Felt a nervous flapping in my chest. Shivered. Heard Charlie swear, "You were the love of my life."

I didn't need the third try. Elf was too short, so I typed it again. ElfElf.

And I was in.

∿

ElfElf? He'd used his private pet name for me as a password? I didn't want to think about why. We'd been finished. Over. Almost divorced. He'd simply chosen that password because no one else except maybe Derek knew about that nickname. It was a practical choice, nothing else. Still, the name felt personal. As if he'd called me to look at the drive.

The screen showed a menu of folders, labeled with initials and dates. I stared at it, hesitating to open anything. Why? What was I afraid to find? Records of embezzlement? Of bribery? Of illegal trading? Even if I saw those records, I doubted I'd understand them. But my hands were cold and damp, my fingers stiff. Difficult to move.

It's just a list of file folders, I told myself. On a flat, two-dimensional screen. What's wrong with you? Get on with it. My stomach twisted, but I clicked on the first file in the list.

The file opened to an array of photos. Initially, I felt relieved. Glad not to see technical writing or spreadsheets or complex financial records. Just photos. I clicked on one, enlarging it.

And went on to the next.

And the next, and the next.

And then, unable to take any more, I ran to the bathroom, heaving.

~

I didn't throw up, just wanted to. Leaned over the toilet, feeling sick.

Children. Charlie had dirty pictures of children.

Children the age of my second graders. With baby soft skin, wide open eyes. Innocent minds. Only these children weren't innocent. These were posing naked, doing things to themselves.

And, oh God—to each other.

I hung my head over the bowl for a while, gagging, trying not to think. But the images wouldn't go away. What hellish secret life was Charlie into? Had Derek known? Had he been covering for him? Or was Derek into naked kids, too? Is that why he wanted the flash drive?

Oh God—I stood up too fast, dizzy, breathing shallowly.

"Charlie," I dared him to face me. I called him names, cursed at him. "Where are you? Come out, you sick fuck."

Charlie didn't appear. Didn't speak. I walked back into the bedroom, saw the bed, the dresser, the nightstands. Darkness out the windows. No Charlie.

I sat on the bed again, looked again at the screen in disbelief. Clicked forward. Saw things being done to children. By children.

I held my stomach. It hopped around like my mind. Had Charlie secretly been into children? A pedophile? I couldn't believe that. But why else would he have these pictures?

Derek popped to mind—what he'd said about Charlie taking client information from the business. Clearly, Derek had been lying. The files didn't contain client information; they contained child porn. So what did that mean? That Derek had lied to protect me from the truth? He might have been trying to contain the photos. To get rid of them and cover up Charlie's perversion.

Charlie's perversion? How was it possible that I'd had no idea? Not the slightest hint of his secret sickness. I recalled his scent, the meshing of our lips, his warm strength against me. Inside me. His gravelly whisper, "You're the love of my life, Elf." Oh God.

I raced back to the bathroom. When I finished heaving, my heart wasn't racing anymore. I wasn't even trembling. I was simply exhausted. Even so, I took a shower, scrubbing my body because I couldn't scrub my mind. Couldn't expunge my memories of the man I'd loved and married, or of the gut-twisting realization of how sick he'd actually been.

～

Some dreams are hard to wake up from. They are too vivid, too full of detail. They color waking life. The dream I had that night was like that. Too real. More real than real. Impossible to shake.

Despite how upset I was, I'd fallen asleep right away. Even in sleep, though, I was disturbed. I dreamed of a writhing pile of naked children with soulless eyes that didn't cry. They surrounded Charlie, who sat on the sofa in the study, oblivious and dead.

"Dammit, Elle," he croaked, "the plane's taking off. You killed me, and now I'll miss my flight." I smelled his blood.

Then he wasn't in the study anymore. He was underground on a black stream, sitting Indian-style on a raft with Somerset Bradley, who had a hanger sticking out of his eye. Rodents swam and swarmed, gnawing at Charlie. Dark slime was everywhere. "This is your fault, Elle," Charlie's mouth didn't move. But I heard his voice. "Your fault."

I woke up shaken. Repulsed, feeling slimy. Wondering about Somerset Bradley. Why had I dreamed of him with Charlie? Because they were both dead? Because I'd killed one and was a suspect in the death of the other? Possibly. But those answers didn't feel true. My head was foggy. I looked at the clock, trying to rouse myself. Almost eight. Out the window, bright, blinding sun behind red and orange leaves. A car parallel parking. A pedestrian walking a corgi. Life as usual.

But inside, nothing felt usual. Brushing my teeth, I looked in the mirror. Saw the tangle of hair, the bruise on my head turning yellowish-green. And my eyes reflecting knowledge of something unbearable. Something too shameful to say.

Inside my head, bare children grunted. Charlie scolded. Inhabitants of my dream found tenements and took up residence, planning to stay.

You didn't do anything wrong, I told myself. Whatever happened to those children wasn't your fault. But my eyes contained the unacceptable truth, the culpability I'd somehow inherited from Charlie. I splashed my face with cold water, trying to shock the dream, the knowledge away. Then, avoiding the mirror, I hurried downstairs, trying to escape.

My newspaper at the door. The smell of brewing coffee. The sweet and tart tastes of granola and yogurt Morning routine comforted me; after a few minutes, I began to relax. I opened the paper, scanned the headlines. For a welcome change, saw nothing about anyone I knew. Skimmed the editorials. The advice column. Movie and book reviews. The gossip page. Apparently, there was still a world beyond my doorstep. It was comforting to see that, despite my personal havoc, life on Earth was continuing, basically undisturbed. I finished my yogurt, poured a second cup of coffee, turned to the obituaries. And saw a familiar face.

A listing for Somerset Bradley.

∿

I put down my cup. Felt a jolt, sharp like a slap on the cheek. Hadn't expected to see his face. His death notice.

Well, I should have expected it. They'd bury the man sooner or later.

I squirmed on my seat, uncomfortable. I looked away, then back at the page. Away again. Back again. Picked up my coffee cup. Put it down again. And, finally, I turned to the photo, bracing to face the man I'd killed.

I remembered the feeling of thrusting the hanger—the sound it made. His scream. Or wait—did I really remember? Or was I imagining it, filling in the blanks?

I didn't know. Wasn't sure. Hadn't remembered stabbing him when I'd talked to the police, so why would I remember now? God. I needed to call Susan, to get the name of that shrink, make an appointment. Find out what was wrong with me, why my memory was so riddled with holes.

The bump on my head throbbed. And Somerset Bradley smiled from the newspaper. He'd been kind of handsome, had certainly looked better without a wad of metal in his eye—Oh God. Did the obit mention his cause of death? I scanned the listing, afraid that they'd name me and my twisted hanger. But no, they'd just written, "Suddenly." Much more polite than "stabbed in the eye."

I read on. "Aged forty-six. Beloved husband to Gwynneth.

Father to Edmond (Heather), and Rupert. Also survived by a sister, Millicent (Haywood Reynolds) and three nephews. Memorial service at St. David's Episcopal Church in Radnor, tomorrow at noon. Interment private. No mention of flowers or donations.

I closed my eyes, covered my face with my hands. Took a deep breath. Recalled being slammed against the floor of Charlie's apartment, hitting my head. Seeing the shiv in my hand.

I put my hands down, opened my eyes, saw my hands. Studied the cut on my palm, the thin dark scab. Tried to remember how I'd cut myself. An orange? Slicing an orange? I pictured Charlie, dead on the sofa. The knife in his back. No—I hadn't cut myself stabbing him, must have done it cutting an orange. I closed my eyes again.

Finally, I looked back at the paper and read the obit again. Somerset Bradley. Beloved husband. Beloved father. Beloved uncle and brother.

Gwynneth. Edmond. Rupert. Millicent.

Service at noon. Interment private.

Rupert. Edmond.

Gwynneth.

I'd made a wife into a widow. I'd taken their father from his sons.

I'd killed a man.

"This is your fault, Elle," Charlie growled. I looked at the wound on my hand, remembered my knife in his back. Was it possible? Maybe I'd killed two?

I sat at the table, frozen, staring at the page.

Somerset Bradley, aged forty-six, smiled back. In the photo, he had two eyes.

~

The waiting room was small and indefinite. No way I'd be able to talk to a person who'd created an environment of colors so neutral that they weren't colors at all. Not definite enough to be labeled tan or gray or taupe or beige. Just blah. Blah-colored chairs, carpet. Blah walls. And a big blah piece of modern art that wasn't even definite enough to serve as a Rorschach test.

I was four minutes early. In four minutes, if he was on time, I'd meet the doctor Susan had recommended. I'd casually asked her that morning if she knew any shrinks. I was careful to make it low-key, said I was thinking of following up on our conversation about my memory. But she must have heard urgency in my voice because, within minutes, she had me set up with an immediate appointment in a shrink's swank Society Hill office, furnished in postmodern American blah.

Truthfully, it bothered me more than a little that this shrink had been referred by Susan's friend Zoe, who, as an art therapist, knew lots of them. But Zoe—and this was the bothering part—Zoe was married to none other than Detective Nick Stiles. The very same Detective Nick Stiles who was investigating Charlie's murder.

It felt too close. Worse than too close. It felt crazy to see a doctor who was friends with the wife of the homicide detective who considered me a person of interest, if not a suspect in a murder. But Susan assured me that doctor/patient privilege would prevail. That I could confide anything I wanted and the psychiatrist wouldn't disclose what I said to anyone—not to the courts, not even to her.

The waiting room had no magazines. Not one. The lighting was bland, an off-white lamp on an end table. The only color in the room was from a potted fern. I crossed my legs. Uncrossed them. Two minutes. If he was on time.

"There's a guy who can see you today," Susan had called back, not ten minutes after I'd called her. "Zoe says he's excellent. Smart. Teaches at Penn. And he's no bullshit."

"No bullshit?" I had no idea what she meant.

"He doesn't play shrink games, like answering your questions with questions. Or letting you lie on a sofa talking aimlessly. Zoe says his approach is focused. He'll tell you his thoughts, give you feedback, right then and there."

I wondered what his thoughts and feedback would be about child pornography. I hadn't told Susan yet about the flash drive or its contents. Hadn't even told her about Derek's blackmail insinuations. I knew I should, that the pornography might be important, might play a role in Charlie's murder. But I couldn't talk about it. Not yet. Couldn't say the words "pedophile" or "child pornography" out loud in the same sentence as Charlie's name. I felt too sickened. Too ashamed.

I checked the clock on my cell phone. It was time. The top of the hour—

"Mrs. Harrison?"

He was balding and blond. Lighter than blond. His hair was almost white. Glowing. His clothes the same color as his waiting room.

"I'm Don Schroeder." Not Doctor. He shook my hand. Firm. Warm. Strong. My hand wanted to stay in his.

And then I was sinking into a brown leather sofa in his book-lined office, accepting a cup of blah-colored mint tea.

～

"Do I call you Mrs. Harrison?"

"No, no. Call me Elle."

He smiled. His cheek muscles were thick. So were his fingers. White blond hairs on his hands. "Good. Call me Don."

So. We were on a first-name basis. Now what?

He sat in an easy chair, facing me. Not pushing. Waiting to see what I'd do?

"Thanks for seeing me so quickly."

"I'm glad I had an open spot."

Silence. We had run out of amenities.

"I guess you want to know why I'm here."

"Why don't you tell me?" He tilted his head. Watching me gently. Maybe wondering how I'd hurt my forehead. Or maybe he knew. Maybe Zoe—Susan's—friend had told him. Or maybe he'd read about it in the newspapers. He probably knew all about Charlie. And about Somerset Bradley and my head bump. Probably, he was just waiting to see what part I'd tell him first. I sipped tea, stalling, not sure how to begin. The mug was heavy. Soothing in my hands. Too hefty for tea, better for coffee.

Dr. Schroeder—Don—waited. Crossed his legs. Sipped tea. I didn't start with the flash drive and the pedophilia. Or with Somerset Bradley's death. Or Charlie's murder. Or the holes in my memory. There was something I needed to find out first.

∾

"Because I'm color-blind."

Oh. So that was it.

"Rather than make dire mistakes, I go for things that, I'm told, will blend. Does the lack of color bother you?"

No, not anymore. Actually, I was relieved. I hadn't meant to make an issue of it. But not one item in his waiting room or office had any but neutral tones. Not even Dr. Schroeder, whose hair was colorless and skin was pale. And the bland tones had disturbed me, seemed too passive and indefinite. But now I understood. The man lived in a colorless world, couldn't comprehend, much less, select colors. I wondered what it would be like, not to see reds or purples or yellows or blues. How different life would be. Would it be like tasting only one flavor? Hearing only one sound?

But time was passing. I had only an hour, needed to use every minute. Decided to be direct. But I had plenty of reasons to give him for why I'd come. Like hearing Charlie's voice after he was dead, seeing him at the funeral. Or stabbing a man in the eye. Or finding Charlie's photos of naked children. But I didn't mention any of those. Instead, I said, "I'm here because I have holes in my memory."

He uncrossed his legs. Folded his hands on his lap. "Holes?"

"Yes. Lately—no." I started over. "See, my friends—I've always been spacey. I wander in and out of conversations. I go off in my head. It's like I'm watching from the ceiling. Or taking a break from being in the room—"

"Sorry—This 'spacey' faraway feeling. Is it new?"

"No. That's normal for me. And it's not all the time. I can actually kind of control it. If I get bored or nervous or tired or stressed, I just kind of wander mentally away. Why? Is that bad?"

"Bad?" He smiled, leaned forward. "Nothing we talk about here is 'good' or 'bad,' Elle. Those are judgments. We're here to understand, not judge."

Right. Psychobabble. Probably it was bad.

"So tell me what you mean by wandering mentally away."

Why? I didn't want to get bogged down in normal stuff. I wanted to get onto the important parts. Like how I couldn't remember if I'd killed Charlie.

"I don't know. Like at the funeral. I kind of drifted off. I saw and heard everyone, but it was like I'd floated away. Like I was there but not there. Kind of outside myself."

"Outside yourself."

"Yes. Like I was watching."

"Watching."

God, was he going to repeat everything I said? "Yes. The way you'd watch a movie, only you're in it and it's real."

He paused, watching me with gentle eyes. He asked more questions. I answered. Told him about drifting in and out of conversations and events. How usually I could be in charge, coming back into focus when I wanted. I explained that drifting was normal for me, didn't seem strange. That my friends found it quirky, called it, "pulling an Elle."

He tilted his head, raised his eyebrows.

"And you've been 'pulling Elles' for how long?"

Forever. For as long as I could remember. In fact, at that moment, I was tempted to drift off and watch the session from a safe distance. Maybe from the colorless ceiling.

"Despite these wanderings, you've been functioning with no problem. You said on the phone that you teach school."

Yes. I functioned pretty well. And, yes, I taught school. Second graders. I thought of my class, saw sparkling eyes and shining faces. Benjy. Tommy. Molly. Aiden. Lily. Josh. An unknown child, posing naked.

"I'd like to spend more time on this subject. But you said it's normal for you. Which leads me to think that 'pulling Elles' is not what you meant by 'holes' in your memory."

No. It wasn't.

"So what did you mean?"

"Just—I'm having some trouble remembering stuff."

"Remembering stuff."

Oh God. The man was a living echo.

"Are we talking about short term? Like remembering appointments or, say, where you've put your keys?"

I met his eyes. "No. It's more about specific events. Like, for example, I can't remember whether or not I murdered my husband."

∿

He didn't flinch. Didn't pause. He continued as if I'd said I couldn't remember where I'd parked the car. "Tell me about your husband's death, Elle. About what you don't remember."

And so, I did, sort of. My telling was hurried. I was afraid that my hour would run out before I finished. And what I said was out of sequence, in flashes, like my memories. But, in no particular order, I told him about the night I'd found Charlie's body. Not remembering the hours between coming home from school and going to Jeremy's bar, including cutting my hand. I told him about the rose that moved around the house. And that I didn't remember the actual killing of Somerset Bradley.

Dr. Schroeder—Don—asked few questions. When I finished, I couldn't look at him. I hadn't told anyone the things I'd told him. I'd never articulated it even to myself. And, having done so, I felt exposed. Naked. My chest hurt. I couldn't breathe.

For a moment, Don said nothing. Then, slowly, he leaned forward and met my eyes. Put his hand on my arm, squeezed gently.

"My goodness, Elle, you've had a terrible time all on your own, haven't you?"

My eyes flooded. I wanted to ask what was wrong with me, why I couldn't remember significant events like, for example, killing a man. But I couldn't speak. Would have choked if I'd tried.

"We're going to work on this, Elle. But first of all, most important, I want to reassure you."

To reassure me? Tears gushed suddenly over my lashes, down my face. Dr. Schroeder—sorry, I couldn't think of him by his first name—he wanted to reassure me. He would work with me. I sniffed, swallowed a sob. He handed me a box of tissues and sat back, waiting for me to collect myself.

"Do you want me to tell you my initial thoughts?" He watched me blow my nose.

Of course I did.

"Let's start with what we talked about first. About 'pulling Elles,' okay? Normally, I wouldn't come to so swift a conclusion, much less share it. But in your case, your descriptions of your 'Elles' are almost textbook examples of a certain dissociative disorder."

Wait. Dissociative disorder? I remembered the term—"Dissociation disorders" from college psychology classes. It was the term they used for people with multiple personalities. Like Eve, in *The Three Faces of Eve*. I crossed my arms. And my legs. Was Dr. Schroeder saying that I was like her? That my personality was divided into different distinct identities? No, that wasn't possible. Was it? Was one of my parts a killer? I took a breath. Made myself speak. "You mean like split personalities."

He smiled broadly. "So you've taken psychology courses."

Yes. A few.

"Well, no, not nearly as severe as split personalities. There is a whole spectrum of disorders that involve dissociation. Some are severe. Others relatively mild. And treatable."

He paused, letting his answer settle in. "Specifically, you seem to be experiencing something called dissociative depersonalization disorder. Have you ever heard of it?"

I shook my head. No. I didn't think so.

Dr. Schroeder got up, surveyed his bookshelves, pulled out a volume, rifled through pages. "Let me read a couple of phrases from this book—it's a pop-psych book written by a Mayo Clinic doctor, but it's pretty good at getting ideas across. Here: depersonalization disorder. Typically, it involves—quote, 'the feeling of being outside yourself.'"

I stiffened. My face felt hot.

"Symptoms include: 'the feeling of watching your life from afar.'"

That was the way I'd described my mental wanderings. Almost verbatim.

"Or of 'viewing life as if you were viewing a movie.'" He closed the book, looked up at me. And smiled. "Sound familiar?"

I wasn't able to smile back. Something was wrong with me. A doctor had described it, even used the same words. I had a disorder. And that disorder didn't even address the more serious problems, the gaps in my memory that had brought me to get help.

～

"The good news," Dr. Schroeder sat again, "is that these symptoms are often associated with depression and anxiety. So there has been marked success at reducing them with antidepressives and antianxiety medications."

"And the bad news?"

He grinned. "Elle. Is there always bad news with good?"

I tilted my head. "Isn't there?"

He sat up, lost the smile. "Well, it's not exactly 'bad' news. Just possibly not so good. From what you've said, your condition sounds long term. Chronic. So it might—mind you, *might*—be more complicated to treat than something more acute, short term or temporary."

Another pause. From his expression, I could see that more "not exactly bad news" was coming. "And?"

"And," his eyes didn't leave mine, "you've mentioned memory loss centered around specific events. That kind of memory loss isn't typical of depersonalization disorder. It might be indicative of a second dissociative condition."

A second dissociative condition.

I heard myself breathe, "Oh God." Felt blood drain from my head. I was sick. Very sick.

Dr. Schroeder frowned. "Elle? Are you all right?"

I reached for my mug. Sipped sweet, now tepid tea. Nodded. Yes, I was fine. In a depersonalized kind of way.

"My theory, as of now, is that we're dealing with a compound situation. On one hand, you have a preexisting tendency to depersonalize—or go away when things are stressful or difficult. And you have an acute condition that manifests itself during confrontations with severe traumas."

He'd paused again, letting me absorb his points.

"Normally, Elle, when you face mild stress, you let your mind drift off and carry you away. You drift back when you're calmer. This has worked for you for years. But now, traumatic events have occurred that were so severe that your mind couldn't cope by doing its normal drifting routine and watching from afar. The events were too terrible, too horrible, to cope with even from the roof or a movie screen. So your mind went a step farther. It actually rejected the experiences, refusing to record them. Or possibly, it buried them so deeply that you wouldn't be able to retrieve them. Either way, your mind protected you by not allowing these unacceptable, unbearable events into your consciousness. Do you follow so far?"

I thought so. When really bad things happened, my mind essentially shut down my memory.

"We psychiatrists like to give names to things, even amorphous conceptual things. We label them so they seem manageable and definite, even when they aren't." He smirked. "The name we give memory losses like yours is amnesia. But not the kind of amnesia one might get from a car accident or a blow to the head. This type has no physical cause, so it's called dissociative amnesia. In your case, because the memory loss is limited to specific events and windows of time, it's called localized dissociative amnesia."

He paused again. Looked from me to his watch. Apologized with his eyes.

"It's a lot to digest."

It was.

He'd diagnosed me with conditions that sounded serious and had a lot of syllables. And might take a lot of time to work out. But because of the urgency of my situation, he arranged to see me daily, even on the weekend for the first week of therapy.

Leaving his office, I still couldn't remember what had happened in the hours before I'd found Charlie's body. Still couldn't quite recall killing Somerset Bradley. But, despite that, I felt optimistic. Hopeful. I wasn't alone, covering up, trying to appear normal. Someone knew what was going on with me. Someone was going to help me. And, so far, no matter what I'd told him, he hadn't appeared shocked or appalled.

But then, I hadn't yet mentioned pedophilia.

~

When I left, I felt so cheery that I took some time to walk around Society Hill. Past historic homes and old churches to

Washington Square, where I sat on a bench, drinking a yogurt shake I'd bought along the way. It was Friday, warm, breezy, almost seventy. Sunlight flickered through colored leaves, warm, like rays of hope.

Sitting on the bench, though, I began to question my mood. Charlie had died eight days before. Nothing had really changed. He was still dead. I was still a suspect in his murder. I had still killed a man. And I still had a flash drive full of child pornography. So what the hell was there for me to be cheery about? Was I not just dissociative, but also delusional?

Seeing Dr. Schroeder had changed nothing. If anything, my problems had become more complicated by what I'd learned. I had a personality disorder. No—I had two. I'd need to take medication, which might or might not help. My conditions might or might not be treatable. My symptoms might or might not get worse.

My cell rang. Susan's ringtone. I sighed. Pulled the phone out of my bag.

"So?"

"So. Like you said, he tells you what he's thinking. No bullshit. Thanks for finding him."

"So did he help? Do you remember anything else?"

Did she think he was a magician? I thought of Joel. He was a magician. Maybe he could cure me. "Not yet, Susan. It'll take time."

She was quiet. I recognized tension in the silence. Pictured her, as usual, pushing hair out of her eyes, figuring out how to word something troubling.

"What?"

She exhaled. "We have to talk."

Oh God. What now? I pictured Officer Moran slapping handcuffs on my wrists. "Tell me."

But she wouldn't. "Not now." Susan sounded urgent. "In person. How's your house? In an hour."

She would tell me nothing, insisted on a meeting. By the time we got off the phone, my mood had darkened. What did Susan have to tell me? How catastrophic would it be? Why did she have to tell me in person?

I watched a squirrel scamper up a tree, across a branch. Saw a couple of tourists snap pictures of the memorial to the Unknown Soldier. And, from a great distance, I watched the woman on the bench down the last of her shake. Stand. Toss the empty cup in the trash. Begin walking slowing north toward Walnut Street to hail a cab.

~

I admit I wasn't paying attention. I was deliberately drifting. Dulling my emotions by pulling an Elle. But I made my way across Washington Square without incident. I stopped the intersection of 7th and Walnut, waiting for traffic to break. Looking for a taxi. Seeing none, I walked west, aware of people on the sidewalk. Of engine noises. Of glass windows, restaurants, and shops.

But I was a safe distance away, watching myself and my surroundings. Oddly aware, though, that I was in the act of depersonalizing. Or was it dissociating? Disordering? What an odd word, disorder.

I walked up Walnut Street, thinking about words and prefixes. The meaning of the names Dr. Schroeder had given to my conditions. The aroma of Chinese food interrupted. Szechuan chicken? Peking duck? I wasn't on Walnut Street any more. I'd drifted too far, hadn't paid attention where I was going. I was on 9th Street in Chinatown, heading north.

I stopped, getting my bearings. Looked again for a cab. Saw one, down 9th Street at a stoplight. Stepped off the curb, through the row of parked cars so I could hail it as it approached. Didn't notice the bicycle a few car lengths down or its rider watching me.

When the bike sped forward and came directly at me, I didn't have time to be surprised. For a stunned nanosecond, I stood immobile, simultaneously gaping at the cyclist, noting the purple helmet, the lowered shoulders that braced for collision, grasping the danger, figuring the calculus of the bike's speed and direction. And deciding that I'd better move. As fast as I could, I whirled around, pivoting, dodging the bulk of the impact, diving between parked cars, aware that I was too late, too slow.

From far above in the rooftops, I saw myself leave the ground and fly. Saw myself hit the pavement. Heard a passerby ask, "Miss, you okay?" And struggled to my feet too late to watch the cyclist with the purple helmet pedal away.

~

The bruises didn't seem bad at first. Not as bad as the scrapes on my knees from tiny glass shards and pebbles and whatever else coats the pavement on 9th Street. Or the raw patches of skin on the heel of my right hand and along my forearm.

The good news was that I caught the cab I'd seen. He stopped along with the other cars, as drivers gawked at the woman who'd been knocked down by a hit-and-run bike rider. Pedestrians offered help. A woman took my arm, guided me out of the gutter. My body was tingling, rattled. But nothing was broken; my parts moved. I gathered up my handbag. Checked myself, saw that my khaki Capris were dirty and stained. Brushed them off with sooty, prickling hands. People were staring. The woman asked if I needed an ambulance. Someone suggested calling the police.

No. No thank you. No ambulance. And certainly, definitely no police. Thanking the woman who'd helped me, I hopped into the cab and recited my address, felt the vibration of the engine as the cab took off. As we drove, I watched out the window for a cyclist with a purple helmet. Didn't see one.

A few blocks later, it sunk in that someone had just tried to kill me. Or at least to mess me up. But who? Why? Was it the same person who'd killed Charlie? My hands stung. I kept re-living the moment before the impact. Trying to see the person's face. But all I could recall were the whooshing of wheels and the sense of flying. And the image of watching myself fly. My dissociative disorder. Lord.

Blood oozed out of my scrapes, but the driver asked no questions, made no comments. He simply drove. His license, posted above the meter, showed his photo and name. The name had lots of consonants. Looked foreign. Maybe he was quiet because he didn't speak English well. Or maybe he didn't like fares who'd been lying bloody in the gutter. I saw his dark eyes watching me in the rearview mirror. Maybe checking to see that I was all right. Or to make sure that I wasn't bleeding onto his upholstery. I understood how he felt, having lost a sofa to blood myself.

The initial numbness of shock was wearing off. Sharp pain began stinging my hip, my arm, my elbow, the palms of my hands, my cut, which had ripped opened yet again. And the cab jerked and wove, bouncing over potholes, swinging around double-parked trucks, skirting SEPTA buses, lurching to sudden stops for pedestrians or red lights. Hurting all over, I clung to the armrest, hoping to survive the two- or three-mile ride from Chinatown to my home in Fairmount. I needed to get inside, figure things out. I looked outside the window, watching the street numbers increase, still watching for the bike rider and the purple helmet.

Finally, we pulled onto my street. Home. I wanted to pay the driver, dash into my house, sink into the bathtub, soak my wounds, and try to figure out who'd just run me down. But I didn't do any of that.

Because when the cab stopped in front of my townhouse, Susan was on the doorstep, dressed in a lawyerly green suit. I'd forgotten. She was waiting to give me bad news.

～

"Where've you—" she began but stopped as I emerged and she got a look at me. Her mouth opened. "Now what? You look like you've been rolling in the gutter."

How odd.

"Hit-and-run. By a bicycle." My jaw felt stiff. All of me did.

"Seriously?"

I paid the silent driver, took my keys out of my bag, limped up the front stairs. My right hand stung and trembled.

Susan took my keys, unlocked the door. Inside, she looked me over, assessing the damage. "You're bleeding. You're a mess."

She threw me into the shower. Moments later, wrapped in a soft oversized towel, I sat wincing and whining on the toilet seat as she tweezed gravel out of my scrapes and examined my bruises. The bloody cut on my left hand balanced the oozing scrapes on my right. Both knees, my right arm, and left hip were darkening, blossoming with varying shades of red, purple, and blue. Contrasting with the yellow-green tones on my forehead.

No question. Susan was right. I was a mess.

"So where were you? What happened? Someone just rode past you and knocked you down?"

Again, I pictured stepping onto 9th Street. The rider speeding up. And then, the taste of gutter dirt.

Hot water, the rough washcloth stung on my elbow.

"Think back. Do you remember anything about the bike? What color was it?"

The color of blur.

"Or the rider? Was it a man or a woman?"

"No idea. But the helmet was purple. And the cyclist wore black spandex with yellow accents."

"There. That's something."

Well, not really.

"Were there witnesses? Did you get their numbers? They might have seen—"

No. I didn't get any numbers.

Susan fretted. She scolded. Finally, she took out her cell phone, made a call. Told me the police would look into it, though we both knew there was nothing, not a piece of evidence to lead them anywhere.

"What's wrong with you, Elle? Why didn't you get the witnesses' information?"

I was shaking. Cold. Had no idea what was wrong with me. No, not true. I had a list of defects. And Dr. Schroeder had just identified two more.

Annoyed with me, Susan finished her doctoring. Told me I'd live. Asked if I wanted some tea.

I was still braced for her to give me the news she wouldn't say on the phone. I opted for something stronger.

At the bar in the study, Susan poured two generous servings of Johnny Walker Black. I looked before I sat, but didn't see Charlie on the sofa. Of course I didn't. Charlie was gone, buried. Hadn't shown up since the funeral.

"Want an ice pack?" Susan offered from the bar. "It'll stop your swelling."

"No, I'm okay." I wasn't. I sat gingerly, protecting sore spots, took a long swallow, leaned back, felt soothing heat slide down my throat.

And braced myself to hear whatever Susan was about to say.

~

She sat beside me. Sipped. Held her glass on her lap. Her suit was a soft hunter green. Professional silk blouse. Her heels low, practical. I had rarely seen Susan in lawyer garb. She sipped again. Put her glass down.

"So." She pushed hair out of her eyes. "Two things. About Sherry McBride."

I swallowed booze. Picturing her with Charlie, her fiery hazel eyes.

"Here's the thing: According to Detective Stiles, there's no definitive evidence that Sherry McBride ever dated Charlie. No evidence that the two ever even had a drink together. Or a hot dog. Nothing."

"What kind of evidence would they expect?"

"Witnesses. Friends who'd seen them together, or whom they'd talked to about seeing each other. Or souvenirs. Or e-mail. Or phone records. There's nothing."

"But she acted as if they were involved—"

"Yeah. Because, more than likely, she wanted to be involved with him. Knowing Charlie, he encouraged her. Smiled, took an interest. Talked to her. Charmed her. You know how he was. But he was probably an unwitting participant in what limited relationship they had. Probably had no clue about her fantasies." She took another drink. Set it down again. Leaned back, stretching her arms out on the back of the sofa. Loosening up.

Charlie had the gift of remembering not just everyone's name, but their stories, as well. Their details. As if each one he spoke to was the most important person in his life. It was how he got people to trust him. Hell. It was how he got me to marry him.

"Bottom line," Susan continued, "no one who knows either of them says they ever saw each other romantically or even socially anywhere outside of work."

"But they must have." At the viewing, Sherry McBride had commented on my wedding picture. She must have seen it. "She's been in Charlie's bedroom."

"Elle. I'm sorry. How could you possibly know that?"

I told her about the remark. And about the wedding picture on Charlie's bureau.

She tsked. "Really? Do you seriously think that the photo in his bedroom is the only wedding photo Charlie had? He probably had one in his office. On his desk. For all you know, he papered the walls with pictures of you."

"Okay." I got it. Took a sip. Another.

"Elle, the fact that she saw a picture of your wedding doesn't mean she saw it in his bedroom or that she was involved with him. In fact, even if she did see it in his bedroom, we can't conclude that they were involved. Knowing her, she could have been stalking him and broke into his place."

I was unconvinced. "It doesn't mean anything that nobody knew. People see each other secretly all the time. Especially if they work together."

"Elle. Seriously." Susan frowned. "Why would Charlie bother to sneak around with her? He was single again. Could date anyone he wanted. No reason to hide."

True.

"But beyond that, think about it. About Sherry McBride."

I did. Saw her cornering me at the viewing with fury in her eyes.

"Look how she behaved at the viewing. How she dressed. The woman has no class. She's loud and foulmouthed. Cheap. Crass."

Sherry McBride was also long legged, athletic, womanly. With an ample bosom. Actually, men like Charlie might consider her amusing. Or wait, no. Not men like Charlie. What was I thinking?

"Trust me. Charlie wouldn't as much as look at someone like her."

Actually, she was right. Charlie wouldn't as much as look at Sherry McBride. But not for the reasons Susan had listed. Sherry McBride was simply way too womanly. Way too adult.

I swallowed Scotch, thinking of Charlie. How many times had we had sex? A few thousand? More? During all those times, had he been fantasizing that I was a child? Oh God. I took another gulp. Another. How was it possible that I hadn't suspected anything? Hadn't seen any signs? Obviously, I hadn't suspected because Charlie hadn't wanted me to. Had been good at keeping secrets. Well, the secret was out. I was going to tell Susan, show her the pictures. But she was still talking. I needed to pay attention, find out why she looked so upset. So animated.

"—bad news. Her alibi checked out."

Wait, whose alibi?

"She was seen. Just like we thought, she followed Charlie to your house. But she didn't go up to the door or ring the bell. He didn't open the door to let her in."

Oh. Sherry McBride's alibi. I put my cup down, closed my eyes. "How do you know?"

"Your neighbor, Charlotte Fox, came home from work around five thirty and took her dog out. The dog found Sherry on their property and, being a guard dog, he did his thing. Went crazy. Of course, Mrs. Fox made her leave. But the important thing is when she found her, Sherry was crouching behind a planter, watching your house. She insisted that her boyfriend was in there, that she was just waiting for him to come out."

I knew Charlotte Fox. She took great pride in her horticulture, didn't like people messing with her planters. But wait. The encounter didn't necessarily give Sherry an alibi. "Susan. You said Charlotte took the dog out at five thirty. Charlie wasn't killed until after six. Sherry could have come back without Charlotte seeing her."

"Well, no. She couldn't have."

Susan sighed, met my eyes. More bad news was coming.

"Stiles and Swenson did their homework. Records at the University of Pennsylvania Hospital emergency room show Sherry McBride showing up at 5:55 p.m. and being discharged at 8:15 after receiving twenty-two stitches on the ankle and calf. For dog bites."

～

Damn. Sherry wasn't a suspect in Charlie's murder. I lifted my Scotch. Winced as the cool glass touched the raw spot on my palm. "So. Sherry McBride's off the hook."

Which put me more firmly onto it.

"I don't suppose that, while she was surveilling my house, she saw the killer go in or come out?"

Susan looked glum. "Stiles asked."

"And?"

"Not a soul."

My cell phone rang. I picked it up, saw the name on the screen. Ted Harrison. No way I was going to talk to Ted. He hadn't bothered to show up for the viewing or the funeral. Had nothing to say that I'd want to hear. I let the call go. No sooner had it stopped ringing than it started again. This time: Derek Morris. I cursed, grimaced, let him go to voice mail. Wasn't going to talk to him, either. Was not going to deal with his desperate search for the porno flash drive.

Susan saw my reaction, tilted her head. It was time to tell her. But when I opened my mouth, I didn't mention the flash drive. Instead, I asked, "How about lunch?"

I stalled. Made use of my refrigerator full of cold cut trays from the funeral. We would eat sandwiches in my kitchen, talk about normal stuff. How I missed my class. Who was feeding the hamsters. If the substitute was being good to my kids.

Susan talked about her daughters. How Lisa and Julie were like pit bulls, fighting constantly over nothing.

We stood at the counter where I'd heard my dead husband call my name, felt him kiss my neck. I recoiled at the memory. The thought of his touch now repelled me. Susan saw me twitch, raised an eyebrow as she spread mustard.

"I mean, all siblings fight. It's not unusual." She assumed my twitch was a reaction to her daughters.

"I'm sure it's just a phase." I tried to look calm.

Susan smirked. "Like my brother and me—we really fought. Remember when Scott broke my arm?"

"No, I remember that you fell out of a tree while you were trying to lasso him."

She laughed. "I got him, too."

"If you don't count the part where he pulled on the rope and you fell."

She dished out potato salad. Roast beef and cole slaw on rye for me. Baked ham and Swiss for Susan. Dessert of brownies with walnuts and dark chocolate chips. Cream sodas. Heavy, comforting food.

But eating ended. Chitchat was over. It was time to tell her about the porn. I didn't know how to begin, how to bring the subject up. We had, after all, just finished eating. Lunch didn't seem an appropriate time to say I had a dozen or so computer files full of naked children. Maybe I should start by talking about Derek. About his assertion that Charlie had stolen client information. How he'd come over, asking to look around the house for missing files, maybe for a flash drive.

But I didn't. Because it didn't matter how I got around to it, I'd still eventually have to talk about the porn. I'd have to admit that Charlie had possessed it, brought it into my house, hidden it there. Might have died trying to protect it. And, even though the porn wasn't mine, even though Charlie, when he'd brought it into the house, had no longer been my husband except technically, even with all of that, I was still ashamed to tell Susan about it.

After all, Charlie had been my husband for a long time. I'd loved him, and somehow, his secret—his depravity—felt personal. As if it reflected on me.

I drank more Scotch. Tried to build up nerve. I'd known her forever, but wasn't sure that our friendship could withstand my connection, however indirect, to something as vile as child pornography. Susan was, after all, the mother of three. A homeroom mother at the school. An officer in the PTA. The mom whose house all the neighborhood kids played at.

No. Susan would not be tolerant of abusers of children. Or of those who tolerated, let alone, married them.

"So," she swallowed a gulp of soda, "why do you think

Derek Morris keeps calling you?" She took another drink. "Knowing him, it's about money. Did the firm have life insurance policies? Or death benefits?"

Not even close.

"By the way, did Charlie have a will?"

A will?

"Do you have a copy of it? Because you should."

I didn't have a copy. In fact, I didn't even know if he had a will. Nor did I know if Charlie's firm had death benefits or life insurance.

"We never discussed dying." Hadn't planned on doing it in the short term. Wills, life insurance—none of it had seemed important yet.

Susan shook her head. "Seriously? Never? Lord, Tim and I already have our burial plots. We have everything—a funeral bank account, life insurance, trust funds for the house and investments, wills. The whole enchilada."

Good for them.

She shrugged, still amazed at my poor planning. "I'll call his divorce lawyer. Maybe he knows. Hell, maybe he drew up Charlie's will."

I swallowed the last of my Scotch. And decided to just get it over with. Time to tell her. Friendship aside, Susan was my lawyer. She needed to know about the porn. After all, Charlie might have been killed because of it.

And so, I took a deep breath. "Did you like him, Susan?"

"Who, Charlie?"

I nodded. Yes. Charlie.

She stuttered. "Of course. Well, I . . . I mean, in a way. He was charming. Not that I liked the way he lied to you. Or how he stole your inheritance—"

"But he seemed decent?"

"Basically."

I took her by the hand, then, and led her to the study. And opened my computer.

~

Before I opened the files, I asked Susan to take a seat on the sofa and told her about Derek. "He told me that Charlie had stolen private client files. Important information that could ruin prominent lives."

"Wait, what?"

I sat sideways, so I could face her. "He indicated that Charlie was going to blackmail one of their clients. And he thought Charlie might have hidden the information here. He asked if he could look around."

"Tell me you didn't let him."

"Of course not."

"Good. I don't trust him. So what are you going to show me? You found the pilfered files?"

I nodded. "I found the flash drive after the funeral. Charlie hid it on the bar."

"So?"

"Susan. It's pretty—"

"No, I'm asking if you told Derek that you've found it."

I shook my head, no. "See, the stuff on the drive isn't what Derek said it was. It's not private client information."

Her eyebrows lifted. "Okay. Maybe this isn't the same drive that Derek was looking for. Maybe it's something else entirely."

I bit my lip. Folded my hands. Sat tall. Why was she asking so many questions, making this even harder than it already was? "Trust me. It's the right drive. It's just not what Derek said it was. Actually, I think it's possible that Derek made up that whole client story to cover for Charlie and, indirectly, protect himself and the firm."

She watched me. Mildly interested.

"Susan. Charlie might have been into something awful—"

"What is it, a snuff film?"

"No, but—"

"Let's take a look, why don't we?" She turned to the screen.

"Be prepared, Susan. It's bad."

And with that, I opened the first file.

~

I didn't look at the pictures. I'd seen them. Instead, I watched Susan's face, her reaction. As she advanced through the photos, her eyes changed, became grim. Her jaw became set. I expected outrage and shock. Revulsion. I'd even left the door open to the bathroom, in case she had to expel her ham and cheese.

But she didn't need the bathroom. Didn't express any of the emotions for which I'd been prepared. She simply viewed the photos, one at a time. When she'd viewed the entire file, she sat back. Pushed hair out of her eyes. Looked at me.

"How long have you had these, Elle?"

I shrugged. "A day or—"

"Because you realize these might change everything."

I nodded. Yes.

"You never saw Charlie with any images like these before?"

"Of course not."

"His sexual appetites never seemed—"

"Susan. No. I never had a clue. How can you even ask me that?"

She shrugged. "You never know what goes on in people's bedrooms."

I let that pass. Bristling.

She turned to face me. "So. Do you know any of the children?"

What? "Of course not." Did she think I'd taken the pictures myself? Perhaps posed my students?

"Nor do I. You know what? I don't think they're local." She started through the shots again. "The settings—look at the furniture. And that telephone? Its design? It looks foreign."

Really? I wasn't sure. There were all kinds of phones anymore.

"And look," she pointed to a magazine on a nightstand, "that's not English."

The letters were too small to see. No way she could know that.

"I think it's Greek. Maybe Russian."

"So?" What difference did it make where the pictures were taken? "I don't see—"

"Have you looked at the other files on the drive?"

"No. I couldn't stand it."

She clicked away, moving on to a new file. "Damn it, Elle, why didn't you tell me about this right away? What's the matter with you? These pictures might cast a whole new light on Charlie's murder. It might take the heat off you."

She opened another file. The images were poorly lit. Candid, not professional like those in the first file. The hands were adult, male, faceless. Touching a child.

I choked on my question. "So, Susan. You don't think Charlie had these because he was—"

"Was what?"

I hesitated. She looked up at me from the screen.

"Are you asking me if I think Charlie was a pedophile?"

Adult male hands caressed a boy's buttocks.

I just looked at her, couldn't speak.

She looked back at the screen. Then at me again. "I learned a long time ago that people can surprise you, Elle. I've represented people whose spouses have had not the slightest idea that they've been robbing convenience stores or stealing cars. Even raping women. But this? Could Charlie have hidden a sexual aberration like this?" She paused, thinking.

Could he? Had he? Bed had been the one area where, even at the end, our marriage had been strong. Thinking of it made my throat feel thick.

"No. Sorry. I don't buy it. You'd have had some indication."

She clicked forward through the file. Opened the next one to find more of the same, this time with young girls, as well. And the next.

Finally, she opened last file on the flash drive. The first photo showed a young tow-headed boy in Moscow, outside the Kremlin. Holding Somerset Bradley's hand.

∾

That file didn't show sex acts. The photos looked perfectly innocent, showed men, sometimes alone and sometimes with children, mostly candid, eating ice cream and walking like tourists in the Russian capital.

Susan recognized the children. "Remember the kid in the shower stall? This is him. And that's the girl from the bondage thing."

But in this file, they were dressed. Like children. Smiling. Skipping in a park. Kicking a soccer ball.

Altogether, there were pictures of four men. Somerset Bradley. Jonas Walters. One I didn't know. And another that I did.

Charlie's partner, Derek Morris.

Derek. With Somerset Bradley and Jonas Walters. In Russia.

My stomach twisted. I tasted a mixture of recycled roast beef and anger. Susan was talking, but I couldn't listen. I was trying to make sense of what I was seeing. Were all four of these men pedophiles? Even Derek? Jonas Walters? And Somerset Bradley? Had they gone to Russia on some kind of pedophilia tour package? Were the candid shots in these files mementos of their trip?

Oh God. Now it made sense why Somerset Bradley had gone to Charlie's condo—he'd been looking for these photos. They could have destroyed him. And Derek. And the other men.

And what about Charlie? What was he doing with these files? Planning to blackmail the others? Or to blow a whistle, exposing them? Was he threatening Derek, trying to force him out of the business? I had no idea.

Susan was talking, or rather, shouting. Angry. Escalating. "—think I can represent you if you don't tell me everything? Now that Sherry McBride isn't a suspect, don't you realize that you are the only one the police are even looking at? You are this close," she put her thumb and pointer a quarter inch apart, "from being arrested for Charlie's murder. If I hadn't begged and pleaded and used every ounce of pull I have in my friendship with Nick Stiles, you'd already have been arraigned. Probably be behind bars. Are you completely insane, Elle? Why —what possibly could have led you to keep this from me?" She looked at me, exasperated. Panting. Waiting for an answer.

I owed it to her. She was right. "I'm sorry, Susan. I thought the photos were Charlie's." I paused. "And if I showed them to you, you'd think he was sick. And by contagion, that I was. That you'd be disgusted."

"You thought I'd be disgusted." She shook her head, rolled her eyes.

Yes. I nodded.

"Disgusted with Charlie. Who was divorcing you. And who's dead. And whose death might send you to prison for a long, long time."

Yes, yes, yes, and yes. "See, I didn't look at all the files. I didn't know about the other men in the pictures."

"Elle. Whether or not Charlie was a pedophile—whether or not the other men are—it makes no difference."

"How can it make no difference, Susan? It's unspeakably sick. How can you not be disgusted?"

"Because my personal disgust or lack thereof is not relevant—"

"Not relevant?"

"No matter what I think or feel, you are my client. And in this country, as you may remember, even the vilest suspect accused of the most heinous of crimes is entitled to zealous, impartial legal defense. So my reaction—"

"Wait. You're saying I'm vile?"

"Good God, Elle. What I'm saying is that all that matters here is you and your legal situation. Are you daft? Don't you get it? These files raise the possibility that someone else—in fact, four someone else's—had motive and opportunity to kill Charlie. For example: Derek thinks Charlie is going to blackmail a client over these pictures; Derek kills Charlie to prevent it. Substitute the names of the other men in the photos if you want other theories. Bottom line: the files take the heat off you."

I got that part. But not the part about her attitude. I wanted her friendship and respect and affection, not just her representation. "But Susan, the kids in those photos—they're the age of the kids in my class. Seven or eight years old. They're just a little older than your Emily. Can't you see why I couldn't stand it—"

"Oh, get over it, Elle. So you were shocked. Well, welcome to Earth. This is a planet where people do terrible things to each other. It's part of reality."

"How can you say that? You're a mother—"

"Yes, I am. And, believe me, I'd jump in front of a tractor trailer to keep my kids safe. But ultimately, I know I can't protect them from everything. The world has ugliness and cruelty. Crime galore. And you can't just pretend it's not there and hide it—especially from your attorney. It won't go away."

She asked if I had a blank flash drive. Busied herself downloading and copying the files. And I went to the bar and poured myself another Scotch, feeling chastised. Not offering her one.

I swallowed booze. The images of the children, of the men abusing them wouldn't leave my head. Got confused among memories of Charlie. His kisses. His shoulders. Our steamy nights in bed. Despite what Susan said, I felt ill. Something primal boiled in my rib cage, threatened to erupt. From above, I watched myself swallow Scotch and turn to Susan. Heard myself speak.

"You know, Susan? If Charlie was involved in child porn

and I found out? I don't know what I'd have done. I might have—it's possible that I'd have killed him."

Susan didn't even look up. "But he was nowhere in those photos. So, according to what's on those files, he wasn't involved." Susan was finished copying the flash drive, popped it into her bag. Looked at me directly. "So you wouldn't."

Long after she'd gone, I stayed in the study, watching myself sip Scotch. Not entirely sure.

∾

Over and over, I replayed my dream of stabbing Charlie. The feeling of steel slicing through fabric, skin, tissue.

And I replayed Dr. Schroeder's explanation of localized dissociative amnesia. It was specific to a particular event so traumatic that the mind refused access to it. The way my mind refused access to the hours around Charlie's murder.

I pictured what might have happened. I might have encountered Charlie in the house. Hell, I might have even let him in. Either way, I'd have demanded to know what he was doing there.

"You can't just come over whenever you want. You don't live here anymore. You need to call first."

"What's the matter, Elf? You afraid I'll steal the silver?"

"No. You already took the silver. And everything else of value."

We'd have argued. But that wasn't new. We'd argued a million times. An argument didn't explain his murder.

I started over, redesigned the confrontation. Maybe I'd found him at the desk in the study, on the computer.

"What the hell, Charlie? You scared me. You can't just show up here any time you want. You need to call first." I had a knife in my hand, would have grabbed it when I'd heard someone in the study. "Don't tell me you came here to answer your e-mail?"

"No." He wouldn't have looked up from the screen, would have clicked through the photos. "I'll be just a second."

"What are you looking at?"

I'd have looked over his shoulder. Seen the naked kids. Discovered Charlie's involvement in pedophilia.

"Oh my God—" I'd have backed away, repulsed and shocked.

"It's not what you think, Elf."

How often had he said those words to me?

"I swear, just let me explain."

He'd have come after me, trying to convince me that I had misconstrued, misinterpreted, misunderstood what I'd seen. And in a fight filled with fresh revulsion and rage on top of festering betrayal and rejection, maybe I'd used the knife. Maybe I'd killed him.

That would explain the precise details in my dream. And the way I'd found the drive. Maybe I'd tossed it into the cork jar myself and subconsciously remembered doing it. Maybe part of my mind remembered what I'd done and was trying to surface, to tell me the truth.

Oh God. I could hear Charlie whining. "You didn't have to kill me, Elle. Divorcing me was bad enough."

But his voice wasn't a memory. It was there, in the room. I looked around. Saw what looked like a man's shadow in the corner, behind the desk.

"What the hell were those pictures, Charlie? How could you have pictures of naked children?" I asked these questions out loud, as if the shadow were Charlie's. As if it would answer.

"Maybe I had a good reason."

Wow. It did answer.

"Did you see me in any of those pictures, Elf? No, you didn't. Because I wasn't in them. Not a single one. Go ahead. Look. And also look at who *was* in them."

I already knew who was: Somerset Bradley. Derek. Jonas Walters and another man. "So what were you going to do? Blackmail them? That's almost as bad as being in the pictures." Well, no. It wasn't nearly as bad. But I was talking to the shadow of a dead man that wasn't really there. I didn't have to be accurate.

"Maybe you're right. Maybe I was going to blackmail them. But maybe I wasn't."

Wait, what?

"Maybe I was going to expose a ring of powerful business-men who share an unfortunate appetite for sex with children. Who spend fortunes investing in child prostitution. Who have actually organized lists of places to go and people to see so they and those like them can satisfy their perverse desires."

Charlie was going to expose the pedophiles?

"But no, you would never think of that—you have to think the worst of me."

I had no defense. The fact was, he was right. I'd assumed that either he'd been involved in pedophilia or he'd been plan-ning blackmail. Had only briefly considered that he'd been try-ing to be a hero. I tried to picture it: Charlie as a hero. The man who'd lied to me about our savings, who'd secretly pilfered my entire inheritance to invest on his own, who measured people solely by the size of their bank accounts, who'd scammed people into investing in semilegal, high-risk financial schemes. Could that same deceitful, ambitious, money-driven Charlie actually hand his business partner and several very rich clients over to authorities in order to save some poor, anonymous sexually abused and exploited children?

Hmmm. I tried to see it. Almost could. But not quite.

"Sorry. I don't know what to think, Charlie." I lifted my Scotch, emptied the glass.

"No? Well, think about this: why wasn't I in those photos?"

"Maybe you were holding the camera."

The shadow sighed. "You have so low an opinion of me. It hurts."

Charlie was hurt by my opinion? Not likely. I was beginning

to doubt that the voice was Charlie's. Maybe some other dead guy was impersonating him. "Where did you get those files, Charlie?"

Silence.

Of course there was silence. I had been having a conversation with my imagination. Constructing the answers in my own mind. But now, my mind had no answer, and there was silence. Lord. I needed to talk to Dr. Schroeder. I wasn't just depersonalizing any more, I was hallucinating. Actually seeing and hearing things. Probably having a breakdown. Odd expression, "breakdown." Like a rusted car, abandoned along a deserted highway. Or a rotted barn, caving in. Was I like them? Breaking down?

"They were from a sex trip they took. I made copies of Derek's files to use as evidence. The photos were Bradley's."

"Charlie, Somerset Bradley's dead." I didn't know if he'd know that. Did the dead know about each other? Was there some kind of roster? Welcoming parties? "I killed him. In your apartment."

"You killed him?" The shadow rose, as if standing to see me better. "God, Elle. Did he hurt you?"

This wasn't a real person. I didn't have to respond. But I did. "No. He tried."

"Son of a bitch was looking for the flash drive."

Yes. He was.

"Derek swore they'd never let me give the photos to the police."

"How would they stop you? By stabbing you?"

Charlie's voice sighed. The shadow slumped. "They might have, Elf. If you hadn't done it first."

Damn. I didn't want to argue. Wasn't sure he was wrong. But how could he be sure who'd stabbed him? He couldn't have seen the actual attacker; the knife had been in his back.

"So you were going to give the flash drive to the police. You didn't offer them an alternative. Like buying it back from you?" I set my glass on the coffee table, got up. Walked over to the desk, addressing the corner where the shadow had been. "Swear to me that you weren't blackmailing those men."

I stood alone at the desk, demanding an answer from the dark space behind it. I hadn't vacuumed in a while; a cobweb had formed near the floor, connecting the bookshelf to the hardwood. I wondered for a moment where cobwebs came from. They weren't spiderwebs, weren't free-floating dust. I waited, but Charlie didn't swear his innocence to me. He didn't answer at all. The space in the corner behind the desk looked empty and bare, without the slightest sign of a shadow.

～

I'd been seeing things again. It wasn't like pretending, not like imagining. What I saw and heard seemed real, even though I knew it couldn't be. I wasn't merely depersonalizing or dissociating or having amnesia. I was over the edge. Not having a breakdown. I was already broken. Real and not real were interchangeable to me. I was, in scientific terms, nuts.

Agitated. Unable to stay still. I kept moving. Pacing in circles. Okay, time to get out of the house. I grabbed a sweatshirt and my keys, hurried outside, felt the reassuring slap of cool October air on my face. Saw normal traffic, normal parked cars. Normal people walking normal dogs or riding normal bikes. Gradually, I began to calm down.

I headed across Fairmount Park toward the Schuylkill River, following Kelly Drive, passing the Museum of Art, the row of elegant old boathouses, the Girard Avenue bridge, the clusters of sculpture in the gardens above the river's banks.

I walked among joggers, skaters, and bike riders for maybe half an hour before I sat, looking out on the water. Watching its motion, the ripples of silver flickering on the surface. Ducks in pairs. Geese and gulls in flocks. Turtles of all sizes crowding onto an immersed tree trunk near the riverbank. Scullers rowing by. I sat, unaware of time, almost calm.

In truth, I was relieved. I'd shown Susan the files. The awful secret wasn't mine alone anymore. And, for all her scolding, she'd survived. Hadn't fainted or puked or even stopped speaking to me.

But that wasn't all: I was relieved about Charlie. The conversation with the shadow had almost convinced me that he wasn't—hadn't been—a pedophile. Those pictures weren't his. They were, as Derek had said, stolen "personal client information." The pictures could ruin careers, shatter lives, lead to blackmail. And provide motive for murder.

Which meant, as Susan said, that there would be more suspects in Charlie's death. I would no longer be alone on the list. Might even not be at the top.

I closed my eyes, felt the late day-sun warm my face. Let the tension out of my shoulders. Recalled the photos. The smiling boy, holding Somerset Bradley's hand. The spindly young girl holding an ice cream cone, walking with Derek Morris and Jonas Walters.

In front of the Kremlin.

In Red Square.

I was on my feet again, hurrying. Jogging—no, despite my bruises and sore muscles—I was running home. Obviously, the men had been in Russia. In Moscow. I ran along the river, absorbed, not noticing the cyclist coming up behind me.

"To your left!" A guy walking a bulldog screamed at me, and reflexively, without looking around, I jumped off the path onto the slope of grass leading down to the water, stumbled, twisted my ankle, and fell, protecting my already sore hands and knees, so that I rolled over the cement and splashed right into the Schuylkill. I landed sideways, felt the cold wet slap, then the immersion, then my hands and knees sinking into muck. I tried to stand, but the river bottom sucked at whatever body part I leaned on for leverage. With a final burst, I thrust my torso upward to a standing position, felt my head emerge, then my chest, drew a hungry breath of air, and let my legs sink calf deep in muck, turned to see a small crowd standing at water's edge, gaping in alarm. A wiry, bearded guy had taken his shirt off, ready for a rescue. In shallow water.

Voices called to me, asking if I was all right. Telling each other what had happened. "This bike went right at her, knocked her over."

"She just rolled right into the water."

"They ought to make bike lanes."

"There. She's climbing out. Grab her. Pull her up."

From far away, I watched the bearded guy and a woman in jogging clothes reach out, take my arms, then my waist, pulling me out of the mud and water. Finally, I was again on solid ground. I watched myself thank them, tell them that I was fine. That I lived nearby. The skinny guy offered me his shirt. Another one wrung out my sweatshirt and hung it on my shoulders.

Someone said that the cyclist should be arrested. That the bike had seemed to aim deliberately at me. Someone else agreed. I thought of the incident in Chinatown. What was with these bike riders, coming at me wherever I went?

Unless it wasn't riders. Unless it was just one. One rider, following me. Deliberately trying to run me down. I was shivering. Dirty. Dripping and soggy. Was I also paranoid?

"You're bleeding," the jogger woman pointed at my leg.

Yes. I was. My knees were scraped raw, and bloody water trickled down my legs, into my sneakers. But I didn't feel pain. I just felt wet. And numb. And I wanted to get away from this well-intentioned group so I could get home.

Laughter was what did it. I don't know how I started laughing, but I did. The others were angry at the cyclist, worried about me. But when I started to giggle about my clumsiness, retracing my fall, everyone relaxed. Began laughing, too. Thanking everyone, I refused more help and finally broke away.

By the time I got to Green Street, I'd become accustomed to the stares of passersby. I was bleeding, drenched, cold. And limping. Wounds, old and new, were nagging and annoyed.

I went inside, peeling off wet clothes, looking at my latest scrapes and bruises. Ready to wash off the river in a hot bath. But while the water was running, I went into my bedroom.

The envelope from Charlie's pocket was on the dresser, where I'd left it. And among the itineraries, just as I'd remembered, was a trip to Russia's capital.

~

The papers gave departure and arrival information, hotel accommodations. For a party of five, but the only name listed was Derek's. Nothing incriminating.

Even so, combined with the photos, the itineraries built the case that the five had traveled to Russia together to have sex with children.

I was trembling. Limped to the bath, sunk into steaming water. Felt the sting of heat on my scrapes and cuts. Leaned back. And soaked. When the bath cooled, I turned the faucet on again, adding more hot. Washed my sores. Watched my skin turn rosy.

Finally, when my blood was again running warm, I stepped into my soft chenille robe, sat on my bed, and called Susan. I didn't mention falling into the river. Just the itineraries.

"Trips to Russia?" She'd already spoken to Stiles, had told him about the flash drive.

"Travel plans. Flight schedules. Hotels."

"Get them to me pronto, so I can give Stiles everything at once. This is great, Elle. It proves that other people besides you had motive. It should take the heat off you."

After the call, I sat on the bed, holding my phone and the envelope. Wondering how Charlie found out about the sex vacations. About his partner being involved in something so vile. And then I wasn't sitting anymore. I was lying down. Watching myself, curled with my knees tucked against my chest. Missing Charlie. Wanting to talk to him—not just to the shadowy image I kept conjuring—but the three-dimensional, still breathing Charlie. To hear his rich baritone lie to me again. To touch his face, his hands. Look into the darkness of his eyes. How was it that he was dead? What had happened to him? To us?

I knew, of course. There had been lots of little frictions. Unanswered questions. Unspoken suspicions. Underlying doubts. And then one day, I'd opened a statement from Fidelity, the investment company handling my portfolio.

I'd called him in a panic. "Charlie, Fidelity says I have $17.34 in my account. What do I do? They lost my money."

He'd been busy. Distracted. Half listening. "Calm down, Elf. What?"

I repeated myself. Asked if I should call them. Or get a lawyer to call them.

A tiny hesitation. "It's okay, Elf. Don't worry. I'll take care of it." He'd sounded confident. Smooth. Like it was no big deal that over two hundred thousand dollars had been misplaced like car keys. "It's probably a simple computer error."

"Charlie, it's an investment account. With lots of separate investments in it. How can it be just a simple computer error?"

"Let me get on it, Elf. Just be patient and calm down. I'll take care of it."

And I'd believed him. That night, he'd assuaged me, saying Fidelity was "working on it." And the next evening, he told me he'd been busy all day with a big client, had played phone tag with Fidelity. He'd poured me a glass of Shiraz, held it out. Looked into my eyes.

And that's when the walls crumbled. The floor shattered. The sky collapsed. I'd known. There had been no computer error. No phone tag. Fidelity had made no mistake. No. What had happened was Charlie. Charlie had taken the money. Had emptied my account, used it for some business venture. Hadn't bothered to ask. He'd stolen it.

And lied about it.

And that was it: the end. After all the other little lies. After years of Charlie's slick explanations and questionable excuses, it was that one flash of realization, that one final lie that crushed all trust between us. And with trust went everything else. That night—that instant—our marriage ended. It took another fourteen months for us to admit it. Nothing was said out loud. But we both knew. Our marriage died even as Charlie stood there, looking into my eyes, offering me a glass of Shiraz.

Well, there was no use going over the aftermath. The blame, accusations, excuses. The pitiful efforts at patching things up. No point. I never found out why he took the money or what happened to it. He'd promised to pay it back. But he'd promised a lot of things. Never mind. That was history. And Charlie was dead.

I watched the woman as she lay on the bed for almost an hour, not moving. Still holding the phone, staring blankly at the papers. I could see the heading on the itinerary in her hands, could read the name of the travel agency. Magic Travel. Its address was on Sansom Street in Center City. I knew the street. It wasn't far from Dr. Schroeder's office in Society Hill.

Before I left the house first thing the next morning, I went to the computer, opened the files of photos, clicked through, looking for pictures that clearly showed each of the four men's faces. And I printed them out, one by one.

～

Magic Travel was a small storefront located between a nail salon and a pizza parlor, across from a parking lot. Outside, a rack supported a couple of chained bikes. Something I'd never have noticed before, but now everything involving bikes seemed to flash red alert. Maybe I shouldn't have come. What did I really hope to accomplish? The travel agent might be a criminal—maybe hooked up with the Russian Mafia, arranging sex workers for travelers who booked with them. Maybe I was getting into dangerous territory, should let the police do the investigating and forget it. I could still leave.

But I didn't. I wanted to find out what was going on, and I knew that the travel agency wouldn't reveal to the police what they might to a prospective customer. Derek Morris would never have known where in Moscow to go for child prostitutes. Someone had advised him. Maybe someone online or in Russia. Or maybe the travel agent.

I stood in front of the agency, figuring out what I'd say. How I'd approach the topic of unconventional services. I watched the flashing neon sign in the window—a wand and top hat with a neon airplane flying out of it. The name of the business arched above them in gold and green neon cursive. I peeked inside, saw a bike helmet dangling from a coat rack—dark green, not purple. Maps, posters, and displayed brochures lining the walls. Toy model airplanes hanging from the ceiling. A model of a cruise ship mounted on a table. Nothing unusual.

Go on in, I told myself. What was the harm? I'd stay just a minute. Just get a feel for the place, ask a couple questions, and leave.

The receptionist had red hair and blunt fingernails bitten almost to the quick. When she smiled, two dimples popped up, both on one side of her face. The name plate on her desk said, "Cindy."

"Can I help you?"

Great. What was I supposed to say? I smiled. Hesitated.

A man's laughter boomed from one of the three cubicles at the back of the room.

I looked around. Saw myself standing at the counter, looking

nervous. I could say, "Hi. Do you by any chance arrange international sex tours?" Or maybe, "Do you have special packages
for pedophiles?"

Lord, what was I doing there? I should go.

"My husband, actually his friends, booked a trip here a few
months ago. They went to Russia."

She nodded, waited for me to go on.

I took out the photos. "Do you recognize any of these guys?"

She leaned over, glanced at the photos. "Ma'am, I'm sorry.
I don't understand. Was there a problem with the bookings? Because if there was—"

"Oh, no. No. It's—I just wanted to know what their travel
package included."

Her eyes shifted. Her brows rose. Her smile faded, dimples
disappeared. "Because?"

Because? What should I say? "Because they're thinking of
going back. With more friends. And I'll be doing the arrange-
ments."

Good answer. Quick thinking. She nodded, sat back, asked
for information. Names, dates of the trip they'd already taken,
so she could look it up. I handed her the itinerary. She typed information into the computer. In the back offices, men were
laughing.

I stood at the desk, clutching my bag, waiting. Watching
Cindy. Looking around. Wondering what I was doing there.
Why I hadn't left the investigating to the police.

Cindy's eyes were on the screen. Reading. She punched more
keys. Read some more. Frowned. Bit her lip. Then looked up at
me. "Ma'am," she hesitated, "the trip you're interested in—I'm
afraid it was a deluxe customized package, arranged directly by
Mr. Lowery."

My stomach twisted, warning me to leave. "Mr. Lowery?"

She nodded. "The boss. He has a list of clients he handles
exclusively."

Oh, of course he did. Clients with exclusive requirements.

"So all those records will be in his private files. If you want, you can ask him about them directly."

Uh-oh. Ask him about his exclusive clients?

"Actually, he's stepped out for a moment. He should be back soon." She glanced at the rear cubicles, where men were talking. Bit her nail, took a shallow breath.

Instantly, I thought that she was lying, that Mr. Lowery wasn't out, that he was one of the men in the back, and she was covering for him. But then I thought that, no, he wasn't in the back, that Mr. Lowery didn't exist. That "Mr. Lowery" was a code name indicating trips arranged for sex or other illegal purposes. That the men in the back were thugs from the Russian Mafia who would want to know that someone was out front, asking about one of those trips. That Cindy was trying to stall me until she could get their attention.

She was still talking. Watching me too closely. "—get you started. Why don't I take the preliminary information. Like your name and address, the names of your friends who want to travel, dates, and destinations."

"No, no." I backed away. Not about to identify myself. "It's fine. I'll come back another time—when Mr. Lowery is here."

"Are you sure?" She eyed the cubicles again.

"Yes. Thank you." I turned, heading for the door. Hurrying.

"Ma'am? Hold on, ma'am. Wait—" Oh God. She was coming after me. Running around the desk.

I turned the knob, opened the door. Stepped out onto Sansom Street, where there were cars passing, people walking. But she was fast, caught up to me. Put her hand on my arm. Tight. Grabbing, pulling. What was she going to do, drag me back inside? Let the mob interrogate me? I saw myself in a cubicle, tied to an office chair, being tortured by Russian travel agents.

I wheeled around, facing her. Saw red hair, freckles, twin dimples in one cheek.

"You forgot these, ma'am." The hand that wasn't touching me held out Charlie's itinerary papers.

I took them and thanked her. She tried to smile, but her eyes looked unconvinced.

～

I walked, head down, occasionally looking over my shoulder to see if anyone from the travel agency was following me, scolding myself. I'd accomplished nothing. All I'd learned by going to the travel agency was that the men who'd gone to Russia had been on a special client list. But that didn't necessarily mean they'd been involved in illegal or immoral activities. For all I knew, "special" meant corporate. Or rich. Or repeat. Or complaining and difficult.

In fact, "special" could mean anything. My eyes focused on the sidewalk, the cracks in the cement, old wads of gum, cigarette butts, the shoes of passing feet. What was wrong with me? Why had I even gone there? I could hear Susan, screaming. Telling me I was interfering with the investigation. Influencing possible witnesses. Messing with minds, tampering with truth. Whatever. That she couldn't help me if I continued to insert myself—

"Elf?"

Elf? I stopped walking. Listened. The voice wasn't Charlie's. Not as deep. I spun around.

Joel, the magician, smiled broadly, looking me over.

Joel? Really?

"Wow. I wasn't sure it was you, but it is." He put his hands on my shoulders, studying my face. Smiling.

I stood immobile, blinking like a stunned rabbit. Aware of each bloodshot eye, every forehead bruise. Damn, I should have worn mascara. Joel?

"How've you been doing?" He took my hands, leaned over and pecked my cheek. As if pecking my cheek was perfectly normal. As if we knew each other. My cheek tingled, no longer accustomed to the brush of whiskers. He didn't release my hands, and the cut and scrapes began throbbing from the pressure of being held.

Say something, I told myself. Tell him you're okay. "I'm okay. Thanks." And then I said, "What are you doing here?" Great line. Like it was surprising that a guy from Philadelphia would be walking on a Center City street? But I was stunned, seeing him. Aware of my breathing, my pulse.

"I work nearby." He let go of my hands, finally, and pulled a Hershey's Kiss out of my ear. Held it up, handed it to me. Grinned.

My face got hot. "Doing tricks? That's your job?" I thought of Magic Travel, the wand and the top hat.

He laughed. "If only. No. I'm just a working slob. A paper pusher, even on Saturdays." He stared with dancing eyes. Too long. The moment was awkward.

I looked away, then back at him. "Well, it's nice to see you—"

"Elle, are you free? Want to go for coffee? Or there's a frozen yogurt place nearby." His eyes flirted, teasing and impudent, as if asking not about getting me a latte but about getting us a room.

Stop it, I scolded myself. You're imagining things. But my neck was heating up. Blotching. Adrenalin was rushing, speeding up my heartbeat. Signaling a warning. Fight or flight? What was wrong with me? Joel was merely being personable. I was way overreacting.

"I can't." Finally, I managed an answer. "I have an appointment. With a doctor." Why was I telling him that?

He kept his eyes on mine. "Okay, then have dinner with me."

Dinner? With him? My mouth opened. No words came out.

"Come on." His eyes held onto mine. Not giving up. "I'd—

Elle, I'd really like to spend some time with you. To get to know you. Quite honestly, you've been on my mind since I first saw you that night at Jeremy's. And then, when Charlie died and I saw you at the viewing, I realized you were his wife. Sorry. I mean his widow. Well, I told myself to forget it. The timing was wrong. You wouldn't, you know, be interested—I mean, having just lost your husband. But now, here you are, and I'm talking way too much. Look, just say, 'yes.'" He smelled fresh like the forest. Like autumn.

But no. What was I thinking? I'd just buried Charlie. I couldn't go to dinner with him. No way.

"Eight o'clock? I'll come by for you. How's Rembrandt's?"

And then I was walking away, heading for Dr. Schroeder's office. Crossing Washington Square, watching the sky through colored leaves. Feeling the light filtering through. Recalling Joel's strong jaw, playful eyes. Wondering how he'd known Charlie. Reminding myself to ask him that at dinner.

∾

I was in a daze the whole way to Dr. Schroeder's office. In shock. A man—a very attractive—no, let's face it—a very hot, sexy man had just asked me to dinner.

I was going on a date. I'd been asked out. Technically, I hadn't accepted. I hadn't said anything at all. But my silence hadn't fazed him. He was like Charlie that way. Simply assuming that he'd get what he wanted. Not allowing for the possibility of "no."

And so, we were going to dinner, Joel and I. I arrived at Dr. Schroeder's office a few minutes early, sat in the colorless waiting room, preoccupied. Lord. Who'd have thought I'd ever see Joel again? Or imagined that he was interested in me? "You've been on my mind since I first saw you at Jeremy's." Wow. I'd been on the mind of a guy who did magic tricks to make sad strangers smile. I replayed bumping into him on the street, realizing who he was. The shock of his hug, his cheek brushing mine. His voice thickening as he told me I'd been on his mind. His shoulders—

Lord. I was getting carried away. Needed to put reins on my mind. It was, after all, just dinner.

Except, what was I thinking? For me, there was no thing as just dinner. I wasn't some normal woman reentering the singles scene. I was a recent widow. Whose husband had been murdered just ten days ago. And who was still a suspect.

I could hear Susan screeching, Are you crazy, Elle? How do you think this looks to the police, to the press? Who is this man? What do you even know about him?

Maybe I shouldn't go. I could call and cancel. If I'd taken his number. Which I hadn't.

Or I could go and simply not tell anyone about it.

Dr. Schroeder opened the door, beckoned me into his inner office. He didn't usually have Saturday hours, had come in just for me, to jump-start my therapy. I sat on the neutral-toned sofa. Accepted warm spiced tea, still debating what I should do.

He sat opposite me in his bland, well-worn easy chair.

I realized I shouldn't go. I should meet him and explain that I couldn't, at least not now. Not for a while.

"Have you thought about our last session, Elle?"

Wait. Our last session? "Of course. Yes."

"And?" Dr. Schroeder watched me, tilted his head.

And? My mind clicked and whirred, shifting gears, trying to remember the session, to figure out what he was talking about. Oh, of course: The holes in my memory. We'd talked about how I'd killed Somerset Bradley but couldn't remember it.

"Any new thoughts about your amnesia?"

I shook my head, no. Sipped tea. "But I talk with Charlie. I have conversations with him." I blurted that out, impulsively. Without thought.

He nodded, unsurprised. "Perfectly understandable, and probably healthy."

Was it also healthy that Charlie talked back?

"You're working out your loss. Talking to him can help."

Really. "And my dreams—I have nightmares." Like the one about a heap of naked writhing children. "They're very detailed. There's one about stabbing Charlie."

"And you're afraid that the stabbing dream is a memory. Am I right?"

Was he? How could it be a memory? How could I dream about events I don't even remember? I shrugged, didn't have an answer.

He put his fingertips together. He wore a wedding ring. White gold. Colorless like his hair, his skin. His clothes. Was his wife color-blind, too? Why didn't she help dress him—at least a red tie or green sweater.

More silence. Patient, watchful eyes.

I thought of the night Charlie died. I'd been at Jeremy's, alone, awkward. I'd felt a physical jolt when I first saw Joel. Powerful, sexual. Almost like fear. I was off guard, unsure of myself. Surprised by the magic and the rose. But not troubled, not guilty or sad. Not at all aware that Charlie was dead.

At least, not consciously.

So maybe I was aware subconsciously? Which meant I could dream about it?

"How do I know the same thing didn't happen with Charlie that happened with Somerset Bradley? I don't remember stabbing Somerset Bradley either, but I know I did. So how do I know I didn't kill them both?"

"How do you know?" Dr. Schroeder let out a breath. "That's the question, isn't it? Tell me, Elle. Do you think you'd be capable of killing your husband?"

No, of course not. But I'd never have been able to kill Somerset Bradley, either. Or anyone else. And then, there was the child pornography. If I'd seen it, if I'd had reason to believe Charlie had participated in it—if my temper had erupted and we'd fought—And he'd escalated the fight with barbs and taunts—

Well. That was the question, wasn't it.

I didn't answer.

Dr. Schroeder went on. "Here's what I'd like to do, Elle. I'd like us to become a little aggressive with your disorder. Not because I think you killed your husband. But for two reasons: First, because there's a police investigation going on and it would be good if they could rule you out. And, second, because you don't want to have to spend your life worrying and wondering about whether you killed him."

Both good reasons. "Aggressive. How?"

"First, I want you to begin a regimen of antianxiety medications. These should relieve some of your depersonalization tendencies. But they also might help you relax in general. Which might—or might not—help you recall specific incidents that have caused major anxiety or even trauma."

Would I remember killing Somerset Bradley?

Did I want to?

"Along with the meds, I want to try hypnosis. If we can take you back to the times when trauma occurred, maybe we can help you reexperience some degree of what happened, enhancing your memories."

"But you said I don't know because my mind didn't record it."

"Your conscious mind."

Oh.

"So, what do you think?"

Fine. It was fine. Except that acid roiled in my abdomen, burning my organs.

"Why don't we begin. Relax, Elle."

Relax? Seriously?

"Lean back against the cushions. Sink into them."

I saw myself on the sofa, sitting in the neutral office, across from a man who couldn't see colors. I tried to sink, felt the upholstery supporting my weight.

"Let the tension out of your scalp."

My scalp? Was there tension in my scalp? I focused on it, tried to loosen it. The top of my head, the crown felt lighter. The upholstery held me up, hugged me.

"Now your neck, your shoulders, your back."

Was he kidding? Nothing—not hours of massage could get the tension out of my neck and back. Did he think that his mere suggestion would? His voice was monotonous, toneless, steady. Did he really think he could hypnotize me?

"Your hips, your thighs, your calves."

His voice was gentle, patient. Not hurried at all. But it wasn't working. I was hearing everything, totally aware, not in a trance.

"Let go of any troubling thoughts. Let go of thinking altogether. Let your mind float to a place where you're completely relaxed. Safe. Carefree. Completely at ease."

Where would that be? Where had that ever been? The womb? I pictured my mother, rest her soul, sitting on the side of my bed, reading to me. Was childhood a place? Did it count? I saw my mother, her hair pulled back in a loose dark bun. Saw her show me the pictures on the page, "There once was a beautiful doll, Dears, the prettiest doll in the world. Her cheeks were so red and so white, Dears—"

I heard Dr. Schroeder's voice and opened my eyes. Somehow, my nose was stuffed, my cheeks wet. I'd been crying? I was still on the sofa. Dr. Schroeder watched intently, still sitting in the armchair. He handed me the tissue box.

"Why am I crying?"

"You'll remember everything we talked about. If you want to. You did very well."

"Tell me." I blew my nose. "What happened? I thought I remembered everything but I don't."

"You were quite easy to hypnotize, Elle. You went under right away."

I did? "Did I say anything? About the murder? About Charlie?"

"Like I said, you'll recall whatever you want to. Don't you remember anything?"

Not a thing.

"You talked about your classroom. About your second graders. About wanting to get back to work."

I did? I had no memory of it. But I missed my kids. Benjy. Audrey. Lily. Aiden. William.

"Mostly, though, you talked about Charlie and your marriage."

About Charlie. Our marriage. What had I said? Why couldn't I remember? Was the hypnosis session another memory hole? More localized amnesia? Had I uncovered another trauma? I had a million questions. But, oddly, I didn't feel like asking them.

I was too relaxed. Almost at peace. Almost optimistic.

Dr. Schroeder glanced at his watch. It was 4:49. He stood, made our next appointment, and gave me a prescription as he walked me to the door.

I was outside before I realized that, damn, once again, I hadn't told him about the pedophiles.

～

"A date? Tonight? You do? With who?" Becky screamed into the phone.

So much for not telling anyone. I hadn't planned to tell her. But it slipped out when she called to tell me how my students missed me, how the substitute was bumbling and pathetic, how Romeo and Juliet, the hamsters, might be expecting babies, how the art teacher was cheating on his partner with the music teacher. And, almost as an afterthought, how Sherry McBride had shown up at school.

"She what?"

"I'm sure it was her. I mean, I wasn't there. I personally didn't see her—"

"She came to school?" Good God. "Why?"

"You're not going to like it. I mean I wasn't even going to tell you. But then I decided you should know."

"Duh, yes. I should know." I ran a hand through my hair. Sherry McBride had gone to my school?

According to Becky, Sherry McBride—or someone Becky assumed was Sherry McBride because "who else could it have been?" had been at the school, looking for me. Had wandered through the hall, pretending to be a parent, asking Jack, a janitor, where my classroom was. Telling Jack that she had a child there. That he'd forgotten his lunch. Jack thought it odd that the woman didn't know where her own son's classroom was, so he asked her name.

"And that's when she got weird." Becky stopped.

"Weird?" Weird how?

I could hear Becky breathing. Considering how to phrase things. What to leave out. "Dammit, Becky, just tell me."

"Okay, Elle. But don't pay it any mind. I mean nobody believes any of it."

"Any of what?" My voice was shrill, impatient.

Another hesitation. A big inhale. And then Becky let it out. "She told Jack that you'd had an affair with her husband. That you were unfit to teach. That you would corrupt the children. She called you names. I don't have to repeat them, do I?"

No, she didn't. Oh God. I slumped onto the bed. Leaned over my knees. The whole school must be buzzing about this.

"Jack—you know how he is, won't take any shit from any-body—well, he finally escorted her out of the building and told her to stay off school property. And he told the office about her. So now we have tightened security. She won't get in again."

I tried to make sense of the incident. "Did she actually go into my classroom?"

"She never went in, no. Jack realized she wasn't really a par-ent before she could get inside."

Well, at least she hadn't disturbed the kids. But why would Sherry McBride want to go to my classroom? What had she planned to do? Was she dangerous? My stomach burned. I won-dered if I had an ulcer.

"Listen, Elle. You should get a restraining order against that woman. She's psycho."

Probably I should. Yes. I'd talk to Susan about it. Stalking me was bad. But going to my classroom? No. That was too much. Way beyond too much.

"Sorry, Elle. But I had to tell you—"

"Don't be sorry. Yes, you had to."

Silence. "So. How are you doing?"

How was I doing? I meant simply to say, "Fine," or "Not bad," but when I opened my mouth, what came out was, "I have a dinner date."

And Becky screeched. "A date? Tonight? You do? Who is he?"

And, for the moment, the conversation shifted from Sherry McBride.

≈

I could almost hear her mouth drop.

"His name is Joel."

"But where—when did you meet him?"

I told her I'd met him the night we'd gone to Jeremy's.

"But no—you left early. And alone—and you never said any-thing about meeting somebody."

I reminded her that Charlie died that night. Meeting some-body hadn't been on my mind.

"So what's he like?"

I sat up in bed and told Becky a little about Joel. Not about the rush I felt when I was with him. Or the jolt of physical contact. But about his magic tricks. How he'd given me the rose.

Becky gave advice. "Okay. This is your first date. Whatever you do, don't talk about your marriage or your separation. And, oh God, don't mention Charlie's murder. Or that you're a sus-pect—keep it light. Talk movies, music. You know. Ask him his job. His opinions. Make him do the talking—but then, do NOT pull an Elle. Pay attention to him."

Becky went on, an expert on first dates. She'd had hundreds, maybe thousands of them.

"And wear some makeup, Elle. Give yourself an edge."

An edge? Like in a competition?

"And don't forget our deal. Call me the minute you get home. The minute he leaves. Don't make me worry that you've gone out with Joel the Ripper."

She kept on giving advice, imparting wisdom as if I'd never been on a date before. As if I were her kid sister or child.

But I let her talk, knowing she meant well, was trying to ease my way back into the singles world.

Two minutes after we hung up, before I'd even left the bed-room, Jen called.

"You have a date? You didn't tell me? Why didn't you call?" She went on, barraging me. "Where are you going? What are you wearing? Make sure you put on mascara. And eye shadow. Highlight your features. Why don't I come over and help you get ready?"

It wasn't the prom, I told her. It was just dinner. Down the street at Rembrandt's.

"Rembrandt's? Kind of pricey for a casual date." Jen always noted price tags. "Becky said he works in Center City. What does he do? And has he been married? Any kids? Be careful, Elle. For all you know, the guy's an FCA." Fucking Con Artist. "Or he has a wife and kids and is stepping out."

"Thanks, Jen. I appreciate your confidence in my judgment."

"I'm just saying. You don't know who he is, so be careful. Ask questions. Find stuff out."

I told her I wasn't marrying him; I was having a meal.

"You never know, Elle. Keep your eyes and your options open."

I said it was my first date ever, since Charlie. I wasn't thinking ahead. Had no long-range goals.

Jen backed off. But only momentarily. "Well, whatever you do, don't sleep with him. Not tonight. Not even next time. Make him work for it."

Really? Work for it?

She continued warning me about the pitfalls of sexual relations in a postmarriage world. She'd heard horror stories. Men our age were no better than boys in high school. My phone beeped; I was getting another call. The screen said: Susan Cummings.

Becky must have told her. Oh dear. I braced myself, took a deep breath.

And told Jen I had to take the call.

❦

"I was just about to call you." I was ready with an agenda, hoping to avoid getting scolded about my date by distracting her, telling her about Sherry McBride, asking her to get a restraining order. But I didn't have a chance to tell or ask her anything. Susan got right to business, didn't even bother to say hello.

"How was the shrink?"

The shrink? She wasn't calling about Joel?

"Good. Fine."

"What does 'good, fine' mean?"

Apparently, Becky hadn't called her. Susan didn't seem to know about my date.

"It means we're working on my issues."

"But are you making progress? And don't tell me it takes time. I know that."

What did she expect? An instant cure? I left the bedroom, walked downstairs to the table in the hall where I'd left my bag. "He prescribed some pills that might help." I took the vial out, opened it. Took out an oblong white tablet. Swallowed it without water. Thought for a nanosecond. Swallowed another. Jump-starting the effects.

"Pills? What kind of pills?"

"The antianxiety kind." Why did she need to know the name?

"And they're supposed to bring back your memory?"

"I don't know, Susan." Lord, she could be abrasive. I walked back upstairs. "He's also hypnotizing me. He's doing everything he can to help me remember things." Went into my bedroom. "But it's been just two days. Not enough time."

She let out a loud, frustrated breath, no doubt pushing hair out of her eyes. Pursing her lips. Impatient.

"Come on, Susan. Realistically, you didn't expect my amnesia to disappear in two fifty-minute sessions." I opened my closet, glanced at my drab selection of tired, mostly two-years-ago-styled clothes.

"I was hoping it would. If not disappear, at least that it might leak a few dribbles of what happened."

Her impatience made no sense. Made me nervous. "Susan, what's really bothering you?"

Another deep sigh. "I gave the flash drive to Stiles today. He looked at the pictures."

Her voice didn't sound happy. Not even a little.

"Good. So he sees that there are others who might have hated Charlie."

She sighed. "Yes. And no."

And no? "What the hell does that mean?" I sat down on the bed. Clutched the comforter with my bandaged hand.

"He recognized the men in the photos, including Somerset Bradley. He was understandably appalled. But he didn't necessarily draw the conclusions we hoped for."

My fist tightened. So did my throat. I closed my eyes. "Tell me."

"He's my friend, Elle. He's bent over backward to fend off an arrest. But he's worried about your amnesia. He thinks it's a little too convenient, and that not everyone will believe that it's real. Some people will believe that you knew about the pedophilia and the photos longer than you say you did, that you fought with Charlie about them. And that fight might have been what led you to kill him."

"But Charlie wasn't in the pictures. So, even if I had seen them, why would I blame Charlie?"

"Elle." Her voice was tired, parental. Slow. "You're right. Charlie wasn't in the pictures. But think. Somebody held the camera. So that somebody wouldn't be in the pictures. Who do you think that could have been?"

I didn't answer. I'd thought of that very same possibility, had confronted Charlie about it earlier. And he hadn't actually denied holding the camera. Instead, he'd dodged, complaining that my suspicions were hurting his feelings, and then he'd changed the subject.

Except that Charlie was dead and buried. So, in fact, I hadn't confronted him and he hadn't dodged or changed the subject. In fact, I'd had the whole conversation with myself.

"So, bottom line: Stiles admits that the four men in the photos might be guilty of traveling for the purpose of exploiting minors and engaging in pedophilia, and he agrees that they might be worth looking at for Charlie's murder. But he's also aware that you've killed one of those men and claim not to remember it. And that you had the means, opportunity, and motive to kill Charlie, and you also claim not to remember that."

"Claim? I'm not *claiming*—"

"Yeah. Well, I don't think he's buying your amnesia."

"Stiles thinks I'm faking?"

"It doesn't matter. Stiles isn't your problem. He's not the D.A."

Oh. Something smoldered in my belly. Fizzed and burned like acid.

"So, here's the deal." I could almost see Susan's face. She was sitting at her desk, head on her hand. Frowning. Eyebrows furrowed. "Stiles wants to meet with you privately. Tomorrow morning. Nine a.m. I'll pick you up at eight."

At eight. Tomorrow morning. And then what? After he met with me, would he arrest me? Right then? Damn, was I going to jail? In a matter of hours? I glanced at the clock on the night-stand. The digits made no sense. Green numbers with a colon in the middle, blinking, like the top hat and wand in that travel agency window. Where I'd gone just before I'd bumped into—

Oh God. Joel. I was supposed to meet him for dinner. How was I supposed to do that, knowing that I might be arrested in the morning? My first date promised to be my last. I pictured bars all around me. Long ones, thick and solid.

"Tomorrow, Susan, are they going to arrest me?" I made myself let go of the comforter. My nails had dug into my skin, and the cut on my hand had opened yet again.

She hesitated. "I doubt it. Not yet. He'd have given me a heads-up." And then she added. "I think."

She thought?

"That's why I was hoping you'd had a breakthrough at the shrink."

I got it. The police were focused on me. Closing in. I imag-ined living in a cell. Unable to see the sky. Walk along the river. Teach second grade. Feel the sunlight or have a Scotch or hang out with my friends or raid the refrigerator—

Suddenly, my earlier emergency—getting a restraining order against Sherry McBride—seemed unnecessary. Trivial.

"What color do prisoners wear, Susan? Orange?" Orange made my skin look sallow.

"Stop, Elle. You're not in jail yet. Don't fret and start imagining things. We'll talk details in the morning."

Don't fret? Seriously? Why was she suddenly so casual? Acting as if an arrest for homicide was no big deal.

"For now, don't even think about any of this. Go out and have a couple glasses of wine. Have fun on your dinner date."

Really? Have fun?

We hung up. There was nothing else to say.

The clock flashed numbers, 7:16. I had to get ready.

I stood, looked into my closet, faced the same sorry clothes. And realized that, even though she hadn't fussed over it, Susan had known about my date all along.

～

Clothes were strewn all over my bed. Laid out as outfits. My nerves were jangled. I couldn't choose. Couldn't focus. Kept fighting pictures in my mind. The bunk beds of a narrow jail cell. Sherry McBride skulking into my schoolroom. A shiv like the one in Somerset Bradley's eye. Sherry McBride lurking outside my house, watching for Charlie. A prison tray of white bread and mashed potatoes.

I took sweaters out of my wardrobe—a red cable-knit, a dark-green cowl neck, a black cardigan decorated with patches, a comfy, bulky camel. I grabbed pants from the closet. Camel, black, brown, gray. Denim. Wool. Skinny legs, relaxed legs.

Wobbly, unsteady legs.

I felt nauseous. My insides rippled, squirmed, even as I tossed a corduroy blazer and a long-sleeved T-shirt onto the pile. And a loose, ankle-length flowery skirt. I had no idea what I was doing, amassing a mountain of clothing. But there it was, growing. I didn't really see it, though. My thoughts seesawed between a crazed stalker and a prison sentence.

I told myself to get a grip. Get ready for dinner. Take a shower. And I did. I stepped into the shower. But suddenly, showering felt unfamiliar, luxurious. Precious. And private. Steaming water pounded the vanilla-scented shampoo on my scalp, streamed down my lathered body. Lord, I would miss this in prison. I'd heard that they only let you wash twice a week there. And then, you hosed down as a group. And the women were violent; they raped each other regularly as they soaped up and guards watched, pretending not to. Oh God. Were those stories true? Where had I heard them? Stories about how your hair gets oily and your skin breaks out, turns yellow because you get no sunlight.

"What's with the pile of clothes, Elf? Are you packing? Going on a trip?"

Well, maybe I was, but the trip I'd be going on wouldn't require packing. "No. Just out to dinner." I wasn't surprised to hear him. Or embarrassed to answer. "I can't decide what to wear." I didn't look out of the shower to see him. I knew he wasn't real.

"Dinner? Wait. You have a date?"

I turned off the water. Stepped out onto the mat. "Why not? We were separated. I'm single. I can date if I want." Wrapped myself in a towel. Felt queasy. Pressed my arms against my stomach. Heard Susan declaring that my problem wasn't Stiles, but the district attorney.

"But I'm not even cold yet. I only just got buried. It's — disrespectful."

"I'm not getting married, Charlie. I'm having dinner." I crossed my arms, suddenly indignant. "And seriously, how can you complain about me seeing someone else? At least I waited until you were dead — "

"Okay, here we go — "

"I wasn't the one who cheated and lied, Charlie—"

"Come on, Elle. You know the only woman I loved was you. Only you."

"Stuff it." I imagined Charlie sulking. His mournful eyes. I poured moisturizer onto my hands.

"So who is this guy? Do I know him?"

I didn't answer. I applied cream to my face.

"Is this your first date?"

Massaged it deeply into my cheeks.

"Or have you been seeing him all along? Is that why you were so eager for a divorce?"

Oh Lord. "Stop it!" I meant myself, not Charlie. I needed to stop bringing him back. To do what Susan said, go out and have a few glasses of wine. Enjoy what might be my last night of freedom.

"You're right. I should let you have some fun. After all, you might be going to prison soon. Besides, I have no business asking about your love life. I relinquished all rights—"

"Charlie, enough. Let's not go there. Not again." I was already frazzled. No way was I going to dissect the corpse of our marriage. I needed to dry my hair, pick out some clothes. Somehow get my stomach to settle. Stop spiraling.

"I'm just saying I want you to be happy."

He did? "Thank you." My hands were unsteady as I rubbed herbal skin cream onto my legs.

"I mean it, even after what you did. Even if you get away with it. After all, I'm dead, and that's not going to change. No use blaming you forever."

Blaming me? Would he never stop? "Let it go, Charlie. I didn't kill you."

"Right. I stuck the knife in my own back."

I saw it, jutting bloody from his body. Touched the bandaged cut on my palm. Pictured myself in an orange jumpsuit, with pimples and greasy hair. Saw Sherry McBride stopping by on visiting day. I stood up, escaping the images. Wanting Charlie's voice to stop, not sure where it was coming from. Beside the hamper? Behind the door? Inside the linen closet? Inside my head?

"Just tell me, Elle, why were you so mad at me? Why don't you just say it?"

"Not now, Charlie." I rubbed my temples, avoiding a headache.

"It wasn't just the investment. And it couldn't have been a woman. There was nobody—"

"Not even Sherry McBride?"

"I swear. She was nobody. Truthfully. Nobody."

Was he protesting too much? Never mind. It didn't matter. And he wasn't there. I would ignore him. I opened my jewelry box. Maybe I'd start with accessories. A gold bangle bracelet? Gold hoop earrings? Or maybe diamond studs?

"So," Charlie started again. "Why did you do it? Was it for the money?"

What?

"Because there's quite a bundle. And you get all of it, Elle. Every penny. You were still my wife, and I didn't have a will."

I was appalled. Hurt. And mostly angry. "You think—you believe that I killed you for your money?"

"It would make sense—"

"To you, maybe." Exasperated, I grabbed my tweezers, leaned into the mirror, plucked at an eyebrow. His money? Really?

"Damn it, Elle, be honest. You were pissed as hell when I borrowed your inheritance—"

"You didn't borrow it. You stole it."

"See? You're still angry. You even said it was the last straw."

"Meaning I was divorcing you, not killing you."

"And yet, if I'm dead, you get all my assets. Not just the half you'd get in a divorce."

The idea was absurd. Outrageous. I yanked another eyebrow hair.

"One small catch in that plan, though. If you're convicted of killing me, you get nothing. Not a dime."

"But I didn't kill you." Ouch. I pinched skin. Put the tweezer down, grabbed the hair dryer.

"Nevertheless—"

I turned it on to drown out his voice. I didn't want to hear any more of his implications, excuses, and accusations. "Go away, Charlie." I shouted above the whirr. "You're dead. So go be dead. Leave me alone."

"You can't mean that, Elf." He shouted, too, to be heard. "Not really."

"Oh, but I do. Trust me." In the mirror, my face looked distorted. Nostrils flaring. Eyes fierce. I whirled around, facing the empty room, holding the hairdryer. "Dammit, Charlie. Why wouldn't I mean it? You accused me not just of killing you, but of doing it for your money? Money? After everything else you've done—"

"But I can explain all that—"

"I'm not talking about your shenanigans. I'm talking about the pictures of naked children you brought into my home. And the trips abroad you arranged for your pervert clients to have sex with kids."

"Now wait, Elle."

"How old were those kids, Charlie? Eight? Ten?"

"What makes you think I had anything to do with those trips?"

"You and your slimy partner. You're the reason I'm in all this trouble. I fucking killed a man—I killed Somerset Bradley because of your sick pictures. And I'm about to be arrested for your—"

I stopped abruptly, mid-sentence. My voice had become guttural, scraping my throat, erupting hot and raw from my belly.

I saw myself, but didn't recognize the raving, stark naked woman standing in my bathroom, raging, screaming over my blow dryer into empty air. Jabbing her fingers at nothing. Belting out the exact sort of rage at Charlie that the police saw as my motive for murder.

I held still, panting, watching her slowly reclaim her temper. When she was calm, I turned off the hair dryer and looked around. The clock in the bedroom read 7:41. Charlie said nothing.

"Go away, Charlie." My voice was flat now, and final. "Leave. Go wherever dead people are supposed to be. And stay there. Don't come back."

Holding my head with both hands, I stared out the bathroom door at the heap of clothing on my bed, unable to move.

And realized that the doorbell was ringing.

~

If Jen hadn't stopped by, I probably wouldn't have made it to dinner. I might have stood in the bathroom for an eon. But she did stop by, and she chattered nonstop as she picked out sleek but comfy black pants, a dark-red sweater, low-heeled boots. She talked as she helped with my makeup, reminding me that I needed to highlight my eyes, emphasize my cheekbones, moisturize my skin. I drifted in and out, hearing part of her monologue, letting her take charge, becoming rag-doll passive. I did not mention Sherry McBride or Susan's call or the possibility of my arrest. I let her think that my nerves, my trembling were about my impending date.

"You'll be fine, DSI." Don't Sweat It. Her voice sounded faraway, like a memory. "Being with a man—it's like riding a bike. You learn it once and you know it forever."

She dabbed perfume under my earlobes. A complicated scent. Sophisticated. She'd brought it with her, knowing I wouldn't have any.

I tried to thank her.

"Don't thank me. We do for each other. Christ, do you want me to thank you for everything you've ever done?" She messed with my hair, restarted the blow dryer. "Okay, here goes. Starting with high school: Thanks for letting me cheat off you in geometry. Thanks for pretending the cigarettes were yours. Oh, and for double dating with me and that kid Alex—remember him? Junior Mister America—"

"Okay, Jen. I get it." I didn't have to thank her.

"So," she fluffed some kind of goo onto my head, "this guy's got SA?" Sex Appeal.

"Jen. It's just dinner."

"Right. Don't be coy, Elle. I can tell you're nervous. He's got to have some serious SA."

Well, she was right. He did. I pictured him. Eyes teasing. Lips hinting at a smile. Shoulders rippling under his blazer.

"You've got to think positive, Elle. Don't get stuck on the past and the mess with Charlie. That's over. Sooner or later, you have to take charge and envision what you want. Maybe it'll be this guy, maybe not. But whatever, it's up to you to create your future. Go for it."

I nodded. Wondered if she'd visit me in jail, decided that she'd come by dutifully, once. Maximum twice. Prison didn't fit into Jen's safe, shiny world. The orchestra fit there. And charity benefit balls. And luncheons and pedicures and Lexuses and landscape architects and Super Bowl tickets, but not prison. I closed my eyes to let her apply shadow, opened them for the mascara brush. Let her manicured fingers play with my face, rearrange my hair. I wanted her to stay. Felt that if Jen were with me, prison couldn't happen. I watched her, wondered what it was like to be Jen. To be able to eat anything, never gain weight. To spend anything, never run out of money. To take yoga, Pilates, gardening, golf lessons, never need an actual career.

But it didn't matter what it was like to be Jen. I was stuck in my own skin. And it didn't matter how that skin was made up or what fabrics it was wrapped in. It didn't matter where or if I had dinner, or with whom. In or out, with or without wine or the dinner date, the night would pass. The morning would come. And I would have to meet with Stiles.

At 7:57, Jen declared me ready to go, pecked me on the cheek as I thanked her, and darted out the door. I was still in the entranceway when the doorbell rang. I opened the door, thinking Jen must have forgotten something.

Joel stood there, eyes dancing, holding a single red rose.

~

It went by in an eye blink. No, it hung, suspended in time, separate from everything else. Unattached to before or after. Isolated. Protected, like a pearl in a shell.

And then it was over. I signaled Becky with a quick text to say that I'd returned safely, that we'd talk in the morning. Then I got undressed and lay on my bed, staring at the ceiling. Replaying my date long into the night.

When I opened the door, he told me I looked breathtaking. Breathtaking. I liked the sounds of the word. "Breath" sounded soft, gentle. Air passing around tongue and through teeth at the end. "Taking," though, sounded sudden, sharp, cutting. Sexual. Dangerous. So, I looked soft and dangerous? I liked that idea. That he couldn't breathe when he looked at me.

But it was only a word. And Joel, I already knew, was a flirt. A player with teasing eyes.

I accepted the rose, put it in a tall thin vase. And we walked to Rembrandt's, were given a table in a dimly lit corner in the room behind the piano bar. Candlelight. Couples all around us; two tables of four. Some looked up as we walked by. The women eyeing Joel. I tried to see us, what we looked like, but couldn't drift off. I was solidly planted in the moment.

He seated me. Pulled out the chair, waited for me to settle, then to lift myself up so he could slide the chair further under me. I was aware of him being aware of me, my movements, my balance. Of the rhythm of sitting and rising and sitting again. I was aware of his hands on my chair, his eyes watching my nether parts lowering onto the chair. Thank God Jen had helped me pick out pants that fit snugly, flattering my butt. And when I was seated, his hands lingered for a moment on my shoulders, giving them the slightest, most tender squeeze.

I wanted to moan.

Lord. I needed a drink. My moods over the last several hours had risen and plummeted repeatedly. As Joel took his seat, I glanced around the restaurant, felt cushioned by the flicker of candles, the hushed voices, the oil paintings on dark walls. The slow, patient background of piano music.

He leaned forward, eager eyes on mine.

I needed to cool down. I didn't know anything, really, about this man. Except that he'd somehow known Charlie well enough to come to the viewing. And that looking at him, being near him made my blood roar. But he was talking. I needed to listen. "—even at Jeremy's, I found you hypnotic."

Hypnotic? "Oh, please." My neck felt hot.

"I'm serious. Afterward, I couldn't stop thinking about how stupid I'd been not to get your number. When I was walking away from you, I was hoping you'd stop me—you know, ask for my phone? Punch in your number? But you didn't."

No, I didn't.

"Why not?"

Why not? It hadn't occurred to me. I'd never given my number to a stranger. But I couldn't say that. It sounded prissy, even to me.

"I mean, did you feel anything like what I did? Any attraction? Tell me the truth."

The truth? What had I felt? I remembered him offering me a coin, producing from nowhere a scarf, a rose. His eyes had singled me out, focused on me as if I were the only woman in the room. But why? He was so handsome. So practiced at flirt-

ing, and paying so much attention to a self-conscious, inexperi-
enced, not-as-glitzy-as-he-was woman. So, what had I felt?
Panic. The desire to run for the door. But another feeling
stopped me.

Kind of a déjà vu, a familiarity. A sense that—almost that
I'd met him before. That something other than chance had
brought us together. Maybe fate.

But I wasn't going to admit any of that. Would never have
said any part of it out loud. Certainly not to him.

He chuckled at my silence. "Okay. I guess not. I was hoping
it was mutual—"

"No, that's not fair. Remember, I had a headache. And, truthfully, it was my first time out since—" I stopped. Heard both Jen
and Becky yelling at me: *Do not talk about your marriage!*

"Actually," the words popped out, "I felt familiar. Kind of
like I already knew you."

Joel smiled, tilted his head. Reached out. Touched my hand.
A bottle of Rosenblum Petite Sirah arrived. Warm fresh bread.
We ate red meat. Joel's lips were neither too full nor too narrow;
they looked firm, smooth as they parted to admit his fork. And
his jaw rippled, made shadows on his cheeks when he chewed.
He didn't look at all like Charlie. Longer, slimmer, he moved
more gracefully, like a river. And his voice flowed more
smoothly. I told myself not to think of Charlie. He had no business here. This was my night. My first date with another man.
I knew I needed to ask Joel for information. Find out about his
relationship with Charlie. But there was no rush. My questions
could wait. It was all right to take it slow, to savor the attention.
The subtle seduction of conversation, the maddening, almost
accidental touches, the slow embrace of wine.

We talked, laughed. Never ran out of topics.

"How did you get into magic?"

"Magic?" He grinned, reached over, touched my wine glass,
and suddenly there were two of them. Two glasses of wine.

What? "How did you—"

"You mean how did I do this?" He smiled. And now there was a third. Three in a row. Full of wine.

I was baffled. Alarmed.

Joel shrugged. "I took up magic to cover my shyness."

"Your shyness?" Was he joking? "You don't seem shy."

"See? It worked. Magic gives me a way to approach beautiful women without using the same old tired lines—instead of asking, 'Do you come here often?' I can reach into her ear and say, 'Is this yours?'" He reached behind my ear and, this time, presented a bracelet. A gold bangle just like the one I'd been wearing. I checked my wrist, saw it was bare. Took the bracelet, replaced it, puzzled and impressed.

"You're good." I laughed. Lifted my napkin, realized it wasn't a napkin anymore, but a lavender chiffon scarf. Wrapped around my house keys. Wow. My napkin, it seemed, had moved into my purse. I found it when putting my keys back. When—how had he done all this switching right in front of me? His tricks made me uneasy. As if I didn't know what he was up to. How to keep my privacy and protect my stuff.

"Don't worry. I'll stop—I was just showing off. I make it a personal rule never to abuse my skills."

Apparently, he wasn't just a magician, but a mind reader, too. "Good. Because you'd be a great pickpocket." I had the urge to check my wallet, restrained myself.

He lost his smile. "Making money wasn't my goal. Girls were. I was a skinny, bashful teenager, afraid to talk to girls, much less ask them out. Magic was my ticket."

His ticket? "Magic" and "ticket" in the same sentence made me think of the travel agency. Magic Travel. Maybe he'd heard of it. But why would he? Just because of the word, "magic"? "So you've gotten a lot of women to pay attention to you?"

He smiled. "Well, yes. But so far, no one's been right. I'm still looking." And he looked into my eyes. Deeply.

My face got hot. I reached for one of the wine glasses. Sipped. It tasted real.

"Elle, honestly, I'm at an age where I've done enough singles bars and traveling alone. My friends tell me I'm a born bachelor, but the fact is, I'd like to settle down."

I felt his gaze. The heat of it ran down my neck, my chest. I didn't dare look back. Busied myself with the stem of the wine glass.

He paused. "But magic—it's more than a gimmick to help me meet ladies. It's a way of life. Kind of a philosophy."

"Oh?" I swallowed more wine, dared to look at him.

"Really, there is no such thing as magic. It doesn't exist. It's all illusion, just like everything else in life. People see what they want to see, or what they expect to see, and they miss everything else. They want to believe there's a trick. But the only trick is in their perceptions."

I was confused. Must have looked it.

"An event only seems magical because the audience doesn't see—or doesn't pay attention to all the pieces of the puzzle." His voice lowered, became private, almost a whisper. "You don't see where the coin is hidden. I distract you, or move in a way that you don't see the sleight of hand that takes your keys. You don't know the scarf is there all along. You don't expect it, so it seems like magic. That's how life is, isn't it? We see what we expect, what makes sense. What we want to see. What we can bear to see. And we reject the rest."

I stopped breathing, replaying his last few sentences. Lord. Could Joel possibly know about the holes in my memory? The things I couldn't bear to recall? Had he created his little speech about rejecting pieces of reality just for me?

I swallowed more wine. Smiled. Nodded. Tried again to do an Elle and mentally float up to the ceiling and watch our table from a safe distance. But I couldn't. Why not? Maybe it was Dr. Schroeder's pills—I'd taken a double dose. Maybe they'd begun to work. Or maybe it wasn't the pills. Maybe it was Joel. The square line of his jaw. The hint of a smile on his mouth, flickering in his eyes.

"So," I scrambled for a comment. "Is all magic fake?"

His eyes narrowed, thoughtful. "No, not fake. Just a manipulation of perception."

Perception? As in perceiving the presence of a dead husband? I thought of Charlie's kiss on my neck, our conversations. The rose that had moved through the house. Was that illusion, too?

"What about, say, the supernatural?"

"The supernatural?"

"Yes. Is any of that real? Like Ouija boards. And mediums who contact the dead. Or ghosts—"

"Whoa—Hold on, Elle. What's this about? Are you thinking of holding a séance? You want to contact your—"

"No." My answer came too fast, too loud. Before he could mention the word *husband*. "No, of course not." I looked away. Mentioned or not, Charlie had somehow joined us. "I was just wondering if you thought it was all illusion like magic."

He told me he had no idea, never messed with the dead, doubted that any of it was real. And then he changed the subject. Talked about me. Asked about my work.

I told him about my class, that I missed the kids. I mentioned Abbey's fabulous spelling, Benjy's photographic memory. Lily's art. Roxy's lisp. Aiden's mischief. I told him about our hamsters, Romeo and Juliet, that Juliet might be pregnant.

I talked too much, expected him to be bored. But he asked questions about curriculum planning, about gifted and slow learners. He was asking about trends in children's literature when the waiter brought our entrées.

Charlie had never asked me about my work. Not ever. Not in ten years.

I picked up my fork. Looked at my hand to make sure that the glow was just inside me, that it didn't show on my skin.

I watched Joel's knife slide smoothly into his steak, the juice spilling onto his plate, soaking his potatoes red. I watched him chew. His jaw muscles flexed and rippled. His tongue flicked across his lips. He dabbed his mouth with his napkin, reached for his wine. I was fixated, crossed my legs, pressed my thighs together. Thought about what his chest would look like without his shirt.

Lord, I'd been without a man too long. Did it show? Did he know?

I tried to cover my thoughts, but stumbled. Forgot what I'd been saying. Laughed at myself. Pretended it was the wine. That it had nothing to do with the glimmer in Joel's eyes, the reflection of the candles glowing there, making them look like dancing fire, the heat of which made my skin sizzle, the rhythm of which shook my bones.

I'd had too much wine. Needed coffee. Needed to cool down. Over espressos, I realized that we'd talked a lot. About where we'd grown up—he was from Quakertown—how we were both only children, what pets we'd had as kids—Joel had raised cockatoos—our worst first dates—his had thrown up in his vintage Triumph—where we'd gone to college—he'd gone to Penn State, majored in Business Administration—how we'd chosen our careers—he'd always wanted his own business. Talking had been easy. We'd had no clumsy silences, no hesitations. We'd laughed. We'd told stories about our families, ethnic backgrounds, favorite foods. But there was one significant topic we had not talked about: Charlie.

Charlie was the elephant in the room, obvious and huge but not acknowledged or discussed. I hadn't asked how Joel knew him, had been avoiding the subject, almost not wanting to know. I heard Becky warn: *Don't talk about Charlie. Don't bring your marriage on the date with you.*

She was right. I didn't have to ask him. Didn't absolutely

need to know. I could find out later, if we kept seeing each other. Which was a ridiculous idea, considering my impending arrest. I wondered if Joel would write to me in jail. Decided that, no, of course he wouldn't. I'd had too much wine. Felt sorry for myself. Wanted to cry.

He was watching me, eyes gleaming. He tilted his head, as if aware something had shifted. Silently asking what it was. Waiting.

I didn't want to mention jail. Didn't want to talk about it. I lifted my cup, not intending to speak, but the words came out on their own. "So, Joel, how did you know my husband?"

~

Joel blinked, his face blank, revealing nothing. "Through his partner, Derek Morris. Derek did some investing for me. For my business."

"What kind of business?" He hadn't told me.

He paused, cup in the air. "Travel. I have an agency—"

"Magic Travel." My stomach knotted. I saw the neon hat and wand.

"Yes." He grinned. "You've heard of it."

Yes, I had. A chill snaked up my spine. My hands got cold. I was having dinner with the man who owned the travel agency that had arranged the sex-with-children trip to Russia. I clutched my coffee cup, mind racing, deciding what to do. Ask him about his connections to child prostitutes? Accuse him of abetting pedophiles? The list went on. Got more aggressive as it progressed, until mentally, I was shouting and throwing utensils at him and storming out of the restaurant.

Actually, I sat still, saying nothing, watching his fingers holding his cup, the economy of his motion, his easy grace. I told myself to hold on. Not jump to conclusions. I had no evidence, not a single reason to believe that Joel knew anything whatsoever about the child sex trade, much less that he was involved in it. In fact, he was probably an innocent travel agent, simply booking flights and hotels. I needed to relax. Stop assuming the worst. I took a breath. Tried to listen to what he was saying.

"Over time, we referred more and more clients to each other, and eventually I met Charlie."

When he said, "Charlie," I actually felt a pang. I bit my lip, waiting for it to pass. I had to get over it, had to get used to Charlie being mentioned in conversations, couldn't fall apart every time I heard his name.

"And I liked him. Your husband was a good man."

A good man? My husband? I sat up tall, bristling. Obviously, Joel hadn't known him all that well. But Becky had been right. I shouldn't have mentioned Charlie. The mood, like the espresso, suddenly cooled.

All three wine glasses and the bottle were empty. I looked at the candles, suddenly recalling the dozens—no, hundreds of times I'd sat in restaurants with Charlie. Comfortable. Watching his face across the table. Not talking much. Not needing to.

"What's wrong, Elle?"

What should I say? Should I talk about my unresolved feelings for Charlie? Or maybe the naked children? How about my impending imprisonment? "Sorry—it's nothing."

"Is it me? Did I say something?"

"No. Really. Of course not."

Lord, I wished I could drift away. Why now, of all times, couldn't I pull an Elle?

"Another espresso?" The waitress had black fingernail polish, a rose tattooed on her neck.

I shook my head, no, before Joel could reply.

On the walk home, he took my hand. Confidently, as if he had a right to hold it. But gently, as if he knew I was upset. His touch was soothing. Made me feel cared for, even safe. The night was chilly. And by the time we got to my doorstep, his arm was around my waist. Warm. Protective. I didn't want him to remove it, didn't want the evening to end. I opened the door, and we stood on the stoop like teenagers. Saying goodnight awkwardly. Was I supposed to kiss him goodnight? If I tilted my head back, most certainly, he'd take that as an invitation. All I had to do was lift my chin. I looked at his lips, imagined kissing them. Joel waited, talked about what a good time he had. The moment, the decision, the outcome were up to me. I took a breath, thought about the elegance of his fingers on the steak knife. The candle's fire in his eyes. I looked at his lips, and then they were ever so softly brushing mine, tentative, flitting away. And then they were back, this time lingering, pressing, open and moist, tasting of coffee and wine. Suddenly, his arms wrapped me up, pulled me against him. His hands moved down my back, cradling my bottom, pressing me close so I could feel him, his heat. I didn't resist, didn't hesitate. I clung to him, surprised by a tidal wave of desire that had been building up since Charlie left. Closing my eyes, I had the sense of being swept away, caught in a current of rushing water. I needed air. I pulled away, inhaled deeply. And smelled the distinct, familiar scent of Old Spice.

Old Spice?

Oh God. I turned away, flushed, fumbled with my key. *Ask him in,* I heard Becky urge.

WTF? Jen cried. *I told you: no sex on the first date.*

"Thanks for dinner, Joel." I was breathless, my voice low. "Tonight—was great." Before I could reconsider, I separated from his embrace, squeezed his hand and went inside, alone.

For a long time, I lay in bed, thinking. Replaying the evening. The chemistry. The conversation. The waves of desire. Oh man. Those waves of desire.

But I couldn't have asked him in.

Not because of Jen's advice or my worries about being arrested. Not even because of Joel's unlikely yet possible involvement with travel packages for sex.

No. The sole reason I couldn't ask him in was that I'd smelled Old Spice.

I was afraid of bringing Joel into the house. Of what Charlie might do.

‿

The knife rose and fell, splattering blood. But this time I wasn't stabbing Charlie. This time I was trying to grab it away from the killer.

I reached for the handle, but the fist held it too tight. Moved it too quickly. Plunged it down again, aiming for Charlie's back. I tried to stop it, reached for the killer's hand. For the wrist. But the knife was already arching upward, slashing my palm. Blood gushed, smelled warm and coppery. Made my grasp slippery, and caused pain that was thin and precise. The knife came down again, slowly this time. Like a feather or a leaf. Lord. Why didn't Charlie run away? Why didn't he turn and fight? I watched the hand rise and swing down again, determined now, going for the kill.

And then, as from above, I saw the whole room—Charlie and a woman. Tall and strong. She held the knife in her right hand—she wore a ring on it. A wedding ring? And she kept stabbing at Charlie while her left hand tried to grab the knife away. I watched, confused. The right hand went up; the left opened, ready, and when the knife came down, the left hand reached for it, closed around the right, but got sliced by the blade, not able to stop it. The blade slid through the left hand's grasp, cut through Charlie's clothing, skin, muscles, and bones and came to rest, embedded and deep in his heart.

The right hand released the handle; the left surrendered, wounded and bloodied. I watched, but no longer from above.

Charlie turned to me, dying. Asked, "Why?"

I tried to answer, to tell him that it wasn't me. That I hadn't killed him. But words wouldn't come out—I could make no sound at all, so I stood there, speechless, bleeding, watching him die.

I woke up suddenly, still trying to speak. My throat was dry, and I was breathless, clutching my bandaged hand. Oh God. I grabbed the comforter, pulled it up to my chin.

What the hell was that dream? I looked around, orienting myself. Trying to shake off the details. The smell of blood. The pain of the knife. The clock said it was almost six. I blinked. Sat up, fluffed the pillows. Lay back down.

My fingers hurt, ached from clutching.

Had the dream been telling me what had actually happened? If so, was my memory coming back? Dr. Schroeder's pills, the hypnosis—were they working? I closed my eyes, saw the hand rising, holding the long thin knife. Saw it tighten its grip, poised to swing. Wearing a wedding ring.

And opened my eyes. I'd recognized the ring, knew it well. Had worn it for over a decade. The right hand in the dream, no question, had been mine. I looked at the bandage on my left palm, wondering again if I'd cut my hand while stabbing Charlie.

Of course not. The dream wasn't to be taken literally. The battling hands were probably symbolic of my conflicted feelings for Charlie—love and hate. And of my feelings of impotence about not being able to prevent his death. The dream was my mind trying to work out irrational unresolved emotions, nothing more.

Almost six. Susan would be coming by in two hours. I needed to sleep. To be rested for the meeting with Stiles. But I didn't dare let myself drift off. The dream was too fresh. I could still feel the slash of the knife. Hear it whooshing through air. Almost taste the blood.

So, no. I wasn't going back to sleep. Instead, I got out of bed, went downstairs to make coffee. Opened the door to look for the newspaper. And found a long white box there.

It looked like flowers.

～

How sweet. How amazing. They had to be from Joel. But how had he sent them so early? Who delivered flowers before six a.m.? Before the newspaper came? Well, never mind; Joel was a magician. Could simply have made them appear, like the chiffon scarf that was still in my bag.

I stepped outside, looked around. Nothing moved. Not a single car. Not one jogger or dog walker. Soon, the street would burst to action. But for that moment, I was alone. Had the street to myself. The city slept, blanketed by early morning light. Completely still.

The box was long and white, wrapped in red ribbon. I picked it up, looked for a card. Couldn't find one. Maybe it was inside? I took it into the kitchen, laid it on the counter by the sink. Got a vase out of the china cabinet. Remembered the last time someone had sent me flowers. Charlie, of course. Last Valentine's Day, even though it was an empty gesture, as we were about to separate. Charlie had been big on flowers. Gave me a dozen roses for every occasion: birthdays, anniversaries, Christmas. And a single rose to apologize, to flirt. To cover a lie. Best of all, roses were a way for him to avoid having to shop. They were easy, didn't take time or thought, and no one, not even I, could complain about getting them. Toward the end, though, they'd annoyed me. I saw them as just another of Charlie's smooth manipulations. But now, looking at the box, I misted up. Wished that they were from him. Missed him. Missed his stupid roses. His quick twisted thinking. His scheming. And I felt disloyal, getting flowers from another man.

Still, flowers deserved water. I wiped my eyes, sniffed. Untied the ribbon, opened the box. Thought, as I lifted the lid: Please be snapdragons or lilies or anything else; just don't be roses.

I got my wish. They weren't roses.

⋰∿

A hoarse bark burst from my throat, piercing the morning stillness, and I recoiled, shoving the box off the counter, spilling two tiny charred bodies onto the floor beside it. One hand on my mouth, the other on my belly, I raced to the door to look for whoever had left them. But, of course, the culprit wasn't there. No one was. Just the newspaper. A man walking a black Lab. Trees with orange and yellow leaves. And the white noise of morning.

Half gagging, half wailing, I ran back to the kitchen, knelt beside the tiny corpses. Stiff little paws. Fur all gone. Skin seared. I wrapped them tenderly in a dish towel. Who could have done this? Who would traumatize second graders by killing their pets? Who would torture hamsters?

And who would deliver their dead bodies to me?

∿

Only one person. She must have gone back to the school, gotten past security, and kidnapped them. Killed them as part of her obsessive hatred of me. Really? Oh God. She'd killed the hamsters? And the worst part was she'd get away with it. After all, what could I do? Call the police? 911? Report some murdered rodents? I stood in my kitchen staring at them, shaking with anger. Tears streaming down my face. This was a crime, wasn't it? An act of sadistic murder and cruelty to animals. And a terrorist threat. Wasn't her whole point to terrorize me?

I wiped my eyes, had to calm down. To think. Was I even sure that these were our hamsters, not just random ones from some pet shop? In a way, it didn't matter. Murder was murder. But in another way, it mattered a lot because, if they were Romeo and Juliet, the killer had invaded my classroom. Had stolen pets from the children. Her aggression was escalating.

Small animals were already dead. Who knew what she'd do next? The woman needed to be sent away. Locked up. I pictured her in an orange jumpsuit, sharing my jail cell. Oh God.

My hands were fists; my nails penetrated the scab on my palm. No, this time, the bitch had gone too far. It was one thing to confront me at a wake or run me down with her bicycle. But messing with my kids? Killing their hamsters? That, I wouldn't tolerate. And I wouldn't hide behind the cops or the courts or restraining orders. It was personal, and I would end it personally.

Gently, swaddling Romeo and Juliet in the towel, I put the tiny bodies back into the box. And pulled on some clothes.

∾

I opened my laptop, Googled the phone directory. Found her address. She lived on 20th Street, near the Franklin Institute. A couple of miles away. I put on sneakers and sweats. Put a note on the door for Becky. Left the house about six thirty.

It was easier, less painful to jog than to walk fast. So I jogged. Blended in with the early morning urban athletes. Lord, who'd known how many people were up and running that early? The street was loaded with them. Traffic was beginning to flow. The city was stirring.

And I was thinking about what I'd do when I got there. I ought to set fire to her, let her find out what it was like to have her flesh melt away, to sizzle and flame the way Romeo and Juliet had. First, I ought to run her down with a bike. Knock her into the river. Punch the living crap out of her. I ran, breathing in rhythm with my pulsing rage, picturing the aftermath. Imagined her flattened, bloodied, fingers broken, eyes blackened, gasping for mercy. Mercy? I had the corpses of Romeo and Juliet. A dead husband. Fury blazing in my belly. But mercy? No, I didn't have any of that, not a milligram.

I ran down 20th, crossed the tree-lined parkway, headed toward Arch. Saw the street numbers getting close. Kept going.

Breathing. Planning. Saw myself ringing her buzzer, calling her out, grabbing her by the hair when she came outside, twisting it tight. Heard myself hiss into her ear: Coward. Worm. You messed up when you tried to ram me with your bicycle. You don't have the nerve to take me on face-to-face, so now you're going after my kids? Second graders? Killing their pets? Really? Tell you what. How about I settle this and tear your fucking head off?

And there it was. Sherry McBride's building. Her last name and first initial on the buzzer. She lived on the second floor. Panting, sweating, pumped with adrenalin, I pressed the button. Waited. Cars passed. Pedestrians. Dog walkers. Joggers.

No one answered. I hopped from foot to foot, unable to stand still, about to press the buzzer again when the front door opened and a man in a business suit came out, nodded a greeting.

"Thank goodness. I forgot my key." The lie popped from my mouth as I reached to grab the door, but he smiled and held it open. Without hesitation, I thanked him and stepped inside.

~

She hadn't answered the buzzer. Maybe she was out on her bike, riding past my house, stalking me. Fine. I'd wait for her, confront her when she came in. Climbing the stairs to her apartment, I pictured her seeing me at her door. Panicking. Trying to run. I'd tackle her. Sit on her and twist her arms until she caved and cried, begging me to let go.

Her door was open. Cracked just a bit.

"Hello?" I knocked, but she didn't answer. Cautiously, I stepped inside. "Anyone home?"

Silence.

The place smelled of air freshener and unwashed laundry. And vaguely of something I couldn't define. The curtains were closed, the entranceway dark. I stumbled over what felt like shoes. Reached around for a light switch, snapped it on.

And came face-to-face with Charlie his arm around Sherry McBride, almost big as life. Poster-sized. She was holding carnations. He was in a business suit, handsome and dapper on the hallway wall.

He startled me, being there. Large and alive. Grinning broadly. In color.

What was my husband—okay, almost-ex-husband, doing with his arm around Sherry McBride? And hanging on her wall? Over their heads was the edge of a banner: "—ppy Secre—" So, it had been Secretary's Day. Even so, she had no business with Charlie's arm around her. Furious, I ripped the poster down. Rolled it up, held it like a club.

Realized I was making a lot of noise.

But she didn't come running into the foyer to see what the commotion was. Didn't tiptoe out with a baseball bat to see who was there. Of course she didn't. She wasn't home. Must have left the door open by mistake. Even so, I stood by the front door, holding the poster, listening, hearing nothing. I called out her name again, just to be sure. Got no answer. So I plowed ahead, not sure what I was looking for. Not sure anymore what I hoped to accomplish. Blinking at the confused jumble that Sherry McBride called home.

The place was a wreck. Total havoc. Sofa cushions tossed on the floor. Lamps overturned. Clutter all over the living room: clothing, magazines, bottles, plastic bags. I waded through the mess into the kitchen, which was small, just a row of appliances covered with towels, and empty microwaveable dishes. The cabinets were open. As was the oven. I kept moving. The door to the bedroom was half closed. I opened it slowly, cautiously. Her bed was unmade, mattress crooked, covers and pillows all over the floor. Biking clothes, a sports bra, a chiffon scarf tossed on top of the rumpled comforter. A musty smell hung heavy, complicated by something else, primal. Not sweat, but something like it. I breathed through my mouth, tasting something metallic, pivoting, scanning the upheaval.

It wasn't normal. Not even a slob would create this kind of disorder. Someone else had been there. Had ransacked the place, left the door open. I stood in the room Sherry the stalker/bicycle attacker/hamster murderer slept, holding the rolled-up poster. What was I doing there? Somehow, I'd lost it, had crossed a line. Had become as bad as she was, trespassing, stalking the stalker. And for what? I couldn't confront her. She wasn't even home. I needed to leave—couldn't afford to get blamed for ransacking the place. But turning to go, I glimpsed her open closet door. The inside was papered with photos.

There had to be a hundred of them. Tacked or taped or pasted up in clusters. Charlie smiling. Charlie drinking coffee. Charlie talking. Charlie walking. Charlie conferring with Derek. Charlie close up and Charlie far away. Charlie alone and Charlie with others. Some photos had been cut, removing anyone who wasn't Charlie. Others showed Charlie taped to photos of Sherry. As if they'd been together.

I stared, imagined her putting the montage together. Gathering the pictures, cutting and pasting. Lord, what had Charlie done to attract this level of obsession? I wondered if he'd even noticed it. Decided, no. He'd had no clue. Would have been oblivious. Would have complimented and charmed Sherry just as he complimented and charmed everyone. "You look gorgeous this morning, Sherry." And, "Sherry, your smile always makes my day." Or, "Sherry, great job! I don't know what I'd do without you." Charlie made everyone feel special. Unique. Needed. Valued.

But Sherry must have taken his words to heart. Believed that he alone appreciated her, understood her. Cared deeply about her.

If anyone understood how that worked, I did. I'd taken his words to heart, too. *You're the love of my life, Elle.*

The clock on her nightstand said ten after seven. I'd have to get going if I wanted to be on time for the meeting. But I wasn't ready to go. Even if she wasn't home, I still wanted to make a statement to Sherry McBride. And, looking at her closet door, I realized what that statement would be. I wasn't there only to avenge the hamsters, but to rescue Charlie, as well. One by one, I peeled his photos off the closet door, collecting them. Stuffing them into one of Sherry's empty plastic bags. Feeling a pathetic sense of satisfaction as I strutted out of her bedroom. Smiling smugly as I passed the cracked bathroom door to be sure no more pictures were in there.

I could see part of the sink from the hallway, but not the walls, so I pushed the door. It bumped into something, wouldn't budge. So I leaned in, peeked around.

And saw Sherry McBride's nude body splayed against the shower stall, covered with a blood-soaked bath towel. Dead.

∾

I couldn't move. I stood frozen, gaping at her, not breathing. Trying to interpret what I was seeing. Her eyes were wide open, staring past me at the sink. Her face was bruised, nose bloodied as if she'd been beaten. An ice pick—at least, I thought it was an ice pick went in one side of her neck and out the other.

I blinked. Tried to think. Couldn't. Sherry McBride was dead. Murdered. Who'd killed her? Oh, and wait—when? Because it had to have just happened. She'd been at my house, leaving the hamsters, not an hour ago. Hadn't I seen her there, riding her bike? I knelt beside her, touching her forehead. Her thigh. Her arm. She was still warm. Oh God—she must have died just moments ago. Must have been lying there, bleeding to death, choking on her blood as I'd been going through her house, ripping down photographs. Had she heard me? Had she tried to call out for help? Oh God.

Okay. Okay. I had to collect my thoughts. Call for help. 911. The police. But I didn't have my phone with me, hadn't brought my bag. So I'd have to find Sherry's. I backed away from her, out of the bathroom, across the hall, into her bedroom. Where was her phone? How was I supposed to find it in this mess?

I scanned the bed, the nightstand, the dresser, hurried out to the kitchen, found her phone on the counter there. Picked it up, began to punch. 911. I stopped breathing. My fingers—they were bloody from touching her body. They left blood on the numbers of her phone.

Alarms clanged in my head, telling me to run, to get out of there fast. To pretend I'd never been there or seen her. Sherry was the third dead person I'd either found or killed in a little more than a week. How would I explain that? Or my presence in her apartment? And her blood was on my skin, my hands. The police would find out about Romeo and Juliet, and Sherry's stalking me. And they'd see her photos of Charlie—all of that would look like motive. And I had no alibi.

Quickly, without thinking, I grabbed a dish towel and re-traced my steps, wiping and washing everything I'd touched. Erasing my presence. Trembling, trying to remember where I'd been, where my fingers had been, even on Sherry's body. Again, I pictured her lying there, dying. Listening to me rifle through her things. Hoping someone had come to rescue her.

But I needed to stop that. To focus on clearing up all signs of my presence. I rubbed the closet door, the knob. My mind spun. Whirled. Wait. I was destroying evidence—wiping away my fingerprints only made me look more guilty. And I might be destroying the real killer's prints, too. Oh God. The real killer—he must have been in the apartment just minutes, maybe seconds, before I got there. I might have walked in on him—might have bumped into him as he left. A shudder passed through me. Had I seen him? That man who'd let me into the building. The one in the business suit who'd held the door open for me. Was he the killer? I pictured him. Fortyish, something familiar about his face. Graying hair, long nose, thin lips. His gums showed when he smiled.

But it made no difference what he looked like. If the police arrested me for Charlie's murder, they wouldn't believe what I had to say. Might not consider any other suspects if they learned I'd been here. I'd had motive, means, and opportunity to kill Sherry, and that, as it had been with Charlie, would be enough. I needed to get out. Hurried back into the kitchen, tossed the dish towel into the sink. Started for the door. Stopped myself.

Before I left, I needed to think. Collect myself. Make sure I wasn't forgetting anything.

Relax.

I took a moment, repeated Dr. Schroeder's mantra, letting the tension out of my body, my back, shoulders, and neck. Looked around. Double-checked that I'd picked up every piece of evidence, erased every sign that I'd been there.

Finally, carrying the bag of pictures and the rolled-up poster, I dashed out of the apartment and hurried home, stopping only to wipe the prints off the doorknob.

∿

Susan arrived early. I'd just gotten out of the shower. My hair was wet, and I was still shaking when I let her in. I ached to tell her what had happened, needed her to assure me it was all right. But I couldn't. I'd destroyed my fingerprints, messed with a crime scene. And, even though she was my lawyer, I wasn't sure how much she'd feel comfortable hiding from the police.

And I didn't know how much she'd believe.

"Hurry up, get dressed." She shoved me back up the stairs. "I'll make coffee."

I was halfway up the steps when I heard the scream. Damn. I hadn't thought to warn her about Romeo and Juliet, had left them on the counter.

"Elle?" She ran into the hall, wide-eyed. "What the hell—"

"Sorry." I started down the steps, deciding to tell as much of the truth as I could. "Sherry McBride was here. She left—"

But Susan's hands were up. She turned, headed back into the kitchen. "No, don't get distracted. Get dressed and we'll talk."

Oh God. How much could I tell her without including the murder? Should I say I went to Sherry's, but she wasn't there? What about the guy in the suit? Should I mention seeing him leave? Because when the body was found, that would make them look for him—

"Come and sit."

Susan hadn't waited for me to get dressed. She came into my bedroom with two steaming mugs. I pulled a sweater over my head, fluffed my hair, and sat.

"So. What the hell are those dead mice?" She held a mug out for me.

I told her about the box on my doorstep. About finding the hamsters. But not about going to Sherry McBride's apartment. Not about the pictures of Charlie I'd stuffed into my closet. Not about the murder.

"So, for sure, we'll get a restraining order against her. She's a sick puppy."

I nodded. Saw Sherry's dead staring eyes. Stifled a wave of nausea.

Susan sipped coffee. "But we need to triage our issues. Before we get distracted by Ms. McBride, we need to assess things."

We did? Uh-oh. She was being professional Susan. Not warm big sister Susan. Not let-me-bake-banana-bread Susan. Her voice, her eyes, her posture were stiff. Impersonal.

"So. I finally heard back from Charlie's divorce attorney. And I found out something interesting: We're not the only ones who've called him to ask about Charlie's will. He's heard from Emma and from Ted. Because you were about to be divorced, they think you shouldn't inherit Charlie's estate. Emma hired a lawyer and intends to sue if you do inherit."

No surprise. Emma was convinced I killed him, wouldn't want me to profit from the murder.

Susan cleared her throat. Sipped coffee. Sat perfectly straight. "Anyway, Charlie had no will. He'd been talking about writing one. But he died before he got around to it."

Okay. So there was no will. I sipped coffee. "So?"

"So?" Her tone asked how stupid I possibly could be. "As his legal wife, you're the beneficiary of Charlie's entire estate. Which you wouldn't have been if he'd lived long enough for his will to be written or for the divorce to become final."

Oh. I got it. Inheriting gave me motive.

"I also found out Charlie that had three life insurance policies."

"Three?" I'd known about one. He and Derek each had one, for the business.

"Derek is beneficiary of one. He gets a million dollars. The other policies name you as beneficiary. For a total of two point five million dollars."

I inhaled, choked on coffee. Coughed. Didn't hear what Susan said next.

But she kept on talking, didn't wait for the coughing to stop. " —if you're convicted of killing him. In that case, you get nothing. Not from the estate or the insurance policies."

I patted my chest. Tried to breathe. Tried to float away.

"He named his siblings as secondary beneficiaries."

Okay. I closed my eyes, saw Sherry McBride with an ice pick in her neck. Lord. I wondered who would find her—and when. It could be days. Or the phone might ring any minute with the news. My mouth tasted coppery. I sipped coffee. Tried to stay with Susan, follow what she was saying.

" —know you're innocent. But, to an outsider, to the police, to the press—when this financial information—especially the insurance stuff gets out, well, it doesn't look good."

No, it didn't. "But I didn't even know about the insurance policies."

"I believe you." She pushed hair out of her eyes. "But it's hard to prove a negative. How can you convince people you did not know something?"

She was right.

"So, be prepared. The press has got hold of this, so it'll probably be on the news—"

"Oh God. They'll say I killed Charlie for money." Actually, Charlie had said the same thing. And somehow, money seemed a baser motive than jealousy or rage or revenge. I took a breath, saw walls crumbling, the floor giving way. A couple of charred rodents. A blood-soaked bath towel. "Because—oh man. If the school hears this—what about my job?"

"Your job?" She cocked her head. Crossed her legs. Sighed. Looked at me with guarded eyes.

"Yes, Susan. My job."

"Elle," she spoke carefully, "we have far bigger problems than your job right now."

Yes, we did. She had no idea how big. Maybe I should tell her. If I didn't, the truth would fester and churn inside me. I couldn't hide it, needed to let the truth out, no matter the consequences.

"Susan, something happened this morning—"

She squeezed my arm. "Something about Charlie's murder?"

"I don't think so. Not directly."

"Then save it, Elle. We have a lot to deal with before the meeting. Let's take things one at a time."

~

"This meeting today with Stiles." She met my eyes. "It's important."

She paused for me to absorb her words. Okay. I knew it was important.

She went on. "And I have a feeling it won't be good." Again, she paused.

I held the mug close to my face, felt its warmth. Braced myself for whatever was coming.

"Stiles's wife called me to say he's upset. She knows you and I are close and doesn't want to be in the middle. Stiles doesn't usually talk to her about ongoing investigations. But this time, he's dropped hints. And even though she doesn't want to break his confidence, she told me he's not happy about what's going down."

Which means?

"To me, that sounded like he might have to arrest you."

Her words reverberated, sounded far away. Arrest. Not a scary word; it sounded like "a rest." Not bad, to take a rest. But Susan was talking about me taking a long one, behind bars, wearing orange. Susan's face lost focus. Something heavy dropped inside my chest. Crashed into my bowels. Sherry McBride's bludgeoned face grinned at me, and I saw the hanger protrude from Somerset Bradley's eye. In slow motion, I watched myself set down my coffee mug, stand, run to the bathroom. I heard Susan call my name, slow and elongated. Saw her stand and come after me.

Outside the door, Susan was talking. Telling me that it would be all right. That there were recourses. Recourses? Another odd word. I thought about it. Recourse. Something you take if you flunk math? The path of a dammed-up river? It didn't make sense in the context of murders and arrests. But she was still talking, now saying the word, "bail." I heard her voice more than her words. My body cramped and twisted, rebelling.

When I finally came out, my face damp with sweat and hair feeling matted, Susan was waiting. She reached out and took me in her arms, and when she released me, I saw that her mascara was running, her face wet with tears. She swallowed, touched my chin, nodded.

And said, "It's time, Elle. We have to go."

On the way out, I stopped to swallow a couple of Dr. Schroeder's pills. They might not help, but they couldn't hurt.

～

Even with the scar on his face, Stiles was handsome, in a rugged, craggy sort of way. Strong jaw. Direct, intelligent eyes. An aroma of soap. His bones were long, and he looked awkward, out of place on the swirling floral print of Susan's living room sofa.

Don't look guilty, I repeated a list of don'ts to myself as he began talking. Don't think about Sherry McBride or her brutalized body. Don't avoid Stiles's eyes.

"Frankly," he leaned forward, resting his elbows on his knees, "I'm not convinced you did it."

I shrunk into the cushions of the easy chair. His tone indicated that he was leading up to a "but." Like, but the rest of the department does. But the DA does. But I have to arrest you anyhow.

"But here's the thing, Elle. The other suspects that we've looked into? They all have alibis."

I blinked. Said nothing. Waited.

"Sherry McBride was in the ER for a dog bite. Derek Morris was out, entertaining clients. Somerset Bradley was home with his family, and neighbors corroborate that. The other men in the photos of Russia were not even in town. One was in Thailand; the other in Houston."

He paused again.

"Bottom line. You stood to inherit millions from your estranged husband's death. He was killed in your home with your knife, at a time when, by your own account, you were home. From a prosecutor's standpoint, you and you alone have no alibi, yet you had motive, means, and opportunity to commit the crime."

I was still breathing, barely. Seeing myself from far away, pulling an Elle despite the pills. They weren't working, not strong enough to tether me. I drifted away, watching myself sitting motionless, bloodless, white, fading. Waiting for the handcuffs to appear.

Susan stood up. "Let's cut to the chase. Are you arresting my client?" She sounded ferocious. Abrupt.

Stiles hesitated, looked from me to Susan, back to me. Back to Susan. His voice was edgy, cautious. "Susan, we've discussed this. I told you I couldn't promise—"

"Just answer me, Detective. Are you arresting her or not?" Her hands were on hips. Eyes fierce, daring him.

He leaned back. Put his hands together. "Sit down, Susan. We're here to talk."

Susan huffed and puffed, but sat. Crossed her legs. Folded her arms. Sliced him with her stare.

"Personally, I don't think this case adds up. There was a partial fingerprint on the knife that doesn't match Elle or Charlie—"

"That gives reasonable doubt," Susan interrupted.

"It doesn't match any of the people we've looked at. Might be old. A guest who touched the knife. We can't be sure. But from my point of view, if you wanted your husband's money, would you be dumb enough to kill him in your own home at a time when you had no alibi?"

"Of course she wouldn't." Susan spoke for me.

"I don't think so either. Trouble is, the DA disagrees. Seems you failed to mention to the police that your husband lost your entire personal savings—your whole inheritance—in a bad investment."

Susan was on it. "Her finances aren't relevant—"

"And then there's the matter of the kiddie porn—and, by the way—thank you for that flash drive. There's an investigation already underway, since it's a crime to travel abroad for purposes of illegal sexual liaisons."

"And you wouldn't have that evidence if not for Elle." Susan interrupted. "She's cooperated fully, assisting law enforce-ment—"

Stiles kept talking, silencing her with his eyes. "But let's talk about how the porn applies to your situation—maybe you thought your husband was on that trip to Russia. Maybe you thought he funded it or planned it or was the guy holding the camera—well, that's what the DA thinks. You found the pic-tures and, with all the friction in your marriage, they were the last straw—they led you to a crime of passion."

"Bullshit—where's the evidence? There is not a shred of proof that Elle found those pictures before the murder." Susan was on her feet again. Voice booming. "In fact, she handed them over as soon as she found them—and that was *after* Charlie's death."

"Susan, sit." It was a command.

Susan huffed, but sat. I watched from the sky, silent as a cloud. And as weightless.

"Again. We don't know when Elle found the flash drive. Or when she first saw the images on it."

He talked about me as if I wasn't there. The way my friends often did. His voice rumbled in the distance. Dangerous like thunder.

"In fact," he went on, "even Elle doesn't know when she found it. She says she has no memory of the entire chunk of time surrounding the murder."

"What do you mean, she *says*? An eminent psychiatrist is treating her for localized dissociative amnesia. He says her mem-ory loss was caused by a trauma."

"Yes, you've told me all about it."

"Well, I'm telling you again. Because you don't seem to accept the fact that she can't remember despite the fact that a nationally renowned, highly respected professional believes her and has diagnosed her—"

"Susan, save it." Stiles leaned forward again. Spoke softly. "It doesn't matter what I do or don't believe. But, obviously, the psychiatric information will be part of your defense."

Our defense? Oh God. I was going to be a defendant. In court. In a murder trial.

"Fine. So answer me, Detective Stiles. Are you arresting her or—"

"Susan, relax. I asked for this meeting as a courtesy to you. Out of respect for our friendship." He sounded peeved. "I could easily have waited until the warrant was drawn up and simply gone and picked her up. But I didn't. Out of our friendship. And because I know you and Elle go way back." His eyes drilled her. Pulled rank.

"Okay." Susan's shoulders sagged. "So what's the deal?"

Air currents carried me higher; the air was thinner. Too thin to breathe.

Dimly, I heard them talk of a choice. An offer. Elle could surrender at the Roundhouse. Within forty-eight hours.

The wind had grown louder, was almost deafening. Maybe I'd misheard. Gotten it wrong.

"Bail?" Susan's voice defied gravity, floated up clear and bell-like.

Bail? I strained to hear.

"The DA has agreed, even though it's a murder charge. A quarter million. But only because I personally guaranteed—"

Wait. A quarter million? That was the amount Charlie stole from me. The amount that I didn't have anymore.

How did it work? Would I have to sell my house? Sign it over to the warden? The judge?

Well, what was the difference? I wouldn't need a house anymore. I'd live at a state facility. I was not in orange, but butt naked, being body-cavity searched by burly prison guards. Being thrown into a cell with tattooed, greasy-haired witches. Being raped in the shower and shivved in the cafeteria line—

"Elle!"

I dropped fast and hard, crashing into my body as it sat perfectly still on the cushions. Susan was jostling me. "Dammit, Elle. Pay attention—" To Stiles, "She gets this way. Drifts off." To me, "Did you listen to what we've just discussed? Do you have questions?"

Questions? Seriously? I was going to jail. I would be arraigned. Searched. Locked in a cell. I would have to mortgage my house to raise bail. Would lose my job, have my face in the papers and on the six o'clock news. Wouldn't die right away, but was definitely losing my life. Another casualty. Our names seemed like a song title: Charlie, Somerset, Sherry, and Elle.

I looked at Susan and shook my head. No, I had no questions.

Susan and Stiles stood. Susan thanked him, said she appreciated his going out on a limb for her. He assured her that he was following his gut, doing what he thought was right. They parted with a tentative, yet warm, embrace. Stiles met my eyes, nodded once, wished me well. And left.

The meeting was over.

～

Susan plopped onto the sofa, running her hands through her hair, cursing. "Okay. We've got forty-eight hours to comply."

She went on, telling me what to expect, the procedures I'd have to undergo. Assuring me that she'd have me out within a day. That I wouldn't spend more than one night in jail. That I should keep to myself while there, speak to no one. Leave my valuables at home. She took my hand.

"This will be the worst of it, Elle. They really don't have a strong enough case."

I nodded.

"Are you okay?" She eyed me, assessing.

I nodded again. My chest threatened to explode. I debated telling her about Sherry McBride.

"Well, let's plan the next two days. We want to get there early day after tomorrow." She looked at her watch. "Before ten. So nobody gets nervous."

I managed another nod.

"This must be terrifying for you. Look. Let's do business, and then spend the next two days pampering Elle. I'll treat you to a spa day. How about a massage? A facial?"

Was she serious?

"Because we'll have plenty of time to plan our defense strategy after the arraignment. First step is just to get you past that hump and back home on bail. You'll need ten percent, twenty-five thousand dollars for bail. You have it?"

"Barely. It would wipe out my retirement account."

"Fine. You'll get it back. Now, think. We have two days."

Two days. It sounded like a death sentence.

"So what do you want to do—let's go somewhere great for dinner—you choose. I'll call Becky and Jen."

I blinked at her, silent. Did she think I wanted to party? The thought of food was sickening. Repulsive. Why didn't she know that? Susan meant to be helpful. She sat beside me, holding my hand. But she seemed out of reach, miles away. In another universe. Susan had never stuck a hanger into a man's eye. Never discovered that her husband kept dark secrets and lies. Never found murder victims practically everywhere she went. Never been a murder suspect. No. Susan's life was protected. Perfect. She had a husband, kids. A career. A future. Freedom.

Suddenly, I resented her. Wanted her to back off and stop looking at me. I was about to say that I wasn't up for dinner. Or even for a massage. But she'd moved on, wasn't thinking about pampering me anymore.

"When do you see the shrink again? Do you have an appointment today?"

Yes, I did.

"Where are your pills? Did you take them today? Well, take more. Double the dose. Because, Elle, we need you to have a breakthrough, and we need it now. You've got to remember what happened the night Charlie died. Because if you can just remember where you were, what you saw, who the real killer is, all these charges will go away."

Wait—who the real killer was?

Susan faced me, smelling of Burberry. She spoke slowly, eyes misty. "Elle. I believe you saw Charlie's murder. That seeing him killed was your trauma, the source of your amnesia. We need your brain to unlock what it knows. And this whole nightmare will end."

I tried once more to remember Charlie's murder. And once more couldn't. All I could envision were jail cells and bars. "I'll try."

"Of course you will." She looked disappointed. Or maybe sad. She took a breath, straightened. "Look—I don't want to sound negative, because I don't feel that way. But, whatever happens, Elle, remember, I'm with you all the way. You are not—and you never will be—in this thing alone."

Whatever resentment I felt instantly vaporized. Ashamed of myself, I hugged her, thanked her. Realized how completely she believed in me. How she'd never dream that, even now, I was hiding something from her. Damn. I should have told her about Sherry McBride right away. Now it was too late. The window of opportunity had passed. I'd committed to secrecy, to hiding inconvenient truths. Just like Charlie. I was no better than he was.

She offered to drive me to the bank to arrange bail money, and we went to the car. But on the way, I changed my mind. Bail money could wait, and I had a few hours before my appointment with Dr. Schroeder.

Before I went to jail, there was somewhere else I needed to go.

‿

I told her not to wait. I'd walk or get a cab home. For a while, Susan refused to leave, but I insisted. Told her I appreciated her devotion to me, but for now, I needed solitude. So, reluctantly, promising to see me later and go with me to the bank in the morning, she pulled away, leaving me alone at the gate of the cemetery.

The quiet felt like an embrace. I stood at the entrance, absorbing it. Admiring the brilliant red-and-yellow foliage of the trees. Releasing the tensions of the morning. And, surrounded by graves, I began to walk.

I remembered exactly where Charlie was. It had only been a few days since I'd left him there. I followed the hilly path, crossing the oldest part of the grounds, passing crowded, often crooked headstones weathered by time, the carvings fading, almost illegible, covering bones of lives forgotten. Came to a newer section where monuments were more elaborate, more evenly spaced. Ornate obelisks, carved columns towered overhead. Heavy mausoleum doors marked rocky slopes of hills. The only sounds were my footsteps, rustling leaves, and occasionally the chirping of birds, and I kept walking, aware that, for as far as I could see ahead and to either side, I was the only person still breathing. I walked between, around, and over bodies, throngs of them, stepped directly above their bones. A cool breeze tickled my neck, maybe the protest of a soul I'd disturbed. Maybe just a breeze. I passed through a sea of sculpture and stillness until I came to the newest section, where graves were marked with uniformly tasteful granite slabs that lay at their heads like stone pillows. Some were dotted with flowers or flags, photos or mementos, but there was one so new that it still lay bare without a slab to mark it, the grass above it newly sodded. No flag. No name. No flowers. No mementos.

The grass was thick and moist, flittered in the breeze. I let myself sink down on it, stretched out right on top of Charlie. And began to sob.

~

I couldn't sense him.

"Charlie?" I wiped my face. Listened for his voice. Heard nothing. I closed my eyes, tried to feel his touch. Felt nothing. Just damp grass on cool, indifferent ground. Another breeze, a cloud covering the sun. A chill, hinting of winter.

All around me were headstones. I lay among them, aware of Charlie's body beneath me, and wept. "What happened?" I whispered into the ground. "How did this happen to us?"

I listened. Heard nothing. Of course I heard nothing. I'd told him to leave me alone. "Go wherever dead people go," I'd demanded. "And don't come back." For once, maybe Charlie had listened.

Or the pills were helping. Making me hallucinate less. Either way, Charlie was gone.

I let my head sink onto the grass. Closed my eyes, willing those same pills to help me find my memory. To replay what happened the day of the murder. I saw Charlie in the study. The knife in his back. Opened my eyes.

Why couldn't I see what happened before that? I tried. Went back to the morning, the day at school, Benjy's birthday party. Coming home. Writing the note about birthday snacks. And then—nothing. Until I was at Jeremy's with Becky.

And Charlie was dead. Lying in the earth, beside the plot of ground where someday I would lie, inside the casket I'd picked out, encased in concrete to keep him dry. I ached for his hug. His scent. His quick wit. His surprises. Despite everything, I still loved him. But how? Maybe it wasn't love. Maybe it was just habit. Or an illusion.

An illusion. I thought of Joel. Heard him talking about illusion at dinner. Oh God. Why was I thinking of Joel while I was lying over Charlie's body? In fact, why was I thinking of either of them—I was going to go to jail in a day and a half. I saw myself locked in a windowless cell, much like a coffin. Unable to see the sky. To feel the breeze or hear the rustle of autumn leaves. Oh God. I'd go crazy there. All because of Charlie. I sat up, angry.

"And what about Sherry McBride?" I demanded. "Did you have an affair with her?"

Silence. Charlie wasn't even defending himself anymore. I'd banished him. I wanted him to answer. To swear, *You were the love of my life.*

He didn't. I couldn't conjure him up. But I talked to him anyway.

"Did you get her involved with that kiddie porn? Is that why someone killed her?"

I wondered if he knew she was dead. If she'd come after him, stalking him through heaven or hell.

I wanted him to talk to me, but wasn't sure what I wanted him to say. What would have helped? Maybe nothing. Probably nothing. Hearing nothing, I stayed there, lying down, sitting up, thinking, remembering, wondering, worrying, talking, regretting, crying. Even laughing. Almost forgiving him. Definitely missing him. But finding out nothing new about who'd murdered him.

When I finally checked the time, it was half past one. Almost time for Dr. Schroeder. I didn't know how to say goodbye. So I whispered that he should save my place. Then I stood, brushed myself off, straightened my clothes, called a cab, and retraced my steps to the cemetery gate.

∾

Dr. Schroeder understood the time constraints, and, assuring me that I should relax, began to hypnotize me.

"Sit heavily in the chair." He droned in monotone. "Let your body sink into the cushions and relax."

I tried to listen, but images and voices kept interrupting him: Sherry McBride lying bludgeoned and bloody. Charlie slumping, knifed in the back. Children posing for sex photos. Stiles warning that I had forty-eight hours to surrender at the Roundhouse. Susan insisting, "We need you to have a breakthrough, and we need it now."

The interruptions didn't help. They distracted and pressured me. I told myself to ignore them. To follow the doctor's suggestions and relax my body parts. So far, my toes and feet were cooperating, but my mind wouldn't. It bounced from image to image. The taxi ride from the cemetery, blue tape on the seat, the smell of cigarette ashes and sweat. The awareness of Sherry McBride lying in her apartment, waiting to be discovered. The ringtone of my phone. Becky's cries.

"Oh God, Elle. This can't be true. Susan told me not to tell you that she told me, but I can't help it. They're actually going to arrest you? You? While that maniac McBride walks around free, killing hamsters?"

Stop thinking, I scolded myself. Empty your mind of thoughts. Let your muscles relax. Your ankles. Your calves. Your knees.

But I was back in the cab again. Hearing my phone again. Answering it.

"I had a wonderful time last night." Joel sounded untroubled. Cheerful.

"So did I." Dear God. My voice was weak. A whimper.

"Why don't we have another, even more wonderful time tonight?"

He was asking me out. Fabulous. I'd met a sexy, eligible, irresistible man just in time to be locked up for murder. I thought about bail, that I needed to arrange the money. Must have hesitated too long, messed up the conversational rhythm. Joel had gone on without me.

"How about La Buca. Eight o'clock?"

And so we had another dinner date. And Sherry McBride would soon be in rigor mortis—might be already. Who would find her? And why couldn't I remember the hours around Charlie's murder? What was my mind hiding from me? I had to stop thinking. Had to focus on my session with Dr. Schroeder.

And on my thighs—I had to relax my thighs. My hips. Had to let the tension out.

But was I crazy? What was I doing, accepting a date? Visiting the cemetery? Even sitting in this beige toneless room, trying to get hypnotized? I should be packing, getting on a plane, taking off for—what countries wouldn't extradite me back to the U.S.? I didn't know. Should be finding out, Googling the question on the way to the airport.

My eyes were teary again. Dr. Schroeder was telling me that all my troubles were lifting away, lightening my weight. That my back was relaxing, feeling lighter. And my shoulders. And my arms. That nothing could hurt me. I was going to a happy place, where there were no worries. Where it was safe. Where I would be without fear, without grief, without pain.

~

I was completely relaxed, mentally transporting myself to my father's study, sitting in his big leather easy chair. Surrounded by his books and papers. His musky scent. Safe and protected from all harm.

But I couldn't sustain the illusion. Somewhere down the hall a memory surfaced. Charlie was yelling. Odd, because he almost never yelled. Even when we fought. When he was angry, he kept his voice maddeningly calm and controlled, as if he were a mature rational adult and I a premenstrual, chemically imbalanced hysteric. But now, Charlie's voice was raised. Furious.

I stood and followed it, walking toward the study. It was Sunday. Late morning. Warm—maybe summer? Yes, mid-July. I was in tan shorts and a yellow tank top. Barefoot. Toenails painted hot pink. Charlie was in the study with the door closed. Why was the door closed? It was just the two of us in the house. Maybe he was on the phone? No—someone else was there. Another voice, yelling back.

"Go fuck yourself, Charlie, you self-righteous son of a bitch—"

Derek?

"You have no idea what you're messing—"

"Oh, but I do." Charlie's voice trembled, thundered. "I know exactly what and exactly who—and how to get to them."

"What are you talking about?" Derek tried to outshout him. "You're not—"

"And where. And why."

"—talking about blackmail?"

Silence. They both stopped at once. I stood in the hallway, watching the door.

"I said nothing about blackmail."

"You said everything but the word."

More silence.

"God Almighty." Charlie's voice quieted, sounded grave. "This is ruinous. What have you gotten us into, Derek?"

"Me? I believe it was you who hired that bimbo—"

"Sherry's not a bimbo—"

"And you who had the genius idea that she could back up all the files."

All the files—Did he mean the files of the pornographic pictures? I tried to make sense of what I was hearing. But I had to listen—they'd stopped yelling, spoke softly. I strained to hear, could make out only small random phrases. Nothing that made sense. Something about dates. Decisions. Papers. Weeks—or maybe leaks? And adoption?

Adoption?

Then a third voice spoke up. "Look, I'm out of here. You two settle this between you. Just make your minds up soon. Because, if you cancel, there'll be fees."

The door opened in my face. A man stepped out, nodded my way, hurried down the hall to the door.

Dr. Schroeder was telling me that I'd remember everything I wanted to, that I would awaken refreshed and renewed. That I would remain relaxed all day, able to unlock my memories at will as the day progressed. And then, he counted to three.

I felt refreshed and renewed, remembering Charlie's argument with Derek. And the third voice, too. It was probably just business, not necessarily anything nefarious. But, over dinner, I would ask Joel why he hadn't mentioned meeting me months ago, in the hallway of my house.

~

I spent the next hours at home, swallowing extra pills, sitting in the room where I'd found Charlie's body, trying for a breakthrough. Sometimes my mind tickled, as if a featherlike memory was touching it ever so lightly, just beyond the range of my consciousness. Too many fragmented images. Who would have wanted to kill Charlie? The investors, to conceal their child prostitutes? Derek, to protect the business? Sherry McBride, to protest his rejection? Or maybe, if she'd indeed copied the photo files, to blackmail the investors? Maybe Joel? No, I couldn't believe it, didn't want to think so. But possibly. He might have sold something besides travel packages. So, even with Somerset Bradley and Sherry McBride dead, there were still at least four people with possible motives.

But the police weren't arresting them.

I sat in the study on the new sofa, leaned back, trying to rest. Letting thoughts surface on their own. Hoping my memory would offer up something new. I sunk into the cushions, relaxing my body à la Dr. Schroeder, starting with the toes. Took slow deep breaths. Watched dust floating in the air. Saw a knife glimmer in my own bloody hand.

I stood up, releasing a groan of self-pity. Hugging myself. Forget relaxing or trying to remember. Nothing was going to save me. I was going to jail. And, for all I knew, I deserved it—I might have killed Charlie. Please, I told my brain, let go. Let me see what you've hidden, no matter how bad it is. I'm going to jail anyhow. If I killed him, I might as well know it. Tell me what happened.

My brain didn't react. I remembered nothing. Head in hands, I slumped back onto the sofa. My chest was tight. Breathing hurt.

I sat for a while. Minutes. Leaned back against the cushions. Hopeless. Drifting. Remembering my last talk with Charlie. Before we'd fought about his affair.

The money. He'd seemed to think I'd understand. *You get all of it, Elle. Because I had no will.*

I'd been appalled. "You think I killed you for your money?"

You were pissed as hell about your inheritance.

I'd explained that it hadn't been just the inheritance.

You said the money was the last straw. And if I'm dead, you get it all, not just the half you'd get in a divorce. Unless you get convicted of killing me. Then you get nothing.

Charlie seemed to think I'd get nothing. That I'd be convicted. And, if Charlie thought I'd killed him for his money, certainly a jury would. But Charlie didn't think that—he didn't think anything. He was dead. I'd hallucinated that conversation, imagined it, gone over the edge. Well, why shouldn't I? In my situation, what was the point of staying sane? And why was I thinking about Charlie's money?

I walked in circles, worrying my hands. Stomach knotted. I pictured the blood that by now would have gravitated to Sherry McBride's back, turning it purplish-gray. Heard the phone rang but ignored it, afraid to hear that she'd been found. Afraid to hear anything from anyone. Pacing, I finally began to replay the argument I'd heard at Dr. Schroeder's. Derek and Charlie yelling about blackmail. About the mess they'd gotten into. Maybe I was thinking of Charlie's money because of that conversation—the mess the business was in. Blackmail.

The faces of the dead spun through my mind. Somerset, Sherry, Charlie.

And the face of the one person connected to them all.

I didn't like Derek, had avoided him all week. But I'd known I'd have to confront him sooner or later. It was time.

~

His secretary's name was Roxy. She was about twenty, had short red hair, blue eye shadow, pearl-polished nails. Roxy was generally spunky, but she slunk away when I burst in and demanded to see Derek. I was, after all, the partner's widow.

Derek stood as I stormed in. "Elle, what a surprise!" He opened his arms for an embrace. I must have glowered. He aborted the hug, offering me a chair instead.

I sat. I glared.

"M and M's?" He took a dish off his desk, held it out.

I narrowed my eyes.

"I've been trying to reach you all week," he popped a handful of candy into his mouth, took a seat opposite me on a plush leather chair that matched mine.

"I know." I'd ignored his calls.

"How are you doing, Elle?" Derek paced himself, trying to sound sincere.

"How would you expect?"

He nodded, looked at his lap. An exaggerated expression of sympathy. "It's been hard for me, too. But I'm glad you've come by. We need to talk."

"Yes, we do."

He waited a beat, leaned forward. "This is difficult for both of us, Elle. I don't know where to begin—"

"How about with the naked kids?"

He started, recovered quickly. "What did you do with the—"

"With the flash drive? You mean the kiddie porn. That's what you were looking for, right? The files you said Charlie took from the office. The confidential client information."

Derek's eyes shifted just slightly. He crossed his legs, put his hands together, fingertips forming an arch at his lips.

I kept going. "That was all bullshit, wasn't it, Derek? The truth was that you were taking your clients on perverted sex trips—a pedophiles' holiday."

"Oh Jesus, no." His hands slapped the arms of his chair as he cut me off. "Elle, you are dead wrong. Absolutely, completely off base. Although, given the pictures in those files, I can see where you got that impression." A slow, snaky smirk.

I said nothing, waited for him to slither into his hole.

"Okay. So you looked at the images on the flash drive." He tilted his head. "And you saw—what exactly? I'm not sure how to address this unless I know what you've seen."

I mimicked his position, crossing my legs, placing my palms on the arms of my chair. "Enough. I saw enough to get you and your friends arrested. And you will be."

He lost the smile, the pose. Sat forward, hissing. "The hell we will. If anyone gets arrested, Elle, from what I hear, it's going to be you."

I didn't bite. Didn't react.

"Sorry. I shouldn't have said that." He was trying to shake me up, divert my attention. "We're talking about the kiddie porn."

"Yes." I stared him in the eye, not flinching.

He watched me for a moment, shifted positions in his chair, leaning forward. "Elle, clearly, you have no idea what you saw. Or what the images mean. You have no context in which to put them."

"Context?" Was he kidding? "Sick is sick no matter how you frame it."

"Again, you're dead wrong." He sat farther forward, too close. I could feel his breath on my face, smell the sweet chocolate. "Poor Elle. So confused. Just like your pain in the ass husband—sorry to speak ill of the dead. But you see, the world is far larger than what your narrow provincial views can imagine. Full of a vast array of cultures whose norms, rites, and traditions you in your self-righteous, ethnocentric naïveté would find revolting." He leaned back, finally, lecturing, gesturing professorially. "Did you know, Elle, that there are communities who stretch their women's lips to the size of their heads, and their necks to the length of their femurs? People who pierce pubescent boys' penises with quills and feathers. Chinese who still bind and stunt the growth of women's feet. There are people who circumcise their girls—often without anesthesia, using shards of glass. Mothers who circumcise baby boys with their teeth. Does any of this offend or shock you? I can go on—people who eat monkey brains and dogs. Men who practice polygamy or marry children or wed their brothers' widows or take their nieces' virginity—"

"What's your point, Derek? That sometimes having sex with children is normal?"

He didn't answer. Simply leaned back, watching me. And let his snaky grin slide across his face. "You know, Elle, it's too bad that you were so quick to give that flash drive to the police. Given, I mean, that your own livelihood still depends on the success of this firm. Charlie wouldn't want his former clients to be involved in a scandal."

"No, he wouldn't." My voice trembled. I tried to control it. "But Charlie had limits. He wouldn't stand for exploiting and abusing kids. That's what you were fighting about, wasn't it?" Suddenly, I could imagine what had happened. Derek coming after Charlie, trying to convince him to give back the files on the flash drive. Charlie refusing. "Is that why you killed him?

Because he wouldn't stand for his company sponsoring pedophilia?"

"What?" Derek's mouth opened wide, revealing two gold caps on the lower left. A coughlike laugh erupted from his belly. "Really? That's what you're saying? That *I* killed Charlie?" He shook his head. Stood, checked his watch. "Look, Elle. Nice try, but we all know who killed Charlie." His eyes pierced me as if my guilt were an established fact, as if there were no doubt.

Derek walked back to his desk and took a seat. Folded his hands. "This has been fun, but I have an appointment in a minute. So let's wrap this up. You've made entirely false assumptions, Elle. What you saw on that flash drive was merely a record of a worthy attempt by well-meaning clients to rescue some exploited children from abroad."

What?

"Those sex shots showed the children's former lives as child prostitutes. Our clients were attempting to pay cash for their freedom—essentially to buy them from their pimps—and to legally adopt them and bring them here to the U.S., so they could develop normal, or at least seminormal lives."

I blinked at him, silent. Remembered the photos. Some had seemed purely innocent. Men, holding hands of kids eating ice cream. Walking with them near the Kremlin. Not all the photos were sexual. Could Derek be telling the truth? Had I misinterpreted everything? I couldn't be sure, couldn't remember seeing adult faces in the sex shots. If their faces weren't shown, there was no proof that Derek's investors had actually abused the children.

"I can see where you'd jump to the conclusion that you did. But, in fact, by causing all this ruckus, you've probably done nothing more than embarrass and frighten off some very wealthy, well-intentioned potential adoptive parents, costing the firm a ton of money." His tone was condescending. Cold. "Hell.

I'll be lucky if none of them sues us. That is, if you leave any of them alive long enough to sue us."

Derek watched me, waited for me to apologize and go away. But I did neither. Instead, I leaned my elbows on my knees. "So these men, the clients who went on your trip—they were philanthropists."

"Exactly."

"Rescuing children."

"As I've said."

"I see." I waited, letting him breathe. "But, if that's the case—If they were trying to do good works—why were you upset that Charlie took the files? Why would Somerset Bradley go so far as to search his apartment for them?"

For a nanosecond, Derek sputtered. "Well, it's obvious." He cleared his throat, stalling, shifting in his chair, trying to come up with an answer. "We were all upset, foreseeing the possibility that what's happened could happen. Someone could make copies. Could distribute them. The images could be taken out of context. People could draw false conclusions just as you did."

He went on, forming phrases repeating his theme, until an intercom buzzed on his desk. His secretary's voice declared, "Your four o'clock."

Derek told her to tell him to wait, but the door swung open, and the four o'clock appointment strolled in.

"Good news, Derek, we got it. But it wasn't easy. That fuckin' bimbo—" When he saw me, Joel froze, closed his hand around the small object he'd been holding up. Twisted his face into a smile. "Elle, I didn't know you were here."

Eyeing Derek, he walked over to me, bent to kiss my cheek, and, as seemed to be his habit, from nowhere, produced a rose.

~

Okay, the rose thing was getting old. I stood, telling myself to get out of there. To act normal. Smile. Take the rose. Thank him. Not let on that I'd seen the flash drive in his hand. Or that

I'd heard what he said about the bimbo. No. I had to leave, had to act as if I hadn't seen or heard anything, as if Derek had convinced me that I'd imagined the whole pedophilia thing. That the clients were a bunch of wealthy do-gooders who wanted to help children. That everything was fine.

My cheeks hurt from smiling. "Well, thanks for explaining things, Derek. I guess I got it all wrong."

Derek stood, didn't return the smile.

"So." I looked from him to Joel. "Okay, then. You guys go ahead with your business. I'll be on my way."

Derek moved closer.

"No, don't bother to walk me out, Derek. I'm fine. I'll be in touch, okay?" I was talking too much. Chattering. Told myself to shut up. I turned toward the door. Wanted to run, made myself move slowly. Calmly.

Joel stepped in front of me. "Elle, don't hurry off. I didn't mean to interrupt whatever you were — "

"Oh, you didn't. Really. We were pretty much finished." I moved to the door. "No problem. So, I'll see you later."

The change in his face was sudden. His mouth opened as if to say something. But no sound came out. His eyes shifted to look at something behind me. Seemed to be asking a question.

As if from above, I saw Derek standing behind me, a brass statuette in his hand. A voice in my head screamed: Run.

So, I threw my body forward, shoving Joel, diving for the door.

～

Through the fog, from far away, I saw Charlie's brother. Ted walked into our kitchen, unexpected, unshaven, smelling damp and oily like a subway station. I wondered why he'd come, how he'd managed to get from Virginia to Philadelphia without money. Probably by using his thumb. Getting rides from truck drivers. He was drinking a beer, whining to Charlie. "Come on, man, you're my brother."

I couldn't hear Charlie's answer, but it agitated Ted. He winced. "Why don't you just say it—you think you're better than me."

Another muffled response from Charlie.

Ted slammed the beer bottle onto the counter. "For real? I'm not worth a few grand to you? Your money's more to you than your blood?"

Charlie's words faded away, as did Ted's, their fight drowned out by other voices. Closer and clearer. A tenor and a baritone. Pain clanged in my head, and I tried to remember where I was, to locate my body parts. Too groggy to move, not alert enough to make a sound, I took silent inventory. Found one arm sprawled out to my side, the other twisted uncomfortably underneath me, my weight pressing my fingernails into the still tender cut on my hand. My hips faced the heavens. My legs lay limply, separated from each other at an indelicate, graceless angle.

I drifted back into shades of gray, hearing the voices dimly as, gradually, I came awake. My skull raged where it had been hit. My neck ached, turned at an unnatural angle. My cheek burned against wool carpet. None of me felt stable enough to move.

So I lay motionless, waiting for my brain to rewire. Hearing fuzzy conversation. Maybe one of the voices was Ted's? Was he actually here, asking Charlie for money? Wait, no. Of course not. A sharp pang reminded me: Charlie was dead. Seeing Ted in the house—it must have been a dream. Not real.

So what was real? I tried to remember. Listened to the voices. Picked up random phrases.

"—out of control." I knew the voice. Not Ted's. Joel's.

And I remembered where I was.

Joel went on. "—didn't sign up for this—where's it going to stop?"

"—messier than expected." Derek sounded condescending. Miffed. "—in it together—"

"—body count—"

"—no surprise—Ms. McBride chose—hardball with the big boys—shouldn't have—against Ogden—"

More fog. The voices drowned in blurry waves. In my haze, I wondered how badly I'd been hurt. If I was dying. Were they going to just let me lie there? I tried to open an eye, took a while to find the nerve circuit connected to my eyelid. Concentrated on lifting it. Saw shadows, vague shapes. Closed it, opened it again. Concentrated. Saw a fuzzy expanse that slowly took definition. A fibrous flat surface and a nodule of red. A carpet. And, in front of my face, a rose. The rug was plum colored. I hadn't noticed that before. Derek must have picked the shade himself, was a master of the details of appearances. Men's cologne. Manicures. Hair gel. Shoes.

I could see those now with my one opened eye. Expensive, soft leather. Black slip-ons. With black silk socks. Charcoal pin-stripe pants. They were all I could see of him. The rest was hidden by the bulk of the leather easy chair. I closed my eye, let my face rest on the plum-colored carpet, and listened.

Joel sounded urgent. "—can't just leave her here—"

"Obviously not." Derek snapped. Impatient. "She has to go."

To go? My eye opened again, looking for the door. I wondered if I could unobtrusively crawl out.

"Go? What are you going to do?"

"I? What am *I* going to do?"

"You're the one who knocked her out—"

"Get it straight, my friend." Their voices were loud, easier to hear. "We all have a vested interest in the outcome."

"No, man. Not me. I haven't done one illegal thing."

"Spare me, Houdini. Who was it again who arranged the trips?"

"But that's all I did. You can't prove that I did anything else."

"Let me remind you that your entire business venture depends on this firm. I own you." Derek's feet moved. He placed them flat on the floor, backed against the base of the easy chair. I pictured him jabbing his finger at Joel. "If I go down—if any of us go down—you go with us. Understood?"

Silence.

"And don't pretend you had no part in this. Your girlfriend Elle gave Charlie's file to the authorities. So go ahead. Try telling an overzealous DA that, although you planned and arranged every detail of every travel package, you had no idea whatsoever what was going on—or any culpability in the subsequent murder of Ms. McBride. Or any part in concealing evidence in the death of Mr. Bradley. Please. You're as much in this as the rest of us, and the only way out is for us to stand united."

More silence. I opened my other eye. Derek's feet stretched out again, rested on their heels.

After a while, Joel said, "I don't like it."

"Really? How surprising. The rest of us think it's ducky."

Some shuffling. Repositioning of feet.

"How long do you think she'll be out?"

"No idea. Frankly, I'm surprised she's not stirred. I didn't think I'd struck her with much force."

I closed my eyes, in case they looked at me.

"Do you think she did it?"

"Did what?"

"Charlie."

Wait. Didn't *they* kill Charlie?

"I never doubted it." Liquid sloshed. Drinks being poured? "Not until today."

"And now?"

Derek hesitated. "And now, I realize how little tolerance our friend Ogden has for scandal. And what great lengths he'll go to in order to prevent one."

So Derek didn't do it. Ogden killed Charlie? But who was

Ogden? Was he the fourth man in the photo? He had to be. Except Stiles had said that everyone in the photos had alibis that checked out, and that would include Ogden.

"Charlie. Somerset. The bimbo. It's got to stop, Derek."

Liquid sloshed again, more drinks being poured. "It will. You have my word. This is the end. It stops here and now."

There was a long pause. What were they doing? "To those we've lost," Derek toasted. "And are about to lose."

They were quiet as they drank.

∿

They stood over me. I felt the air stir as they approached, smelled woodsy cologne, Derek's dry-cleaned wool and polished leather.

Someone knelt beside me, pushed locks of hair off my face, felt my skull. Hold still, I told myself. Do not twitch. Do not shiver or stir. I felt Joel's eyes on me, his hand lingering on my face. Tender. Comforting.

"She's got quite a bump on her head."

"Don't worry about it."

The hand left my face. The air swirled as Joel stood. "So. What now?"

Derek let out a long sigh. "It's a sad turn of events. Elle Harrison came to see me. She was despondent over her husband's murder."

I was? Past tense?

"Guilt-ridden, she confided that she'd killed both him and his girlfriend."

Wait—his girlfriend? Charlie swore he was never involved with Sherry. Another lie?

"Elle was terrified of going to prison. When she left here, I was troubled about her state of mind. My worries, it turned out, were valid. Bereft and overwrought, the poor woman committed suicide."

Oh God. They were going to kill me. Joel? Joel was going along with it? No. Of course not. He'd never allow it. My face still tingled from his touch. He must be playing Derek, just so he could stall him. I remembered his kiss, greeting me as he'd come in, lips lingering and gentle. And the kiss after our dinner date. No question, Joel cared about me. Ultimately, he'd stand up to Derek and protect me. Or magically make a gun appear in my hands. Or make me disappear out the door.

"And the file? Those photos—what will we tell the cops?"

See? He was stalling. Coming up with a rescue plan.

"Ogden's foundation will confirm the adoption stories. He's had paperwork drawn up, proper applications. Even proposals for building schools in two or three of the countries."

A pause. I tried not to tremble. Waited for Joel to slip me a letter opener, a scissors.

"Suicide, huh?"

"Unfortunately."

"Are you serious? People don't kill themselves by hitting themselves on the head. No one will buy that it's suicide."

"Joel, please. No one will see the lump."

"Of course they will—look at it. You'd have to be blind—"

"Trust me. There won't be a lump. The bullet will blow away half her skull."

～

Even lying down, my knees melted. If I'd been standing, I would have fallen down. It was time for Joel to perform his magic, but he didn't. He didn't take a stand to protect me, either. I was on my own. Had to get the hell out of there. But how? I hadn't moved anything but an eyelid yet, would probably be dizzy and sluggish, clumsy and slow getting to my feet. And they were both right there, fit, strong, and agile. Watching me.

Maybe, at the last minute, Joel would fight Derek off.

But maybe he wouldn't.

Derek opened the door, said goodnight to Roxy. When she was gone, he said he'd bring his car around. Told Joel to wrap me up so I couldn't move if I regained consciousness and to bring me down in the elevator.

Good. I'd be alone with Joel. Could talk to him. Get him to help me escape.

But Joel said, "No. You bring her down. We'll take my van. There's more room and no windows."

No windows? Oh God.

Apparently, Joel wasn't planning to rescue me.

Unless—maybe he was waiting. Planning to knock Derek out and shove him, not me into the back of the van. Maybe?

My heart was pumping too loud, too fast. They'd probably hear it and figure out that I was faking unconsciousness. Which would mean I couldn't take them by surprise. Not that I knew what sort of surprise. Not that I had any coherent thoughts at all. Even the pain in my head was dull. All I could feel was fear of having half my skull blown away.

The door closed, Derek's long, lanky arms slid under me, squashing a breast, jostling me, rolling me over onto some kind of fleecy fabric. A blanket? An afghan? Then, gracelessly, Derek wrapped, shoved, rolled, lifted, tossed me over his shoulder, swathed in cloth. Through all of it, I remained limp.

He slapped my butt, jabbed me with elbows and fingers. He grunted and cursed, complained that I was too big, that I weighed more than he'd thought. I did not react. Did not stiffen or resist or let on that I was aware of insults or pain. Or of blood dripping from my head, getting bumped against the edges of desks and the frames of doors. I didn't tense up even though his sharp shoulders dug into my belly and, more than once, his grip slipped, threatening to let me fall.

I dangled, rump up over Derek's shoulder, completely passive, trying to come up with an escape plan, sensing that inaction was my best choice. That, for the moment, lifelessness was my best chance at staying alive.

∾

Joel didn't knock Derek out and shove him into the back of the van. The person Joel shoved there was me, and he did it roughly. But lying there by myself, I was finally able to open my eyes. A red eye blinked at me. Another. Two of them, surrounded by white fur. A bunny? Yes, huddling beside me in a cage. Nibbling a carrot.

I moved my head slightly. Pain rumbled in my neck and skull, but I was able to look around. A blue blanket wound tightly around me, wrapping me like a mummy. I was wedged between the rabbit cage and magic equipment. A trunk. Boards and slats. Posters. A long, silver-and-black box, coffinlike, divided in half for sawing a body in two.

I turned my head, looked around for the saw. There had to be a saw. Or maybe a hammer, a screwdriver. Nothing.

And nothing cushioned me from bumps or ruts in the road. I bounced against the van's hard floor, banging my already sore head. In between bumps, I tried to unwrap myself and free my arms. Squirmed. Wiggled. Realized that I'd have to sit up to unwrap the blanket. Which would mean rolling over. I swayed from side to side, rocking to build momentum. But there was nowhere, no room to roll. I kept knocking into the bunny cage and gave up.

But I couldn't give up. Couldn't just let them kill me. I envisioned breaking out of the van, leaping onto the street, running home. Getting ready for my dinner date as if none of this had happened.

But it had happened. And my date with Joel wasn't going to. Thumping and bumping in the back of the van, it hit me that my life was over. Nothing I'd hoped for or planned would occur. I was going to be dead, like Charlie. Becky and Susan and Jen would pick out my coffin. I pictured them, my best friends, shopping for flowers. Selecting the clothes I'd wear at the funeral. Writing my obituary. Arguing over how to word the cause of death. "We can't say 'suicide,'" Jen would insist.

"Just leave it out," Becky would sniffle. "It's no one's business."

" 'Suddenly,' " Susan would suggest. "We'll just say she died, 'suddenly.' That's enough."

And then they'd plant me in the plot of dirt beside Charlie in the cemetery, under fresh sod. I would never see another sunrise, never teach another class. Never love another man. Or even have another date. Or another dinner out. No more soft candlelight or smoky red wine. No flirtation. No seduction. I pictured Joel across the table, fire dancing in his eyes. Damn. I might have—no, definitely would have slept with him this time. Pictured his shoulders. His lips. God—what was wrong with me, fantasizing sex with a man who was about to murder me? I was an idiot, a fool. And soon, if I didn't come up with a plan, I would be a dead idiot fool.

But on the bright side, if I were dead, I wouldn't have to turn myself in to the police. I could see Susan, waiting at the bank, sputtering and furious that I hadn't shown up to withdraw my bail. She'd think I'd gone on the lam. Odd expression. On the lam. On the lamb. Why did the same sound that expressed purity and innocence also describe a criminal running from the law?

And why was I delving into the oddities of the English language and dating and sex and everything except what was important? Two men were driving me somewhere to kill me.

I needed to stop dissociating.

To focus.

Okay. I lay back and closed my eyes, determined to make a plan. But when I closed my eyes, I saw Ted in the study with Charlie. Standing beside Charlie's desk. I saw details. The chain around Ted's neck with the big silver cross. The Chinese letters tattooed on the inside of his arm. The chip on his front tooth. The check in his hand.

"You expect me to say, 'thank you'?" He waved the check in the air. "Okay: Thank you." It was sarcastic.

"Get lost, Ted." Charlie stood, walked to the bar. "And stay there."

When had that conversation happened? I had no idea, couldn't remember. And didn't know why was it coming back to me now when I needed to be making an escape plan. Maybe it was the pills. Maybe they were finally working, helping me remember things. Or maybe it was the knock on the head.

But damn, if not for the pills, I could have just floated away. Escaped mentally by pulling an Elle. Instead, I tried again to shimmy out of the blanket, couldn't. Didn't have wiggle room. The engine was loud, hoarse. Another bump. Another hit on my head. Oh God. How could this be happening? It couldn't be. I had to be dreaming. Derek and Joel couldn't seriously intend to kill me.

The van lurched—hit a pothole? I flew. Landed with a harsh thud. Closed my eyes in case they turned to check on me. Wondered if the rabbit was okay. With the engine, I couldn't hear them talking. Could barely hear Willie Nelson singing about getting on the road again.

Suddenly, after maybe ten minutes, the van stopped. The engine went off. Willie was silent.

Derek groaned. "Jesus, Joel. There are bulls that give a smoother ride than this heap of scrap. I need a chiropractor."

"Sorry, princess. Forgot you were so delicate."

"You said you made keys? Let me have them."

Keys jangled. Van doors opened and closed. I heard footsteps. And Derek calling, "Okay. Bring her in."

Even with my eyes closed, I saw light splash over me when

the rear doors opened. "Let's go, Elf." Joel grabbed my ankles and yanked.

I didn't make a sound or open my eyes, but Joel handled me like a side of beef. He dragged me across the floor of his van. His touch had changed, was callous and indifferent as he hefted me up onto his shoulder, the same shoulder I'd envisioned bare in my bedroom. His cologne smelled too sweet, made me sick. I inhaled, worried that my lunch might erupt all over him.

"Hey, there, sweet girl," he cooed, almost a whisper. "Sorry about that bumpy ride."

Thank God. Now that Derek was gone, Joel was going to help me. I opened my eyes, started to say his name. "Jo—"

But he didn't hear me, was still talking. "Well, you must be okay. You ate your whole carrot."

The rabbit? He had me slung over his shoulder like a sack of fertilizer and was sweet-talking the damned rabbit? He slammed the door, shifted me around on his shoulder where I bounced and swayed with his every step. His scent had overcome the cologne, become raw. Like sweat, like blood. And to think I'd been going to sleep with him.

～

"I didn't think you packed much punch, Derek. But you sure KOed her. She's still out." Joel dumped me onto a cold, hardwood floor. I struggled not to break the fall, made no sound when I landed hard. And didn't let on that I recognized the wood, that floor. Hell, as soon as we crossed the threshold, I recognized the air. Didn't have to open my eyes to know I was home.

"Come on, Prince Charming, give her a kiss. Wake her up."

"Wake her? What for?"

"So she can write a note."

No way. I wouldn't do it.

"You're kidding." Joel laughed out loud. No. It was more

of a scoff. "You think we can just wake her up, like poof? She's probably in a damned coma."

"Nevertheless, give it a shot, will you, Joel?" Derek sounded impatient. "Just for goddamned fucking once, can you not question everything I say and simply do as I ask?" Derek's voice rose in pitch, sounded over the edge. I imagined he was running his hand through his oiled hair. Blinking rapidly. Clenching his jaw to regain self-control. Finally, cleared his throat, spoke with forced calm. "Look. It's better for us if there's a note. A note makes the suicide more credible."

Joel snorted. "Derek, think for a second. Let's assume that I can actually wake her up—which I probably can't. Why would she cooperate and write a suicide note? So we can get away with killing her? Forget it. She'll tell us to fuck ourselves."

He was right. Only I'd be less polite.

"Fine." Derek clucked, perturbed. "All right, then. Never mind the note. We don't need it. Let's just get on with it."

Oh God. Now? They were going to kill me now?

"So where's the forty-five?"

Forty-five?

"I don't know. It's around here somewhere."

Joel cursed. "Jesus, Derek. When you said Charlie had a gun—"

Wait. Charlie had a gun?

"—I thought you knew where it was."

A gun? In my house? Not possible—I'd never have allowed it. But then, I'd never have allowed a lot of what Charlie did. For all I knew, we had Uzis and grenades. For all I knew, we had an arsenal.

If only.

"We were in the study when I saw it—I assume it's in there. In his desk."

Their voices trailed off. I waited a beat, listening. Had they really left me there, unguarded and alone? I opened an eye. Another. Yes. I was alone on the wooden floor of my foyer. Wrapped in a flannel blanket.

Quickly, before they'd realized their mistake, I rolled, unraveling the fabric. Shoving it off me. Climbing onto my knees, wobbling to my feet. Aware of dizziness and pain and the need to hurry. The room was swaying, but I had to move. Heard them sniping at each other.

"Okay, genius. There's no gun here. So where is it?"

"I swear. It was right here. In the desk—"

"But he moved out. Didn't it occur to you that he might have taken it with him?"

Using the walls to steady myself, I started for the front door. It was just across the foyer but seemed miles away. I took a labored step on legs of oatmeal, then another. The door seemed no closer. The voices faded. I couldn't make out what they were saying. Until suddenly, Joel came into the hallway.

"Gotta piss like a racehorse. Where is it?"

Before Derek could answer him, I was out of sight.

～

As Joel hunted for a toilet, I lunged for the coat closet, closed the door gently behind me, pushed through the wall of coats, cleaning bags, and jackets, tiptoed over and around the jumble of storage, and slipped into the cramped cobwebbed triangle of space at the far end, under the steps. Huddling there, I realized that I'd been spending a lot of time in closets. Too much time. This one wasn't as comfortable as Charlie's had been; it lacked carpeting and air. And this time, I didn't have even a hanger to make a weapon with. Damn. Why hadn't I grabbed one from the coat rack? Or a nine iron from the storage compartment? Or even an umbrella? I had nothing to defend myself with. Didn't dare go back to scrounge, couldn't risk making noise.

Crouching, panting, I waited and listened. Out in the hallway, Derek and Joel discovered my absence. They shouted at each other, panicking, searching for me. Scolding each other, casting blame.

"Damn you, Joel." Derek was sputtering. "You said she was unconscious."

"Don't put this on me, Derek—you told me to look for the gun."

"But obviously, you were supposed to secure her first. Can't you think of anything by yourself?"

"No. Not a thing. This whole fucking thing was your—"

"Never mind culpability, Joel. Please try to stay on point. We need to take care of business. Let's assess. She's wounded, so she can't have gone far. Unless—Did she manage to get outside?"

"I checked the kitchen door. Everything's bolted from inside."

"So she's still in the house, somewhere. Start looking."

"Hold on. Quiet. Let me try something." I heard footsteps.

"What the fuck are you—"

"Derek, will you just shut up?" More footsteps on the hardwood. Then, "Elle?" It was Joel, calling out, sounding urgent and concerned. "Elle, honey. Where are you?"

Honey?

"I know you're confused and scared. But, Derek's gone. I think I broke his neck. So you don't have to be afraid. It's just me now, so come on out. You're hurt. You need a doctor."

The son of a bitch was trying to coax me out of hiding. Silence, as he waited for me to emerge. I huddled, listening to pathetic, transparent lies. Did he think I was stupid enough to believe him?

"Okay. I get it. You don't trust me. But honestly, I was just playing along with Derek. Waiting for a chance to take him down. You know I could never hurt you."

Joel walked as he called to me. The floorboards creaked

under his weight. "Derek lost it. He got way over his head in some real bad business. But he's not going to hurt you now. No one is. We need to get you to a hospital. And we—you and I—need to talk."

His footsteps came closer. Stopped outside the closet door.

"So why don't you come out and talk, Elf?"

Oh God. Had he figured out where I was? The closet door opened. The lightbulb came on. My chest did a drumroll. Pounded like hooves of stampeding horses. I was sure they'd hear it, feel it shaking the walls. I curled into a ball, grabbed my knees, pressed my head against them, positioned for a plane crash. Held my breath. Armloads of coats got pulled from the racks. Boxes and suitcases got yanked from the storage compartment. Joel grunted and cursed, called my name again and again, repeating that he'd never hurt me. That we still had a dinner date at La Buca.

I pressed back into the underside of the stairs. Heard the blood rushing in my head. Watched a hand—Joel's fingers reach through shadows back into the dark space where I huddled, groping blindly, touching the floor beside my feet, tapping slowly across the space. Resting not an inch from my hip. Would he feel my body heat? My fear? Would he crawl deeper into the closet and see me?

I waited. Wondered if my chest would explode from not breathing. If I'd lose control and mess my Capris. I watched the hand as it traced the underside of the lowest step, then the second. As it followed the riser to the third, I knew it'd find me.

This time, though, I wouldn't go down easy. This time, I'd hurt them back.

～

I would become my own weapon. My nails weren't long, but they were long enough to dig. And my jaw was strong. I made fingers into claws, ready to grab Joel's wrist, opened my mouth, prepared to clamp my teeth into his flesh.

His hand crept up the riser, felt its way across the bottom of the third step. Millimeters from my face. I ached to breathe but didn't. Swimmers could hold their breath for minutes. Surely, I could last a few more seconds and take him by surprise. My nostrils flared, teeth ached, ready to chomp and draw blood. Ready to tear skin and rip away meat. I was no longer a helpless victim. I was a beast, a predator about to strike.

Maybe Joel sensed danger. Maybe he just gave up. Either way, he suddenly withdrew his hand and backed away. The closet door hung not quite closed, but, finally, I drew in air. Closed my mouth. Relaxed my talons. Felt like heaving. Didn't dare. Didn't even move.

I don't know how long they kept looking for me—an hour? Two? But my back was cramped and legs numb from crouching. I heard them arguing, slamming doors. I felt the stairs shake over me as they stomped up stairs and down. Pictured them opening cabinets and closets, tearing apart the attic, the basement.

Several times, I heard my cell phone ringing just a few feet away in the foyer. Once, I heard the doorbell ring. Becky, probably. Maybe Susan or Jen.

I sat in the darkness until, hearing no sounds, I dared to straighten out my legs, gently, slowly, letting them lengthen into the cubby. I bumped some shoes and boxes, and knocked an umbrella, which fell against the wall. I froze, expecting the door to fly open and Derek or Joel to drag me out. But the door didn't open. I waited, listened. Wondered if they were still in the house. If they'd heard the thump.

The numbness in my legs became pins and needles. Sharp, painful. I shifted my weight. Heard nothing.

My head ached. Whole body hurt. How long was I supposed to cower in the closet? How long would they wait in the house? Hours? All night? Into the morning?

My stomach growled. The doorbell rang again. And cobwebs tickled my neck. My skull throbbed. I closed my eyes, let go of a tear.

"No, don't cry, Elf."

I jumped, startled. The lump on my head bumped against the bottom of a step.

Charlie? Really? He hadn't talked to me since I'd told him to go away and be dead.

"Charlie." Thank God. I wiped tears away with the back of my arm.

"I've been thinking, Elle. You had every reason to tell me to get lost. I'm sorry. This is all my fault."

Yes. It was.

"At least I got him out of here."

"You? How?"

"I told Joel that you weren't back here. He thought it was his own thoughts. But it was me. I'm finding I can do all kinds of things. Like suggest ideas."

Really? Had he suggested ideas to me?

"That's how I bought you some time to hide. I wanted them to leave you alone, so I told Derek that the gun was in my desk."

The gun? "What gun, Charlie?" He wasn't making it easy for me to be grateful. "You had a gun? Here, in the house?"

"Elf. Can we please not fight? I just saved your life."

I knew that he wasn't actually there. That I was alone in the dark. Hallucinating. Nonetheless, I had to ask.

"Saved my life?" Was he claiming to be a hero? One minute apologizing, the next wanting credit. Would he never stop twisting the truth?

"Yes, of course I saved you. I love you, Elle."

"You love me."

"Always and forever."

God, he was good. Convincing. I wanted to throttle him. "That's nice, Charlie. You love me forever." Sherry McBride came to mind. Not dead. Taunting me at the viewing. "Why would she do that, Charlie?"

"Oh, come on, Elle." He sounded beaten. Persecuted. "We've been over that a hundred times."

We had?

"I've told you—"

"Was she your girlfriend? Because that's what Derek said, that she was your girlfriend."

"Derek's a psychopath."

"She said it, too. She told me she was your girlfriend. So? Was she?"

I felt his breath on my face. Smelled Old Spice. "You're the only woman I ever loved, Elle."

So. It was true. He'd had an affair with her. Otherwise, he'd have insisted, No. Of course not. She was crazy, obsessed. She made it up. But he didn't say any of that. Didn't even try to deny it. Even now, when he was dead, my gut twisted with betrayal. The air got sucked from my lungs.

"Damn you, Charlie."

"You're right. If I were you, I'd have killed me. I was a shit."

Wait. He was agreeing with me?

"You were right about all of it. I lied. I cheated. I did shady business deals, got involved in things that even I thought stunk. I was a skunk, Elle. I didn't deserve you. I'm sorry."

He sounded sincere, but I wasn't convinced, had long since steeled myself against Charlie's charm. But my shoulders tingled as if enclosed by a soft warm cloud. As if Charlie was there, enfolding me. Embracing me. And for that moment, while he held me, I was comforted. Not afraid of dying. Willing to be dead as long as he would be there with me.

"I wasn't a good man, Elle." His whisper was a caress. "I wasn't always good to you. But I loved you when I was alive. I still love you. I always will love you. That's really all that matters in the end."

In the end, he was probably right. But was it the end? I pictured the grassy plot of ground, twin headstones. Charlie lying encased beside me. Suddenly, none of our problems—money, secrets, lies, infidelity, even murder—none of that seemed important. In the end, facing eternity, all that was important was that the two of us would be together.

"I love you, too, Charlie." I said it out loud. I meant it, too. But I don't know if he heard me. Because just then, something in the hallway crashed or exploded. Men were shouting. Somebody screamed. Somebody cursed. Footsteps pounded, fast.

Maybe they'd found the forty-five.

~

It didn't matter anymore if I made noise. Whatever was going on in my house was loud enough that no one would notice anything I did, chaotic enough that no one would care. I crawled into the storage compartment to grab a nine iron.

"No, not that." Charlie stopped me. "Take this."

I looked in the corner, on the shelf. Noticed a small black case.

"Open it."

I took it down, unfastened the clasp. So, they hadn't found the forty-five. It was here, in the closet.

"Why didn't you tell me about this before?" I'd been hiding there all that time, could have used a gun.

"I was hoping you wouldn't need it."

But now I did?

Footsteps stampeded down the hallway. Something shattered. Someone yelped. I turned on the closet light, looking at the thing. It was ugly, dark blue, dangerous. Smelled oily. Weighed a ton. I wondered how to load it. Had no idea.

"Hold it like this," Charlie instructed. "And slide the clip in here, into the grip—"

Clip? Grip? I didn't know the terms, but he guided me.

"The cartridges are already in the clip—"

"Cartridges?" I thought of ink.

"Bullets."

Oh. Right. Those kinds of cartridges. There were boxes of them in the case.

"Pull the slide back, that's right. And release it. Now you're ready to shoot."

Was I?

Armed and powerful, I stood tall, stretched my back, took a deep breath. And stepped into the outer closet.

Charlie warned me to stay back. To ignore the commotion and stay hidden. To use the gun only as a last resort.

But I was tired of being passive. I stood opposite the closet door, knees slightly bent, aiming the gun at it with both hands, ready to shoot anyone who opened it.

Something crashed in the hallway. Damn—the table. Grandma's Wedgwood— What the hell was going on? Did Derek and Joel think that, since they couldn't find me, they might as well trash my house? Were they turning on each other, frustrated that I'd gotten away? What was wrong with them? Why couldn't they just leave?

More pounding footsteps, shouting. A grunt, close by.

"Who the fuck is that guy?" Joel's voice seemed to come from the living room.

"What's he doing here?"

"Damned if I know." Derek panted, sounded as if he was just outside the closet door.

He was. The door flew open and Derek dove in.

"Stop, Derek." The forty-five stared at him, maybe six feet away, ready to fire.

He didn't stop.

"I swear I'll shoot."

He kept coming, wide-eyed, arms outstretched as if to tackle me.

Not this time.

Charlie called, "Elle, wait!" but too late. The recoil knocked me against the closet wall. The bang rattled my ears, pounded my already throbbing skull.

Derek was still staring at me when he went down.

Grasping the gun, shaking, I stared at Derek, confused. He was facedown, dead. A heap on the floor of my closet. I'd just shot him in the chest. So why was there a knife protruding from his back?

~

I recognized the knife. It was mine. From my kitchen.

Not again, I thought.

Not again? Wait. What?

Déjà vu. Something told me this had happened before. That I'd found this very same knife once before, in someone else's back.

Why was that? Why couldn't I remember? And what was I doing in the closet holding a gun? Where were all the coats—I opened the door, saw coats strewn all across the hallway. Loose hangers. And Grandma's Wedgwood collection, broken. Shards everywhere on the hardwood floor.

What had happened here?

The knife, I thought. I had to find out about the knife in the man's back. There were voices in the study, and I started down the hallway, stepping over cushions, books. Broken bottles. Shoes. A vase. It looked as if someone had gone through the house throwing things. Confused, I waded through clutter, following sounds.

The study door was open just a crack. I peeked in. Saw the bar in disarray. Bottles overturned. Scotch and beer spilling onto the floor. Voices coming from the desk. I closed my eyes, strained to hear.

"I've said all I'm going to say."

Was that Charlie?

"We're done."

It was, yes, Charlie. What was he doing in there? He didn't live in this house anymore, had no business showing up unexpectedly. He had his own apartment now. And who was in there with him?

I stood in the hall, unable to see them without opening the door. But I didn't want them to notice me. Wanted to hear what they were up to. I pushed the door just a hair, then another. Trying to see without being seen.

And somehow, I could. I didn't have to open the door. I simply could see inside the room. Charlie sat at the desk. The other man faced him, his back to me.

"You have so much, damn it. You wouldn't miss it." Whose voice was that?

"It will never be enough. If I give you money this time, what about next week? Next month? Do you think I want to support you? Why should I? No one supported me. No one gave me a check every time I messed up. I made my money all by myself, like a grown-up." Charlie stood, leaned on his desk. "You want money? Grow up. Go get a job."

"Christ, don't get self-righteous on me." The guy stood, too. Faced Charlie eye to eye. "Don't pretend you sweated and toiled in honest labor. You're just like me, only you con richer people."

"In no way am I like you. We share parents. Nothing else."

Parents? The guy was Ted?

And Ted didn't give up. "Think of it this way, Charlie. You're divorced now. You don't have to support your wife anymore. And what I need has to be a lot less than she cost you."

"Your point?"

"Even if you help me out, you'll still come out ahead."

Charlie shook his head. "My wife fucked me. What have you done?" He huffed off to the bar. Reached for the Scotch—

but the bottle was upright. The glasses, too. Nothing had spilled or been knocked over. "I'm not giving you another dime."

Ted followed him. Stood behind him. "I'm asking one more time. Last chance, Charlie."

Last chance?

Charlie poured a drink. "Get lost." Waved goodbye, dismissing Ted without even turning around.

Oh God. I needed to call out—to warn Charlie—I remembered. I knew what was going to happen. The knife. Ted was going to grab it off the bar and stab Charlie.

"Look out!" I raced into the study, shouting. "Charlie—he's got the knife."

Both men whirled around, facing me, agog. Neither of them was Charlie.

∴

But one of them was Ted.

Ted. Looking at him, I remembered. All of it. In a flash.

I'd been in the kitchen, making a snack. Cutting an orange. And I heard a sudden shout—the knife slipped, stabbing my hand. Oh God. Who was in the house—prowlers? Burglars? Holding the knife like a dagger, I crept down the hall, following voices to the study. I stood outside, listening. Recognizing who was in there. Charlie and his brother. Arguing again. Ted asking for money again. But this time, Charlie refused. Ted stormed out of the study, irate. Fuming. Not even noticing me there in the corner.

What were they doing in there? In my house? Indignant, I flew into the study. "What the hell is going on?" I reminded Charlie that we were separated, that he had no right to barge into my home, much less to bring his drugged-out junkie brother with him. I demanded that he leave. That he give me his keys. That he respect my privacy. That he stop drinking my liquor.

Charlie swallowed Scotch, watching me, waiting for me to

finish. When I did, he put the glass down on the bar, held out a cocktail napkin. "Elf, your hand is bleeding."

I looked. Lord. It really was. Blood ran down the knife I still held, dripped onto the carpet. Charlie took the knife, set it on the bar, pressed the napkin against my hand. But I pulled away, hurried across the hall to the powder room. Rinsed the wound, wrapped it in a towel.

I was coming out of the powder room when Ted ran out of the study. Wait. He'd already left. Had he come back? Why? I watched him run down the hall, heard him slam the front door.

And then I went back into the study.

~

Charlie dropped his glass of Scotch. Stood facing the door, eyes meeting mine.

"Elle—"

I was still angry. Didn't care what he had to say. "You better go."

His eyes were too steady. Intense. "Elle—"

Why did he keep saying my name? He took a step toward me, awkwardly, sloshing his drink, spilling some. He steadied himself, took another unsteady step.

"Charlie?" Something was wrong. Was he drugged? Had Ted slipped something into his drink?

His eyes were fixed on mine. Didn't waver.

"What's wrong?" I got to him just as he fell into my arms, knocking me backward. We both fell, tumbled to the floor, me under him, a pile of legs and arms. I called his name, examined his face. Was he having a heart attack? A stroke?

Charlie tried to get up. Pulled himself onto all fours. I scrambled to get out from under him, and he held onto my shoulders to push himself to his feet. I put an arm around him. My hand was bleeding. At first I thought it was my blood that had soaked his shirt. I twisted to look at his back.

And that's when I saw the knife.

~

My knife. The one he'd taken from my hand. The one I'd cut myself with. But, what had happened?

Ted. Of course. He'd come back, seen the knife on the bar and, when Charlie dismissed him again, stabbed him. That's why he'd run away.

Charlie squeezed my arm. A death grip.

"Charlie, let go. I need to call 911."

"Why?" Charlie looked baffled. Maybe he didn't grasp what had happened. Was in shock.

"You've been stabbed."

"Why?"

"Come, sit down." I helped him to the sofa, aware that the wound was deep, near his heart.

"Was it money?" His voice was raspy.

Probably it was. Money was what Ted always wanted from Charlie. "Sit, Charlie. Be careful. Here, lean this way so you don't move the knife."

"Why would you do this?"

Why would I? "I didn't—it was Ted."

"No. Ted left."

"No, Charlie. He came back—" Hadn't he seen him? Ted must have come from behind, stabbing him in the back without saying anything. Not even asking for money again.

"Elf. Why? Tell—"

Again why? "We'll figure it out later." I started to pull away, but his hand clutched my wrist. "Let go, Charlie—I have to call—"

"No. Please."

He pulled at me. His eyes begged.

So, God forgive me, I didn't call 911. I sat beside Charlie on the sofa, cradling his head against my chest, holding him until, a short time later, he let out his last breath.

~

They were staring at me. Frozen, wearing twin expressions of alarm.

It took a moment to realize that it wasn't me they were alarmed about, but the gun. I was still holding it. In fact, I was holding it up, aiming it at Ted's gut.

"Thank God, Elle." Joel started toward me. "You have to help me—"

"Shut up, Joel." I moved the gun, pointing it at him.

"Elle—" Ted smiled at me. He looked like a younger, scruffier, skinnier Charlie. "Who are these guys? Did they hurt you? Because, I swear—"

"I mean, shut up both of you."

"Wait, Elle." Joel was suddenly my best friend. "I don't know who this creep is, but it's obvious he came here to rob you. He has keys—"

"Of course I have keys." Ted was indignant. "I'm family. I have a right to be here. Who the hell are you?"

"No, Ted, I never gave you keys. You have no right to be here." Why was I even responding to him?

"Charlie gave me his. They were Charlie's."

No. Charlie hadn't given keys to Ted. "Cut the crap, Ted. You took them when you killed him."

"When I—what? You're saying I killed my own brother?" He squinted at me as if I'd gone out of focus.

"You think he killed Charlie?" Joel tried to ally himself with me. "Why?"

"I wasn't even here the night Charlie was killed." Ted's hands were up, protecting himself, making a wall. "I was home."

"No, Ted. You were here. I saw you. I saw you stab him."

"No, you couldn't have. You weren't there."

Silence. At first, he didn't realize what he'd just said. Gradually, the stupidity of his reply dawned on him. How could he have known I wasn't there unless he was? Essentially, he'd confessed.

Joel looked from Ted to me. "So, Elle, you didn't do it?"

Wonderful. Even Joel had believed I'd killed Charlie.

"Nice try, Elle. Blaming me." Ted tried to look smug. Failed. "But the cops—they already know it was you."

Joel watched Ted. "You piece of shit. You were going to let her fry for what you—" Before I could react, his fist landed on Ted's jaw. Something cracked, probably a bone. Maybe teeth. Blood spurted from Ted's mouth as he sunk.

"Joel, stop—" Was he seriously trying to make up to me by knocking out Charlie's killer?

Except that Ted wasn't out. He reached for Joel's leg, grabbed it and rolled, taking Joel. Joel yelped, thudded.

"Okay, enough!" I yelled, waving the gun. "Keep your hands to yourselves!" It was as if I was talking to my second graders.

Blood dribbling down his chin, Ted pummeled Joel in the face, punched his throat. Joel was larger, more muscled, but the throat jabs winded him. Coughing, red-faced, he walloped Ted in the belly and, as Ted doubled over, he got him once more in the jaw. Blood spattered on my new carpet. I smelled it, heard grunts, groans, fists colliding with flesh.

I yelled at them again to stop, but they didn't care. I threatened them, but they didn't hear. Finally, bracing myself, I closed my eyes and fired the gun into the corner.

They both looked up. Twin expressions, frozen in alarm. Only this time, bruised and bloodied.

~

The police were on their way. So was Susan.

Joel sat beside Ted on the floor of the study, leaning against the bookcase beside the door. They'd already bled onto my new carpet. I didn't want them to ruin my new sofa, too.

Joel eyed Ted. "This ugly prick is Charlie's brother?"

"Mind your fucking business." Ted cursed through swollen lips, missing some teeth. I saw one lying near his foot, didn't pick it up.

Joel tried sweet talk. "Elle, really. This has all gotten out of control. Come on, put the gun down."

I didn't answer.

He waited a moment, asked, "Where's Derek?"

I didn't answer that, either. The gun was heavy. My hands ached from holding it.

"You heard that shot before she came in here." Ted touched his jaw. His toothless "s"s were "th"s. "That's where he is."

"You shot him?" Joel looked at me wide-eyed, feigning disbelief.

Again, I said nothing.

"Of course she shot him. We both heard the gun—"

"He was dead before the shot. Somebody stabbed him." I leered at Ted. "One of you."

"You fuck—you fucking stabbed him?" Joel twisted his body to face Ted, his hands tightening to fists.

"I swear if you hit him again, I'll shoot you both." I didn't mean that. I needed Joel to testify that Ted had killed Derek, needed Ted to confess to killing Charlie. Which meant they had to stay alive.

"Elf, you got to listen to me." Joel tried to bargain. Still thought he could get to me. "I told you before. I had no part in Derek's mess. I wasn't involved in any of that kiddie stuff. All I did was book trips for your husband's business. Honest."

The gun weighed a ton. My ears were ringing, and I felt unsteady. I moved to the bar so I could support my elbows on the counter. Any minute, I told myself, the police would storm in. They'd arrest Ted and Joel. I'd be exonerated. It would be over.

"Seriously," Joel went on. "That stuff with the kiddie sex? That was all Derek and Somerset. George and Jonas. Those guys were pervs. But Derek said he'd pull the plug on my agency, ruin me unless I helped them out. Believe me, Elle. They make me as sick as they make you."

I tossed a wad of cocktail napkins at them. "Wipe the blood off your faces. You want to look good for the cops."

Ted held a few to his mouth, leaned his head against the bookcase, closed his eyes.

"Elle. Please. Be reasonable. I'm not one of those scumbags."

"No? Is that what you told Sherry McBride?"

His eyes shifted. "Who?"

"Before you killed her. Did you tell her you were a good guy? That you weren't like the others? What did you tell her? That you were trying to stop them? Or expose them as pedophiles? Did she trust you and actually hand the files over?"

"Pedophiles?" Ted's eyes opened. "What are you guys talking about?"

"Oh, her." Joel ignored him, furrowed his brows as if in thought. "You mean the bimbo. Charlie's—his secretary." He sighed. Rubbed his eyes. "Okay, here's the truth."

The truth?

"Sherry was blackmailing them. Derek, Somerset, Ogden, Jonas. They wanted to get rid of her, but that's all I know. Ogden took care of it. But I have no idea if he killed her. He might have hired somebody."

"Yeah. Probably they hired you. Otherwise, how would you have her flash drive?"

"Her flash drive? Oh, the flash drive I brought Derek?" He shook his head, smiling, as if I had it all wrong. "That was delivered to me. By a messenger."

I shook my head. Lies. Lies. Lies. Lies. Joel never ran out of them.

"You killed a woman?" Ted looked disgusted. "Dude. That's lame."

"You knew I was Charlie's wife." I might as well clarify. Not that it mattered. "You went out with me to try to find his copy of the files."

"No. Not true—well, at least the part about why I went out with you."

Ted eyed Joel sideways. "You're dating this asshole?" One eye was swelling. He was going to have a shiner.

"Believe me, Elle. You're wrong. That part was real. I care about you."

"Aww, shameless bastard." Ted scowled. "Moving in on a grieving widow."

My wrists ached from holding the gun. But things were beginning to make sense. Even little things. Derek must have told Joel that Charlie called me "Elf." So Joel used that name to get my attention. It had been no coincidence. And Derek had known that Charlie gave me red roses for every occasion.

"Come on, Elle. They had me by the balls." Joel held his hands out as if to say, "How can you blame me? Nothing was my fault."

I remembered meeting him. The rose he gave me. The rose that later moved through the house. Appearing magically on the floor of the kitchen or the bedroom. And suddenly, I had a theory.

"You have keys." Did everyone have keys to my house? He must have lifted my keys and somehow made copies—or Derek had copied Charlie's and gave the copies to Joel. No matter how he got them, he was able to get in.

"Keys to what?" Again, the innocent expression. Joel, acting ignorant.

I moved away from the bar, stood beside the sofa. Pictured Joel sneaking into the house to search for the flash drive, taking the rose from spot to spot to spook and distract me. To toy with me. Had he also whispered to me, pretending to be Charlie?

"Don't pretend, Joel. You know to what. You came here after I left Jeremy's. You let yourself in and snuck around, looking for the flash drive."

Joel's eyebrows rose in the middle. He looked perplexed.

"Elle, honestly. I have no idea what you're talking about. Are you saying someone was in your house the night I met you? Because it wasn't me. Maybe it was this guy. He's the one who had Charlie's keys."

"Fuck off. Sicko bastard." Ted hissed. He met my eyes. "It wasn't me."

"Well, it wasn't me. The truth is, Elle, whatever you think of me, our time together was real. And I—Let's just say I'm disappointed that tonight didn't work out."

My head was ringing. The voices drifted, sounded muted and faraway. Was I going to pull an Elle now, with a gun in my hands? No. I couldn't. Probably I was experiencing the aftereffects of the gunfire. Or a concussion. Probably I needed more pills.

At any rate, I'd had enough. Derek was dead in the closet. Ted had probably stabbed him, just as he had Charlie. Joel or Ogden had murdered Sherry McBride. I didn't want to look at either of them or hear any more. I leaned on the back of the sofa, holding the now two-ton gun with both fatigued hands. The police would be there any second. All I had to do was hold on until then.

～

Apparently, they both saw that I was weakening. And neither wanted to wait for the police. Suddenly, as if they'd rehearsed it, they bounced to their feet and ran in opposite directions. Maybe they knew I wasn't a good shot. Maybe they gambled that I couldn't hit a moving target. Maybe they didn't believe I would actually hurt them. Whatever their thoughts, they sprinted at me, Joel from the left and Ted from the right. I tightened my hand around the gun, shouted, "Stop," before I fired, missed Ted, blew a hole in the wall over Charlie's desk, and stumbled backward with the recoil as Joel rammed himself into me, grabbing my left arm. I twisted my right arm to aim at him, ready to shoot. But Ted took hold of my right arm. Two against one. I still held the gun, but couldn't aim it at either of them. I remember telling myself to kick. Or try for a head butt. I squirmed to get free.

"Got to go, Elf," Joel grinned, eyes twinkling.

I glared and thrashed, wishing I'd blown his head off.

"Rain check on dinner?" His whisper was throaty. Suggestive.

Suddenly, my jaw slammed backward. I saw a flash of white. And then I was on the floor beside the sofa. Without the gun. Ted was gone, Joel darting out the door.

I tried to get up. The walls, the floor wouldn't hold still. I held onto the back of the couch, anchoring myself, hearing commotion in the hall.

"What the fuck?" Joel's voice pierced my sore head, an octave too high.

"It wasn't me, Charlie—" Ted squealed like a puppy. "It wasn't. I swear."

I crossed to the doorway, off balance. Stepped into the hallway, clung to the wall.

Joel and Ted stood by the coat closet. Derek's shoes protruded into the hall.

"What are you doing, man—" Joel gaped at Ted. "Put that thing down."

"All I wanted was for you to share. I'm your fucking brother."

"Dude—who are you talking to? Stop playing around. We got to go."

"Don't, Charlie. Please—"

I heard Charlie, like a rumble of distant thunder. I moved slowly, unsteadily, unable to hurry.

Ted chattered. "You wouldn't help me. You turned me away like I was garbage. What was I supposed to do?"

Another ominous rumble. A shadow rising in the corner. Charlie, gathering rage.

"You're freaking me out, man." Joel danced around, edgy. "I'm gone—" But he didn't leave. He was fixated on Ted.

"Okay. I'll tell you why. I thought you were divorced. Single. And if you died single, I'd be next of kin. Me and Emma would inherit the money." Tears rolled down Ted's cheeks. "I'm sorry, Chuckie. I am. I asked you nicely, but you told me to get lost. Your own brother—"

"What the fuck is wrong with you?" Joel jabbed Ted's shoulder. "Let's the hell out of here."

Joel stared at Ted. Ted didn't notice. He held the gun to his temple, bargaining with a shadow.

Sirens wailed outside.

"Come on, man," Joel urged. "Put the gun down."

Oh God. The shadow swelled, and I swear I heard a bellowing roar.

Ted whimpered like a scared little boy. He pressed the gun against his head. "Please, Chuckie. Don't—"

"Charlie!" I ran, holding the wall. "Stop—"

I needed Ted alive. To talk to the police. To confess.

The sirens screamed. The doorbell rang. Someone yelled, "Philadelphia Police! Open the door!"

Joel looked around, backed into the dining room.

Ted pleaded. "Charlie—Chuckie—Please—"

I yelled, "No—Don't!"

But Charlie didn't listen. The gun went off one more time.

~

Even with half his forehead blown away, Ted lived long enough to tell the police that he'd killed Charlie. Well, not exactly. What he said first was: "It was. Me. Charlie."

I stood behind the freckled redheaded cop kneeling beside him. I called out, "Tell them why, Ted. Tell them why you did it."

Ted gurgled.

A burly black cop bellied up to me. "Move back, ma'am."

The redhead asked, "Who's Charlie? Where is he now?"

"Tell them, Ted." I called. Didn't budge.

"What's he saying?" A skinny mustached cop turned to the burly one.

"I don't know. Bus here yet?"

"No, but he won't make it onto the bus—"

"Officers, please. Listen to him, will you?" I interrupted. "It's a dying confession."

"Ma'am," the burly one put his hands on my shoulders and began shoving me, physically, from the scene.

"That's my brother-in-law. He's dying. He killed my husband. Listen to—"

"Ma'am, move away. You don't want to make this hard on yourself. Let us do our job."

I argued. He threatened to arrest me. Like I cared. If they didn't hear Ted's confession, I would go to prison for the murder he'd committed. I tried to get around Burly, back to Ted.

"Ma'am, I'm warning you—"

Over his high, wide shoulders, I could see more cops. They swarmed in with the EMTs. And someone I never thought I'd be happy to see, Detective Nick Stiles.

～

Hours must have passed. Darkness deepened and lifted. I noted location changes. My house. An ambulance. The emergency room. And, finally, Susan's house.

I leaned into the cushions of the floral sofa, and Becky handed me steaming tea. Susan sliced the freshly baked lemon poppy seed cake she'd brought to the coffee table. Handed out plates.

Jen grabbed the first one, complaining. "You cut such skinny pieces, Susan. Are you saying we're getting fat? Or just charging by the slice?"

"Behave, Jen." Becky smirked. "We have company."

Detective Stiles accepted a plate, smiling. "No need to behave on my account." His smile was lopsided, marred by the scar that crossed his face. Even so, I adored it. Thought it was fantastic. Hadn't seen it before. Was elated to be with him when there was reason to smile.

Susan took the last plate and took a seat on a wingback chair. "So. Should I do the honors?" She reached into a bucket of ice, lifted a bottle. When the cork popped, everyone cheered. Well, not Detective Stiles. He sipped coffee. But the rest of us whooped without reserve.

Susan poured. Toasted. "To the end of a terrible ordeal. And justice."

"And Elle surviving." Becky chimed in, squeezing my arm.

"And the Fantastic Four." Jen added. She occasionally called us that, like the comic book.

"To friendship." I lifted my glass, looking at them one at a time. Becky, Jen, Susan. And finally, Detective Stiles. Who wasn't really my friend. But at that moment, I loved him as if he were.

Detective Stiles was on duty, couldn't have champagne, but he raised his coffee cup, silently accepting my toast, and we drank. We ate tart and sweet moist cake. Breathed freely, without fear.

~

"I think you owe Elle an apology, Detective," Jen drank her glass in one gulp. Poured herself another.

"Well, actually—" he began.

"No, he doesn't, Jen." Susan scolded. "He was doing his job."

"Oh, KMA." Kiss My Ass. Jen swallowed, as usual, bickering with Susan. "We all knew she was innocent."

"Look. Even Elle didn't remember what happened and couldn't give herself an alibi."

Detective Stiles didn't try to interrupt. Just sipped coffee, listening.

"But she'd never have killed anyone. Especially Charlie."

"Detective Stiles was just following evidence and procedure—and he went out of his way to bend rules for Elle. We should thank him. Just back off, Jen."

"FY, Susan." Jen glowered. Downed her second glass. Poured a third.

"More cake, Detective?" Becky offered.

Jen said she wanted more, cut several slabs. Thick ones.

"So," Susan sipped champagne, "it's over."

Detective Stiles shifted in his chair. "Well, not entirely."

"What do you mean?" Susan stiffened. "She didn't kill anyone. Derek was dead before she shot him, and Ted gave a dying confession—"

"Whoa, hold on, Susan." Again, the crooked smile. "Relax. No charges are being filed against Elle. But still, four people are dead. It's not over. We need statements. There's a ton of paperwork. Elle's house is still a crime scene. And she might have to testify, if we can ever find the creep behind all this."

"Who was behind it?" I had no idea which creep he was talking about. "Was it Ogden or Walters?"

"No. All those guys were just members."

"Members?" I closed my hand around the stem of my glass. "Of what?"

"Oh—she doesn't know," Becky swallowed cake. "She was in the hospital."

I'd stayed overnight for observation, due to a concussion. But I insisted on leaving, got released by lunchtime. Hadn't slept. Felt woozy. Wanted to go home. But couldn't until the police were done there. Lifted my glass and sipped cool bubbly.

Two men had died in my house—counting Charlie, three.

Then again, Charlie wasn't quite dead. I considered telling them that he'd killed Ted. That it hadn't really been a suicide. But I decided not to. Last time I'd mentioned Charlie, no one believed me. They'd said it was my imagination. My need. This time would be no different.

"Are you listening? Elle? Hello?" Susan clapped her hands in front of my face.

"She does that," Becky explained to Detective Stiles. "She wanders in her mind. We call it 'pulling an Elle.'"

"I wasn't doing an Elle." Was I? "I was just thinking." Wondering, in fact, how my hallucination of Charlie's ghost—something I'd imagined—could have killed Ted. Unless Ted also hallucinated Charlie—maybe out of guilt? And he'd been talking to his conscience? His own imagined Charlie? Or maybe—could Charlie really have been there? Both Ted and I had sensed him. Was it possible? And if so, would he still be at the house when I got back?

Would he ever leave?

Did I want him to?

I couldn't be sure. I still didn't know what Charlie had been intending to do with the flash drive. Blackmail the men? Blow the whistle on them? And I didn't know why Sherry McBride had a copy of the drive. Was it Charlie's backup? Was she operating on her own, blackmailing the men independent of Charlie?

Damn Sherry McBride. Charlie's "girlfriend." But he hadn't loved her. Had he?

My head hurt. I sipped champagne, watched the five people gathered around Susan's big round kitchen table. Encircled in a glow. Tea, coffee, cake, champagne.

Listened.

"—But that's just one of the names." Stiles had a soothing baritone. "He kept changing it so he wouldn't get caught—"

"Because he has it online, and the servers could catch on, shut him down, and get him prosecuted." Susan interrupted. " 'Kid Love' is less erudite than most of the names. But he hops around, changes sites and names. Basically, it's an international pedophile club. He arranges travel to countries that look the other way and tolerate adults using child prostitutes."

He arranges travel? I'd lost the thread of conversation. Were they talking about Joel?

"He hooks his pervs up with kids as young as they want," she went on. "Infants. Toddlers. The site offers 'erotic experiences that supercede—' what was it again? 'The narrow limits of gender, race, and age'?"

"No, the 'bourgeois limits,'" Becky corrected.

"Sickening." Jen grimaced, stuffed more cake into her mouth.

But Joel had said he only made travel arrangements for Derek's clients, nothing more. Another lie? Why did I still want to believe he was innocent? The man had lied to me, kidnapped me, helped Derek try to kill me, maybe even murdered Sherry McBride. And still, I had trouble accepting that he was the one who arranged trips for pedophiles. Joel was unquestionably the group leader they were talking about. Not Derek or Somerset or Ogden or Walters. Joel. The travel agent. The leader of the group. The one holding the camera? I pictured him, standing with me at my door, pressing his lean, long muscled body against me. Kissing me ever so gently—it was all fake. Every word, every gesture, every touch had been calculated. Designed to manipulate me and get his hands on Charlie's flash drive.

Even so, I needed to hear it.

They were still talking. The conversation had moved on. I interrupted. "What's the name of the guy with the website? The one who organizes the pedophiles?"

"Right now, he's going by Lowery." Stiles sucked a poppy seed from between his teeth. "Joel Lowery. Has a local travel agency called Ma—"

"Magic Travel."

"So yesterday wasn't your first contact? You know him?"

Yes. I did.

And no, I didn't.

I wondered where he'd gone. How he'd gotten out of the house so quickly when the police arrived. He hadn't driven away. His van was still parked in front of my house, loaded with equipment. Joel. I remembered his charm, his smile as he pulled a quarter from my ear. A scarf from the air. A rose from nothing.

Actually, it was no surprise that he'd vanished; the man was a magician.

～

I stopped seeing Dr. Schroeder at our next session. He wasn't happy about it. Said he was concerned that I was stopping therapy so suddenly, just as my memories were beginning to surface.

"I can't insist that you continue, of course." He frowned, crossed his legs. "But we've just begun making real progress. We've uncovered the trauma that triggered a major incidence of your amnesia. You remember that you witnessed the murder of your husband by his brother. That you held Charlie as he died. Your ability to recollect those events is most significant."

He held his fingertips together, his thoughtful pose. "But I'm convinced that there's much more to do. You also had amnesia regarding the death of Somerset Bradley. Which implies that there may be other events that you don't remember."

He paused, letting me think about what he'd said. I wondered if it were true. Because if it was, I wouldn't know. Wouldn't remember.

"As we've discussed, localized amnesia like yours is a defense mechanism. But it's also a symptom of a dissociation disorder. I think we can surmise that you've buried other memories. We haven't uncovered them yet. Nor have we examined why you protect yourself from traumas in this manner. Nor have we satisfactorily treated your dissociative pattern of separating yourself from your surroundings by 'pulling an Elle.'"

No, we hadn't done those things. "But I do feel much better.

I don't 'pull Elles' nearly as often. And I remembered what happened to Charlie. Which is what I came here to do. I'm satisfied. I think I'm done here. Really."

He exhaled. Uncrossed his legs, leaned forward, elbows on his knees. Speaking directly. "Elle, given that your localized amnesia occurred at least twice in a short time period and that you are beginning to recall the triggering events, I have to warn you. Other repressed traumatic memories might surface. Unexpectedly. Out of nowhere. Suddenly. You should be prepared for—"

Dr. Schroeder warned me about memories that might pop out at me like jacks in the box. Or was it jack in the boxes? Jacks in the boxes? Who knew? I saw myself bundled in a parka. Coming home from school early due to the snow. Skidding and sliding on the roads, then wading through knee-deep snow to the door. Water was running upstairs. How fabulous. Charlie was home! Taking a shower? Perfect. We'd start up the fireplace, open a bottle of wine. Make love on the sofa. Or the rug. I ran up the steps, straight to the bathroom, still holding my schoolbag. Calling to him, telling him I was home. Flinging the bathroom door open.

"—and you might very well need support." Dr. Schroeder looked concerned. "These memories will no doubt be unsettling. There were, after all, reasons your mind refused them."

Finding Charlie in the shower.

Washing Sherry McBride.

Wow. Dr. Schroeder was right. The memories could arise suddenly, out of nowhere. Charlie must have wondered why I kept asking him about her as if I had no idea they'd been involved. As if the shower incident had never occurred. He must have assumed I remembered it. That I was playing some bizarre guilt game.

She had a single red rose tattooed on her butt.

They hadn't seen me. I scooted into the closet as they

emerged, dripping. Heard her moaning and cooing. Reached into my schoolbag, retrieved my scissors, ready to take them by surprise. Kill them both.

"Have you had any other disturbing memories? Because we should talk about them."

"No." I answered too fast, dismissing Sherry McBride's ample naked parts from my mind. "No, no others."

He stopped talking, watched me. One eyebrow raised. I looked away.

Saw the remains of Charlie's hand-tailored, thousand-dollar suits piled beside me on the closet floor. Cut to pieces. A cuff in my hand. A sleeve on my lap. Lapels, flies, chunks of material everywhere. Sherry McBride's voice no longer oozed through the door. The bedroom was silent. I replaced my scissors in the schoolbag, went downstairs to make dinner.

Dr. Schroeder told me to call him if I changed my mind. Not to hesitate. He reminded me that avoiding him wouldn't mean I could avoid my memories. And that he was there to support me anytime.

I felt guilty about it, as if I was letting him down. But I didn't want to continue. Already, I drifted less frequently and, mostly, only when I wanted to. And I decided that I didn't need to be helped. My mind knew what it was doing. Carrying me away to keep me safe. Burying memories that would hurt. There was no reason for further treatment. Maybe my "disorder" was a gift.

~

Days passed. The press found other people to hound, other stories to attract eyeballs. My headaches eased. The lump on my temple shrunk. My bruises faded. The cut on my hand, allowed to rest unmolested, finally began to heal.

Susan invited me to stay with her family again, but I passed. As soon as the police allowed me to return home, I did. The cleaning crew and carpet installers came the same day, removing final remnants of Ted and Derek. I didn't even have to see any of it.

Becky came by every day after school; Jen every morning after hot yoga or Pilates or spinning class. Susan called at least twice a day, sometimes more. Mostly, I was alone.

I looked and listened for Charlie. I called out to him. Talked to him. Asked questions. But he didn't reply. Maybe he was gone. Maybe he'd only been hanging around to avenge his murder. Lord. At first, Charlie had thought I was the one who'd killed him. If he hadn't found out about Ted, what would he have done? Shot me? Often, I relived Ted's death. Saw the gun at his head. Heard him beg and whine, pleading for his life, and then, the ear-shattering bang. Ted's head exploding. Where was amnesia when I wanted it?

I slept a lot. And when I was awake, I fought my memories. Not to rediscover them; to quell them. Dr. Schroeder was right. I'd hidden away more than just two painful incidents. There were others, beginning with childhood. And they ambushed me unpredictably. As I bathed. As I ate. As I folded laundry. As I tried to sleep. I struggled, trying to erase them as they surfaced. Searched for the mental mechanism that had wiped them away before. Had no luck.

I stopped taking the pills. Took long walks through Fairmount Park. Along Boathouse Row. And finally, it occurred to me that, if I wanted to stop dwelling on the past, I needed to be busier in the present. It was time to go back to work.

～

Monday morning, a month and three days after Charlie's murder, I was up and dressed by five thirty a.m. Ready to go. Eager. Nervous. Would the kids be happy to see me? Would they have become too attached to the substitute, disappointed that she was gone? Would she have kept up with the lesson plan? Would I have the energy to make it through the day?

I couldn't wait to see them. Their shining eyes and open faces. I prepared myself for direct questions and comments. Mrs. Harrison, did you hear what happened to Romeo and Juliet? Someone stole them! Is it true your husband's dead? My mother went to the funeral, did you see her? We sent you cards, did you get them?

There would be a lot of questions. Lots of time getting reacquainted. I paced. Sat. Stood. Made coffee. Checked myself in the mirror. Changed my outfit from pants to a skirt. Then back to pants. Checked the mirror again. Did I look pale? I was more nervous than I'd been for a date. Oops, damn. Pictured my last date. Joel. My stomach twisted, just thinking of him. Of all the dates I'd turned down after my marriage fell apart, I'd finally accepted one. With the Official Pedophile Travel Club Tour Guide and Club President? Didn't want to think about him or my judgment or dating or pedophilia. Wanted to get back to work. To the kids. I could almost smell the classroom—that unmistakable mixture of bagged peanut butter and jelly sandwiches, paste, soap, kid sweat, squirminess, curiosity.

I went downstairs, took out two mugs. Sweetener. Lowfat creamer. Looked at the clock. Paced.

Finally, the doorbell rang. Becky, arriving with scones.

Don't answer it, Elf.

I froze, smiling—Charlie was back. God help me, despite everything, I was glad. "Where've you been?"

I'm dead. Where do you think?

I had no idea. "You stopped talking to me."

I wasn't far, just waiting for you to cool down. I knew you were mad.

I was. Beyond mad. "You were right."

I was wrong to blame you for killing me. I'm sorry. I was wrong. But if anyone had motive to kill me, it was you. I gave you cause after cause.

No argument there. "So now what?"

I'm back, Elle. For as long as you want.

"As long as I want?" Did I want?

It's up to you. Your choice. But you need to decide now.

Now? Really? "Why now?"

Elle. I can't explain. Just know that I love you. I'm here for you if you want me.

The bell rang again.

I hesitated. Yelled, "Coming!" Reminded myself that Charlie wasn't really there, that I didn't really have to decide anything right then or ever. Obviously, I was conjuring him again, creating an imaginary companion to ease my loneliness and grief. "Look, Charlie. I can't ask you to stay. It would be wrong. You're gone. You're not supposed to keep me company. You're supposed to—to be dead. And I'm supposed to go to work—" I started for the door.

Wait, he sounded tired. Be honest, Elf. Tell me what you want. You need to say it out loud.

"Charlie, don't you see? I can't say it." Besides, it didn't matter what I said or didn't say. He wasn't really asking, wasn't really there. Was just my imagination. "This is your time to rest in peace." I sounded like an obituary. "It would be selfish to make you hang around just because I want you to—"

But you do want me to?

Did I? God help me, I did. Even though I remembered him washing Sherry McBride's butt, I still loved him. "Yes, okay. Selfishly, in a way, I do. Yes. I do." My voice was choked.

And I had to let Becky in. "Give me a second—I'll ask Becky to wait while we talk."

The doorbell again. This time twice in a row. Wow. Becky was in a snit.

I hesitated, picturing the empty plot waiting for me in the cemetery. What had I just done? I'd just asked a dead man to stay with me. I ran a hand through my hair and closed my eyes, collecting myself. Then I stopped and turned back to the voice.

"No. I'm sorry. This is wrong. I have to let go, Charlie." My eyes filled up, already missing him. Wanting to change my mind. "It's okay. I mean it. You can move on."

"Elf, wait—"

"No, Charlie. It's fine. We'll be together when it's time."

Blinking away tears, biting my lip, I hurried to open the door.

But it wasn't Becky.

～

Becky, in fact, was just getting out of her car, parked right in front of the house. Grinning, she held a paper bag from Saxby's. "Look at the lucky spot I got. A van just pulled out."

A van? I stepped onto the porch. Looked down.

She hurried up the sidewalk. "You're nuts, coming back to work, Elle. If it was me, I'd milk it and stay out for—" She stopped, following my gaze. "Whoa. What's that?"

I didn't answer. She could see what it was as well as I could.

"Great idea," she was impressed. "Wonderful. They were so upset about the guinea pigs—"

"They were hamsters." I didn't look up. Couldn't take my eyes off the thing.

"Whatever. What a great way to come back—they'll love her—or is it a him?"

I had no idea. I felt sick just looking at it, recalling when we'd met.

"She's so white. Hi there, pretty." Becky knelt, cooing to the thing. "So who knew you could get pets delivered to your door?"

I didn't move. Heard the blood rush from my head. Looked up the street, down. Saw nobody who looked like Joel. Of course I didn't. He'd driven away in the van. Vanished.

Becky carried the cage into the house. Set it in the foyer. Brought the scones into the kitchen. "Come on," she called. "They're still warm."

I stared at the rabbit. Watched its nose quiver. How had Joel gotten hold of it? Had he taken it when he'd escaped? I didn't remember if the police had found it in the van, had been too upset even to think of the rabbit. But why had he left it with me? And why now? To scare me? Should I call the police?

"Elle?" Becky called. "You coming?"

I moved away from the cage. Stepped into the kitchen. Poured coffee. Brought the mugs to the table.

I was shaken, not thinking anymore about Charlie. But then, on the counter by the coffee pot, I saw the rose.